MISHIMA'S LEGACY

Ian McKinley

MISHIMA'S LEGACY

DOUBLE DRAGON

ACKNOWLEDGMENTS

Thanks to Linda for putting up with me when I'm in writing mode, to Denis and Susie for proof-reading and editing, and to Jim McKinley for the cover artwork.

ACKNOWLEDGEMENTS

"Anything can become excusable when seen
from the standpoint of the result"
— Yukio Mishima,
The Temple of the Golden Pavilion

CHAPTER ONE

I was just about to cut into the thick kangaroo steak when the alarm went off. *Fuck! The advantage of shifts in the emergency response unit is that you get served the best food. The problem is that, half of the time, you never get to eat it!* I glanced at my watch – only four hours left of the compulsory week my team had to spend at the sharp end, keeping up to date on counter-terrorism actions in the field. *A bit different from our usual foreign threat assessment work.*

I gulped a large mouthful of alcohol-free Grand Cru Shiraz, determined not to let this fine wine go to waste, while searching through details on my pad and ignoring the bodies around me as they scrambled out of the canteen. Some kind of nerve gas had been released at the St Louis border checkpoint, just outside Basel. *Shit! That area's still cooling off after the dirty bomb there, eight months ago.* I cast my eye over a wall screen that had already been updated with this incident by the time that I reached the operations room. *Fortress Switzerland!* The map of this small country showed its border delineated by colour-coded circles recording terrorist attacks. Nuclear in blue, chemical in green, bio in red. Grey for conventional weapons although, given the latest developments in compact thermo-baric weapons, these were less trivial than they sounded. Orange was new: directed cyber using miniaturised EM-bursters. These had yet to cause any significant problems, but we always respond to them as if they have the potential to do so.

Of course, despite our tight entry regulations, attacks occurred also within this perimeter. These were, by international standards, few and far between – maybe helped by our Draconian anti-terrorist laws. Even incitement to terrorism could lead to the death penalty – or immediate exile together with all immediate family members, which might be worse than a clean execution in many cases. *Maybe not enough to stop fanatics, but at least it ensured that we had no concerns about repeat offenders.*

Details of the gas attack were now coming in. All eyes were glued to another screen, which showed a video of an old woman pushing a pram at the French side of the kilometre-wide no-man's-land that separated the checkpoints. Our frequency-hopping terahertz scan picked up the package in the baby-buggy and simultaneously triggered its detonator. There were several gasps as the explosion tore apart whatever was in the pram and sent the woman flying backwards in a sheet of flame. *No sense even thinking about her, if she survived the blast, the gas would have killed her quickly enough.*

The Froggies were already squealing, as usual, their protests scrolling down one display, while another that captured gas monitor records confirmed that most contamination was confined to the French sector. *Tough titties: it's their fault for not stopping the incursion at their checkpoint. Of course, they don't have our technology, but that's their problem.*

I hurried to join my team in the chopper for the quick jump to Basel. We were nicknamed 'the Foreign Legion' as, although with Swiss roots, we had all worked as mercenaries around the world – but now with Swiss security clearance and associated passports. We were based in Brugg, in the German speaking part of the country, but the working language for the entire counter-terrorist unit was English.

We struggled into slick, active camouflage *ABC*-suits on board, partnering up to check each other's seals to ensure their nuclear/biological/chemical protection functions. Under other circumstances, the sight of fit bodies in minimal underwear would have been distracting, but now our focus was entirely on safety. Although my main attention was on my partner, Helen, a statuesque, blue-eyed blonde, as team leader I also kept an eye on the others. Slim, Latin Rüdi checking skinny Pirmin, with his shock of red hair, while bronzed, blond Jörg was paired with the compact, raven-haired Rashmi. *A good, highly professional team.*

We began to relax as the expert-system sitrep built up. *Strong south-westerly winds and forecast heavy rain within the next hour or so. Good news for us and the Frogs, but not so good for the Huns, as the cloud of toxin is now dispersing over the southern Black Forest.* As a precaution, we were deploying extra monitors and mist-sprayers on our side of the Rhine, but the risk was minimal. The Germans would, however, have their work cut out to limit casualties in their rugged terrain.

11

As always, our approach was to respond first and sort out the fine details afterwards. Threats were immediately neutralised, as visibly as possible for whatever deterrent value it might have. Thereafter, we went into silent mode, tracing back to find the source of the attackers and their equipment. Then we followed the technique developed to perfection by the Israelis – focused overkill to remove anyone at all remotely responsible. This was never acknowledged, but everyone knew we did it.

Switzerland survived for centuries due to its policy of armed neutrality. Absolutely no offensive capability, but enough defence to ensure that any attempt at invasion wasn't worth the effort. Of course, over the last two centuries, the banks were an even more important reason why nobody attempted to attack the Swiss. Now, unfortunately, the banks were the justification for many of the attacks, being identified as the safe-havens for the wealth of the mega-rich. In many cases antipathy was now further inflamed by the exclusive communities set up in the Alps for their top-level clients.

The bottom line, however, is that money management takes up the slack from the general demise of tourism as an industry in Switzerland, mirroring that of the glaciers. We provide a base for a significant fraction of the very richest tycoons, oligarchs and internet whiz kids who, between them, control 90% of the global economy. This now contributes significantly more to our national budget than pharmaceuticals – our only other major industry.

My musing came to an abrupt end when we dropped heavily onto the helipad behind the heavily reinforced bunker that marked the Swiss side of the border crossing. A four-man squad bailed out and assembled the kit needed to monitor, and if required neutralise, any residual toxin. My team sat on the ground for a further five minutes, engines still running, while the final input from the attack trace-back was integrated.

"We've got them," Jörg announced, with a grin evident despite his face mask, "confidence over 99%."

"How close to the border?" I asked, knowing in advance that the answer was going to be the one I dreaded.

"Hop, skip and a jump; just by Colmar." I found it hard to believe that the young communication engineer had recently served as a Pontifical Swiss Guard: he seemed to relish the hands-on aspects of our work, the bits I really hated.

"OK, pass the coordinates to the cockpit and set up attack mode, I guess we're the ones who get to handle this." The copter slowly lifted, now silent as speed was sacrificed for stealth. The five ducted rotors made the machine resemble a giant version of an early drones – *not very elegant but, when combined with active electronic shielding, this black beast is effectively invisible on a dark night.*

"Cloud base is just under a thousand meters, so incursion will be no problem," the pilot reported. "With this rain, we'll be on the ground before anyone notices us. What's the attack profile?"

"The terrorist was transported to the border

from this building…" Jörg transferred the image to my pad. "There are apparently four families living on the ground floor. Above that there's a children's clinic."

"Fuck!" I cursed aloud. *It was so much easier in the old days when the raghead fuckwits based themselves in remote farmhouses, believing this would keep them out of sight. We could then simply go in with guns blazing and eliminate the entire nest. Napalm was then the weapon of choice: suicide bombers may not be deterred by images of their comrades being shot to buggery, but the videos of our victims slowly burning to death certainly had shock value, even if they did lead to widespread international criticism from the goody-goody lobby.*

"Okay, we'll hover over the building and abseil into the back alley. There's an empty car park just a few hundred metres away where the chopper can land when we need a pickup. Tool-up guys: Jörg, EM attack on ground and basement levels; Rüdi, shaped charge to go through the back wall from the alleyway; Pirmin, gas and smoke drones. Helen and Rashmi, we'll lead the incursion while the others mop up. Monitoring drones will be handled by the co-pilot."

"Do we have any images yet?" Rashmi asked while she strapped light armour over her ABC suit.

"Only poor satellite stuff so far," Jörg answered just before these appeared on our pads. Profiles of an old two-story building that looked like it may have once been a small hotel were overlain with thermal images. "It looks like only a couple of children in the apartments on the ground

14

floor. About a dozen adults in the basement. I'd guess that's where the explosives and toxins are, but we'll get confirmation from the drones. The integrated map will be on your visor displays."

"And the clinic upstairs?"

"About a dozen kids and three adults, who'd probably be nurses."

"ETA ten minutes," came a disembodied voice from the cockpit as the internal lighting dimmed to a red glow and our visors switched to night-vision. "There's a local curfew after the gas attack, so nobody on the streets apart from a couple of police patrols. Do you want a diversion for them?"

I quickly ran through the continuously expanding database on this terrorist cell. "This bunch seem to pray in a mosque about two kay to the northwest. Put a small yield missile on it."

"Any likely collateral?" Helen asked. I knew that, like me, she was a rather reluctant executioner.

"Maybe a cleric or two, but they're known supporters of female circumcision..."

"Genital mutilation, that is," Rashmi scowled. "Okay, fine with me, blast the fuckers."

There was only the slightest jolt as the missile was fired. "Consider the fuckers blasted," the pilot confirmed. "Drones are also dispatched and you should be getting first images very shortly. Hover in five..."

The lights went out completely, the side door opened and the winch arm deployed. "Right, boys and girls, we're fast-roping just to be on the safe side." I ignored the usual groans. "Okay, not strictly necessary here, but good practice for the times when it is. In order, Jörg, Rüdi, Rashmi, Pirmin and Helen…"

"Just to ensure that you have somebody soft to fall onto…" whispered one of the girls, causing general laughter.

"The two guys who drove the bomber to the checkpoint got back only fifteen minutes ago, so they're all going to be wired at present. There's no room for error, so let's get this done cleanly."

We waited in silence until a small LED over the doorframe glowed green, then rapidly piled out, slipping down to the rain-soaked roadway in seconds. The monitor drone images were now coming in, allowing us to identify our opponents in the basement: from their sizes it looked like eight adults, four children and a baby.

"I thought the children were sleeping in the apartments," Helen whispered in my ear.

"It looks like three small children and another three babies upstairs at ground level, but there are certainly others down in the basement."

"And you're still going with gas?"

"It's the safest option. As soon as Jörg puts the lights out, we need to incapacitate them all ASAP."

"Something that puts an adult down has a good chance of killing a child," she pointed out.

"True, but if there's any way that those fuckers manage to set off the bombs that they've probably got on the premises, all these kids will die anyway – together will all the innocents in the clinic upstairs."

Helen sighed, as I knew she would, and squeezed my arm. Just then my visor flashed to show that the EM-burster had done its job and,

16

almost simultaneously, a hole blew in the wall with a loud bang and a whoosh of air as debris flew inwards.

Before the cloud of dust and smoke could disperse, the gas attack drones flashed into the gap and disappeared into the depths of the building. I followed slowly, with the girls close on my heels.

The thick stone wall that we had blown out gave access to a large kitchen, directly beside a staircase leading to the basement. The charge had done its job to perfection, with rubble scattered throughout the room, but only dust slowly settling onto the stairs. The false-colour, heads-up display made it seem as if the house was brightly lit, but this was a synthesised image from passive IR and microwave sources dropped by the drones – in reality the building was pitch black.

"No signs of movement from the basement," Pirmin reported, "but there are kids scrambling about in a back room. I'd need to blow a door to gas them."

I was already moving down the stairs while I responded. "Just leave it. I can't hear anything, so the room must be reasonably soundproof."

"There's certainly more of a racket from the clinic. The explosion must have woken some kids and the power being out is making things worse," the pilot reported, monitoring the entire building as the copter hovered silently above.

"They've got no communications now, so shouldn't get in the way unless they try to leave. Keep me posted, but position drones in the hallway and at the fire escape ready to knock out anyone who emerges." *Fuck, just the kind of complication I don't need!*

I peered cautiously into a huge cellar that seemed to correspond to the entire area of the building, broken only by occasional supporting pillars. *Originally a garage, by the looks of it.* In the far-left corner, a couple of dilapidated sofas and a rocking chair were set round an ancient 2D television screen. Bodies of adults and children were sprawled about, clearly unconscious before they could respond to our intrusion. "All clear here," I reported. "Helen, get me a head count from across there," I waved a finger to indicate her target.

As opposed to the bare concrete walls elsewhere, the right-hand wall was smooth plastic with a heavy sliding door in the middle of it. I tagged it with a laser. "Pirmin, you got this?" What's behind that door?"

"Odd, I don't have any trace of this. The sensors seem to indicate it's a solid wall."

"Fuck, that's not good news!" *An understatement if ever there was one. This setup is typically low tech, so there should be nothing that could spoof the kit that we're using.*

Rashmi strode past me and switched on a head torch for a closer look. "Looks like a tight seal on the door, so gas wouldn't penetrate it."

"Is it locked?"

"Nope," she slid it open, "but it leads into an airlock. We have light, so there must be independent power within this Faraday cage." She disappeared inside. "The inner door is solid, though. Probably a mechanical interlock. Should I blow it?"

"Given that this is probably where they prepared the nerve gas, maybe that isn't the smartest idea. Let me join you and then we can close the outer door. Helen, I'll probably lose coms when we go in, so you're now leading the team."

"Okay, boss. All the bodies we registered are accounted for here. One old woman and the baby are dead, though, and the other kids seem in bad shape."

"OK, start interrogating the adults. Rüdi and Pirmin, come down and help. We're short of time, so just bind their wrists and knee-cap them before you wake anybody up. Also, put a bullet through the heads of the old woman and baby first: that may help to show we mean business."

"On it." Helen sounded very uncomfortable about torturing our captives, but knew it had to be done.

There was plenty of space for Rashmi and me in the airlock, which I could now see was equipped with a sophisticated decontamination cell. As soon as I sealed the outer door, the inner one silently slid open. Without conscious thought I threw myself to the side, an instant before Rashmi flew backwards in a hail of bullets.

As a conditioned reflex, I blasted a full clip from my machine pistol in the general direction of the attack, while my other hand pulled a grenade from my belt and threw it into the room in a single movement. The sonic blast would burst any unprotected eardrums but, hopefully, avoid damage to any containers of gas.

I quickly slapped in a fresh magazine and fired

19

a couple more shots to ricochet off the ceiling. Reassured by the absence of a response, I followed this with a handful of sticky microcams, which produced a ghostly image of a well-equipped laboratory on one half of my visor. Two figures in sleek, top-end isolation suits clutching assault rifles were sheltering behind a solid-looking laboratory bench to the left of the door, while another stood flat against the wall to my right.

Fuck, playing possum! My banger's achieved nothing, as their suits offer enough protection. On the positive side, though, they don't seem to be aware of the cameras. I ejected the large capacity magazine, replaced it with a smaller one holding armour-piercing ammo and switched my pistol to single shots. I then removed a grenade and changed from the default sonic setting to a high intensity flash. I took a deep breath and then threw the grenade into the lab. *Showtime!*

My visor flashed black just before the grenade exploded, being coupled to the firing unit. *Even if the bad guys have flash-shielded visors, these won't react as quickly as mine.* I side-stepped into the laboratory with my pistol in a classic marksman's two-handed grip and shot the figure on my right full in the face, absently noting as I did that the form-fitting suit showed my victim to be a well-built woman. I then twisted round and threw myself onto my stomach, using the images from the cameras to put a shot into the centre of mass of each of the bodies behind the bench.

Even for armour-piercers, a lot of punch was taken out by the heavy wood, so my targets were both alive, but writhing in pain. I cautiously put one more shot into each, before swapping back to my original magazine and wriggling forward on my elbows to carefully peer around the bench. One of the figures was immobile, but the other was screaming in a pool of blood, her cries muffled by her helmet. *Another well-endowed woman...* I peered through her partner's visor *...and a swarthy, bearded man. Just need to ensure that they don't get up to any mischief.* I shot the man point blank in the throat and put bullets through both of the woman's hands.

I checked my monitors – no traces at all of toxin – then rose and hurried back to Rashmi's side. She was still breathing, protected by her body armour, but knocked out by the impacts and bleeding from a wound in her neck. *Probably broken ribs, but lucky indeed as her ABC suit's completely shredded.* I quickly scanned through the medical kit indicators on my colleague's shoulder and found the required button to inject a potent mixture of stimulants and painkillers. Her eyes immediately opened and she gave a gasp of shock, followed by a sigh as the pain relief kicked in.

"Let's get you out of here," I helped her stagger to her feet and then quickly summarised the situation in the lab. "Anyway, I'll sort things out here. You should be able to open the outer door after I go back in and close up. Get evac organised while you're still mobile: you've got about 30 minutes before that jab wears off and I want you strapped in the chopper by then."

"Okay, boss. Take care of yourself," she gave

me a wan smile.

I could hear Rashmi muttering under her breath until the inner door closed and comms were again blocked. *Now to torch this place,* I looked over the glove boxes and analytical equipment within the lab, *although there's something not right about it. This is much more sophisticated than needed just to cook up nerve gas and the associated dispersal system. Even if it was justified, it should have been kept well away from the front lines and certainly not so easily traceable from a failed attack.*

Working on autopilot, I set thermite-based demolition charges while struggling to solve the puzzle presented here. Pulling back a curtain on one blank wall revealed another airlock, which led through to a ramp containing a van and a large stockpile of explosives. Without a detonator, these were stable, so could be left as a gift for the local police when they eventually arrived on the scene.

I re-entered the lab and checked a work station that was linked to all the analytical equipment. A crushed memory chip lay on the floor. *Doubtless done immediately after our incursion was noted.* I picked it up and dropped it in a pocket as a present for our forensics team, before returning to the two bodies behind the lab bench. The woman was unconscious, but woke with a scream after I removed her helmet and administered the interrogation drug. *A very brutal combination of stimulants and suggestion enhancers, but with no analgesic properties at all, which'll make the few remaining moments of her life a veritable hell.*

"What are you doing here?" I asked in English,

repeating the question in French.

Between grunts of pain, I could make out "Fuck off!" in what sounded to be a Scottish accent.

I pulled one of her mangled hands away from her wounded chest and slammed it with the butt of my gun, eliciting another scream of agony. "I can do this all day," I lied, "so why don't you give me something so I can take away your pain?"

"Fuck you and fuck that stupid cunt Achmed! Fuck…" Her eyes rolled upwards and her ragged breathing stopped.

Could probably bring her back with another shot, but doesn't seem worth it. I'm on the clock here. I set the demolition timer for forty seconds and headed for the door. *I wonder who the stupid cunt Achmed is.*

As I exited the airlock, Helen waved in my direction. "We didn't get much but…"

"Later," I stopped her, "the lab's going up in twenty seconds. Let's clear this place." Five shots confirmed that the interrogation was completed and I led the way out of the building, pausing for a moment when a mild ground tremor indicated that the charges had gone off, and then trotting towards our extraction point.

***

After the copter lifted off, we stripped off our suits and immediately commenced the debriefing before Rashmi's meds wore off. I started by summarising my findings in the lab and noted the contrast between the high-tech facilities there and the low-tech shambles that seemed to characterise the gas attack.

"I think our chats with the other nutters might clarify some of this. It seems like the families here were only cover for what they called *the scientists*, they were never supposed to be involved in any attacks. But they heard yesterday that Achmed Hassan's three sisters and their families were killed in the retaliation for an attack on a Swiss train, which was organised from a Spanish refugee camp. His mother wanted revenge, so he helped her set up the attack…"

"Ah, so that's the old woman and the stupid cunt Achmed," I smiled as one part of the jigsaw fell into place. "Did you get anything else useful?"

"Not really." Helen glanced for confirmatory nods from Pirmin and Rüdi, "I think Achmed was the only one who had any idea at all about what was going on; the rest were just camouflage. I'm sure that Achmed realised that he had screwed-up as soon as we arrived, but we couldn't break him in the time available. He did make one slip, though, just after we gut-shot him. He was cursing us in Arabic and promising that Allah's retaliation will wipe the nest of infidels in Switzerland from the face of the earth."

"You know, I think we just might have dodged a bullet here," I mused. "We'll have to see what the boffins make of my helmet cam images together with the chip I found. This lab is part of something bigger, I'm sure of it, we just need to find out what."

"The one thing I can't understand," Jörg contributed, "is why this was set up in Colmar, so close to the border."

Helen frowned. "We had no indication if its existence and would still be ignorant if not for stupid Achmed. But this is still a good question, as building a facility like this without ringing alarm bells would be very tricky. So, the location could be chosen to ease access to kit…"

"Or to targets…" I pointed out.

"Or to both," Pirmin added.

"Well, we can set up web searches when we get back to base. You're lead on this Rüdi."

"Jawohl, Herr Gruppenführer," he responded with a smile. "Rashmi usually supports me on this, but she'll be out of action for a bit."

I now noticed that my wounded colleague's eyes had closed and she was snoring softly. "Yes, indeed, we'll need to bring in a reserve. Any ideas?"

"How about Doris from tech support, she's a real hacking wiz?"

"You mean the drop-dead gorgeous Doris?" laughed Helen.

"And? I'm straight gay as well you know," Rüdi fluttered his long eyelashes in her direction.

"Yes, but she's drop-dead in a very androgynous, Annie Lennox sort of a way," I smiled.

"Annie who?" enquired Pirmin.

"Pop star from decades ago," Rüdi answered, "who does indeed somewhat resemble the gorgeous Doris. Very popular with both gay boys and girls."

"Whatever, see if we can bring her into the team until our sleeping beauty here is combat-fit again." *Pretty though she is, it's Doris's hacking skills that may be exactly what we need.* "I'll talk to the commander and get us removed from any further active response shifts so that we can focus on this."

"Do you really think we should manage this, not pass it upwards?" Helen inquired.

"I'll discuss it with Schmidt, but I have a feeling that we're going to have to run with this one." *And also that it's not going to be an easy job!*

CHAPTER TWO

Two days later, we had our first group status update meeting: now including the beautiful Doris, together with Commander Schmidt, two forensic techs and a liaison officer from the Nachrichtendienst, NDB, the Swiss national intelligence service. We sat around a circular table in our newly established incident room, a sparsely furnished, windowless basement that, despite its clinical appearance, had a faint fossil smell of tobacco from the days in the past when these were the traditional smoke-filled rooms from which spies around the world were controlled. The Commander, elegantly clad in a grey suit and with the good looks and silver hair that would have fit an aging actor, formally welcomed everyone and then passed the lead to me.

I presented the operation outline, displayed as a rotating 3D image floating above its centre. It was titled *Zodiac*, the name randomly assigned when the decision to proceed was confirmed. "Okay, ladies and gentlemen, you all have the background on this in your briefing files." All eyes reflexively flickered to their tablets or laptops. "The bottom line is that the Basel gas attack was an unauthorised action by a bunch of terrorist sympathisers, who shouldn't have had any active role in whatever was going on in Colmar. Their lack of experience, in particular in the case of this idiot, Achmed," his photo appeared along with personal information expanded from the *opponents-terminated* sub-file, "allowed us to trace them back to a base with facilities clearly intended to support a much bigger attack. Do you want to summarise the forensics, Urs?"

Urs Wagner, a chubby, bespectacled man who fit the caricature of a boffin, nodded and expanded the forensics overview. "The lab here is completely different to anything that we've encountered previously. The obvious difference is the shielding, which meant that our pre-incursion monitoring, both active and passive, missed it completely. The technology is state-of-the-art, with the additional complication that it was built in the centre of a French town without being picked up by either ourselves or the French intelligence services." He looked at Alex Supersaxo, the smartly-dressed Nachrichtendienst officer who seemed to model himself on a young Sean Connery, and received a silent nod of confirmation.

"The second anomaly is the sophistication of the laboratory equipment, which is set up for high-level biohazard work and, once again, everything cutting edge. The chip that Gruppenführer Berner provided," he nodded in my direction, "was extensively damaged, but Judith here managed to work some miracles…"

The other tech, a nervous-looking young woman who was slim to the point of almost emaciation, took over the presentation. "The computer system was completely stand-alone, with no links at all to outside databases. The chip had about twenty Exa of memory, enough to hold all that was needed. Everything on it was heavily encrypted and then deleted. Luckily the memory was so large that deletion overwriting was incomplete. Nevertheless, together with the physical damage, this greatly limits anything we'll be able to recover. What we can tell, however, is that the focus was bioweapons tailored for aerial delivery."

"So not nerve gas?" I inquired.

"Nothing at all like that: Urs…"

"It looks like the lab was decoupled from the explosives and other stuff the Gruppenführer found in the access tunnel." A number of images from my helmet-cam appeared. "Here you can see racks storing explosives and a few gas cylinders. The way that they're stacked is interesting though: if detonated, this stack would focus blast into the lab and expel gas into the access ramp."

"So, it's a self-destruct system for the lab, with the gas maybe added to distract attention from its real purpose," Judith finished.

"I would guess that there would be a simple mechanical way to trigger it from the lab if nobody could reach the ramp," Urs continued. "If it had been me, though, I'd have added a backup triggered by our incursion, either the EM blast or our active terahertz scanning. I'm not sure why we got away with it."

I looked at Helen and, as one, we said "Stupid Fucking Achmed!" I waved at Helen to let her expand.

"We know that this Achmed nutcase set up the attack to allow his mother to commit an honourable suicide. I guess he thought he could borrow explosives, gas and a detonator, maybe intending to replace them later. He really fucked-up royally in two ways; bringing the facility to our attention and wrecking their auto-destruct system. Truly a fuckwit."

"It does seem to hang together. The scientists found out what had happened and started deletion of files in the database. As soon as we arrived, they destroyed the chip and maybe tried to hold us back long enough for the explosives to be triggered," I added.

"Yes," Urs interrupted me; "we can see it in this blown-up view." Everyone peered as an image of the lab expanded and a cursor pointed out details. "This is the gun safe located below one of the work benches. The door is only slightly ajar, but we can make out at least two more assault rifles inside. Also, looking as if it has been dropped, a small detonator unit."

"Shit!" I muttered. "I didn't spot that. If the wind hadn't been so favourable and we had to focus initially on damage control, we'd never have reached this building before the self-destruct was rebuilt. Our intrusion would have encountered only rubble consistent with gas attackers and their bioweapon team might even have had time to evacuate if they realised what Achmed had done."

"Anyway, we've been extremely lucky," the Commander chipped in. "Do we have anything at all to put this in context, Alex?"

The security officer looked distinctly uncomfortable, which was strangely incompatible with his dapper appearance. Pictures appeared and personal details began to run in ticker-tape mode. "We've been able to identify the three scientists as a professor and two post-docs from Strasbourg University. Their microbiology research seems to be focused on nanobacteria. They carry out astrobiology work for ESA and NASA, but no indications of anything of military significance or links to any terrorist organisations."

"Little, if anything, in common with the other residents, who were all Syrian refugees and an active part of the local Muslim community," he noted. "Professor Miriam Isaacs is third generation French: originally a Jewish family that escaped from Germany at the start of the Second World War. Seems to have no religious or political affiliations. First degree from University of Marseille, Doctorate from Strathclyde, Scotland, Post-docs in Heidelberg and Marseille, before a lectureship in Basel and the Professorship in Strasbourg awarded a couple of years ago." I recognised this as the woman so pissed-off with Achmed.

"The other scientists also had links to Marseille. They both completed doctorates there and were recommended to Miriam by her previous post-doc supervisor there, Professor Christine Jones. Jones is English, but naturalised French, and appears to be a typical ivory-tower academic. Nothing at all in her record since arrests at anti-Brexit demos during her undergraduate days. The post-docs themselves," images of a young woman and the older bearded man expanded, "Marie-Claire Vitorge and Charles Kempe, are both from unremarkable French families located in Nice and Lyon, respectively. Again, no indications of religious or political activities."

"Almost suspiciously anodyne CVs," Commander Schmidt commented. "Could these be covers?"

"Absolutely nothing to suggest so," Supersaxo replied, "although we're still running double-checks. To tell the truth, it's rather baffling."

"Just like the high-tech lab installation," Helen added. "So where do we go from here?"

"The scientists are clearly the key here," Doris noted, "Maybe we could carry out a focused trace back of all of their activities for the last few years. We'll need access to French security files though…"

"Well, we're certainly not going to go through diplomatic channels for this stuff," Alex responded. "Can you hack everything you need using the standard backdoors, without leaving any traces that could warn the bad guys of our interests?"

"I can do that," Doris smiled confidently. "Maybe it would help a bit if we were to actively spread disinformation, making it look like we had missed the bio-lab and are focusing on nerve gases. The leaders here – whoever they are – will then know only that we wiped out this cell and that, in the process, the lab was destroyed. This is where the complete isolation of this facility, which made it so difficult to find, plays against them."

"I can set up a Nachrichtendienst team to do this. If your group can supply me with a suitable storyboard, Commander, I can pass it on as the actual output of the gas attack retaliation. Even if our opponents are very smart and manage to trace any activities of this team, we have no risk of any accidental slip-ups that compromise the story, because all those involved believe that it's true."

"That should do the trick," the Commander nodded. "What other actions need initiating?"

"The lab itself is the other anomaly," I pointed out. "Pirmin, have a look at what forensics comes up with and try to reconstruct how material and equipment were sourced and how the facility itself was constructed. This may link in with background on the scientists that Rüdi and Doris dig up, so liaise closely with them. Jörg, you haven't said anything, what do you think."

His only answer was a shrug of his shoulders. *Typically taciturn mountain man: does his job but doesn't say a word he isn't required to.* "Okay, you're perfect for secondment to act as liaison with the security team. There's no chance that you're going to blab anything you shouldn't." Everyone but Jörg smiled.

"And what about yourself, Gruppenführer?" my boss inquired.

"I think Helen and I will go on a road trip – pop down to Marseille and check out this Professor Jones. I have a strange feeling that there's more to her than meets the eye."

"Are you going undercover then?" Schmidt asked with a frown.

"I think that's an unnecessary complication. Maybe best if I sort out a holiday next week, which could be my usual summer scuba break. Helen is a keen rock climber, so it wouldn't cause any ripples if two colleagues decided to combine their vacations and the Calanques would be the perfect place for this – somewhere just outside Marseille that isn't too risky for Swiss tourists."

"I've actually already climbed there a couple of times with a SAC group – Swiss Alpine Club," she expanded in response to a raised eyebrow from Doris. "We rented a small villa in the Grande Bastide area of Cassis that would be ideal. I can check its availability."

"So that's the situation, the grunts work while the officers go on holiday," Rüdi groaned sotto voce.

Everyone smiled, but I felt that I had to emphasise how serious our job was. "A holiday would be very nice, but everyone needs to remember how good our opponents are: we have knowledge of their existence only because of a couple of unlikely accidents. The original gas attack, which had negligible impacts on us due to a fluke of the weather, caused a couple of dozen deaths in France and Germany. But this was only a spontaneous action unrelated to the lab, which certainly indicates a very much greater threat. We've got to eliminate this and I'm sure our opponents will play hardball and wouldn't hesitate to take any steps required to block us – so don't think that this desk work is less of a risk than our usual retaliation hits. For Helen and me, if we're nearing key players, it's possible that a bullet in the head would be the best that we've got to look forward to."

All traces of hilarity disappeared and everyone looked distinctly grim. "Well said," the Commander looked around the table, "and, if there is nothing else, I suggest we conclude here and start making things happen. All information exchange on this operation to be restricted to the present participants and requests for any additional resources to be addressed to Alex and myself – we'll sort them out between us."

As we filed out of the meeting room, I patted Helen's shoulder. "We need to plan our holiday ASAP and, if possible, make it look like it had already been booked well before the gas attack."

"Okay, give me an hour to check up what's available and then I'll get back to you."

"Great. I'll get applications for leave next week backdated to last month: the Commander can then sort out any fine details to ensure that they look legit. I must say, though, that the risks may be even worse than I indicated and that I've never looked forward less to a trip to the South of France."

"Look on the bright side: I can take you rock climbing and you may not live long enough for the terrorists to get you!"

"Thanks for that cheering thought." I smiled wanly and waved her on her way.

CHAPTER THREE

Six days later, Helen and I were sunbathing on the wooden deck of a large villa overlooking the port of Cassis. The villa was at the end of a gated cul-de-sac, secluded from neighbouring houses that mainly seemed to be holiday homes, with little evidence of being occupied at present.

Despite continually rising sea level, the harbour still functioned as a base for small fishing boats and, due to the hilly terrain, impacts of flooding were limited. The flourishing tourism of previous decades had suffered from the global economic depression and collapse of socio-political infrastructure, but it was still a centre for diehard sports enthusiasts drawn to the Calanques for climbing, sea canoeing, scuba diving, hiking and mountain biking.

I glanced at my naked colleague, lying on her back with eyes closed, and smiled. *Couldn't look less like a battle-hardened, anti-terrorist soldier.* Smooth, pale skin already beginning to turn pink in the late summer Mediterranean sun, close-cropped blond hair, well-formed breasts tipped by small pink nipples and a hairless Mons that made her look much younger than her thirty-five years. Her face was too thin and angular to be beautiful, but her broad shoulders, slim waist and muscular legs radiated health and fitness.

I looked down at my own body and grimaced. *Almost fifty years old, nearing the end of my active service life – and looking every bit of it. Lots of body hair, maybe compensating for loss from my head, shaved in response to a receding hairline, and all going grey. Muscles beginning to sag. Belly not as tight as it used to be. Scars reflecting the wear and tear of five decades. I could probably pass as a pensioner – if such things still existed on this fucked-up planet.*

I cast my eyes over my comrade again and was painfully aware that the sight of her body was beginning to cause a physical response. *A hard-on is just what I don't need Helen to wake up to – better focus on something else, like how to proceed.*

We knew Professor Jones had an office and laboratory within a university campus conveniently located on the eastern outskirts of the Marseille agglomeration. Although Doris had done a good job of hacking through the university databases, a bit of breaking and entering would be needed to check exactly what the prof and her students were up to. *Should be relatively easy. First hike along the coast and do a bit of climbing with Helen. Camp for the night within a couple of kilometres of the Uni and aim for incursion in the small hours. Doris can spoof any electronic security, so we only have physical barriers and a few rentacops to deal with. Maybe we'll find everything we need, but we can't assume that our run of good luck will continue forever.*

The bad luck would start with the location of the Prof's residence, an apartment in a smart block right in the centre of the city, close to the Saint Charles railway station. Access to the block was strictly controlled, as the lower floors comprised hotel rooms associated with a spa, and the area was busy day and night. Breaking in there wouldn't be an easy task.

I glanced at the trim young woman at my side. *Any slip up at all and things could go very badly for both of us. Even if we hope that we never have to use it, we need a plan to get into Jones' flat. I should probably make this a priority for Rüdi and Doris.*

"Penny for them." Helen's voice startled me from my reverie. "I thought you'd be salivating lustfully over my fantastic body rather than day-dreaming," she teased, playfully.

"Just having a senior moment," I smiled, realising that the woman would have been very close to the mark if she had roused just a little earlier. "Anyway, I have a night dive booked for this evening, with a pick up from the villa at six. I take it that you have everything sorted out for our climbing trip tomorrow."

"We can set off about eight and have some breakfast in the old town. Five hours hiking will bring us to somewhere that we can camp, with some good mixed-grade climbs in the immediate vicinity. With a bit of luck, there won't be anyone else overnighting there. We won't need any active counter-surveillance until we near the campus, and Doris has the required fixes already in place. Weather isn't so good, though, very windy with some heavy rain showers. Miserable for any outdoor activities, but should ensure that we don't have much company."

"And you're really thinking of climbing, even if it's wet and windy?" I could feel our run of luck breaking even sooner than I expected. "You do remember that my experience is limited to a couple of indoor climbing walls?"

"Don't be such a sissy!" she grinned. "It'll be good for you, letting me call the shots for a change."

"Maybe, but it won't help our plans if I fall and break a leg."

"What, break a leg, no chance of that...," she laughed, before spoiling my slight feeling of relief by adding, "...on these climbs you'll break your bloody neck if you fall!"

***

We set off as planned the next morning, wearing shorts, t-shirts, walking boots and matching black, weather-proof ponchos. As forecast, a gusty wind was accompanied by drops of rain, presaging the heavier downpour expected in the afternoon. Our large backpacks were bedecked with ropes and climbing slings and we looked the part of desperate vacationers, determined to enjoy their hobby regardless of the weather.

After breakfast in a harbour-side cafe, we took the Grand Route 98b trail that started at the edge of the town and proceeded to wend our way into the Calanques national park. The well-marked path wound its tortuous way towards the rugged interior, traversing along the tops of sea cliffs with regular descents into valleys and slogs upwards to the cols between them. The wind gradually strengthened and the rain became continuous, making the track of well-polished limestone alternating with granite gravel treacherously slippery and the exposed ridges distinctly perilous. *Thank God for the gecko microfibre patches on the soles of our boots, without these I'd never even make it halfway.*

Our progress was slow and we stopped for a late lunch in the ruins of a hut on the Col de la Candelle. This was not exactly dry, but at least sheltered from the worst of the driving rain. By this point, we had not seen other hikers for about an hour.

"Okay, maybe we won't be climbing today," Helen conceded as we assessed possible camping spots. "Given the worsening weather, we should get as close to the campus as possible, maybe a bit to the north, where the science facility is located," she traced a route on her tablet. "We can fork off the Grand Route after we pass la Tour Carrée, then we're on small tracks where the chances of meeting anyone are negligible."

"I think there's little chance in any case that we'll meet someone else crazy enough to be out under these conditions," I pointed out.

My comrade simply rolled her eyes and continued. "The paths through the forest below the Falaises de Luminy will be out of the worst of the wind and we should find somewhere to camp just beyond the main climbing area there. This'll be only about a kilometre or so from the ring road around the campus."

"Fine with me, anything to get out of this bloody rain for a bit."

"It's not far as the crow flies, but I guess a couple of hours walk, as the wind is getting up."

"Fuck! It already feels like a hurricane out

40

there."

"Stop moaning," she smiled, "it's just a bracing breeze. Tonight, however, it'll get really windy."

"Bugger! And what about tomorrow for our trek back."

"The wind should drop a bit, but the rain'll get heavier."

I groaned as I lifted my backpack. *Yes, definitely, our run of luck has broken. I just hope the weather is the worst of our problems.*

***

The forest turned out to be sparse and evidently burned out by wildfires within the last few years. A hut shown on Helen's GPS chart was a gutted ruin, with only part of one wall still standing. We set up our tent in the lee of this windbreak, but it offered little protection. *At least our camping equipment is top-end, so we can dry off a bit before we head back into the rain later this evening.*

Our ponchos had kept the rain off, but our shorts and t-shirts were soaked with sweat while boots and socks were sodden and covered with sticky mud. Although the tent was big enough to hold four, peeling out of our wet clothing was a struggle in the cramped conditions. Despite everything, we were reduced to laughter by the time we had stripped completely.

The unavoidable flesh on flesh contact had caused obvious arousal in my case...*and probably Helen's, if her rigid nipples were anything to go by.* I grimaced, trying to think of a way to defuse the situation.

"I need a piss – I'll just pop out now," I said

desperately.

"In the buff, in this rain?"

"That's perfect, I'm stinking with sweat and need a shower anyway. It's certainly on the brisk side, but not really cold. I'll dry off afterwards with the microfibre towel we have."

"Actually, that's not a bad idea – I could probably also go a pee. It could be golden shower time," she grinned lasciviously.

Shit, so much for defusing the situation! Anyway, no turning back now.

I clambered out of the tent into the deluge, wondering if the minx was just teasing me. I walked clear of the tent and turned to piss downwind, jumping in surprise as a slippery body pressed against mine and a hand joined mine on my dick. *Well, that question's now answered. Where the fuck are we going to go from here?*

I finished and shook off, then turned into a warm embrace. My hands ran down her flanks to cradle her tight buttocks while hard nipples pushed against my chest. I looked directly into her blue-grey eyes, absently noting for the first time that we were almost exactly the same height, while struggling to formulate a response. "This is not a good idea, in the middle of an op…"

"I've no idea," she interrupted, "as my experience is limited to actions carried out with a combat team. This is new and, to tell the truth, a bit frightening."

"Yes, frightening it certainly is. So, all you need is a cuddle?"

"I could actually go a quick shag, but I suppose

42

a cuddle is a start," she grinned mischievously. "I also need a bit of support when I squat to pee, as otherwise this wind will have me on my arse."

"I can certainly do that, here take my hands. I can be a gentleman and close my eyes."

"What, you don't like to watch girls pee?" she teased while she couched down. "That's quite unusual if my perusal of on-line porn is anything to go by. Very popular with the lads and, quite likely, some of the gals also."

"What, you like to be watched?" I couldn't help staring as she opened her thighs and let rip while smiling up at me.

"Why not? Anyway, bothers me not in the least and you seem to actually find it erotic," she leaned forward to nuzzle my growing erection.

"Stop it, we're not shagging before the mission is complete. Actually, as I'm your commanding officer, we're not screwing at all."

"Mmm, let's see about that…" she tightened her grip on my wrists and took my penis into her mouth.

I can break her grip and drop her on her bum or just take it like a man. Very shortly my indecision led to a fait accompli.

With a look of triumph, she let me pull her to her feet. "Well, that seems to have released a lot of your tension. Hasn't done a lot for me though," she stood with feet apart and pointed downwards.

Bugger! Why not: hung for a sheep as a lamb? I dropped to my knees and rubbed my nose against her clitoris while my tongue roamed further down, a faint trace of urine almost completely masked by

43

the musk of abundant vaginal fluids. *She is certainly ready to rock and no mistake.* Despite this, Helen's relief took a lot longer than mine – but her noisy orgasm made it seem worthwhile.

***

Helen fetched a small bar of soap, which we used for some very intimate washing before clambering into the tent and towelling each other dry. I sorted through our supplies to find the makings of a snack, which we slowly nibbled, washing it down with isotonic sports drinks. I felt rather disturbed by my actions, but Helen seemed to be manically cheery. *Galen must have been right about post-coital tristesse – doesn't affect the human woman. Anyway, need to put this behind us and concentrate on the upcoming action. Maybe putting on some dry underwear would be a good start.*

Helen watched as I donned underpants and a fresh t-shirt, lowering herself onto a bedroll. "I guess this means that a quick post-prandial screw isn't on the cards," she grinned.

I refused to rise to her bait. "We should try to get some shut-eye for a couple of hours before we head off. Sometime about eight would ensure that we have some light for our descent to the campus."

She pantomimed a sad face, but pulled on a pair of knickers before lying down by my side. Already my eyes were drooping and, as I drifted towards sleep, I could hear her muttering. "Typical man: orgasm, a bite to eat and then straight to sleep. Then again I suppose he's not so young any more…"

I awoke to find my partner snuggled against my side, snoring softly. After managing to extricate myself without waking her, I checked the time – six thirty. We would leave all superfluous kit in the tent and make the incursion in form-fitting black body-suits with integrated boots, cowl and visor. *Almost invisible in the dark but, unfortunately, no ABC protection here.* Our belts held holstered machine pistols equipped with silencers; mine also with a pouch containing tools and Helen's with a medical kit. The visors had integrated video cameras while associated electronic aids were uploaded into our over-sized smart watches.

I double-checked this equipment and then sorted out some energy bars before gently prodding my colleague. She awoke with a start and looked confused for a second before grinning at me in a cat-with-cream manner. "I was dreaming that this operation was a dream that I had woken up from. How messed-up is that? Anyway, as long as I'm not dreaming now, I suppose I'd better get kitted up now."

"Did you dream that we had oral sex?" I smiled back. "That definitely was a dream, there's no way that it'd ever happen in real life."

"If it was a dream, how would you know about it?"

I didn't think that'd work, but worth a try anyway. Better change the topic ASAP. "Yes, definitely kitting-up time," I passed over her suit. "It's absolutely wanking it down now," I pointed out unnecessarily, the sound of the rain on the tent

45

making this self-evident, "so we can leave earlier than planned. Better to have as much light as possible for the path to the boundary road, rather than worrying about being spotted by guards. I'll bet that they're all safely inside, confident that nobody without a vehicle is abroad in this deluge."

Helen pulled on a t-shirt then struggled into her suit. "I assume that the hacks have bypassed the monitoring system."

I tapped my smart watch. "Not yet: we're still in fully passive mode, so I can't bring this forward. In any case, I think that getting as far as the road will be okay – no reason for them to have anything outside the fence around the science faculty buildings. By the time we get there, the spoof will be set up."

"Fine, let's get this show on the road," she fastened her belt and then ripped open an energy bar. "The sooner we're started, the sooner it's over and done with and we're back in our little love nest."

"You're dreaming again, that's not going to happen." I noticed her smug grin. *Or, at least, I hope not.* "Anyway, we've got to survive the night first." This bald reminder was enough to replace her grin with a look of grim determination.

***

I slipped onto my backside twice during the descent to the road and even the sure-footed Helen almost fell on a few occasions. *Shame the gecko grips don't come as options on these light combat boots.* The road, identifiable mainly by haloes of light around the street lamps, was completely deserted. We jogged along until we reached the point of the fence closest to the microbiology building and then waited until lights in the entire area went out and our visors switched to night vision. I immediately cut a gap through the chain-link fence. Although the metal was hardened, it was no obstacle to my power shears. Even though the warning system should have been hacked, I was careful to avoid cutting the monitoring cables running along the bottom, middle and top of the fence.

We ran towards a side door, labelled as a fire escape, silent except for the splashing of our feet on the wet grass. The lock on the door should have failed-safe to open, but someone had secured it with a large padlock. *Fuck! So much for health and safety in France!* I drew my pistol and stood back. The shot was almost silent, but the sound of the lock shattering pieced the night. *Should be deadened by the heavy rain, but I hope there aren't any guards wandering about, checking why the power has failed.*

I pulled the door open and we climbed stairs in the faint glow of green emergency lighting, our visors making it appear bright as day. When we reached the fourth floor, the door into the corridor was well oiled and swung open silently. I led the way leftwards, heading towards the laboratories, a student work room and the large office assigned to Professor Jones. As pre-arranged, I made for the Prof's office while Helen split off to check the labs.

The office had one wall of windows, looking out onto the pitch-black campus. There was not the slightest sound from the rain battering against the glass, so very high-quality insulation. When I looked closely with my head torch, I could see faint traces of wires within the window glass. *Faraday Cage: not at all what you would expect to protect the privacy of a normal boffin.* Facing a black leather executive chair, the large oak desk held three huge video screens, an exotic ergonomic keyboard, and a holographic base unit for image display and manipulation. Anachronistic in this high-tech setting were a number of loose cables, which clearly indicated that the central processor and memory had been removed. *Belt and braces here – not only EM shielding, but also shielded hard-links rather than wifi. I guess Jones takes the processor and memory home with her, so there's not much we're going to find here.*

I scanned the rest of the room: a well-polished conference table surrounded by six small and one large leather swivel chairs, three paintings on the wall showing Provence landscapes, a long shelf holding a series of rocks and a small fridge with a capsule coffee machine sitting on it. Given the size of the office, the furnishings were rather Spartan. Although scans picked up nothing, I was checking behind the paintings in case a safe was concealed anywhere when I heard Helen make a surprised squeal.

I dashed back into the corridor, seeing that all the lab doors were now open and noting a trace of the light from my partner's head torch, indicated that she was in the one furthest away. "Buggeration!" I heard her curse, which, strangely enough, acted to reassure me.

I peered cautiously into the laboratory and saw Helen crouched over a body lying on the floor beside a row of glove-boxes, lit also by a torch in its hand. "What happened?"

"Shite! I was scanning the kit here with my helmet cam when this boy surprised me. I guess he was working late or kipping in the student room when the power went off. He shone his torch directly into my eyes when I opened the door. My shot was pure reflex and it's amazing that I even hit him under these conditions. He's dead as a dodo though; large calibre through the neck does that. Bugger!"

"Jesus Christ! That's our plans for undetected intrusion out of the window."

"The smashed padlock was a bit of a give-away anyway, not to mention the hole in the fence," she pointed out.

"I had planned to take the bits of lock with us and hope that, if it was even noticed, it would be assumed that it had been removed for fire safety. The fence I could sort out enough to meet casual inspection with a few spots of super-glue. A body with a bullet in it is, however, rather unambiguous:"

"Sorry, I suppose I buggered things up here."

"Not at all, the risks are so high that you couldn't afford to take a chance. Remember that the scientists in Colmar had assault rifles."

"But this is only a young boy, a student…"

"Whatever, but we need to focus on what to do now. The key thing is to avoid warning our opponents, so that they go to earth and we lose the

49

one good lead that we have. They're bound to be twitchy after Colmar, so we can't reveal that we're targeting Jones. Bollocks!" *Our initial run of good luck now seems to be balancing out by a run of bad!*

"Well, as soon as the body is found the cat will be well and truly out of the bag."

"Right, so I'll take the body and you do what you can to clean up behind us here." I looked around and located a typical laboratory cling-film dispenser. I tore off a large sheet and wrapped it around the neck of the corpse. "Don't need any trail of blood." I grunted as I lifted the still-warm body and hoisted it onto my shoulder. *Lucky this is a skinny sod – I'm definitely not as fit as I used to be.* "Okay, I'll schlep him to the fence and meet you back at the fire door. We're going to have to risk active comms to work out the best way to torch this place."

"You're going to destroy an entire university building in order to cover our tracks," she gasped.

"Dead right," I confirmed before I entered the verbal activation code for my external, line of sight, satellite link. "I'll do this as soon as I'm outside. Okay, five minutes?"

"Five minutes, boss. Buggeration…"

I hurried down the stairs, careful not to trip, and switched on the communication link as soon as I emerged into the driving rain. "Rüdi, Doris, you there?"

"Sure thing, chief, getting a full op download now," Rüdi responded immediately.

"Don't worry about that. We've had a bit of trouble and I need to cover our tracks with a bit of arson. Ideally, I'd like the entire building gutted – but certainly Jones' labs on the fourth floor destroyed completely. Best would be if the source of the fire appeared to be linked to the power cut and at a distance from these labs. Any suggestions?"

"Um, I think I saw something when I was casing the building yesterday," Doris replied. "Ah, here we go. There are extremophile laboratories along the corridor from your target – I guess there'd interactions between the two groups. Lots of work is done under highly reducing conditions and there's a truly stupid amount of hydrogen in their gas store. If you could physically damage the gas supply line and leave the door of the store open, we could turn the place into a bomb. I'd definitely be able to supply a spark when I bring power back. How'd that do?"

"Good enough for me, I'll go dark now, but should have the gas flowing in a couple of minutes. How much time will you need thereafter?"

"Running the simulation now," Rüdi murmured. "If you completely disconnect the gas line… Yes, probably about ten minutes."

"That'd work," I dropped the body by the hole in the fence and raced back into the building. I met Helen half way up the staircase. "It's set up now, but I just need to carry out a quick bit of sabotage. Pick up the corpse at the fence and take it as far into the woods as you can. There's not much cover there, but stuff it out of sight from the road and then start preparing to seal the hole in the fence." I wrenched my tool kit free and threw it to her.

I reached the fourth floor and ran along to the

right, easily locating the gas store by the chemo-toxicity and explosion hazard warning signs. The door was secured by a couple of latches that had not defaulted open on power loss, but were easily wrenched back, allowing the heavy blast door to be slid aside. *Maybe a mystery for anyone doing the forensics after the explosion, but nothing I can do about it.*

There were four racks containing huge gas reservoirs, with the hydrogen clearly marked. As I started to release the gas line with a spanner conveniently tied to the control valve, I noted that one rack contained oxygen cylinders and that a number of plastic 500 litre drums of acetone lay in one corner. *Shit, this place really is an explosion just waiting to happen.*

I raced out of the store, leaving the door slightly ajar, and then clattered down the stairs at breakneck speed. I remembered to lift the smashed padlock as I exited the fire door, just before I switched on the satellite link. "Rüdi, it just occurred to me they may have a log of anyone working nights on the campus. When you get a chance, see if it does exist and, if so, delete the entry for the student who was in Jones' lab."

"Already done. Doris picked this up while we were scanning your video logs. The servers on site are down, but all data is stored in a central facility in downtown Marseille, which we have a back door into."

We certainly lucked out with Rashmi's replacement. "Good job, you guys. The next challenge is going to be extracting us ASAP.

Undetected intrusion with a silent retreat isn't an option now. We're trying to cover our tracks but, if I was Jones, any suspicious event would be enough to trigger a pre-set escape plan."

I clambered through the hole in the fence and watched Helen quickly remove the traces of it before passing back my tool kit. "Won't pass any close inspection, but probably good enough. We should make as much distance as possible on tarmac in the direction of the city before power comes back." I jogged along the road with Helen close on my heels.

"Follow the north perimeter road past the commercial biotech buildings and, at the west corner, there should be a small path through the wood to the Avenue de Luminy," Rüdi instructed. "Two-fifty metres north there's a roundabout. Find somewhere out of sight, but with a view of the road. I'm trying to set up a pick-up by a backup army team who are now in the air, helicoptering up from La Ciotat."

"Actually, we need wheels – ideally a small van or minibus – and dry clothes." I struggled to build a plan while maintaining my running speed. "We need to operate in the middle of the city, so just get us a driver, without the heavy team. Any ideas about how we can get into Jones' apartment?"

"I'm producing this on the fly, as our original concept was a daytime penetration while the professor was at work," Doris apologised. "Anyway, I can get reservations for you both in the spa and just need to set a time…"

"In the spa?" I interrupted. "It's the middle of

the night!"

"Actually, it's not even nine yet and would be quite bright if not for the rain," Doris responded. "Anyway, the spa is top-end but operates twenty-four – seven, so I expect that there may be more than massages on offer."

"Okay, that'll work with me. ETA for pick-up?"

"It'll be at least an hour," Rüdi answered, "and then about thirty minutes to get into the centre of the city at this time of day. I've managed to source minibus, driver and clothes in Marseille, so I'm going to send the army team back to base. I assume that's okay."

"Fine, we just need transport and clothing, so backup is redundant now. You could, however, drop off a couple of grunts at our campsite to recover our gear and trek back to the villa in Cassis tomorrow. Especially if you have a bloke and a gal, this'll remove one potential trace back to us." At that point the lights came back on and we slowed to a walk along the grass at the side of the road.

"The weather will be better tomorrow, so they could fit in a bit of rock climbing," Helen added just as a huge explosion behind us confirmed that Doris's plan had worked.

"That's not a bad idea," I mused aloud, "as it sounds like we may have destroyed the entire microbiology department, so it'd definitely be better if it couldn't be traced back to us."

"Better get into cover soon, as police and fire engines are already on their way," Rüdi recommended.

"Copy that. I see the path that you mentioned and we'll be invisible there. No CCTVs to worry about, I suppose?"

"Nothing at all on that ring road, just cover of access points to the various buildings." Doris responded. "On the main access road that you're heading for, we have one on each of the bus stops, but covering only the pavement and nearby road. You'll be fine if you stick to the edge of the forest. The only tricky ones are a pair covering the roundabout where you'll be picked up – and, of course, dashboard cams on emergency vehicles. Those will be approaching the roundabout from the north, so you should cross the Avenue de Luminy whenever it's quiet and, at the roundabout, turn west along Rue Henri Cochet, towards the stadium. Just find anywhere suitable for pickup beyond the restaurant there and we'll do the rest."

"It's going to get very busy around here soon and we've got an hour before pickup." Helen pointed out. "Shouldn't we try to get as far away as possible? If we jog, we can easily make ten kay."

Just what I need after the exertions of today, but the logic's sound. "We're a bit conspicuous in these suits, so we need to stay out of sight. What do you think?"

"There's a forest road west to the Crete des Escampons, which should be deserted at this time of night," Rüdi responded. "It dead-ends before Baumettes, but there's a path down to a residential area. Only a couple of kilometres as the crow flies, but the route winds about a bit with around a hundred vertical metres up and down. Should be a piece of piss."

I groaned theatrically and then gasped as my feet slid out from below me and I managed to avoid falling only by grabbing the branch of a tree. "Nothing under these conditions will be a piece of piss!"

Helen chuckled. "A walk in the park for anyone not nearing their sell-by date. Anyway, route now confirmed and we're on our way."

"Link should be secure, but we'll go dark now," I added. "Ping us when you have a fixed pick-up time." There was another small explosion from behind us and I could now make out the faint sounds of approaching sirens. *Maybe we've had enough bad luck and we'll get a break or two now but, for some reason or other, I've an awful feeling there's even worse to come.*

CHAPTER FOUR

We were crouching out of the rain in the lee of a shed storing rubbish bins when the minibus approached. It was driven by Robert Lambert, head of security at the Swiss consulate in Marseille. Everything about his rotund, balding, bedraggled appearance indicated clearly that he was not a happy man. Immediately after we piled into the back of the vehicle, he started to list his grievances. "I have no idea what you folk are up to or why I wasn't informed in advance of anti-terrorist actions in my patch," he turned to glare at us, "and I don't suppose you're going to enlighten me?"

"Above my pay grade," I answered. "This op is extremely sensitive and it's completely need to know only."

"So, it's just a coincidence that half a university campus was blown to buggery not far from here? That's not something that I need to know about?"

"No idea at all about that," I looked towards Helen and rolled my eyes. "You just need to drop us off at the station and then we're out of your hair."

"I'll be bloody glad about that!" He lapsed into silence, with his entire body language continuing to present the message of how pissed-off he was.

The minibus had enough space for us to easily strip off our suits and wipe down both them and our sweaty bodies with the towels provided. Towels and underwear were chucked into a plastic bag and I noted Robert glancing into his rear-view mirror as

Helen donned fresh sports-bra and pants, although the sight of her tight, muscular body didn't seem to improve his demeanour at all. *Not into girls? Didn't seem any more interested in my naked bod, though.*

The suits and equipment belts went into a pair of black backpacks and then we dressed in matching jeans, cotton shirts and Nike trainers. The detached visors from our suits now served as designer eyewear. A large, black golf umbrella had also been thoughtfully included. *Due to Rüdi or Doris, I'm sure, rather than surly Lambert.*

Black baseball caps, with integrated comms wirelessly linked to ear buds and throat mikes included our rigouts and allowed us to develop our plans without being overheard.

"En route, chaps," Helen initiated the satellite link to Brugg. "Lambert should be instructed to drop us off at the station and immediately transfer the package that I'll give him to the Consulate for preliminary analysis. You can imply that we're catching a train soon after we arrive, but I don't want him hanging about in any case, as he's really miffed about being out of the circuit on this op. It is more than enough that he knows we're here and can potentially connect us to the lab explosion."

"What's in the package?" Rüdi enquired.

"Just the sticky strips from our suits, in case we got anything from the office or labs. I think it's pretty unlikely though."

"I'll fast track them anyway," Doris added. "We have the full analyses of all patches from the Colmar team, so I'll add an auto-comparison to see if there are any links."

"I hope to hell there are," Helen murmured softly, clearly still upset about the collateral casualty from our incursion.

In the vehicle, the strained silence lasted until we approached the impressive 19th century edifice that was the Saint Charles station. "Here you are," Robert noted superfluously as we drove up to the drop-off point in front of the Ibis hotel. "You have something for me?"

"Thanks a lot, Robert, the lift helped a lot. This is the package," I nodded to Helen, who handed over a small, sealed plastic box before she clambered out after me.

"I don't suppose that I need to know what it is?" He turned it in his hands before slipping it into a glove compartment and driving off as soon as we closed the door, clearly not expecting any answer.

I opened the umbrella to shield us from the downpour, noting that the wind had dropped or, at least, we were sheltered by the surrounding buildings. "Let's get into the station. Jones' flat is on the other side, somewhere."

"Yes, facing onto Place Victor Hugo," Doris responded. "Very fancy building which was once a school." A map ghosted onto the left side of my glasses. "Your massage is confirmed for fifteen minutes from now."

"How will that work?" Helen asked, not bothering to sub-vocalise now that we were on our own.

"As I mentioned before, the spa is top end and caters for what they term *discerning adults*. You have a suite and two personal attendants booked for two hours, with the option of extending for a further two. There are massage tables, a hot tub and a sauna but, from the CCTV, it looks to cater more for bondage than back rubs."

"There's video? I wouldn't have thought the clients would have been happy with that."

I could detect amusement as Doris responded to my question. "Monitoring during sessions only for protection of the staff. Afterwards, everything auto-deleted. I have hacked into the system, though, so we can see everything that's going on."

"So, you'll be able to see us there?" Helen asked.

"Of course. But I imagine that you'll have little time for any hanky-spanky anyway."

"Shame about that. What do you think, boss, maybe a chance of some kinky action?"

I ignored my partner and led the way through the busy station. *The last thing I need is to distract myself with thought of Helen being serviced by a couple of Dominas.*

It took only five minutes to traverse the station and walk along the covered passageway to the Spa L'école, which shared a reception desk with an associated hotel. Just before we entered, I asked why we hadn't simply reserved a room in the latter. Typically, the establishment was fully booked for the night: adding yet another complication to the operation.

"You are booked in as Mister and Missus Smith, but I've prepaid the session so you don't need to show any ID," Doris added.

I simply gave this name at reception and,

moments later, a beautiful young woman who looked as if she might be Thai appeared to take us to our suite. She was clad in white trousers, shirt and sneakers and looked like a conventional masseuse. *Maybe Doris has been taking the piss.*

The girl simply led us to our room, passing an elevator that seemed to access both the hotel rooms and the apartments above them, and waved us inside. "Your therapists will be with you shortly, make yourselves comfortable," she said before shutting the door behind us.

The entrance hall contained a wardrobe, convenient for dumping the umbrella and the backpacks before we removed our jackets and hung them up, keeping our caps on. The main room was large with two rather sophisticated massage tables in the middle, covered by thick white towels. On the left side was an open shower and a sauna with a glass door. To the right was a Jacuzzi, which was gently bubbling, and a couple of sofas. The facing wall was entirely mirrored and contained another door. "Looks kosher enough," I observed.

"Yes, if not for the heavy rings at each corner of the table," Doris pointed out, "and the rack of toys behind you."

I turned to see that Helen had lifted a cover on a large trolley to expose an array of dildos, riding crops, wooden paddles, handcuffs, silk ropes and trays of clips and other kit that I could not identify. "Okay, maybe not so kosher," I admitted.

While I was trying to work out the possible use of some of these implements, the mirror door creaked open and I turned to observe the entrance of

61

the therapists. *Maybe there is some kind of therapy that required practitioners to wear tight black leather bodices, matching thigh-length boots with ridiculous high heels and minute leather tangas, so it's a pity we don't have time to find out what that might be.*

I heard Rüdi's wolf whistle as I inspected the beautiful young women, who looked like they might be sisters, if not twins. They were tall and slim, with black, shoulder-length hair, scarlet lipstick, dark eyeshade and incongruously large breasts, with nipples sporting large silver rings.

"Mister and Missus Smith, I am Valerie and this is my sister, Monica," the one on my left announced. "I think we need to get you out of those clothes first of all."

"Let me look at you first," I replied. "You are both extremely beautiful. Can you turn around please?"

The girls were clearly unperturbed by this request or the feel of our hands as Helen and I each caressed one of the pair of shapely buttocks on show. Their gasps of surprise were almost simultaneous when we applied the hypodermics spikes concealed in small finger rings, causing them to immediately lose consciousness.

I managed to catch Valerie around the waist and slowly laid her onto the floor, noting with amusement that Monica had slipped in Helen's arms and was now held just below her pendulous breasts.

"Stop playing with the girl, fun as it seems to be," I smiled and lifted the Domina, carrying her to one of the massage tables. We then lifted Valerie

62

together and placed her on top of her sister. "I assume you're spoofing the cameras, Doris,"

"Of course, but I can record this for you if you want to add it to your bondage collection." I could hear Rüdi chortling in the background.

I refused to rise to the bait, although it was a very tempting offer. Helen and I stripped the girls, handcuffed their hands and tied their legs to the beds and finally added ball-gags. *The drug should keep the girls out cold for at least a couple of hours, but better to be on the safe side.*

I recovered our backpacks from the entrance hall and we quickly stripped and donned our intrusion suits, stuffing our discarded clothes into the packs. "Do we need to block the doors?"

"Nope, both have electric locks and I can jinx them," Rüdi replied. "We also have the output from cams in the hallway and the elevator. Both are clear at the moment and the elevator is on your floor. You can leave the rucksacks here and pick them up on your way out."

"Okay, Helen, we're on," I quickly opened the door and headed towards the lift, hearing the door softly close and lock behind us. The elevator door opened as we approached it and I saw that it was already set for the second floor, where Jones had her flat.

On the second floor we exited and turned left, standing in front of the professor's door. "She's definitely at home now?"

"There's no cam on this landing, but she came up in the lift just after six. Jones clearly has a cam in the peephole, but I can't hack anything from either

her flat or the one opposite." Doris sounded annoyed by this failure. "I do have an over-ride that will open the doors, however – it's required by the building safety regulations. It won't do anything if she's got manual bolts on the inside, though."

I heard the click as the door unlocked and, to my great surprise, it opened silently when I pushed against it.

"That's strange," Helen commented. "I already had a shaped charge ready to take out the lock. Do you think she's really in there?"

"One sure fire way to find out." I drew my pistol and cautiously peered around the door and into a corridor that led to a living room on the left and open doors leading into what appeared to be a bedroom straight ahead and a study to my right. The study was clearly empty, so I waved a finger to indicate that Helen should check the bedroom while I had a look at the living room.

As I moved down the hallway, open doors revealed a bathroom on my right and a service room to my left. The living room contained a TV area and, beyond that, a couple of sofas around a coffee table. To my right was a dining table and beyond that an open kitchen. The L-shape of these areas contained windows looking onto a large terrace. "All clear here and not a trace of Jones, despite every light in the place being on."

"Same for the bedroom and the en-suite bathroom," Helen reported.

"What do you make of this…?" I started before noticing that our satellite link was gone. "Faraday cage again," I informed my partner while I moved towards the door, knowing that there was a signal on the landing. "Fuck, this bloody door's locked!" I wrenched the unresponsive handle in frustration.

Helen appeared at my side and rapped her knuckles against the door, eliciting only a soft thud. "That's bloody solid! It looked like wood from the outside, but must be steel reinforced."

"This is beginning to feel like the Colmar lab," I frowned. "But why would anyone build such shielding into a residence? Anyway, let's have a look at the office first and then we can blow the door."

"So much for undetected intrusion," Helen muttered, "we're leaving behind a trail of devastation."

The large work desk was reminiscent of that in Jones' office on campus, with the same cables to display and input devices, but no trace of the associated processing unit. Similarities extended also to the style of paintings and the selection of rocks displayed along the ledge of the window that extended for the full length of the facing wall. A bookcase contained further rocks and a dozen or so ancient paperbacks, which seemed to be science fiction in all cases.

Helen was looking through the books when the room door suddenly slammed shut, with a solid clunk indicating that it had locked itself. I ran to check it. "Fuck, it's the same heavy-duty job as the front door. We're going to have to blow it too."

"Lucky that we've got two charges, so..." Helen stopped mid-sentence and the colour drained from her face. "Oh, Jesus, shit!"

I saw she was looking at the monitors on her left wrist, so I immediately glanced I mine, "Christ on a bike, how's that even possible? I'm reading gammas, at a very high dose rate!"

Her fingers blurred as she flashed through menus. "Looks like pure caesium-137." Her arm swept in a circle while her eyes were glued to the monitor unit. "There seems to be distinct sources distributed throughout the floor, I guess shields were removed when the door shut." She clambered onto the desk, kicking a screen onto the floor. "This table must be reinforced, so it provides a bit of shielding."

I clambered up beside her, kicking off another screen and a keyboard. "Hell's bells, why on earth would anyone build a setup like this?"

"I've no idea, but it's a death trap in any case," Helen responded. "We'll have picked up a lethal dose within an hour and, soon thereafter, we'll be vomiting and shitting blood."

"Okay, I'll blow the door…"

"No, I'll do it…"

"You've got ovaries, so get on the window ledge there and check if the dose is any lower."

I quickly walked to the door, set the charge, and managed to climb back onto the table before it exploded with a deafening bang. When I returned to examine my work, I quickly determined that, although blackened with a sizeable dent, the door was intact and completely immobile. "Shit, I guess we need to try again with the other charge although, even if that works, we still need to escape from the house somehow."

"Do you think the second charge will do it?" Helen asked.

"In all honesty, I doubt it. That's a seriously armoured door:"

"Then maybe we'd be better trying the charge here." I climbed back onto the table to inspect the corner of the window where she was pointing. "You can see that the window can be slid open, but must have a latch at this side. This is heavy-duty armoured glass and the walls are certainly also armoured, but a shaped charge might just take out the latch."

"The problem is that we can't actually see where the latch is," I pointed out.

"Halfway down the window, would be the obvious place – which would be here."

"And what if there are two latches?"

"Well, in that case, we're truly screwed," she shrugged her shoulders fatalistically.

"Fine, we're better doing something rather than just hanging about, soaking up Sieverts. You've got the charge, so just set it where you think is best."

We crammed together at the far side of the window ledge, almost falling off when the explosive detonated. At first it seemed as if we had failed again but, as we pulled together, there was a small movement that opened a couple of millimetres before it jammed solidly.

Helen peered into the space. "I can see the latch, but it's not completely released."

"What if we try to shake it back and forward?"

"I think that's more likely to make it fall back into place than anything else." She drew a thin ceramic knife from her belt and placed it against the gap, hammering it into place with the heel of her other hand. "Let's see how this goes. Just keep pulling while I..." There was a sudden click and the window slid silently ajar.

"Thank fuck!" I gasped, following my partner through the gap and onto the wide but very wet outer windowsill.

"Negligible radiation there, but we must be a good seven or eight metres above the ground."

I peered down. "There's another window below us. If I can hang off this one, you should be able to climb down me onto the window ledge."

"And then what?"

"I'm sure you'll think of something. Anyway, I'll need to have a good grip and hang as low as possible." I re-entered the room and grabbed all cables in sight, quickly braiding them together. I then removed my pistol from its holster and crammed it into a thigh pocket before taking off my belt and passing it through a loop of cables tied to the table leg nearest the open window. I closed the belt and tugged on the webbing. *Seems solid enough, but will it hold the combined weight of the two of us?*

Helen looked at me quizzically as crawled backwards out of the window. "You really think that's going to work?"

"I'm sure as hell going to find out. If I don't plummet immediately to my death, you're going to have to be fast. Remember, I'm a crumbly old bastard and won't be able to hang on long."

I dropped my legs cautiously over the edge and

then squirmed backwards until my body dropped free, both hands clutching the belt, which extended just below the window sill. I gave a grunt of pain as my full weight came onto my arms, crushing my hands against the wall.

Seconds later, Helen's legs appeared and I looked down to avoid being kicked in the face. Holding the windowsill, she lowered herself until her legs were jammed against my ribs and then gradually transferred her weight onto me. I groaned again as the pain in my arms and hands increased. Quickly moving her grip to my forearms, she moved her legs lower until they dug into my thighs. Her downwards progress registered by the grabs to grip the tough fibre of my suit. *Thank God she's a climber with the arm strength to do that – I certainly couldn't.*

One moment she was gripping my calves and then her weight vanished. For a second, I thought she had fallen, but then I heard her whisper. "I'm down okay, just hang on for a tick."

Easy to say, but it feels as if my bloody shoulders are going to pop out at any time and I can't feel my hands any more. I jerked in surprise at the phut sound of a silenced gunshot followed by shouting male and female voices and crashing noises of furniture being destroyed. Shortly afterwards, although it felt like an eternity, I felt a hand touch my boot, pushing my legs apart.

"I don't have time to work out anything better, so I'm going to get your feet onto my shoulders. I'll lean out as far as possible, so you can let go and brace yourself against the wall while you crouch down until I can get a hold of your hand. I then squat and you can jump down beside me."

I could feel the support beneath my boots and the pain in my arms dropped to a throbbing ache. Only with my weight fully supported, did sufficient feeling return to my hands so that I could slowly force my trembling fingers to open. I released the belt and placed my palms onto the wall for support. I was painfully aware of my exposed position and fastened my eyes on the wall in front of my nose while I struggled to quell shivers of vertigo."

"God, but you're a heavy bastard. Get a bloody move on," Helen commanded, forcing me to start bending my knees while I slid my hands downwards. "Okay, that should do it, lower your left hand now to the side of your knee."

It required enormous willpower to remove my hand from the wall and then slide it down my chest and thigh. It had just passed my knee when my wrist was grabbed and I seized her forearm with a sigh of relief. I looked down to see that her other hand was gripping the frame of an open window and marvelled as she slowly crouched down with only the slightest tremor of her knees.

She twisted her shoulders slightly to the left. "Right, jump down beside me now. You just need to land on the window ledge, I can stop you from falling off."

My position was extremely awkward and it was more of a fall than a jump. Only my left foot landed on the ledge and I felt a shock of pain before I was hauled through the window to sprawl on the floor of the room. "Fuck!" I gasped while I rolled onto my back in time to see Helen following me, landing with catlike grace in a crouch at my side. "Jesus Christ, I hope I never have to do anything like that ever again. I'm surprised I haven't shat myself."

"Well, I'm happy about that too, considering that you were standing above my head," she grinned.

I bent forward and rubbed my left ankle. "The bad news, however, is that I might have buggered up my foot."

Helen moved to inspect it while I looked around. The bedroom seemed to be organised around a huge bed covered by a rather tacky scarlet satin sheet. I could make out a naked woman sprawled on her stomach on it and a black, hairy, male leg extending over the far side.

"Doesn't seem to be broken, just a bad strain. I'll just strap it up and give you a painkiller shot. Do you want to go back to active comms?"

"Christ, I'd completely forgotten that we'd got this option back after leaving Jones' booby-trapped rooms. Okay." I switched the link on and downloaded the cam output while quickly summarising our situation. "Helen, what the story here?" I waved a finger in the general direction of the bed.

"When I dropped onto the window ledge, I could see into the room but the occupants didn't see me. Not surprising really as a skinny white guy with his wrists handcuffed behind his back was licking off the woman there while being well buggered by a huge Negro. The windows are heavy, but closed by a conventional lock, which I shot off. As you can imagine, they weren't best set up for hand-to-hand combat, so I bludgeoned them down pretty quickly. They're probably all concussed, but we should drug them if we're not going to be clear of this place very soon."

"Do we have enough shots?" I enquired after I was helped to my feet and practiced a few tentative steps while I moved to better inspect Helen's victims.

"I've got two, but, of course, your kit is still on your belt, up there," she raised her eyes.

"Actually, two will be enough – the black guy and the woman. The other bloke isn't breathing. It looks like you caved his skull in."

"Oh, bugger!" my partner looked distraught. "More collateral damage! I'm so sorry."

"Don't be," I put my arm around her shoulder, "you had to sort things out as quickly as possible and there was no time for kid gloves. If you hadn't been so fast, it would have been me pushing up daisies – or, actually, jam all over the pavement,"

"Okay guys," Rüdi interrupted, "how do you want to proceed with extraction?"

"Well, better if we can avoid the main entrance, as leaving before the end of a session would seem strange and start investigations that I'd like to postpone as long as possible. What options do we have?"

"You could bail out the window here," Doris answered, "but that leaves you in your intrusion suits. I'd recommend heading back to your bondage suite, then change clothes and take the staff exit."

"What's that?" Helen enquired.

"You remember the way that the leather girls entered, through the door in the back of the room? Anyway, there are corridors to the back of all suites – I guess to allow kinky costumes to be worn without perturbing residents of the hotel or apartments."

"I suspect that the hotel may have a very similar clientele to the spa from what we can see here," I looked around the room. "But, anyway, how do we then get out of the building?"

"There's a common dressing room for the hookers – or therapists or whatever – that includes a small snack area with food and drink dispensers. It has a sliding door leading to a little terrace that's used as a smoking den. You just need to hop over a railing and then you're in a backstreet."

"That'd work. Let us know when the pathway to the suite is clear and we'll be on our way. How does it look for extraction?"

"I've got a reservation for you on a TGV leaving for Paris in twenty-five minutes. You'll be booked through to the terminus, but change in Lyon for a Eurotransit from Barcelona to Berlin. You skip out at Basel and we'll pick you up there."

"Thanks, Doris – and you Rüdi. The op might have gone totally tits-up, but at least we'll get home in one piece. Any op that you walk out of is, at least, a partial success."

"Or limp out of, in your case," Helen gave me a nudge in the ribs. "Not forgetting about the radiation dose that we accumulated. We got out fast, but were well above the annual limits for radiation workers. Although, look on the bright side, at least you've no hair to fall out."

Now, was our escape from the death-trap a sign that our luck's beginning to change or just something that's prolonging the agony, allowing more shit to be dropped on top of us?

CHAPTER FIVE

After arriving back in Switzerland, we spent a day in hospital for tests and prophylactic treatment for our radiation exposure, which had actually been lower than indicated by our conservative dosimeters. Although I was still limping slightly as a result of my sprained ankle and my hands were extensively bruised, we were considered fit for duty.

Our formal debriefing, with the same participants as for operation initiation, occurred two days later. The Commander looked grim as he opened the meeting and summarised the current status. "On balance, I think we've progressed in terms of confirming that this is a threat that appears more serious than anything we've experienced to date. It's clear that this Professor Jones is not at all what she seems to be and the sophistication of the trap set up at her apartment shows that her organisation has major resources, is extremely well informed and has preparations in place to avoid intrusions to their properties that border on paranoia. Before I hand over to the Group Leader, I'd like Alex to summarise the post-mortem analysis from the security team in Marseille."

Supersaxo initiated the holographic outline of his file, with two nodes representing the University laboratory and Jones' apartment linked to the Colmar database. "First the laboratory. Damage to the microbiology building was much more extensive than expected from the hydrogen explosion itself, suggesting self-destruct systems in one of the laboratories, the one where the student was working, and also Jones' office. This was disabled by our power cut, but set off by the fire, so was clearly less sophisticated than that in Colmar. We guess it could have been put in place about a decade ago, when the Professor moved to this campus and had the labs refitted." The image showing a photomontage of the damaged building that was overlain by simulations with and without additional explosion sources.

"I guess this would fit also with the secondary explosions that we heard," Helen added.

"Yes," Alex continued, modifying the model to show time steps. "The hydrogen blast would have been followed by the lab first and then finally Jones' office. These were both low yield, configured to produce fireballs, thus effectively preventing useful evidence being collected afterwards."

"This leads us to Jones apartment, and I should note that the actions here have really pissed-off a certain Robert Lambert from the Consulate." Helen and I exchanged wry smiles. "Although he's out of the loop, it wasn't hard for him to connect the fracas there to you pair and, despite instructions to stay clear, he's been nosing about our database and picked up our cover team instructions. Anyway, that's a problem for me to sort out."

The campus file closed and was replaced by a French police databank library. "We hacked the official reports on three apparently related incidents – assault of two women in a therapy suite, murder and assault in a hotel room and breaking and entry

76

of Jones' apartment. The absence of any CCTV images is complicating things, but staff reports have identified the couple responsible for, at least, the first incident – a young woman and an old bald man." Photo-fit images appeared. Supersaxo looked at us, "not bad, but searches of records from cameras in the surrounding area haven't resulted in any matches."

"I should hope not," Doris whispered.

"Anyway," Alex continued, "the fact that the Dominas were stripped and tied up after being drugged provides an argument that this could just be some kinky sex thing, unrelated to the other incidents if not for the mysterious absence of all relevant video records. Conceivably, the assault of two prostitutes and the murder of their client could also be sex-related, but access of the room via the window has the police completely baffled." Police videos showed the crime scene, leading to a shot from the window that clearly showed my belt hanging from the room above.

"Jones couldn't be contacted and, although known to have entered the building, has been untraceable since. The door to her flat was found to be unlocked and all internal doors open, but it appeared undisturbed, with the notable exception of the study, with damaged computer equipment, the belt tied to the work table, blast damage to the inside of the study door and the blown-out window latch. It has been suggested that Professor Jones may have been kidnapped, but no credible link of this to the other crimes has been proposed."

A further image expanded from the police file.

"The belt is the only hard piece of evidence that they have from the apartment. Untraceable, but typical armed forces kit that would tie in with the traces of military-grade shaped charges and a bullet from a pistol recovered from the hotel room. The injuries to the surviving couple in the hotel room, known prostitutes apparently, are also consistent with assault by someone with combat experience."

"The police picked up nothing on the gamma death-trap?" I enquired.

"Nothing at all. Presumably shielding went back into place when the door locks opened. The cops are completely baffled."

The display flicked off. "Any other questions?"

"What about the student I killed, anything on him?" Helen asked.

"Identified as Jean Petit from your cam images" Video appeared together with a university personnel file. "Body hasn't been found and, in fact, he hasn't even been reported missing. There are a lot of feral dogs around the outskirts of Marseille, so the corpse may be gone for good."

Urs Wagner, the forensics tech, waved his hand and I indicated for him to speak.

"I don't want to screw-up the flow of things, but first results from the dust-catchers on the intrusion suits could be relevant here."

"Fine, go ahead," I responded.

"Well, flakes of skin that we are currently assigning to Jean Petit match some of those from the Colmar lab. Some that we take to be from Professor Jones also. We can't say for definite that Petit and Jones actually spent time in Colmar, but the labs are certainly linked in some way."

"Thank God," Helen sighed, "at least the student had some sort of link to the conspiracy here."

"It certainly looks that way," I concluded. "The problem is that the great efforts made to avoid us finding any link between the labs or trace the conspiracy further seem to imply that it's part of something bigger. In fact, given the resources needed to set up and booby-trap these laboratories and Jones' apartment, I suspect something very much bigger."

"I feel you may be right," the Commander sighed. "Where do we go from here?"

I called up the Operation Zodiac overview. "Our main lead is certainly the mysterious Professor Jones." Video segments of a stout, rather dowdy, brown-haired woman giving a lecture played, while audio summarised her CV. "First degree from Cambridge, doctorate from the Sorbonne in Paris, where she met and married a French-Moroccan biology lecturer, George Dahan. He obtained a professorship in Strasbourg, where they spent a decade while Jones worked up from assistant lecturer to Junior Professor. Divorced in thirty-five, just before Jones got her present professorship in Marseille. She's been there even since – almost ten years now."

"Any recent romantic links?" Pirmin asked.

"Nothing serious from what we've been able to hack from university and police files, or expert-system mining of CCTV records from around her flat," Doris answered. "Occasional visits to her home from students and university colleagues, both male and female, but no clear indication of any relationships with them."

"What about hobbies, interests?" Pirmin added.

"She's a keen hiker, spending a lot of weekends in the Calanques. Of course, not a lot of CCTV coverage there. A regular destination in good weather seems to have been Calanque Sormiou. The CCTV for a restaurant car park covers the walking path and records for the last five years were stored in the cloud. Just beyond this point..." a map appeared, "...there's a nudist beach, so no video coverage there. I do have a search machine digging for any personal video from this location, but it'll take time and I don't have hopes of finding much."

"Was she hiking alone?" Pirmin continued.

"Good question..." video grabs flashed as image analysis ran. "Okay, over the five years, we see her heading towards the beach eighteen times, in all cases alone. Her return is picked up on fifteen occasions, on six of these accompanied by a woman and on three by a man – in one case with a couple. I guess she could be picking up company at the beach."

"Nothing else from the Calanques?" I enquired.

"There's really very little to hack into between Marseille and Cassis. I have picked up a bar on the Calanque de Morgiou, but no useful images as yet. There's another nudist beach nearby, so it's a possibility."

"Thanks, Doris, that's a lot of useful stuff. See if you can trace any of those appearing with Jones on any image. What about the ex-husband?"

"I already checked that," Rüdi responded and opened a Strasbourg police file. "Died of heart attack only one month after his divorce. Despite that, he left everything to her: quite an amount, as he was independently wealthy with his academic work more of a hobby."

"And the source of this wealth?" the Commander asked.

"His father, who was a political exile after one of the many coups in Morocco. He lived in Paris, but his money was mainly in Swiss banks."

"So, Jones is well-off. It didn't particularly look like it from her flat."

Doris displayed a summary from Jones' accounts with Credit Agricole. "She clearly lives off her university salary. There's no trace here of her inheritance from her ex-husband."

"Well, that's a lot of missing money, so we need to start looking at trails from Swiss banks," I looked at Supersaxo.

"No problem, I'll get you the access required."

I nodded my thanks and returned to the operation overview. "Let's step back a bit and bring in the new material from Colmar. Pirmin, can you summarise what we have?"

"Well, the lab equipment was mainly purchased via Marseille University and then diverted en route to Strasbourg, supposedly as part of a collaborative project between Jones and Isaacs. The Syrians were involved in transportation of kit and construction of the lab: they seem to have been inherited by the academics from an Islamic State group that attempted gas attacks on Geneva and

Zurich eighteen months ago. We thought we'd eliminated the entire organisation, but Achmed's cell must have slipped through the net. As isotopic signatures of both the explosives and gas match those attacks, so I guess these were already in place when Jones took over."

"Your term 'the academics' highlights a key question: how did a university professor manage to link up with a bunch of raghead terrorists?" Rüdi took the words out of my mouth. "Those involved are clearly capable of making bio-weapons, but why and for whom?"

A new branch on the operation chart appeared for each of these questions. "Thoughts anyone?" I looked at the frowning faces around the table. "Jörg, anything from the security team?"

"Nothing at all that we haven't already got. They're working through both internal resources and contacts with partner national security agencies, so their presence should be well known now."

Typically succinct!

"Could the two labs represent a single cell, led by Jones?" Pirmin mused. "They could be part of a bigger organisation, but run in as isolated a manner as possible. The primary unit is in Marseille and must have been established about a decade ago. When the self-destruct systems were built into the labs," he added in response to several quizzical stares. "Outside support would have been needed then to source and install the explosives."

"And the radiation sources for Jones' apartment," Helen pointed out. "She's been in that flat for a while now, hasn't she?"

"Yes, for nine years. Bought the apartment and had it completely refurbished before she moved in," Doris answered.

"Might explain caesium-137 rather than a shorter-lived isotope like cobalt-60, which could be easier to obtain," added Judith. "But I can't work out how the required shielding was managed. Even using DU – depleted uranium – you'd need quite a thickness to allow safe working in that room, or the room under it for that matter."

"I wonder, are plans on file for the refurbishment work?"

Doris scowled while she dug unto her purloined database. "Only 2D, I'm afraid." Before and after plans appeared before us. "Mmm, not the same scale or orientation, but I can rotate, resize and overlap." The images blurred and then integrated, with before in blue and after in red. "Internal walls have been moved but there's a two-by-two metre lost area – maybe a hidden room."

"Or a radiation source safe. I think that'd work, as the building plan shows it has bathrooms above and below. I wouldn't like to sleep every night of my life beside it though."

"Interesting…" I scratched my head, sure that there was some kind of clue here. "Was there any other work ongoing when Jones rebuilt her flat?"

"Um, yes," Doris displayed before and after plans that looked remarkably similar to the ones we had just seen. "This is the flat opposite, owned by a rather reclusive widow, Madame Dupont. She bought her apartment at about the same time as Jones and I guess they saved quite a bit of money by having the two properties done together by the same firm."

"Almost identical work to Jones' pad, but without the radiation store. Is there more on this?"

"Already looking. Seems like the contractor that did the work was in a shaky financial situation and went bankrupt soon afterwards. Not helped by a fire in their office, which destroyed all their records."

"Convenient that! So, what's the story with Dupont?"

Doris presented a summary with a series of pictures and videos. "Age fifty-five, retired as a teacher after her husband, a banker, died leaving her a tidy little nest egg. Sold their large villa in the suburbs and downsized to this place. According to the police interview, she slept through all of the action, but was extremely upset by the break-ins and murder and was going to stay with a friend in Toulon."

"I wonder… You see that, despite significant differences in their facial image scans, she and Jones have similar builds."

"Jones is a centimetre shorter with different colour hair and eyes," Doris integrated data as her search machine ripped it from hacked servers. "Iris scan also completely different. Nevertheless, it could be a disguise. But would it be possible to maintain this for a decade?"

"Dupont was a recluse," Helen reminded us, "so I think we can't preclude it. If Jones actually lived in the flat opposite and her apparent residence was just a front, it could explain a lot."

"It's a hell of a lot of effort for a small benefit in terms of security. But belt-and-braces seems to be a philosophy that characterises this crowd. Do we have anything else to support it?" I wondered aloud.

"Actually, I'm still looking at these conversion plans for the two flats," Judith displayed them together. "There's a cable duct running from Jones' study to Dupont's back bedroom with a central switchbox noted as cable TV. From the building plans," these were added to the image, "the cable input to each flat is located in the living room, just about where Jones had her TV."

"You know, this would work in an extremely paranoid kind of a way," I added. "What if the deadly study serves only to store Jones' processor unit: she lives in and works from the flat opposite. In the event of her identity being compromised without her knowledge, any incursion would lead to intruders being trapped and killed within the study. If the processor was present, it'd be fried by the radiation. If she had time, as in our case, she could retrieve it before we arrived. Radiation would also have the advantage over an explosion of allowing her more flexibility to make her escape."

"But this implies that the processor is extremely valuable. Would she really allow it to be destroyed in the case that she successfully killed the intruders?" Helen asked.

"Yes, but what if it's only a mobile working unit with a full backup that's considered to be un-findable?" Judith responded.

"She'd have to be extremely confident that it couldn't be found..."

"Yes, definitely, but I think I know now where it is," Judith smiled at the blank stares. "Here!" A cursor pointed at the junction box between the two apartments. "It's built into the floor, certainly shielded and accessible only with major excavation, which would probably trigger self-destruction. It could completely mirror everything on the portable unit. If Jones was abandoning her flat with the mobile unit, she could destroy the backup – unless she was sure that it was so well hidden that she could leave it as a secondary emergency backup. However, I'm pretty sure Dupont would have scrubbed its memory before setting off for her friend in Toulon and, as she had enough time, this could be done much more effectively than was the case with the chip in the Colmar lab."

"Well, this would not only clear up a lot of the anomalies here, but also give us another lead to follow – the widow Dupont. I guess that's something for Rüdi and Doris."

"As Jones now knows we're after her, is there any point in maintaining my disinformation team?" Alex Supersaxo asked.

I pondered this question for a couple of minutes while scanning through the operation overview. "Well, she certainly knows that Colmar was a Swiss retribution attack and may well guess that it's linked to our actions in Marseille. I can't imagine, though, that the set-up there was specifically designed with us in mind. There could be other players involved, so maybe we need more disinformation rather than less. How about informing your team about the events on Campus and asking them to check for any links to Colmar, without any suggestion of our direct involvement? They can deal openly with the French police and the Consulate. We will, however, need to take that pest Lambert out of the way to ensure that he doesn't give us away."

"Seems reasonable. Of course, anything they find will be copied by Jörg to your team."

"Okay, I guess we can wrap this session..." a wave caught my attention. "Sorry Urs, was there something else?"

"I'm not sure, it's just that when we were taking dust samples off Helen's suit, I found this business card in her pocket." The image floated in front of us – clearly details of a bar or restaurant, with one side in English and the other Japanese.

I looked at Helen, who appeared completely mystified. "I haven't a clue..." she started before slapping herself on the forehead. "Ah, yes, I remember now. I pulled it from one of Jones' paperback books just before the door slammed closed and things went apeshit. I don't even remember pocketing it, but I guess I must have."

"Yes, well if you did it while facing the door, that'd explain why we couldn't see anything on your cam record. We'll go back through the footage before that to see if we can enhance it a bit to pick out more. Anyway, this establishment, Far Yeast Brewpub Shiodome, is in Tokyo and opened only sixteen months ago. However, there's no record of Jones travelling to Japan within the last five years."

"Interesting. Okay, you and Judith chase this further, liaising closely with Doris and Rüdi. Is there anything else?" I saw heads shaking around the table. "Right, let's get on with it and see if we can either find Jones or get answers to some of Pirmin's questions."

***

Early next morning, Doris reported that she was getting some interesting material, so I summoned the team to hear it together.

"I've been integrating what little we've been able to dig up on Dupont with what we have on Jones." A timeline appeared extending over the last ten years. "You'll see that the professor takes an extended four-week break every year – going sailing in the Med, aboard this rather swanky yacht," the photo of a large vessel with a vertical axis wind turbine appeared, together with a video of a tall, bronzed man, "which is owned by the billionaire Pierre Tan. He has a French father and Vietnamese mother, giving him dual nationality. Made his money in property, investing in cheap, higher land in the coastal areas most impacted by rising sea levels. Seems to spend almost all of his time on the boat or in his villa, on a small private island off the Costa Smeralda in Sardinia. He clearly likes his privacy: I've been able to find a few images from harbour webcams and CCTV from other vessels, but nothing during the periods when Jones was aboard that allow her to be unambiguously identified." A series of videos showing the yacht in different locations appeared, with enhancement to show bleary shots of women that could be the professor.

"I haven't yet been able to nail down the link

between Jones and Tan, but it's interesting that, during each of Jones' cruises, Dupont flies to Tokyo for a fortnight. Last time was seven months ago."

"Do we have anything on the Japanese side?" I asked, peering at the time lines and the flights noted. "And, any idea why she flies Emirates via Dubai rather than the daily, direct, Air France option?"

"Japan searches are ongoing, but the problem with Tokyo is the sheer volume of CCTV available. If I can hack out hotel bookings, however, I'll be able to narrow this down. The flights are interesting: Emirates is certainly a better airline and actually a little cheaper than Air France," details of flight variants were displayed. "Emirates will always involve more time in the air, but there are options with shorter stop-overs than the one she always choses, which requires overnighting. There is, however, a free hotel night included in the package, so maybe that's the attraction."

"Could be, but the oil crash hit the entire Middle East hard and Dubai isn't a place that I'd chose for a vacation. Anyway, Rüdi, see what you can dig up from that link while Doris concentrates on Tokyo."

I noticed Helen frowning and nodded in her direction. "This guy Tan, the name's familiar. I'm sure that he invested heavily in prime land in Switzerland, which he then sold on to oil sheiks when they skipped from civil unrest and brought their ill-gotten gains to safe havens in Europe and Canada."

"Mmm, so Tan could be an active part of this

organisation, with Middle East links. But why would someone like that be involved in terrorist attacks against Switzerland?"

Pirmin looked very thoughtful. "What if the main aim of this organisation has nothing at all to do with Switzerland? We did wonder about an expensive laboratory being located so close to the border, but could that be an accident due to the location of Achmed's cell?"

"That's worth thinking about. This entire conspiracy is so convoluted that I wouldn't write off any possible explanation of what's happening," I projected the operation summary. "In any case, a secret project to develop bioweapons has got to be a threat that we need to neutralise. Any suggestions?"

"If Tan really is part of this, his e-security will be top class and I'd doubt that even Doris could crack it. Do we know where he is at the moment?"

Moments later a satellite image appeared, time-logged only two hours earlier. "Yacht is docked at his villa, so I guess that's where he is." A series of further images appeared as Doris worked back in time. "Okay, he's been home for only two days, so maybe he'll stay put for a bit. Ah, wait a minute, gale-force winds for most of the coming week, so maybe that's why he's home. It wouldn't be much fun sailing in that."

I felt as if I could read Helen's mind. "So, a little breaking and entering could be on the cards again?"

"The protection set up for Jones' database was so extreme that there must be a lot of very valuable information on it. We do, however, need to find

Dupont in order to have a chance to grab it. If we know where Tan is and think he may possess something similar, intrusion would seem to be justified."

"Could be, Helen," I frowned as I tried to assess the implications of such an action. "It'd be extremely sensitive, as this is a very powerful man and we have nothing but the weakest circumstantial evidence to support an argument that he is any kind of threat to us. With justification, we could veetol in a heavy team and toss the place but, even then, he could destroy any databases there before we reach him. It'd need to be a deniable, softly-softly kind of intrusion."

"Do you feel another holiday coming on, boss," Helen smiled at me.

"I think the Commander is certainly worried enough to authorise further direct action, but we'll need better cover to ensure there's nothing at all that could link us to Switzerland or Provence. Helen, start looking at options, based on a team of three on the ground."

"Three?"

"You and I have the most combat experience and Doris is our best hacker."

"Doris!" Rüdi interjected. "She's got no combat experience whereas I..."

"You, yourself, noted that Doris was our best hacker. Isn't that the case?"

I stopped him before he could argue further. "This isn't a Uni or residence block, it's a private island. I'd bet that all communications are impregnable from outside. Even external links will be untouchable: undersea cables or line-of-sight lasers or something similar. We need to get Doris inside that villa, with you providing the link to base and Pirmin providing any support you need."

Doris looked a bit pale, speaking with a slight tremor in her voice. "I don't have the experience, but I'm fully trained and prepared to give it a go. I'm sure our group leader will take good care of me."

I wish she hadn't said that, as it reminds me that Helen and I escaped from our last jaunt by the skin of our teeth – and this is going to be a lot trickier. "Right, Helen, you're lead here while I have a chat with the Commander and Alex Supersaxo. *Well, that's it, alea jacta est!*

CHAPTER SIX

Two days later I was in a rental villa in the village of Romazzino on the Emerald Coast of Sardinia. We had travelled to the island via Glasgow, entering Italy using Scottish passports that Alex had organised for us. Following the economic collapse of Italy after the eruption of Vesuvius and the complete destruction of Naples, Sardinia was a semi-autonomous region with notoriously flexible regulations when it came to anything that supported the local economy. *The ideal place for someone like Tan to be based, but also easy to access for tourists from richer countries like Scotland.*

Putting together an incursion on such a short timescale was tricky, but we decided that we might have a small window before details of Colmar and Provence actions were communicated from Jones to Tan. *This could be an inherent weakness of the isolated cells that seem to characterise this organisation.*

We arrived at midday and set up a comm centre in one of the bedrooms, setting up secure links to Brugg and downloading updates to the database on Tan's island and our intrusion plan. The rocky island, Isola dei Povari, had been uninhabited before Tan bought it and constructed the harbour, helipad, villa and support infrastructure that made the estate completely self-sufficient in terms of utilities. His estate included also the scatter of islets around the main island, with the entire area declared a private marine reserve in which no fishing was allowed.

A series of historical satellite images allowed the building work to be followed but, comparing the volume of spoil that was incorporated into sea defence walls to the visible excavations, it was clear that there had been a lot of tunnelling which, even with multi-spectral imaging, was very difficult to map or interpret in detail. Typically for Sardinia, no construction plans had been submitted and, in a pattern reminiscent of Jones' Marseille flat, all work had been carried out by a single contractor who went bankrupt shortly after the job was complete.

Tan lived with his wife, ex-wife and two mistresses, together with a teenage son from his first marriage and the baby daughter of one of the mistresses. *Not quite sure how that works, but no indication that they're anything but an open-minded happy family.* An older daughter by his first wife was an undergraduate at the Lausanne ETH – interestingly studying microbiology.

No employment records were registered but, apart from the crew of the yacht, satellite records indicated the comings and goings of a large number of villa staff. Most of them seemed to commute daily, transferred by a private launch making regular trips to Romazzino, Capriccioli and Porto Cervo. About half a dozen or so others, probably security, lived in a small block on the island.

We assembled sandwiches for lunch from supplies delivered to the property in advance of our arrival and gathered in our operations centre to go over our plan for the coming night. "Rüdi, any better guesses about our target?" I inquired.

"Ground level of the villa, where we've been able to get some images, contains living, dining and sleeping areas. Everything's completely shielded, so passive monitoring doesn't give us a dicky bird. We had a couple of consulate security guys kayak past yesterday, accompanied by a micro-drone with a high-resolution camera, but they had to stay outside the marine reserve exclusion zone and the angles are poor, so really this just confirms our best guesses of layout of the front of the building, south facing, rather than providing anything new."

"That seemed a bit risky. Could this kind of action possibly frighten off a paranoid billionaire?" Helen enquired.

"Should be okay, as it would be easy to find out that the trip resulted from a bet by the security chief that nobody could kayak the length of Costa Smeralda in this windy weather and the drone was intended to provide video evidence. There's lots of water traffic in this area, even when the weather is poor."

"How is the weather anyway," I asked.

"Latest forecast is for strengthening winds from the south and occasional showers. I think this is maybe good news for the intrusion team, but not so good for Helen on the boat."

This is the weak point of our plan. Helen takes us in an inflatable to the lee of one of the islets and then Doris and I approach the island underwater. "Pirmin, you've been setting up local infrastructure, do you think we could do the intrusion without the boat, swimming from the shore?"

"From the beach of Spiaggia del Principe, it'd

be about two and a half kilometres – doable but you'd need bigger oxygen tanks and a higher capacity rebreather," he answered.

"What about a DPV – a diver propulsion vehicle?"

"To minimise risk of detection you'd need something stealthed, a military swimmer delivery vehicle. If I could get a hold of a couple, it'd certainly make the crossing more practical."

"This is all a bit last minute," Helen pointed out.

"And I've done only a few sport dives," Doris added. "I've never used a rebreather and have not a clue about these underwater scooter things."

"We're flying by the seat of our pants here and want to get into Tan's place ASAP, but we have to be sensible in terms of risks. Although it's forced on us by the weather, I think the SDV option is actually preferable overall." I looked at the revised operation plan. "How's the weather looking for tomorrow night?"

"Much the same," Rüdi answered, winds more south-easterly and possibly stronger, less rain."

"And an SDV?"

"Would have been very tricky to put in place by tonight, but there's certainly kit that we could borrow from a French naval base in Corsica or a US carrier just off Malta." Pirmin paused and then continued, "I'd go for the US carrier option, if possible, as it gives us more options for disinformation to hide the operation. If we route everything via Israel and call in a few favours from Mossad, I'm pretty sure we can conceal any links to

Switzerland."

"It's probably overkill, but we've underestimated this crowd before and this gives me a better feeling. Right, tomorrow's a training day. As soon as the SDVs are available, we head to somewhere secluded in the northeast and set up an exercise with a two point five kay transit to a scooter drop-off point, fin for a half kay to a beach exit, jog around for half an hour in full kit and then work our way back. If the wind holds, we'll be a bit more sheltered there, but that's probably good for Doris's first time at this."

Doris frowned in my direction. "So, you actually have experience with all this rebreather, SDV stuff?"

"Well, not exactly," I confessed, "but how hard can it be? Current technology is just about idiot-proof." *I certainly hope so, as I have to look after Doris as well as myself.*

"Okay, given that we get to this island fortress as planned, what then?" Doris asked.

"That's a good question," I smiled at her. "What do you propose that we do?"

The beautiful young woman smiled back at me. "Well, if it was up to me, I'd take out the guards first."

Helen looked shocked. "Isn't that a bit extreme, especially as we've no solid proof that this Tan guy is actually involved."

"I didn't mean take out in terms of kill: just ensure they don't cause us any trouble." The intrusion plan was displayed together with a 3D image of the island and the assumed people present.

"Middle of the night, so we can assume that, of six guards, only two will be on duty. The other four should be sleeping in the bunkhouse, so all we need is a bit of gas to ensure that they won't wake up until we're long gone. From the satellite images," a time series was displayed, "the guards now present seem to be three couples – two hetero and one homo. The rocky slabs on this beach seem to be the place for al-fresco romantic encounters when the weather allows it."

"What about the guards on duty?" I asked.

"We're fairly sure that this small bunker at the end of the jetty is the security centre, covering both the villa and the yacht, when it's docked. This should be our target, as it must have links to the villa itself – hardened buried cables, I'd guess. If I can hack in via these, we can maybe access what we need. In any case, the guards here need to be immobilised. Then, if we need to, we can also enter the house. We could probably ignore the skeleton crew on the yacht, assuming that they'll be sound asleep and far enough away to be undisturbed by anything we're up to."

"But this seems to be the crux," Helen pointed out. "The guards on duty are in a building that's accessed by a biometric sensor," a selection of images expanded on the screen, "which involves face recognition and / or iris scans. There must be some kind of ventilation, but nothing is shown on the walls or roof. Probably some external air conditioning serving both this building and the main house, which would probably be hardened against intrusion, even if we could find it."

"As far as I can see, there's no alternative to entering the guardhouse by the door. If I scan one of the guards from the dormitory, I'd be able to spoof the lock."

"And then what?" I waited as the silence drew out. "Okay, that's Helen's main job for tomorrow, while Doris and I are playing in the sea. Liaise with base and polish Doris's outline so that it's doable. Meanwhile, we'll download manuals and start studying up on rebreathers until we get specs from Pirmin on the SDVs and can get onto their operational instructions.

***

After returning from dinner in a nearby Pizzeria, we drank bottles of the local beer and chatted before it was time to hit the sack. Although I felt that I knew Helen much better after our time in Provence, Doris was a stranger. I was amused to learn that the seemingly demure woman lived in a three with two 'husbands', who were both male models. *Must be a spectacular sight in bed.*

"We're pretty relaxed, though," she concluded, "so you could join us one time if you're into groups. Either of you, or both I suppose."

"That's a very kind offer," I was suddenly feeling my age, "but I'm more of a one-on-one kind of guy."

"That's a shame," she smiled salaciously, "I'd just talked Helen into sleeping with me tonight, so you're missing out on some wet-dream fun."

"Oh, I thought you were into men – seemingly in a big way."

"Yes, well, my husbands are great. Truly

99

tireless studs," she crossed her eyes for emphasis. "But, they're mainly just into sticking their dicks into orifices: anything at all that's on offer. They can suck cock like sword-swallowers, but oral work on a pussy isn't their strength. That's why I like a girl, now and then. Gals can really work wonders with fingers and tongues. Actually, Helen did say that you were very good with your mouth and into kinky stuff, like wet sex."

"A woman well known for her vivid imagination." I interrupted, glaring at Helen, who shrugged her shoulders in an apologetic manner, but with a gleam in her eye that I recognised from the Calanques.

"So, what, you didn't give her a blow job?"

"Well, kind of…"

"While she was having a pee?"

"Well, not simultaneously…"

"In the open, in the pouring rain?

"Pissing down, it certainly was…"

"Me and the rain, both!" Helen laughed, starting Doris off, the ladies revelling in my discomfort.

"Come on, you old fuddy-duddy!" Doris pulled me to my feet. "You're not in the twentieth century or some society run by fuckwit religious fundamentalists: you've got to loosen up." A thought seemed to cross her mind. "Oh, you're not married are you, with a beloved wife."

"Divorced, twice," I confessed.

"Well then, what's holding you back? You're not getting gay in your old age, more into a threesome with Rüdi and his partner?"

"Not at all... Shit!" I cursed when Helen, having sidled behind me, suddenly pulled my shorts and pants down to reveal my slowly growing erection."

"Well, that's passable," Doris laughed while I struggled with Helen. "Not as large as my husbands', but with a foreskin, which I like for a change. Of course, also without the piercings, which have their pros and cons. Maybe nice for them, but makes double anal bloody painful, I can assure you." She again crossed her eyes for emphasis.

Yes, that'd make my eyes cross. The image in my mind of Doris getting reamed may have been uncomfortable for her, but was having a visible effect on my erection.

While I was distracted, Helen took my cock in one hand while cradling my balls with the other and starting to nibble at my neck. "I really think he'd rather be with us than wanking alone, while we're shagging each other to death."

"I think so," Doris dropped to her knees and started licking my glans while her partner squeezed my dick harder."

"Jesus Christ!" My last traces of resistance disappeared. "Okay, whatever you want."

Doris sat back and looked up at Helen. "I guess we better get rid of clothes here and get him into the bathroom if we're going to start with some wet sex."

"Bloody hell, yes. I'm completely bursting. If we don't start soon, I'm going to wet myself.

Shit, it wasn't a one-off, Helen is really into golden showers.

"It's your fault, I've been choking ever since we were in that restaurant. Didn't really believe that he was into that, though."

"He is, but just doesn't know it yet. Any time now he's going to be part of the action."

"I did notice that you talked him into beer instead of the wine he intended to open."

"Got to be a full bladder there and, once we get started, he'll have little choice."

"You girls really think you can manipulate me like that? I'm your commanding officer..."

"Yes, but with your nickers round your ankles and a dick like a bowsprit, you're not really in a very commanding position. So, let's get you stripped for a start."

They are, of course, completely correct. May as well lie back and enjoy it. I obediently lifted my feet to allow shorts and y-fronts to be removed by Helen while my now-free hands helped Doris remove her t-shirt to reveal a completely transparent sports-bra. *Even tan and small but beautifully formed breasts topped by hard brown nipples sporting golden rings. Very tasty and clearly ready for action. This cannot fail to be a night to remember – as long as I can keep my mind well away from the risks facing us tomorrow.*

***

My internal clock woke me at six thirty. I drifted into consciousness, aware that I was close to the edge of a bed, pressed up against a warm, nubile, naked body. The events of the previous evening replayed in my mind, contributing to my usual early-morning erection. *The water games in*

102

the shower were tamer than expected, more a kind of teasing foreplay, but the action thereafter wilder than anything I've experienced in my four decades post-puberty. Helen had been fascinated by Doris's domestic love-life and the pleasures and pains of sex with her heavily pierced husbands. Doris was completely unabashed in her descriptions of bedroom escapades and happy to discuss the benefits of her own intimate piercings – clitoral hood and Princess Albertina – while we explored them with fingers and tongues.

For me, the highlight was soixante-neuf with Doris while Helen enthusiastically helped me bring the woman to orgasm before I came seconds later. Thereafter it was a blur as post-coital exhaustion battled with constant stimulation by the two athletic women.

I pulled back the sheet to reveal that it was Helen I was spooned against, who, in turn, was wrapped around our shared partner, their noses almost touching and breasts pressed against each other. I gently rubbed my penis in the crack of a tight bum, stroking it against her anus while rubbing the accessible nipples of both women, squeezing them together. Moments later, release came and I felt strangely guilty, as if I had taken advantage of the sleeping women. *Weird indeed, considering some of the things that they were up to as I began to dose off last night.*

With reluctance I extricated myself from the bed and dragged my very sweaty body into the shower. *Okay, now all of that has to be put behind us so that we can concentrate on the job ahead.*

I had prepared breakfast and was sitting at a table in the kitchen when the two women appeared a half hour later, hand in hand and seemingly oblivious to their nudity. "Morning ladies, but don't you think clothes might be a good idea?"

Helen grinned and rubbed her backside. "I feel strangely sticky this morning, so we'll shower first. Want to join us?"

"I'd love to, but we need to get our collective asses in gear. Delivery of a van with our SDVs is expected in forty-five minutes and we then need to plan our day. So, scoot – and don't get up to any mischief in the interim."

"What, us?" Doris opened her eyes wide in mock innocence. "Although we both have full bladders, so you might, at least, want to watch."

I do indeed, but can't afford to go there. "A lovely thought, but I'll take a rain check on that."

Helen looked like she might remonstrate, but her colleague dragged her off, to my great relief. *Christ, I've already got another erection: not the best thing when planning an operation that could get us all killed.*

I filled a mug with freshly brewed coffee and wandered into our comm centre, firing up the links to Brugg and noting that Pirmin was already online. I checked for updates on the intrusion plan, but no new ideas on how to manage the guardhouse had been posted. I displayed the 3D image of Tan's island, mentally walking myself through the incursion. *All fine as far as taking care of the guards in the bunkhouse, but after that there's a really good chance of things going tits up.* I noted with a wry smile that this thought had solved my tumescence problem.

I could hear the girls breakfasting when a ping on my phone announced arrival of our kit and I went to unlock the gate providing access to our driveway. A swarthy driver parked at the door, took a folding e-bike from the back, handed me the key to the van and rode off without a word. *Good old Israelis, specialise in need-to-know and keeping all communication to a minimum.*

I quickly looked through the diving kit that had been delivered. *Not only everything that we asked for, but also a spare for anything critical. Yes, going with Mossad was the right decision.*

By the time that I returned to our mission control, the women, clad in t-shirts and nickers and clutching mugs of coffee, were chatting to Pirmin and agreeing the location of our test exercise. I sat to the side and watched in silence as details were worked out. *Good, we're go for this morning, which maximises our recovery time before we're off again tonight. Although the wind has dropped a bit, the forecast for heavy rain showers and a high swell should minimise the risk of any company while we're diving.*

Twenty minutes later, Doris and I started to kit-up, pulling ourselves into the skin-tight dry-suits and checking the seals on our full-face masks. Throat mikes and ear buds were wired into the suits to provide short-range communication between us. On the island, satellite uplinks to base would be possible, but used only in case of emergency. Otherwise, we were completely on our own.

There was space for the three of us in the cab of the little electric van, squeezed together on the bench seat. Helen threw a route map onto the heads-up GPS display and we set off on the drive to Capo Testa. This took longer than I had expected, as the northeast of the island was now largely abandoned and this was reflected in the degradation of the quality of the roads as we passed further from the Costa Smeralda. Nevertheless, by ten thirty, we had parked beside the flooded remnants of what had once been a marina and were offloading our kit.

The SDVs were small with two handles, about the size of 20th century underwater video systems, but remarkably heavy. *According to the specs, even travelling at six knots, these are effectively undetectable by submarine monitoring systems and, given the absence of metal in any of our kit, we should have a profile indistinguishable from larger marine mammals like seals, whales and dolphins. Or, at least, that's what I hope.*

It had started to rain when Doris and I waddled backwards into the water, encumbered by our large fins and dragging the sleds until the water was waist deep. A breakwater considerably reduced the swell, but I could see large waves breaking outside it. I slaved Doris's SDV to mine. "Okay we're off now. Just hold on, relax and let me know if you have any problems clearing your ears. We'll stay close to the bottom until we clear the shallows of the harbour and then slowly descend to ten metres and hold that depth."

"Fine, boss, ready when you are," she answered, with only the slightest trace of a tremor in her voice.

Not only a wild nymphomaniac, but also a very brave woman. I tried to block the nympho thoughts from my brain while I concentrated on the controls of my vehicle. *Operation is almost idiot proof, but I need to concentrate on the passive sonar image to ensure that I don't steer us into any obstacles en route.*

It took only thirty minutes until we reached a point on the other side of the peninsula that we had selected as drop-off point for our scooters. We anchored them at eight metres depth, close to a characteristic rock stack. *The problem with undetectable sleds is finding them again afterwards.*

"Right, Doris, we fin the rest of the way, around five hundred metres. You're now neutrally buoyant at ten metres, so it should be easy to maintain depth. Just keep close to me, on my right-hand side."

For the first hundred metres Doris tended to drift towards the surface, needing to active fin downwards to stay level with me but, gradually, as her breathing became more relaxed, she could hold depth without problem. "Very good, you're a natural diver. All the same, I'm glad we could set up this dry run first."

"I'm not sure that you can call swimming ten metres below the surface a dry anything," she replied.

"Okay, pedant, let's now go silent. Touch my shoulder if you need anything and then we can use hand signals. In an emergency we can use comms but, to minimise even this very small risk of detection, only if we can't avoid it."

After just more than ten minutes, we were gradually following the rocky bottom upwards towards our goal – a small cove with a beach accessed from the cliffs above by a small path. Here the swell was higher, bouncing us up and down as we approached shore. We took off our fins in the shallows but, despite this, I was bowled over twice and Doris three times as we fought our way up the rocky beach.

I removed my mask after I left the water and set it with my fins on a large rock just above the high-water mark. "Okay, let me help you with this," I stripped off Doris's diving kit and placed it on the rock, before removing my own rebreather and weight belt.

We then removed silenced machine pistols from their waterproof pouches and clipped their holsters into place on our suits. Even though not strictly necessary in daylight, we also clipped visors into place on our hoods.

"All okay?" I received a nod and then set off towards a rock face, ignoring a well-defined path. "We go up to the top of the cliff here. It should be a fairly easy scramble with the grip provided by our boots and gloves. We shouldn't need to do this on the island, but it's a good exercise in any case."

We set off together, but Doris easily climbed past me, reaching the top when I was only a little more than halfway. "Very impressive, but remember you're supposed to follow me. If we find something surprising at the top, I'm better suited to handle it."

108

"Sorry, boss, I won't do it again."

I noticed that her breathing was steady while I had started to pant a little. *Fuck, old age doesn't come alone! I might have gained experience, but the performance of the old body isn't what it once was.* This thought threatened to bring up memories of the previous night, so I concentrated on reaching the top as quickly as possible, nearly slipping on a couple of occasions, which ensured that I was completely focused by the time I joined my partner.

"We can jog along the path for few kilometres, then walk back quickly through the scrub, just being careful not to twist an ankle." I set off at a five-minute kilometre pace and heard her soft footfalls padding along at my heels. *Well, at least her fitness isn't a concern.*

Just over half an hour later we were back at the cliff, which we down-climbed rather than using the path. Here I let Doris lead as, at the island, by this stage any threat was likely to be behind rather than ahead of us. After kitting up, entering the water was easier than getting out as, with our fins on, we could throw ourselves into the surf and swim on our backs until the depth was enough for us to submerge. Following the coastline back to the SDVs was straightforward, as was our return to the marina using the sleds.

I beeped Helen on the short-range system when I caught sight of our van and she hurried down to help us recover the SDVs and then strip off our kit. Fifteen minutes later, all was stowed in the back and we were heading back to Romazzino. Doris and I munched on sandwiches and drank coffee from a thermos, while Helen updated us on developments while she drove.

"Rüdi has been looking at specs for facial recognition locking systems and reckons that there's a fundamental weakness here which could allow us to hack into the internal communications in the guardhouse rather than simply opening the door. It really depends if the locking device is completely stand-alone, with an isolated power supply, or if it's linked to the security network. The latter seems more likely, as this then allows comings and goings to be logged."

I scratched my head. "How do we know whether it's isolated or not?"

"Only way to check is to test it in-situ."

"Bugger, I knew you were going to say that! If it isn't isolated, can we be sure that Doris can hack her way in?"

"Pirmin is putting together a package of tools that should handle most systems, which Doris will be able to download in a couple of hours. If that isn't good enough, you'll need to use the satellite link to get support of heavy-duty number-crunchers."

"And, if this system is isolated?"

"Well, it seems certain that you'll be able to open the door, probably without forewarning the guards inside. After that you'll have to wing it."

"Mmm, how does the door open?"

Helen was silent while she negotiated a particularly potholed section of road. "As I remember it, electric-drive sliding door, opening left to right. Yes, Rüdi mentioned that if the lock was coupled to the drive motor, it was less likely that the system was stand alone. The most secure option would have been an isolated lock allowing the door to be opened manually."

"Well, that sounds promising. Anything else?"

"We think we've spotted a cable providing a hard link between the yacht and the estate when it's docked. Might just be power, but a potential vulnerability in any case."

"It looks like delaying the intrusion has provided benefits in addition to training time; the job's now looking a little less impossible."

"So, less chance of us dying?" Doris asked, hopefully.

"Well, I wouldn't go quite that far." I smiled at my partner and tried to make it sound like a joke. *It would be nice to be more reassuring, but this is deadly serious and it needs only a little bad luck and we could be truly fucked.*

***

After returning to the villa and servicing our kit, we checked in with base, had a light snack and then a break to ensure we were fresh for the night ahead. Pills tailored to our individual metabolisms ensured four hours of deep sleep, which would do more than a normal eight. The two women left to sleep together in one bed, while I prepared to kip in the neighbouring room. *The building, pre-op tension will make sure that there's no chance of any hanky-panky this evening.*

I awoke just after eight pm and showered, first with cold water to remove the last cobwebs of sleep and then with water as hot as I could bear, stretching to remove aches from muscles in arms and legs. *Could actually do with a massage; that'll be a priority when I get back home. If I get back...*

While I towelled myself down and dressed, I forced myself to a more positive frame of mind by assessing what the minimum op time would be in the best case. *Thirty minutes SDV, twenty minutes to swim in and exit water, twenty to neutralise the bunkhouse and do the scans, say forty to hack the guardhouse and download what we need, an hour back to our entry point. Three hours and it's done. In the water at ten and out at one. A couple of hours to the Special Forces base on the other side of Sassari and then pick-up by a long-range chopper for evac home. Could be having breakfast in Brugg.*

I held onto this cheerful thought while I made coffee and then set out bread, cheese and cold meats, listening to the sounds of the girls sorting themselves out. They finally emerged in shorts and t-shirts, descending on the food as if starved. *Well, at least, nerves aren't affecting their appetites.*

Thereafter, we tidied up and then fired up the link to base. Both Rüdi and Pirmin were online and would support us until we reached our extraction point. Based on my previous musings I decided to sort out the latter first. "Before we run through the intrusion, how are we set for evac?"

"We already have a chopper at the MFC base, which will go on active standby at ten in case of problems, but is planned to be ready for departure from three," Pirmin responded, displaying an updated mission plan.

I smiled when I saw how close it had been to

112

my guesstimate. "Okay, any updates on the island situation?"

A 3D map appeared before us. "Personnel as before. Based on tracking change-overs, we expect the two guys to be on duty from eight to four, so you'll be arriving in the middle of their shift. The couple taking the next shift will probably be sleeping, but it's not obvious what to expect from the one coming off at eight. They could be still eating in the dining room, in the entertainment room or even in the gym."

"But probably not wandering about outside?"

"In this weather, highly unlikely."

"Any more tools I need to upload?" Doris enquired.

"Nope," Rüdi responded, "you've got everything you're likely to need. I've access assured in case we need to link in some Exaflops, but I hope it doesn't come to that."

"Anything on the villa?" Helen asked. "I know the aim is to stay well away from it, but we need to be prepared for the worst case."

I should have been asking that: need to ensure that wishful thinking doesn't get in the way of preparing for inevitable hiccups!

"Tan, the four women, the baby and the son are still present. There are also about a dozen staff. Normally, they'll all be gone by the time dinner is finished, with the exception of a butler and a chambermaid who live in quarters in the staff wing, which includes the main kitchen, laundry and other service rooms. There must be space for them all to overnight any time the weather is too bad for the launch to sail."

"Could that be the case tonight?" I realised that this was a complication that we hadn't included in our scenarios.

"I doubt it: two maids, the gardeners and a couple of other outside staff left as usual at five. It's very windy with a big swell, but the boat dock is well sheltered and the launch is a rugged, all-weather design. I can't see things worsening much over the next few hours." Rüdi presented a weather simulation, showing bands of rain approaching from the southeast.

"How is it for us getting out of the water," asked Doris. "It wasn't very easy during our dry run and that was supposed to be in a sheltered bay."

"I'd actually been thinking about that, especially given the latest satellite images," I displayed blow-ups of the possible exit points we had considered. "Our original preference was for the rock slabs in the northeast that are used for sunbathing..."

"And al-fresco bonking," added Helen.

"Anyway, that area is sheltered from the wind, but the swell makes it problematic." Video images showed large waves breaking over the rocks. "It's doable, but not easy and we don't need to start with somebody getting injured. So that leaves us the yacht jetty, the little rocky beach beside it in the southeast or the launch dock in the west."

"The yacht jetty is approached by a deeper channel and is well protected by the breakwater but, if I was Tan, the narrow entrance to the harbour would be a focus for monitoring," Rüdi pointed out.

"The approach to the launch dock is much shallower and, at low tide, you'd have to watch out for reefs if approaching from the southwest – as you are. We have high tide about ten, so that won't be a problem unless you're on the island much longer than expected."

I looked at the bathymetric charts displayed. "These rocks may be tricky for a boat, but we'll have no problems navigating around them. In fact, they could be useful to provide extra cover due to the background noise of breaking surf. Will the launch be there?"

"Shouldn't be. If the nine o'clock boat sails on schedule, it'll be moored at Romazzino, where the boatman lives. Physically, it's probably your easiest exit point, but it's well-lit, with six obvious monitoring cameras and maybe more that we haven't spotted." Pirmin displayed these with modelled coverage on a 3D display. "The coverage is pretty good, with few blind-spots. Rain will help a bit, but it won't be heavy enough to provide assured cover."

"Any chance of being able to hack them from a distance?" Doris asked.

"I doubt it," Rüdi replied, "I'd bet they're hard-wired to the guardhouse with shielded cable. Pirmin has identified a possibility though..." An animation began to step forward.

"Yes, you can exit the water on the right side of this slipway, hidden by the dock. At the top, you have a bit of cover from this electric cart used by the ground staff and a route that's covered by only one camera – here. Although there are guards, I'm sure that all cameras will have autonomous image analysis to identify anomalies, screening them to cut out minor events due to birds, blowing debris and anything else that would cause false alarms. If you slowly emerge far enough for the shot, you could nail that camera and then your way is free."

"Yes, but knocking out the camera would certainly set off alarms." Helen again took the words out of my mouth.

"Ah, that's the cunning bit," Pirmin sounded very pleased with himself. "Your kit includes a little air pistol that fires gel capsules that contain various fast-acting skin-contact toxins or knock-out potions. The range is only nine metres, so you should be able to nail the camera with one. I checked the number three variant – it's initially transparent but, on contact with air, hardens and becomes opaque within about ten minutes. I would bet that, to smart image analysis, this would look like a splash of rain caused by an odd eddy of wind followed by slowly decreasing visibility caused by fog or heavy rain."

His bet, but we forfeit if he's wrong! "And, if the image analysis is even smarter – linking input from all local cameras?"

"Mmm, hadn't thought about that…" Pirmin halted the animation and reran it in modified form. "Okay, then you clear the water and move to this point, where you can pot two other cameras. Maybe not strictly necessary, but probably worth it to be on the safe side."

"How many of these capsules do we have?" *The range may not be great but it'll be windy and I'll have lights shining directly into my face.*

"Four. But, as I said, it's possible that nailing the other cameras is superfluous. The critical thing is to hit the first one."

"All this assuming that your interpretation of the image analysis algorithm is correct," Doris pointed out.

"Yes, of course. If not, you're probably shafted."

That's a cheerful thought. "Okay, maybe not perfect, but we have a feasible intrusion scenario. I guess we can start kitting up now."

"Just an update for you," Rüdi added. "Satellite images show the staff heading for the launch, so I guess that's one complication removed."

A small mercy, but doesn't alter the fact that this'll be a very tricky mission.

***

At ten we were on a deserted beach, pushing our sleds into the surf while Helen watched from the van, sheltered from the driving rain. The transit to the SDV drop-off point was uneventful apart from a fright when we almost rammed a pod of dolphins, apparently dozing in shallow water, causing an explosion of images in the passive sonar that we were using for navigation. They circled us inquisitively for a few minutes, nosing into Doris's sled and causing her to squeal in surprise, before disappearing off into the gloom.

After mooring the sleds and going silent, we finned around our sheltering islets and headed for the launch dock. About a hundred metres from shore, a series of regularly spaced images appeared in front of us and I signalled Doris to stop and used a luminous pen to write on the slate that I carried. *Buoys, moored just above the bottom, weren't picked up by our surveys.*

Doris's shrug of her shoulders was clear in her sonar image and summarised our position. *We're committed now, so nothing more we can do. Just as well we went silent, though, in case these things are sensitive enough to pick up our short-range comms.*

I signalled Doris to follow me and then finned slowly through the middle of the gap between two buoys and then towards the slipway. It was a bit of a shock to pass from the grey-on-grey of sonar images to the actinic glare of the dockside lights, but our eyes had time to adjust while we stripped off diving kit and got ready for action in the surveillance blind-spot.

Perversely, the rain had stopped but the wind was gusting strongly. *Makes us more detectable to the cameras and my shots more difficult. Bugger!*

Extracting the small pistol, I edged forward on my elbows until I could see my target. Holding it in a two-handed grip, I took aim, held my breath and then fired. My smart optics zoomed in until I could see the lens. *Hit it on the bottom edge, so can't be sure the entire field of view is covered. Got to make sure.*

My second shot was bang-on centre and I backed down to wait for the gel to harden, tensing myself for the alarm that would result if Pirmin's assessment of the software was wrong. After ten nerve-racking minutes without any sign of a reaction, I waved Doris forward and walked slowly to the position where I could target the other cameras. Going down on one knee for extra stability, I fired one capsule at each, without checking on my marksmanship. *Either I've hit or not and it might not even make a difference in either case, so nothing I can do about it.*

I sealed the gun in a pouch and drew my machine pistol, heading for the guard dormitory while Doris followed on my heels. *Just need to pray that there aren't any other cameras covering our route that Pirmin didn't spot.*

The bunkhouse had the expected layout, with bedrooms on the ground floor and other facilities in the basement. Despite the rain, one of the rooms in the back of the building had a window open, blowing curtains aside and allowing us to see two forms sleeping together in a large double bed. The slight hiss of the gas grenade and the sound of the window shutting caused no disturbance of their regular breathing.

There were no locks on either the main door or fire escape. I led my partner through the former on the off chance that the latter might be coupled to some kind of alarm that we had been unable to see. The hallway was well lit, without any indication of cameras. *Makes sense, we're behind their defences now.* Of the six doors leading to bedrooms, five were closed and the other wide open to an empty room. Sounds from the bottom of a flight of stairs indicated where the missing couple were.

"I think short range comms will be okay now, at least while we're in this building. I'll take the couple downstairs while you get a scan from one of the sleeping beauties." I saw Doris nod and fix filters into her nostrils, before I set off downstairs.

The steps opened into a hallway that appeared to run the entire length of the building. Two doors to my left were open and two to my right closed, while heavy-looking bulkhead doors sealed both ends of the corridor. *Probably access to tunnels connecting the basements of different buildings and any other underground facilities present.*

Sounds were coming from the further open door and, as I passed it, I saw the nearer opened into a kitchen and dining area that seemed to be dimensioned for about a dozen people. I peered around the corner and saw the backs of the couple who must be playing some kind of combat video game. They wore total immersion skin-suits and Oculus visors that were leaking the sound of virtual mayhem.

Now the tricky call – knock them out, which will leave a clear trace of our incursion, or leave them be, serving as a potential threat if anything goes wrong. I then noticed holstered machine pistols lying beside clothing piled on a sofa. *Maybe there's another option.* I moved slowly to the guns, careful to avoid widely gesticulating arms and kicking feet. The pistols held twenty-shot magazines, with two spares clipped to the belts. I removed the bullets from all magazines, put them in a plastic evidence bag, and then headed back to the guards' bedroom.

Doris was at the top of the stairs and followed me into the room, watching silently while I explained my plan while I searched for and found a drawer containing three spare magazines and a box

120

of ammunition.

"Do you really think this is going to work?" she asked sceptically as I loaded the magazines and dropped the remaining bullets into the box.

"Depends how soon it is before they find that their guns are unloaded. If our presence isn't detected, it'll seem so bizarre that I wonder if they'd even report it. The obvious explanations would be that they've either been incredibly sloppy or are victims of some practical joke. What other explanation could there be?"

Doris frowned. "I guess you may be right, so we just need to stay under the radar."

"Yup, if we're spotted, it won't matter what the guards think. It'll ensure that we have less of a risk though, especially if they don't immediately notice that their guns are empty. Anyway, it's now up to you. Let's see if you can get all we need with one hack."

I led the way to the guardhouse, moving slowly to check for any unexpected cameras. When we reached the door, Doris pulled the image scanner from one pouch, placed it over the face-reader and then pulled out a tablet, which she hard wired to both the reader and her throat mike. I crouched in the limited cover of a bush behind the building where I could see both the dormitory and the villa. *Now I'm completely in Doris's hands.*

After thirty minutes my legs were beginning to cramp and I was increasingly worried that we were going to have to assault the guards when Doris's voice caused me to jump with surprise.

"Okay, boss, that's me in. I needed a bit of help

from the Brugg mainframe, but I now have complete control of the security system. All relevant monitoring is now bypassed, so we can talk freely."

"Can you access the central processor?"

"Not a chance in the time that we've got available, but I've accessed the security cameras within the house. They're normally locked-out from the guards, but trip open in case of an alarm. I bunny-hopped through this backdoor and now have both live feeds and records for the last six hours. They auto-delete after that, but I've done a complete memory map, so we may be able to get something more from forensics back home."

"Great, so can we leg it now?"

She was silent for a moment. "Well, the thing is that Tan is in an office somewhere in the basement and working on his computer at the moment. The camera is looking over his shoulder and I'm grabbing a lot of interesting looking stuff. Your call."

Fuck! We're a bit behind schedule already and the longer we wait the more chance that we'll get spotted. On the other hand, this could get us the evidence that justifies the entire caper. I momentarily considered going back and taking out the game-playing guards, before deciding that it probably increased rather than decreased risks. *I should have knocked them out when I had an easy chance, but that's all spilt milk now.*

"Okay, let's give it another half hour and see how it goes. Can you spoof the security system so that it warns us of any threats rather than the guards?"

"Already set up and running. These guys seem to be lulled into a false sense of security by the expert-systems assessing the monitoring data. There are screens showing images from all over the island, but they're paying no attention at all. One of them is watching football while the other is in the loo scanning gay porn while he masturbates."

"Jesus, they even have a camera in the bog?"

"Not quite that paranoid, it's just that the toilet door is wide open and one of the cameras for video-calls faces directly onto it. I can even tell you that that guy has an even bigger dick than either of my husbands, but no piercings that I can see." She laughed.

"Well, you keep focused on what Tan's working on rather than the wanking shirt-lifter."

"Nul problemo, though I have no difficulty multi-tasking…"

"If you want another task, spoof all monitoring between here and the boat. If we're going to be here longer than planned, I think it would be worth ensuring that we have no disturbances from the crew on-board. *And it's got to be better doing something rather than just twiddling my thumbs like a spare tool.*

"Oh, wait a tick… Okay, done. Just be careful."

"I intend to be." I walked slowly past the guardhouse and along the jetty, carefully placing my steps to ensure that I wouldn't trip or hit something that would give a warning, even with all electronics bypassed.

The yacht was huge, forty-five metres long,

appearing to dwarf the small island that the villa was built on. From surveillance and construction specs, we were sure that all crew accommodation was at the fore end of the lower deck, which seemed confirmed by lights showing from portholes just above the waterline. I crossed the gangplank towards the open stern, clearly set up as a bar and dining area, but with furniture now cleared away and battened down for the storm. I was suddenly shocked when lights came on as I boarded, but realised that these were probably activated by simple motion sensors and hence not part of the security system that Doris had spoofed. *My black suit must really stand out under these conditions, but there should be nobody to see me – or, at least, I hope not.*

A door into the opulent lounge was unlocked, with lights again coming on as I entered. The grey, satin, over-stuffed chairs and sofas, mahogany tables, thick Persian rugs scattered over a polished wooden deck and gilt-framed paintings of seascapes radiated wealth displayed without restraint. *If this reflects his character, I'd say Tan is certainly not a modest, self-effacing man.*

"Doris, do you have eyes on the lower deck here?"

"There's nothing in the cabins, but I have a clear view along a corridor and there's no sign of movement."

"It just occurred to me that, although there's unlikely to be anything linked to the main database when the boss isn't on board, it might be useful to have a look at his office."

"Why not? Okay let me see… The door in front of you leads to the master suite: a private lounge, huge bedroom, bathroom, dressing room. His office is accessed by a door in the far side and looks towards the bow. I've unlocked all doors."

"Okay, let me know if there's any change below." I quickly walked through the private lounge, which was decorated in similar taste – or lack of it – and then entered the study. The contrast was dramatic: this oblate semi-circular room was Spartan, floored by a black fitted carpet and containing a large oak desk and high-backed brown leather chair facing towards the bow. The straight wall at my back was unadorned matching oak and the curved wall, floor to ceiling glass, was presently covered by shutters. Familiar-looking cables lay on the desk. *Looks exactly like the set-up used by Jones, so this in itself is very good evidence of a link between the two.*

The only other item of furnishing was a low bookcase along the back wall containing sets of leather-bound books that looked old and probably very valuable. Along the top of the bookcase was a display of mounted rocks and minerals. *Again, similar to Jones' office, although what that signifies is beyond me.*

I was just in the process of examining the bookcase in more detail when Doris came on line. "Tan seems to be logging off now, so I guess we can shoot the crow."

"On my way," I started back, carefully closing doors as I went and hearing them latch behind me.

"How long do we need to clear the island?"

"Call it ten minutes to get back to the slipway and another fifteen to clear the offshore monitors."

"Okay, I'll set a routine to clear my blocks on the jetty cameras and remove all traces of the hacks in thirty minutes. All being well they'll never know that we've been here."

By the time I reached the guardhouse, Doris was already clearing up her kit and we jogged together to the launch dock.

"You need to clean the cameras, don't want anything that'd indicate they've been messed with," Doris reminded me.

I dug out a canister and sprayed the three cameras, noting that my last two shots had both been dead centre. *Not bad at all for an old guy.*

We kitted up and, despite the increased swell, were easily able to enter the water by jumping off the jetty. *Maybe our luck was finally turning again.*

We finned to the SDVs, finding them without a problem. "Shit!" I shook my head in disbelief. My machine was tethered as expected, but Doris's was lying on the bottom. On closer inspection I saw a dent on one side that appeared to have cracked a seam. I was baffled. "Doris, you didn't bump into anything did you?"

She was silent for a moment and then cursed. "Those fucking dolphins! I can't believe the bastards damaged my fucking sled."

I removed the mooring line and the control unit and left it on the bottom. "Just have to hope it breaks up without anyone noticing."

"How are we going to get back now?" Doris sounded on the edge of panic.

126

"Not a problem," I stated with a confidence that I didn't feel. "This one can pull the two of us, no problem. It'll just be a bit slower." *So much for luck changing – definitely spoke too soon. The SDV will get us back, but have we enough oxygen in our rebreathers?*

We were half-way back when Doris's oxygen ran out. *Not surprising, really, as she must be really nervous, breathing twice as fast as me.* We surfaced and I switched on the light in the hood of my suit before dumping her tank and replacing it with mine – not an easy task as we bounced in the swell. "The route is pre-programmed, so just let the sled take you back. I'll just swim along after you."

"Are you sure about that? The weather is really wild and you need to find our beach in the dark."

"Set up a bright light pointing out directly to sea and I'll follow it in. I'll need to dump the mask now so I'll have no comms. See you in a bit."

I faced away from the waves and pulled off the mask and the associated rebreather kit. The shock of cold water on my face caused an involuntary gasp that resulted in me getting a mouthful of salt water. I set my wrist monitor to compass mode and started to swim in a westerly direction, using the direction of wind-driven spray as an aid to staying on course.

Despite the fins, swimming in the heavy sea was exhausting and I sighed with relief when, after about fifteen minutes, I spotted a bright light ahead. Five minutes later I could see that the van had been driven down onto the beach and its headlights were the beacon I was aiming for. Another five minutes and Doris splashed in to help me strip off my fins and stagger out of the surf.

"Enjoy your swim, boss?" Helen asked with a smile as she came to the water's edge to support me as I slipped on the pebbled slope. *Definitely sounds like relief in her voice. I guess waiting behind without a word while we run behind schedule might be the worst job of all.*

I had a moment of worry when the wheels spun as Helen tried to reverse back off the beach, afraid that the van might be stuck in place, but they eventually found a grip and we jerked backwards and slowly bounced onto the tarmac. "We've got at least an hour until we're at the pick-up point, so we can uplink everything we have and have a quick debrief en route."

"Everything already uploaded from my side," Doris reported. "We just need the records of your suit-cam…" she reached over to detach the module from my arm, "…right, I'll send them now."

"There's coffee and sandwiches in the pack there," Helen nodded at a rucksack on the floor, "so you can eat while we get started."

All of a sudden, I realised how famished I was. "That sounds like a plan," I murmured while digging out a thermos and pouring three mugs of coffee.

"Okay, me first. I hacked into Tan's security system, but the firewall around the main processor was too much for me." Doris threw up images that appeared faintly above the dashboard. "The internal cameras covered the guardroom…" video of the masturbating guard caused snorts of laughter, "…the yacht and all rooms within the villa, with a six-hour running record. I guess continuous records are kept somewhere, but not in the part of the system that I could access. Image identification of movements allowed me to focus on occupied rooms. In live feeds these were the master bedroom…" the display showed three naked women in a rather rumpled bed, one apparently asleep and two sitting up, watching a 3D soap, "…with the ex-wife and the two mistresses: the ex is the sleeping beauty."

"That looks cosy," Helen commented. "From the look of it, I'd guess that they're more than just good friends."

"We can check on that when I look at the back records. Anyway, this is the son's room…" it was possible to make out the naked bodies of a skinny boy below a well-endowed young woman, engaged in languid soixante-neuf, "…and this is the current Mrs Tan."

"Jesus, this all seems a bit incestuous," I shook my head.

"Vice is nice, but incest is best," Doris smiled. "Actually, the ex is the boy's mother, but it's rather perverse, nevertheless. Anyway, Tan was in his office in the basement. We need to go over his entire session on the computer, but even the live stuff is interesting." The image was enhanced to show the holographic display in the middle of the desk, partially blocked by Tan's body. "There's a flow chart here that seems to represent the logistics for some kind of project and a sequence of charts showing the development of some product with time. There are links to molecular structures, so the forensics boffins should be able to get something from it."

"Apart from this, I've got a full breakdown of the entire security systems for both island and yacht, which should make any future intrusion much easier. I do hope that won't be needed though."

You and me both. "That's great, Doris, it certainly was the right decision to take you along."

"I'm glad that I was able to help, although I was pissing myself at times – literally. Which reminds me that I need to get out of this suit ASAP."

"Don't worry, the suits are designed for that. I must admit that my own is also a bit smelly." *Not actually the case, but it was pretty close at times.*

"Sounds like wet sex isn't on the cards then," Helen laughed.

"It's certainly not the first thing on my mind. Anyway, we should pull over somewhere after we've finished eating and then we can get wiped down and into normal clothes." *I'll also need a pee after all this coffee, but I'm not going to tempt fate by mentioning it.*

"Actually, thinking about sex just reminded me of one strange thing I picked up from the yacht's security system. It included a logged route for the next cruise, with all points noted where the boat would be easily visible from shore or other vessels with known routes, such as ferries and cargo ships. This is linked to automatic closing of blinds in Tan's office. The destination seemed very odd, though, Isle du Levant, back in the South of France."

130

"Isle du Levant," the name rang a bell for me. "That's the nudist colony set up at the beginning of the last century, isn't it?"

"It is indeed. Over the last couple of decades, it's been very popular with exhibitionists who like to have sex in public. And voyeurs, of course. But most of the island is actually a French military base, which could be the goal."

"Although, of course, for this family of perverts it could just be a sex thing," Helen added.

Whatever, it's strange in any case. Although I've no idea how it would fit together with terrorist bioweapons, any link to the French military would be particularly worrying. And, of course, if more direct action was needed, it'd be greatly complicated if we had to do it in our birthday suits!

CHAPTER SEVEN

At the MFC base, which seemed to predominantly consist of firing ranges and urban combat exercise zones, the pick-up went without a hitch with the helicopter lifting off as soon as we boarded, leaving the van and our diving kit with a security officer from the Consulate in Cagliari. I fell asleep minutes after we were in the air and awoke only with the jolt of landing on the pad within our base in Brugg. After breakfast and a short formal debriefing with the Commander, we dispersed for the weekend.

On Monday morning, the full operations team assembled for a status review, with only Alex Supersaxo unable to attend. He had, however, sent a video message confirming that the Nachrichtendienst had picked up no indication that our intrusion had been noted. This seemed to have cheered up the Commander, who opened the meeting by congratulating the entire team on a very successful mission.

"Thanks, Commander. I must say that I'm very impressed with the performance of my team, but must especially mention Doris who was on her first active op." The young woman blushed prettily. "I don't think it was just better luck that prevented a snafu like Provence, I think we're building a better understanding of the organisation that we're up against. Just seeing the parallels in the security systems set up by Jones and Tan is enough on its own to suggest a strong link between them. The security is extremely tight, but inevitably has flaws and we're beginning to learn how to exploit them. I think Doris and Rüdi can fill in now on what we've learned."

Rüdi waved at Doris, who selected a series of video files for presentation. "From the video records, we have a full work session from Tan. He does block the holo image a bit, but log-on is very fast, almost instantaneous as soon as he sits at his desk. It's like waking from sleep mode, without any password or ID. Given the security elsewhere, this seems a bit strange."

"I don't know if there's anything to it, but the chairs in Jones' two offices and those in Tan's Villa and yacht look remarkably similar, apart from different colours of leather upholstery." Pirmin displayed the images. "In particular these pads on the arms." The displays zoomed in to illustrate his point. "Now can you replay Tan sitting down?"

Doris set up a slo-mo replay and talked us through it. "He drops into his chair, swings round to face the desk, leans back to place both hands on the arms of the chair and Bingo! That's the instant the holo kicks in. Give that observant man a coconut!"

"But isn't that inconsistent?" I asked. "Everything else is hard wired to prevent eavesdropping, real belt and braces, given the surrounding Faraday cage, so why have something like this wireless?"

"Maybe it's not so strange," Rüdi responded, his brow furrowed as he worked his way through the logic. "The chair can provide a comprehensive biometric signature that'd be extremely hard to hack, orders of magnitude trickier than the face recognition used for his guardhouse. A cable to the chair would, however, get in the way. A coded direct burst from the chair to the processor would be almost impossible to intercept and, even if it could be picked up, would seem meaningless without knowing its purpose."

"Makes sense," I conceded. "I guess this means that, even if we had managed to access the office with the processor in place, we'd have had no chance of hacking into it."

"Inside a Faraday cage and so with no external support, not a hope in hell," Doris answered. "To break into one of these things, we need to interrupt an ongoing session or physically grab it and bring it back to base."

"And if we managed use gas to knock out Tan while he was working?"

"No good, as you see the display closes the instant Tan leaves his chair – a kind of dead-man's switch." She played the video segment again slo-mo. "Quite clever, actually, but doesn't make our job any easier."

"Okay, we now know a bit more about access security. How about the session itself? Urs?"

The chubby forensics tech displayed an expert system assessment of the recorded images. "Doris's first guess seems bang on: this is a review of the logistics of a project to produce a range of complex biomolecules. It's very convoluted, involving a mixture of state-of-the-art organic synthesis, biosynthesis and nanotechnology. Not doable in anything other than a very well-equipped laboratory. Our best guess is that almost all of the required processes have been defined and the focus is on scaling them up, which could be quite a challenge."

"Scaling up: can we determine what kind of factor is involved?" Helen was again ahead of me with this key question.

"Difficult to tell, but we saw a first step that was milligram to gram and a second gram to kilogram for the biosynthesis processes."

"Kilograms! That's surely a hell of a lot for some bio-active agent."

"Yes, certainly, but there's also a step three mentioned. If that was a further three orders of magnitude…"

"Jesus!" Helen and I interrupted simultaneously and I looked at the shocked faces around the table.

"Of course, step three might not be a further up-scaling – could be improving purity for example" Urs pointed out. "But if this is high-performance bioweapon production, even kilograms could do a lot of damage."

The Commander lost his happy demeanour. "This bloody organisation just looks worse and worse, especially as we've no idea of motivation. A bunch of academics, a property tycoon and WMDs! What's the linkage between them?"

The other tech, Judith, raised her hand and, in response to my nod, opened a new set of video files. "I had a look at the records from cameras in the other room and spotted something strange…"

"Kinky sex," Helen contributed in a stage

whisper.

"Yes, indeed, but have a look. This is the master bedroom after dinner..." There were a number of gasps and a giggle from Doris as the action unfolded. "As you see, the son is the centre of the action, shagging his mother and being buggered by his father while his step-mother is sitting on his face and the two mistresses are egging the action on with rather large dildos."

"Jesus, no wonder the poor lad looked knackered. After this romp, he would have been literally shagged out," Helen grimaced in disbelief.

"All very perverse," the Commander frowned, "but how does it help us?"

"Look at Tan," Judith reran a sequence, "he's clearly running the entire show. The women and the boy do exactly as he indicates. It's a shame we've got no audio, but mouth reading by our ES shows he is ordering everyone about and they obey without question. This gives us another picture: dominant leader, highly intelligent underlings and terror weapons..."

"It's a cult!" This time I beat Helen to the punch. "Like Aum and sarin. The pattern actually fits: these nut cults often have a charismatic leader who uses sex to reinforce their position. Members are usually above average intelligence, often professionals, who provide funding and have jobs that allow them to support the messiah's goals."

"Bugger!" The Commander looked even more worried. "The common or garden terrorist is bad enough, but in some way understandable. Doomsday cults are completely unpredictable, as they follow the whims of a maniac. I think I have about enough here to justify pre-emptive retaliation. The Italians wouldn't be happy with a strike on the villa, but we could take out the yacht when it next sails without a problem and no risk of collateral damage."

"It's a nice thought, but assumes that Tan is the prime mover in all of this." I displayed the complete op database and highlighted specific components. "Jones and the scientists may well be disciples, but they seem to have some kind of stand-alone operation. In particular, what are the Dubai and Tokyo links? Tan's daughter is also a loose end. She must be, or have been, part of the cult. Is she still active or a defector? Tan's next stop is Isle du Levant; what does he get up to there and has he any other ports of call during his cruises?"

There were frowns around the table while the team considered these questions. "I don't know if it's significant," Urs opened a file with analyses and a video clip, "but there's a DNA match for Jones from the patches on your suit, but not from Doris's. So, this confirms that Jones was on the yacht…"

"But we knew that."

"Yes, but this was from a shoulder patch. I've been through the video and the most likely place this would have been picked up was here – you brushed against the chair when you were looking at the cables on Tan's desk. It could just be cross-contamination though…"

I now saw his point. "Ah, yes, but if her DNA was here, then she either accessed the system directly or stood at Tan's shoulder while he worked.

In either case, Jones seems to be at a higher level in the conspiracy than the others. Was there any other DNA on that particular patch?"

"One other individual, female, best guess the ex-wife," Urs smiled as I picked up on his lead, "but could be the daughter, I suppose."

"Interesting, you'd normally expect a lot more from crew – all those who clean the place or maintain equipment. I can't see Tan doing any menial work, so I guess that's handled by his most-trusted underling, which could well be his former missus. From her role in the incestuous orgies, she must be completely under his control."

"So maybe we need a careful background check of the wives – especially the first – and the mistresses."

"Yes, Pirmin, definitely. You get onto that. And the children, of course. Anything more on Jones aka Dupont?"

"Not a sausage, which is extremely odd in itself, given the degree of CCTV coverage in the city and surrounding areas. She must have had a sophisticated, pre-planned escape route and probably another identity."

"Could she have help with the cameras, someone hiding her traces?" Helen asked.

"It's possible," Rüdi answered thoughtfully. "We're hacking French police sources and so can't run the verification routines that we'd use on our own material. Eliminating all traces would need an insider, though, either police or security services."

I blocked out further discussion of the technicalities of how this could be done and closed my eyes. *There's something here that I should be picking up on.* "Or military!" I announced, causing surprised looks from around the table.

"Until Colmar, all the operations in France were carried out without even the slightest trace in their official records. Doable, I suppose, but extremely tricky. Much easier with an insider, acting as guardian angel in Provence and Alsace, eliminating any anomalies before they're picked up by anyone else."

"Seems credible," Helen gave me a hard stare, "but why military?"

"I just remembered that Isle du Levant was primarily a military base. This includes a missile test centre, so must be high security and linked into the entire national security network."

"Bloody hell!" The commander groaned theatrically. "Just what we need, a fuckwit cult with links to the military. Christ on a bike!"

"Well, of course we don't know that yet; it's just speculation on my part. Anyway, Doris, see what you can dig up on Levant connections and coordinate with Rüdi who's still trying to find the elusive Jones. Urs and Judith, keep up the good work on the material that you have, especially if we can get any further hints from the material that Tan was working on. Helen, in your spare time, put together a concept for an op based on Heliopolis. I assume we're clear for that?"

The Commander nodded his head wearily. "And you, Group Leader?"

"I'm going to go through the entire database from beginning to end, trying to identify any possible links to major players in the conspiracy who we haven't picked up on as yet. Until we're sure that there's no risk of frightening our opponents into bringing forward attacks, we're treading on eggshells."

Aum, Jonestown, Waco, Heaven's Gate and the rest – there's plenty of evidence that such nutters are fully prepared to both commit mass murder and sacrifice the lives of their members. That was scary enough decades ago, but I dread to even think about what could be done with the advanced technology that this crowd have at their disposal.

***

One week later we met again, this time without either the Commander or Supersaxo, who were updating a national security sub-committee in Bern. Although we were careful to ensure that details were available only on a need-to-know basis, it required a top-level political decision on whether to maintain this as a Swiss operation or to bring in international partners – either at European or even global lever. *It's a hard call. The threat certainly extends beyond our borders and additional resources would be useful, but a potential mole in the French military also makes the risk of our operation being compromised greater as the number of players increases.*

I summarised this situation at the start of our meeting, noting a general look of unease that was summarised by Helen. "If we expand the op, we not only risk leaks to our opponents, but we can also lose control of things. We, this group here, have the best overview, but I can't see the big boys being

140

happy about little Switzerland being in the lead. They're bound to initiate a bun-fight for control and, knowing most of them, certain to fuck-up things royally while strangling us with red tape."

"I know all that and, if the worse comes to the worst, I'll fight to have liaison run through the security services, letting us run in the background through the Counter-Terrorist Unit. I'm sure that, between them, the Commander and Supersaxo will be able to delay a decision by weeks and, even if collaboration is agreed, it'll take more weeks to establish. I know it's tight, but we should assume that we've got a month or so max to tie this up completely…"

"You have got to be joking," Pirmin interrupted. "In my time at the CTU, I've never seen an operation as complex as this. Despite that, we've got only an active team of five with two support techs…"

"It's not as bad as that, I'm bringing Jörg back on board, so our active resources have just increased by 20%."

"Yes, big man!" Rüdi smiled and clapped him on the shoulder without eliciting more than a wan smile.

"Anyway, as far as I'm concerned, the size of the team is optimal. We need to be fast and flexible and this isn't possible with a larger group. We can also access more tech support, but this should be done via Urs and Judith, as we don't want anyone else knowing details of what we're up to. So, let's start with Tan and his coven. What more do we have on them?"

Doris looked at Pirmin and Rüdi and then opened the relevant files on the op database hologram. "We don't have a huge amount, but some interesting links are emerging. Let's see, first the ex-wife: a very successful lawyer specialising in company law who, after marriage, worked around the world as a very highly paid consultant until the first child, the daughter, was born. Since then, head of legal support in Tan's company. Strangely her twin sister, also a lawyer, lived together with the couple after they wed and is now living with Tan's daughter and her own son in Lausanne"

"What about the twin's husband?" I peered at the complex chart that was emerging.

The chart expanded to show a further level of detail. "Not married, but long-term partner was a banker: Swiss and very well off. Died of a heart attack and the twin inherited the lot."

"Just like Jones, there certainly seems to be a pattern here, Sorry, go on."

"The mistresses, Sandra Baxter and Sophie Ménagier, both originally worked for Tan's organisation and, officially, still do. Sandra was a PA and Sophie CFO. Both high achievers, who worked their way up the corporate ladder. Sandra's married, her wife is the captain of Tan's yacht and the biological mother of their baby. Sophie has had a number of partners, male and female, but nothing long term. No trace of any children."

"Sandra's wife must be pretty broad-minded," Helen commented.

"Um, let's see. Yes, the wife, Olga, Swedish, has taken Baxter's surname. Previously married to a

Danish woman, but that didn't last long: the Dane split and joined a New Age convent. Olga seems to have a girlfriend in Porto Cervo, who she often stays with when the yacht's back in base. Clearly it's a pretty open relationship."

"There's a bit more on the kids, as both were educated from age six in an international boarding school in Switzerland: Rosenberg in Saint Gallen. Nothing stands out though. All looks typical of the scions of mega-rich families to be found in such places. The boy, David, was spending a school break with his parents, but should head back to Switzerland next week for start of the new term. The daughter, Angie, went straight from school to Uni and moved in with her aunt, who has maintained an apartment in Lausanne since her partner died there. She's only in second year, but her academic record is impressive: a very smart girl. Her cousin, Michael, is almost the same age and also studying at the ETHL, in his case physics and computer science. Also seems very bright. The rest of the material on them is in the file, if anyone wants to look into it, but the ES hasn't picked up anything of relevance."

"Everything seems remarkably insular, a group that keeps everything within the family." *As Doris said, nothing stands out, but that in itself seems quite unusual.*

"Yes, and that brings us to Tan. For such a global entrepreneur, he presents a remarkable low profile. Born in Ho Chi Minh City, but brought up in Paris. Degree in history from the Sorbonne and an MBA from LSE, the London School of

Economics. On graduation, set up his own company, presumably with help from his father, who was a management consultant. This enjoyed a meteoric rise in value due to property speculation, based on clever interpretation of the impacts of rapid sea-level rise. After a couple of years, he bought the island and yacht and became a bit of a recluse. This doesn't seem to have influenced his business, as it was set up from the beginning so that everything could be handled electronically. Offices in Paris, Rome, Lausanne and Dubai, but little indication that he ever visits them in person. Of course, in this case and given his lifestyle, absence of evidence isn't evidence of absence."

"Where's Tan now?" Helen asked.

Pirmin threw up a satellite image and a plotted course. "Sailed from his island yesterday and course consistent with the one Doris found, so we guess heading for Ile du Levant."

"Any idea at all what his goal is there?" *I really hope it's not the base.*

"We've been going over long-term satellite records and have a good idea of his peregrinations over the last decade. Levant is a regular stop-off, once or twice a year. Of course, nothing about what he does there: there's no CCTV in any openly accessible part of Heliopolis. In fact, they don't even have mains electricity. We've hacked into the military base, but so far no trace of his presence any time that the yacht was anchored at the island."

"Do we even know that he landed?" I enquired.

"No hard evidence. Satellite images are too indistinct, especially at night, and there are no aircraft or drone images. The entire island is a no-fly area, enforced by the base but covering also the nudist colony."

"There is one strange link between Tan and the naturists in Levant," Doris added, hesitantly. "It may just be a coincidence, but the grandson of a multi-millionaire resident of the island was also educated in Saint Gallen and lives in Lausanne, although he's doing an apprenticeship at a legal firm based in Geneva. In fact, his flat is in the same building as Tan's daughter."

I can't believe this is a coincidence: there's a pattern here if we could only work out what it is. "So, what do you have on this millionaire guy?"

"Millionaire gal, actually," Doris smiled as she presented some images. "Or maybe even millionaire matron: she's sixty, although very well preserved."

Rüdi whistled as blow-ups showed a veritable Amazon. In company, she was a head taller than most of those around her, with powerful, muscular legs and arms and huge breasts. She was naked in all images, tanned a deep mahogany brown and was completely hairless – body and head. "Doctor Lucy McKie, Scottish, worked in the AI group at IBM Zurich and apparently was Nobel-level brainy, at the very front in the field of man-machine interfaces. She left IBM fifteen years ago and managed to take some key patents with her. These were initially considered non-commercial, but she combined them to develop a product that made her millions in license fees. She then bought an estate at the edge of Heliopolis and dropped off the map."

"That's a profile much like Tan, but about five

years ahead of him," Helen observed. "She was in Zurich, so we must have a lot on her."

"More than Tan, certainly, but nothing that would seem to connect her in any way to bioweapons. Her lifestyle, however, fits the sexually hedonistic pattern. Very promiscuous, AC/DC, but with a special liking for much younger men. Seems to have screwed just about all of her male internee students, but there was never any hint of a complaint. Seems to inspire complete loyalty in all who worked with her."

Completely dominating, that's certainly Tan to a tee. "So, what's she up to now?"

"Difficult to tell, as the little material we have is mainly derived from private images stored on social media sites. Lucky that she's so stunning and a clear target for the voyeurs who ignored prohibitions of filming on the island. Officially she lives with two husbands in her villa, but was often filmed in the company of other young men..."

"Wow, just gets better and better..." Rüdi zoomed-in on an image of the woman arm-in-arm with two men who seemed to be in their late teens, both with the physique of professional body-builders.

"Indeed," Doris licked her lips salaciously, while everyone else smiled, "those are a couple of well-hung boys. I thought I was doing well with two husbands, but I take my hat off to this lady, she's really living the life."

"Okay, let's get some work done before you get into the pornography. I'm pretty sure that McKie and Tan are linked in some way, so that's a job for you, Doris. In case intrusion is justified, we need an outline plan, that's Helen."

She looked at me in bemusement. "Really? Setting up a job in a mansion located in a town where nudism is obligatory? You don't think we'll stand out a bit?"

"Not if we're in the buff…"

"Even so, we'll probably need Doris to do the hacking. Where's she going to conceal her toolkit?"

"I'm sure you'll come up with something, so liaise with Doris on it." The women looked at each other and silently raised eyebrows. "And I think we may well need Rüdi, as Lucy here seems to have a taste for young guys."

"I'll have you know that I'm straight-gay and certainly not into wrinkly old women. You can't expect me to prostitute myself for…"

"From the look of some of these images, the young lads involved seem to swing both ways…"

Rüdi looked thoughtful. "Well, if you put it like that, for the sake of the fatherland, I might be prepared to make an exception but…" The rest of his sentence was drowned out by peals of laughter.

"Pirmin, Jörg; anything else on Jones, aka Dupont, or the facilities in the Alsace and Provence?"

Pirmin looked thoughtful. "Both Tan and Jones were at university in Paris, but they fail to overlap by a year. Now that McKie has entered the picture…" a timeline appeared, "…she provides a bridge between them, as she was a regular guest lecturer there for a few years. There isn't actually any evidence that they knew each other, but we haven't explored that in detail as yet."

"Definitely something to follow up on, you two should work together on it."

I noticed Jörg was vaguely waving a finger in my direction. *A most unusual occurrence.* "Jörg, you got something here?"

All eyes were fixed on him as he flicked a file open, summarising the input provided by the security service team. "The guys were looking for terrorist links to the Colmar lab and just briefly checked to see if the subsequent attacks on the ex-supervisor of microbiologist Isaacs could mean anything. Without the background that we had, the hypothesis tested was that this was some kind of cover-up action by the terrorists who were behind Colmar, as they had also seen that equipment had been sourced via Marseille. Jones seemed such an unlikely terrorist that it was assumed she was probably murdered or kidnapped and that the missing student was most likely responsible. We know he's dead, but they searched for Jones together with a young man, who might have her under control in some way. Assuming that both could be disguised, they simply used gross physiological data for the search and thus came up with dozens of hits for a radius from Marseille expanding with time. This was dropped when the line of investigation was deemed pointless, but I do remember that one of the higher probability cases was this couple, boarding an early ferry from Hyeres to Isle de Levant on the morning after the Marseille raid."

The image was poor, showing a woman of

approximately Jones' build walking hand-in-hand with a slim young man. The woman wore an enveloping poncho and a wide-brimmed hat, making it impossible to make a match. The young man's face could, however, be clearly seen. "I personally checked against all of Jones' students, but nobody was even close."

"Jackpot!" shouted Doris, causing everyone to look at her in amazement while she raced through a file of images. "I know that I've seen this guy before, but he's difficult to recognise with his clothes on. His face wasn't his most notable attribute."

The autoscans confirmed the match. Jones was heading for Levant in the company of one of McKie's boy-toys.

I felt ready to shout myself. "Yes, this is definitely the link that we need! Okay, Helen, incursion is a go. Set up details with the rest of the team while I prepare to talk the Commander into letting us off the leash again."

CHAPTER EIGHT

Five days later, I arrived with the incursion team on a fifteen-metre motor yacht, mooring in the Baie de Port Man on the Ile du Port-Cros. From this point, on the outer edge of the bay off the Calanque du Palangrier, we looked directly towards the small village of Heliopolis, only about a kilometre distant. *At least the weather is a lot better – sunny with only a scatter of clouds in contrast to the rain and gales of our last couple of actions. Typical global-warmed autumn, a month of storms with flooding throughout Europe, now followed by a predicted couple of months of unrelenting heat, leading to widespread drought.*

Doris interrupted my musing to announce that the satellite link to base was now set up and I joined the others in the rather cramped lounge cum galley. I smiled as I looked around, Rüdi wearing a minute posing pouch and the girls topless with only small bikini bottoms. *Getting into the mood for the naturist island, making me feel over-dressed in my Speedos.*

A map of Ile du Levant was displayed, along with a view from the camera mounted on top of our radar mast. Blown-up satellite images showed also Tan's floating gin-palace, moored around the headland in the neighbouring Calanque Longue, and McKie's villa, perched on the top of a cliff at the northern edge of the village. "Do we have anything more on McKie's guests?" I asked while I squeezed in beside Helen.

"Not a sausage," answered Pirmin. "We've no direct evidence that Jones landed on the island, as the ferry she took also goes to Port-Cros, or, even if she did, that she's still there. I guess that, if she's in Heliopolis, she'll be living with McKie, as her villa is spacious enough. It was once a sixteen-room hotel." A series of images and video clips showed its previous incarnation as Le Rocher du Secret. "Tan's boat arrived yesterday morning, but no sign that anyone has disembarked. His son is now with his sister and aunt in Lausanne, waiting until the start of next term, but the rest of the harem are on board." A high-altitude drone image showed the four women lying in the nude on the stern sundeck.

"Any sign of Tan himself?" Helen asked.

"We caught this view of him just before his yacht moored. He seems to be having a post-coital snooze after an al fresco ménage à trois with the wife and ex. No sign of him thereafter."

"Could he be on the island?"

"A little motor boat sailed from L'Ayguade, the port, to his yacht and back about midnight last night, so it's quite possible. However, we don't have any images from the Levant side to confirm this."

"Okay, let's assume that both Tan and Jones are shacked-up with McKie," I displayed a range of images of her villa. "How do we spy on what's going on or, even better, get a hold of one of these processor units?"

"I think we'd be pushing it to try a raid on the villa, like we did on Tan's island," Helen expanded the map of building and grounds. "There's no obvious weak point like the guardhouse. Access is either through the village, when we can't be wearing much more than we are at present, or from the sea, requiring a cliff climb. This is technically doable, but I'm sure the security monitoring will be at least as good as Tan's was. Anything that guards the sea approach can be spoofed, but I can't see a way of getting from the shoreline to the villa without being spotted."

"If we want to get a closer look at the villa, McKie hosts an open tantric yoga class every morning in her grounds," Pirmin suggested.

"Sounds interesting in a kinky kind of a way," Rüdi rolled his eyes. "Do we have any visuals to confirm what goes on at these things?"

"I have a couple of old, low-grade images from closed social sites, cameras are clearly not allowed," Pirmin presented a few 2D videos. "Looks to me just like the group sex that's a drawing point elsewhere on the island. As there's nothing recent or 3D, I guess some blocking tool is in place."

"No satellite images?" Helen asked.

"Nothing useful," a series of pictures appeared. "As you can see, there's an awning covering the area of the garden used. It looks like protection from the sun or bad weather, but it's made of a smart fabric: we can't get anything at all from under it in any part of the spectrum. You can also see that there's a covered walkway from the house to it, so we don't even have an indication if and when McKie and her household participate."

"But McKie is clear in a couple of these images," Doris pointed out, zooming in on videos of the bronzed giantess in the middle of groups of writhing bodies, predominantly young males. "Mmm, all orifices filled there, one double: I wonder where that comes in the Kama Sutra? Anyway, I volunteer to have a closer look. Anyone else up for it?" She then zoomed back to show that the youth enjoying fellatio from McKie was, in turn, being buggered by an older black man.

"Oh, well, I suppose someone needs to hold Doris's hand..." Rüdi started, leaning forward to examine the video.

"Yes, but it's not my hand that you're interested in," Doris slapped his increasingly obvious erection, being rewarded by snorts of amusement.

"Okay, this is an obvious starting point and we can decide who gets to join the orgy later. How many outsiders get involved in this gang-bang?"

"That's something we've got records of," a statistical chart appeared, presenting numbers of people recording approaching the villa at the relevant time in satellite images, broken down for different times of the year and weather conditions. "There's a hard-core of about a dozen regulars, Heliopolis residents from neighbouring properties, and usually ten to twenty others – a mix of residents and visitors."

"What do we have on the regulars?" Rüdi asked.

After a few moments pictures and brief CVs appeared while Pirmin talked us through them. "Two retired men and their pair of catamites from the large house next door..."

153

"Are those boys legal?" Helen interrupted.

"Just barely, as age of consent here is fifteen. Anyway, also a trio, man and two wives, who run a guesthouse nearby. A hetero couple, who own the bakery. Two gardeners who occasionally work for McKie, but live in a collective off the estate; seem to be a lesbian couple. They often come together with two boys from the same community; gigolos who specialise in servicing some of the older ladies who visit the island."

"That seems to cover all ages and sexual orientations. If there's any common factor, it's that they all seem to be pretty fit," I added.

"Regular wild shagging tends to do that, from my experience at least," Doris grinned.

"That's more information than I need, thanks. Anyway, we have an idea of the clientele and the action involved. Is there any way we could get a monitor of any sort in there?"

"We could go through town wearing what we have now, maybe with small handbags or something similar." Doris pointed out. "You can be sure that everything will be scanned when we enter the estate and would be left in an undressing area before the yoga starts. Most of the regulars arrive wearing only sandals and hats, if even that. What do you think, Jörg, you're the equipment guy?"

"For something small, almost undetectable and robust under conditions that wouldn't cause bodily harm, we have a couple of options in the kit that you have with you." Specifications appeared. "Scanning could happen anywhere, but I would expect the detection and destruction of any concealed cameras to be in the door of the dressing room. If it was me, I'd use a nanosecond EM burst at relevant frequencies, a naked body provides little shielding for the critical components of a spy-cam. The best option to beat that would be 2D video with all-organic memory." Two specs expanded to provide more details. "These are set in housings designed for clipping onto intrusion suits or micro-drones, however. So, you'd need to strip them out and put them into something suitable."

"Something suitable, when we're in our birthday suits? From the videos, nobody is even wearing a watch, bracelet or necklace. Although not surprising, I suppose, seeing the antics they get up to," I mused while checking the equipment specs for physical dimensions. "These are small but, even then, millimetre scale and have to then be put into some kind of housing."

After a couple of minutes of thoughtful silence, Doris grinned and lifted her well-formed breasts for our inspection. "Piercings! I noticed that there're plenty of them..." video close-ups showed that the majority of the participants were pierced somewhere or other, with genital piercing quite common. "Reminds me of home!"

Looks very painful to me, but doesn't seem to impact Rüdi's state of arousal. "Okay, Jörg, would that work?"

"Don't see why not, get me a design and I'll programme your 3D printer."

"Right, Doris, you're on that."

"No probs, but how many do we need? One each or as many as possible?" She pointed to her

155

crotch, causing Helen and me to smile and Rüdi look confused.

"We really don't want to increase risks of either detection or kit being fried, so I'd suggest focussing on housings that are as large as possible," Pirmin suggested.

"Or with lots of body shielding..." Doris displayed several images of Princess Alberta piercings."

"Thank God I'm not pierced there!" Helen whispered.

"Actually, I could do that and I'm sure I could sort out the required kit from our medical supplies," Doris grinned.

Helen did not look happy. *Thank fuck I'm not a woman!* "Right, well I've got one pierced ear and Helen has two. Doris has lots of possibilities and Rüdi..."

"Both ears and nipples, although I'm not wearing rings now."

"Nowhere else?" Doris teasingly stroked his bulging pouch."

Rüdi blushed and looked uncomfortable. "Not there, although I've tried it a couple of times. Didn't do anything for me..." He looked as if he was going to say more, but squirmed in silence.

"Right, we seem to be well covered, so we can sort out options with Doris." I said quickly to prevent further teasing. "I think we need to carefully assess if there are any scenarios where this could go tits-up and develop recovery plans for these. Helen, you get together with Pirmin on this. Rüdi and I will take the Zodiac over to Levant and have a wander

156

about to check the lay of the land…"

"Not with you wearing those hideous trunks we're not," Rüdi rolled his eyes theatrically. "Luckily, however, I've got a couple of spare thongs that should fit, even if you're not nearly as well hung as me."

"Well, I've certainly not got it on display at the moment," I glanced down at his erection, to his embarrassment and everyone else's amusement.

***

For me, the stroll around Heliopolis with Rüdi was rather surreal, with most of the people we encountered either completely naked or wearing Le Minimum – minute thongs or G-strings that made the posing pouches that we were wearing seem modest. This would have been unremarkable since the formation of the colony in the early 20th century and further loosening of traditions of public nudity at the beginning of the 21st, but open sexual activity on the beaches and house gardens reflected developments over the recent couple of decades. *Possibly a reflection of increasing socio-political chaos in the European mainland and a backlash against growing influences of religious fundamentalism. Alternatives to conventional hetero couples also seem to be the norm rather than exceptions here and an older man in the company of one much younger, like us, matches a significant subset of the couples here.*

Our perambulation took us past the open gates of the drive to McKie's villa, perched on the edge of a cliff looking towards the Hyeres peninsula. Apart from being much larger than most properties in the village and the high wall that enclosed its grounds, the villa gave no indication of its high security defences. We could see the edge of the covered area where the yoga took place but this would be completely blocked when the gate was closed, as it always was for the duration of the orgies. All this was recorded by cameras built into the frames of our sunglasses and coupled to monitoring from the ultra-sensitive detectors in the matching handbags we carried.

Our reconnaissance data was uploaded and discussed over the satellite link after we returned to our boat. "The shielding in that place is impressive," Pirmin concluded. "Even integrating the output from both your detectors when you were in front of the open gate, there's not a peep from the villa in audio or any part of the EM spectrum."

"So, we need to start by getting onto the grounds. Are we go for tomorrow's yoga class?"

"I printed the rings based on Doris's specs and have incorporated the required circuitry," Helen showed me a handful of what appeared to be gold and silver jewellery. "They're all a bit bulkier than I hoped, so it may be better if you get a nipple pierced, boss – unless, of course, you'd prefer to go for an option lower down."

From the ladies' smiles, I was sure that I was being set up. *Go with the flow, anyway, it'll take their minds off how exposed we're going to be – in more ways than one.* "Okay, a nipple if that's absolutely necessary. So, Helen, how do you suggest that we run this?"

"I don't see any benefit of holding anyone in

reserve, so we all go together. The do lasts from ten until noon. Gates open at nine thirty and we should get there early, which will help us distinguish villa residents from outsiders. The group sessions involve at least three participants, so we should split up into two pairs. I suggest Doris with Rüdi and you with me. This is all a bit uncertain, however, as we've no idea how they pair people up. We should try to get ourselves near residents, McKie if possible, and hope for the best."

"I wonder if either Jones or Tan will participate," Rüdi mused. "If so, we should also try to target them."

"Well, given Tan's penchant for kinky sex, I guess he would be a prime candidate for an al fresco orgy," Doris smiled. "Jones seems a bit less likely to me…"

"Oh, wait a minute…" Jörg interrupted. "I just remember that we got a hold of records of interviews of the spa therapists by the Marseille police. They had nothing significant to add on your activities in the building, but noted en passant that Madame Dupont was a regular client."

"Ah, so there's also kinky sex as a common factor linking Dupont aka Jones, Tan and McKie," I felt distinctly pleased that this apparent anomaly seemed to be resolved. "It makes our interpretation of this as involving some kind of cult more credible."

"All the same, after making it so difficult for anyone to trace them to McKie's villa, would Jones or Tan really appear in the open?" Helen's brow furrowed.

159

Good point, let's work through this. "Depends a lot on whether this crowd think they're under threat or not. Cassis and Provence show that Jones' operations have been hit, but they seem to have been prepared for something of this sort and could reasonably expect to have avoided leaving any evidence. The precautions that they've taken would avoid tying the prime actors together using the type of expert systems and knowledge bases that we normally use. Even if they were shagging each other regularly at these orgies, we'd never pick it up unless we knew exactly what to look for and were prepared to participate."

"Well, it's impossible to know in advance. So, I suppose we just wait to find out tomorrow and then play it by ear." *Sums up this entire operation. It's all wing and a prayer stuff. I'd be so much happier gate-crashing with a heavily armed squad, but we've just got to play the cards we've been dealt.*

***

The next morning was clear and sunny, but with a cool breeze from the southwest. We had a light, early breakfast and stripped off before inserting and testing our monitors, in my case in the form of a large gold ring hanging from my newly-pierced right nipple. *This is totally surreal: preparing for action in the nude.*

"Okay, everyone lubed up?" Doris asked, waving a small spray bottle. She must have noticed my confused look. "Boss, you do know how to prepare for sex…"

"Well, of course I do," I could feel that I was

160

blushing. "I'm protected from all possible STDs, like everyone in developed countries these days."

"Duh, of course you are! Even you can't have missed the miracle that caused the new sexual revolution of the thirties. But you do know about anal sex?"

"Sure, my second wife was fairly keen on it, once or twice a month…"

"But you, have you ever had a dick up your bum?"

I noticed the others were now intently following this interrogation. "Well, I'm actually a straight, hetero kind of a guy…"

"You're waffling! So, really, you've never been buggered?"

"Well, as such, not really…" *Where the hell's this going?* "I'm not quite sure how this is relevant."

Doris turned to look at Rüdi, who took over from her. "You've seen the videos of what Tan and McKie get up to. Does it look to you like any of the participants are straight anything? Conventional tantric yoga involves couples, but this is more like the orgies practiced by alt sex groups. We've no idea how groups are selected, so you've got to be a Boy Scout: be prepared."

"And that means what?"

"First an anal douche, I can sort that out for you. Then a lubricated arsehole, especially if you're a virgin," Doris grinned. "Don't worry, I'll get you through this."

"Unless you'd prefer that I do it," Rüdi laughed. "Then we could get in a bit of practice, so that you'd know what you've got to expect."

"Jesus Christ!" I muttered, "This isn't anything I signed up for when I joined the anti-terrorist unit. Anyway, can we get this out of the way in the privacy of…?"

"Privacy?" Helen interrupted. "You don't think there's going to be any sort of privacy in McKie's orgy, do you? You've got to stop being so bloody prissy!"

So, I'm prissy because I'm uncomfortable about my entire team watching as one of them sticks things up my butt? What the fuck am I letting myself in for here?

***

After I had been sorted out, to great general amusement and continuous banter, we prepared to disembark. Helen carried a little handbag containing only an electronic key for the boat and some money and we all donned sandals, sunglasses and hats before piling aboard the Zodiac for the short trip to Levant. We then walked uphill through the village and on towards the villa as two couples; Doris and Rüdi hand in hand with Helen and me following, arm in arm.

As we neared the open gate, we were joined by some of the regulars – the old couple from the bakery and the two gigolos. Bearing in mind the potential of being grouped together somehow, I started chatting to the former, leaving the latter to Rüdi and Doris, who seemed more than happy with this arrangement.

The couple turned out to be French-Swiss, from Montreux, and were happy to chat about life

162

on the island. They had both taken early retirement and were running the bakery more as a hobby than a source of income. Jacques Lanfranchi had been an engineer and Brigit a banker, and they had two grownup children, both now living in a commune in New Zealand. They were open about choosing Ile du Levant in order to bring more variety into their sex life after three decades of marriage, which seemed to be a rather unsubtle invitation to us.

I lost sight of Doris and Rüdi while we strolled with the Lanfranchis to the tent and had them guide us through the process of leaving our possessions on shelves in the undressing area and then choosing mats near the front of the exercise area, which featured a large screen with a digital clock in one corner. Brigit happily talked us through how the class would run, while the space gradually filled with individuals and groups coming from both a corridor to the villa and the changing room.

At the front, a row of six mats set up for the instructors was separated from the others by a gap of about two metres. "That usually includes Lucy, David and Toni – her two husbands – together with a couple of her fit young lads," Brigit giggled. "She definitely has a taste for young meat, that one. With a bit of luck, she'll group us with one of them, or even two."

I noticed that Jacques also seemed happy with this thought. *So, Lucy McKie is the one controlling all the action; not just her household, but also the visitors. This again fits with some kind of cult dominated by a charismatic individual. Also looks like we'll have no chance to select who we're*

163

grouped with, it's just a lottery.

A couple of minutes before nine, McKie made her entrance, with husband David on one arm and a young lad on the other. They were followed by Tan, walking between Jones and another older woman I didn't recognise. *Bingo!*

For the first half hour the class was relatively conventional tantric hatha yoga exercises that I had read up on. At their insistence, I was paired with Brigit while Helen exercised with her husband. *Variants of sun salutation, warrior, side plank, shoulder-stand – all set up for naked couples and a few trios for all possible combinations of male, female and other.* I had to force myself not to stare at the transsexual couple behind us, both very well hung and with spectacular boobs.

Initially, I was uncomfortable by the inevitable arousal caused by a combination of the naked body rubbing against mine and the sights, sounds and smells of the action around us. Although well into her sixties and somewhat on the plump side, Brigit had a tightly-muscled body and was completely uninhibited as she guided me into the poses. Gradually I was able to relax and my focus moved more into trying to avoid premature ejaculation.

After this first part, there was a relaxation and meditation session for fifteen minutes, for which I managed to partner up with Helen as we were folded into a form of double-lotus. Then the bit I dreaded: McKie wandering through the class with the other instructors, assigning them to groups of five or six that she selected. I held my breath while Brigit and the young man she had been meditating with were grouped together with the two ladyboys and Lucy's husband David.

From my position on our mat, I was looking directly at Lucy's groin as she approached us. *Clearly very excited by what's going on, the sex and / or the control that she has over everyone here.* She took hold of my head and pulled it against her engorged labia, encouraging me to lick the musky juices therein.

"Yes, you, I think," she pressed my mouth against Helen's, forcing me to pass on the taste of her vaginal juices, "and you," she slipped a couple of fingers into our kiss and then licked off our saliva, "and..." she looked around, not noticing how I tensed up. "Mmm, Judy here..." she slipped the same two fingers into Jones' vagina before sticking them back into our still joined mouths, "and the girls." She waved to the two gardeners, who I hadn't previously noticed, and indicated that they should join us, repeating the vaginal sampling with Judy doing the tasting procedure. "My love here does like girls and that leaves all the more boys for me," she laughed and then moved on to form the next group.

Helen and I introduced ourselves using pre-agreed aliases, hijacking the identities of a couple working for Zurich Re, who were currently camping in the Alps. Jones introduced herself simply as Judy, an old friend of Alice's, while the girls were Sophie and Cindy. We actually didn't need the precautionary lube, as the first stage of getting to know each other involved applying a coating of a lubricating gel, taking it in turns for the rest of the group to rub it in, with a particular focus on the genitals and anus.

Four women: looks like I've lucked out here and my anal virginity will remain intact. I grinned thinking of Rüdi's disappointment and looked around to see if I could spot him. *Good, he's still paired with Doris, together with one of the seniors and a catamite from next door plus an older woman that I don't recognise.* Even from the distance, I could see that the woman was sporting huge rings through each nipple, joined by a chain, and a number of large rings dangling from her labia. *All very weird, but I'm sure both my team members will find something to make them happy.*

Thus diverted, I hadn't noticed that, after forming the groups, Lucy was now putting them into position. I became aware of this only when she put her arm around Judy and passed her a large, knobbly, strap-on dildo. *Fuck, my relief was a bit premature.* With almost clinical detachment, McKie set up our starting position, but I noticed a feral glint in her eyes. Helen on her back and Cindy on top of her were placed in soixante-neuf position with Judy behind the former and me behind the latter. Lucy instructed Sophie in her Domina role, providing her with a riding crop to encourage performance, while she adjusted penetration of the orifices of the underlying women. She then bit Judy on the buttocks before moving onto the next gang bang.

The occasional shock of pain to my buttocks did absolutely nothing sexual for me, if anything serving only to drive me away from the point of orgasm. *Anyway, could be worse, I dread to think of the action in Doris's group.* Cindy was getting extremely wet and it was increasing difficult for me to get enough friction to stay erect inside her. Noticing this, Sophie removed my dick, sucking it back into hardness before directing it into a tight little anus. I then gasped with surprise at the strange sensation, seeing that Helen's ministration now included some deep fisting of the dripping orifice that I had just vacates, which caused me to quickly come with an inelegant grunt of release. Sophie immediately transferred my prick to her mouth, sucking hard before climbing to her feet and noisily kissing Judy to share the taste.

I slumped backwards in post-coital exhaustion, shocked into full awareness only a few minutes later when I realised that Lucy had appeared and was now lasciviously licking my sticky belly. "Well, young man, let's get things sorted out again here. You're on the bottom now…" she positioned me on my back, "…and need a bit of oral to get you up again," she sucked my flaccid penis before it was passed to Sophie as she slid on top of me, grinding her pubis against my face. "Let's see… we need another strap-on here," she shouted and one of her toy-boys immediately appeared with a curved, multiple-headed dildo festooned with a complex web of leather straps.

McKie frowned while she inserted one end into Helen's vagina and anus, tightening the straps until her victim squealed. *Probably working out how this can be made as kinky as possible.* I watched in fascination as Helen was placed in position and

Lucy and Cindy together moved the toy into the orifices just above my nose, helping her build up a deep thrusting motion without risking coming out. Sophie's grunts and synchronised clenches of her teeth on my willy, seemed to indicate it was having some effect. *Pleasure or pain, though, I've no idea. Just don't fancy her having an orgasm with her teeth clamped around the family jewels.*

To my surprise, Sophie's ministrations were already bringing my erection back, no doubt helped by the view I was presented with while I licked her clitoris. My groan of satisfaction turned to a gasp of surprise as a finger penetrated my anus. *Fuck! Judy or Jones or whoever. I forgot about her.*

In actual fact it was Cindy. "Nice and tight," she commented before adding a second finger and then a third. "Okay, Judy, give this bad boy a really good buggering." I heard a slap and a squeal that indicated that she was providing additional encouragement.

The shock of penetration caused me to gasp and I could feel my erection dissipate as the rhythm of Judy's thrusts built up. Sophie removed my flaccid dick from her mouth. "I think a bit of help is needed here."

After the sound of another slap and a particularly deep thrust, Lucy stuck her finger into my mouth and I had swallowed the small pill before I realised what was happening. The effect was almost instantaneous: I felt a tingle throughout my body while my penis grew to heroic proportions. *Drugs, why didn't I anticipate this?* Despite the clearly stimulating effects, I now seemed remote

168

from the action and passed the next hour in a daze while Lucy directed changes in positions and group members.

I had left the villa and been steered to a coffee shop before I slowly came out of my dwam. Helen was clearly concerned. "Are you okay? What happened to you?"

"I'm fine, I think," I shook my head to clear it and then drained the small cup of strong, black coffee in a single swallow. "There was some kind of drug…"

Helen looked relieved. "Oh, that. Seemed like some kind of homebrewed mescaline analogue, tailored for a fast kick to the gonads. Something like Joy or Bliss, but better, stronger. Everybody was on it. Are you sensitive to that stuff?"

"No idea, never tried it before."

My partner looked at me in amazement. "It's completely legal – or, at least, not illegal in Switzerland. It really spices up your love life."

"Well, it certainly improved my performance," I realised to my embarrassment that I was still partially erect, "but it's all a bit bleary."

"Can be like that the first few times," she smiled, "but you get accustomed to it quickly. Anyway, you seemed to have been enjoying yourself."

"I'll take your word for it. Anyway, we should get back to the boat."

"I thought it would be better to wait until you were fully compos mentis and your erection was a bit less obvious," she grinned. "Anyway, I guess it can't be uncommon for folk to leave Lucy's orgies still a bit Blissed-out, so probably not something that'd call attention to you."

"Yes, well I'd certainly be uncomfortable walking through the village in this state so let's just have another coffee while I get back to normal." I waved at the naked, blonde waitress and signalled for another round. "Did you see what happened to Doris and Rüdi?"

"They left before us, together with a couple of guys. You remember the ones, the call-boys who regularly attend these classes?"

"Christ, they can't be looking for more sex, not after that bloody gang-bang."

"I wouldn't put it past them, but I think they were just chatting. They'll maybe end up having a coffee of something though, while they're waiting on us."

"Oh, shit, I'm sorry, I should have asked about you. Are you okay? That was some pretty extreme, fucked-up stuff."

"Definitely extreme, but nothing really perverse," her eyes sparkled. "I've done a few groups, but nothing at all like that. Wait a minute, you've had group sex before, haven't you?"

"Well, once, my second wife and her best friend…"

"Wow, what a straight arrow! No drugs and only one-on-one hetero. How the hell did you manage to manage to reach your advanced age with so little experience?"

Happy to change the subject, I carefully sat back in my chair and scratched my head. "Well, my late teens and early twenties were during the early coronavirus pandemics. The chances for personal contacts were very limited. It's funny, I remember my father saying it was just like for him in the seventies – missing out on the summers of love of the sixties and stuck in the period after AIDS had been discovered and before it could be cured. Neo-puritan sort of conditions."

"Poor you," she patted my hand in a strangely matronly manner.

"Anyway, I married young, with my first wife being very religious – although randy as a sack-full of ferrets, so I had a very active if straightforward sex life." I quickly added in response to a quizzical frown. "However, she wanted kids and I didn't, so we eventually split up. My second wife was a bit older than me, had no interest in kids, and banged like a shithouse door in a high wind…"

"Sounds like an ideal woman for you," she smiled.

"Yes, regular sex but with occasional variations: dressing up and role play, anal, stuff like that. As I mentioned, we had a threesome one time with her best friend. That didn't work out too well…"

"You didn't like having sex with two women?"

"It was fine, but my wife clearly enjoyed it more. We divorced soon after and she married her best friend. They seem very happy together."

"That does explain things a bit. The tantric sex orgy must have been a real baptism of fire for you!"

That's a good way of putting it. "Anyway, as long as you're fine. Let's get the bill and look for the others, I've just realised that you're the only one carrying a credit stick."

"Not a problem here anyway," she waved to the waitress, "you can pay everywhere by direct debit based on an iris scan."

"Well, better with direct cash transfer in case a scan can be traced. Anyway, we should get back to the Zodiac now that my head's back to normal."

"I was quite happy with the way that you were," Helen grinned salaciously, "although without the spaced-out bit, of course. You really ought to try Bliss again, it'll be better the next time."

"I'll bear that in mind next time I want to be buggered within an inch of my life," I grimaced, as my return to normalcy was accompanied by increasing pain in my brutally abused orifice. "Christ on a bike, isn't your bum sore after all of that?"

"No pain, no gain," she laughed. "Anyway, we can compare war-wounds when we're back on the yacht and get our video files uploaded. I'm sure Pirmin and Jörg will have fun analysing them."

Shit, forgot about that; probably deliberately put to the back of my mind. "Yes, well I'll mark that file confidential, no reason anyone else needs to look at it."

"Some chance, everyone with op clearance will want to see it, starting with the Commander."

This unhappy thought filled my mind while I walked hand-in-hand with Helen to the harbour, deaf to her happy chatter while she recounted details of the orgy that I would have been happy to forget about completely. *And, despite the pain, what have we really achieved? It was all perverse*

172

enough, but nothing remotely illegal, unless those boys are under-age. Why on earth do they want to have bioweapons and what do they intend to do with them?

When Helen and I met up with the others, she had immediately noticed that Rüdi was now sporting unmatched nipple rings and even I was aware of his wide, shit-eating grin.

"How about that?" he pointed to the iridescent, multi-faceted bolt through his left nipple.

"Where's the camera," Helen asked with a frown.

"Inside the villa, I'm pretty sure. This belonged to one of Lucy's husbands, David. I admired it and said it was a shame that I didn't have a camera to get an image so I could have a copy made. Very nice bloke: we just swapped rings so I could get a photo later. We'll swap back tomorrow. I got on really well with him; he's extremely well hung and knows how to use that battering ram. He…"

"Well, we don't need details," I broke in. "I can see the potential advantages, but aren't there risks also?"

"The cameras can record for twenty-four hours, so this has got to be good for us," Doris contributed. "I can't see what the downside would be."

I worried about that for the entire return trip in the inflatable.

***

Back on the boat we took turns in the small shower and then dressed, rather minimally in Rüdi's case, while the files from our pieces of body-jewellery uploaded to Brugg and underwent a first

173

automated clean-up, focusing on identifying the participants. While eating a late lunch, we discussed the output with the team back at base, enhanced by Rashmi who was now fit for duty. *Nice to have another pair of hands, but she would turn up just when we're going through these bloody videos.*

After she was welcomed back by everyone, it was Rashmi who took the lead. "I've been running the image analysis," she appeared not to notice my groan, "while Pirmin does identity traces and Jörg checks for links within the entire operation database. By the way, nice ring Rüdi." Helen and I looked at each other in confusion while Rüdi blushed and Doris broke into a fit of giggles.

"Anyway, apart from the locals, known residents of the villa and three others like you who are visitors to the island, we have two folk who must be staying with McKie. The most interesting is this woman."

I stared at the image of the late-middle-aged blonde. "She came in with McKie, was one of the instructors."

"Yes, Ingrid Deutscher, who, despite the name, is Dutch," Pirmin contributed. "Doctorate in Biochemistry and owner of a small, specialist pharmaceutical company based in Heidelberg. Believe it or not, also overlapped with McKie while studying in Paris."

"Bugger, so this is even bigger than we realised," I peered at the scrolling CV, "and we have someone else with the capability of producing bioweapons. Any link with Jones?"

"Nothing obvious, but I'm still digging," Jörg

174

reported. "Heidelberg is pretty close to the Alsace, though, so there could be something there. For example, the Colmar lab contained two bioreactors that we haven't been able to trace to either Marseille or Strasbourg."

"Okay, keep on it. Who's McKie's other visitor?"

"Helena, Deutscher's daughter, a twin," Rashmi presented a photo of a beautiful young redhead. "We think her sister was there also, but we don't have a good enough image for a match." A second picture appeared, seemingly identical to the first, then a couple of enhanced video clips of wild copulation including a red-headed woman or red pubic hair trimmed to a landing strip. "In any case, there was another ginger present."

"Open-minded mother, taking her daughters to a gang-bang," Doris smiled.

"It certainly fits with the profiles of McKie, Jones and Tan." *Maybe an indication of incest here also.* "Do we have any idea about the Deutschers' home life?"

"Ingrid's not married, but has a common-law husband and wife. Both work for her company, research chemist and CFO, respectively. Wife has two sons, who bracket the age of the twins. Boys and girls are all home-educated, so records are a bit sparse."

"All you'd need is a couple of live-in lovers and you'd have a mirror of the Tan household," Helen noted before I could.

"Fine, so this has turned out to be a worthwhile exercise: we now know both that the conspiracy is

175

wider than we expected and a consistent pattern is emerging."

"More than that," Rashmi presented a series of clips of Lucy directing wildly copulating groups, "I think it's clear that McKie is the top guru of the cult. We know that Tan is a control-freak, but here we see him being ordered about by her."

"It doesn't seem to have been captured on any of the video here, but I saw Lucy forcing Tan into something that looked like a yoga plough pose. She was sitting on his face and egging on one of her young studs, the black, well-hung one," Rüdi squeezed his eyes tight for emphasis, "who was giving him a serious rogering."

"Yes, that all fits," I agreed, "sexual domination seems to define, or at least characterise, the organisational hierarchy here. But we're not getting much closer to what the bioweapons are all about. We really need to get into the files of someone at, or near, the top of the tree."

"Maybe we'll get something useful from my ring tomorrow, although that means back to the orgy again," Rüdi leered lasciviously.

"Shit, I'd almost forgotten about that. I'd been thinking more about Tan's yacht."

"We now know more about his security," Doris frowned in concentration, "and I guess I could hack through it sufficiently to get us on board. The question is if it would bring anything. This crowd don't seem to leave anything accessible."

"What about Jones' backup at her apartment?" Helen asked.

"Um, I've something on that," Pirmin cut in.

"After the police finished their forensic work, we managed to check on the cable node that Doris had spotted. We didn't even attempt to excavate it; remote sensing showed that it was a quantum dot mega-memory. Or had been, as an inbuilt UV burster had fried it completely. Once these are disrupted that's end game, not a hope of recovering anything at all from it."

"So, even if Tan has taken the primary files with him when he moved in to Lucy's villa, there could be a backup somewhere on his yacht." *But, probably, somewhere physically inaccessible.* I noticed that Doris was still frowning. "Is there something we're missing?"

"Well, if it's also a quantum memory on the boat, we have an almost impossible job of breaking into it. But we could easily check if it was there, if we had a squid."

"A squid?"

"Oh, a superconducting quantum interference device – smart," answered Pirmin, without clarifying things for me in the slightest.

"Indeed," Doris smiled. "The memory would need to be really well shielded and we could probably pick that up. A few laps around and under the yacht and the rest's just CT – computer tomography," she added in response to my quizzical stare.

"I'm not sure what it'll bring us, but can we get a hold of one of these squid things and any other associated kit?"

"I'll check," Pirmin responded, "but I'm fairly sure that we could get it droned to you before sunrise tomorrow."

"Okay, so we can start planning for Rüdi and Helen on orgy duty tomorrow while Doris and I have a swim with a squid."

Helen looked less than happy. "I'm sure that Doris is better at gang-bangs than I am and would be happy to…"

"Yes, but what do you know about squids?" I interrupted.

"Not a sausage," she confessed. Then she brightened up. "Well, what about me teaming up with Doris and you going with Rüdi?"

"It'd be good for you," Rüdi laughed, "teach you to be less of a tight arse."

"My arse has already had more than enough new experiences to last me a lifetime," I groaned to general laughter, with even Helen forcing a smile. "Anyway, let's have another run through the file updates and see if we can tie anything more to the prime movers here: McKie, Jones, Tan and, probably, Deutscher." *And, hopefully, pick up some clues to what any of them need with bioweapons. The sex cult front could easily cause us to underestimate this crowd – these are terrorists with the potential to go far beyond the attacks that we are used to, a threat that isn't just national or international, but could even be global in extent.*

CHAPTER NINE

Next morning, over an early breakfast, we reviewed plans for the day. Rüdi had scanned and 3D printed copies of his borrowed nipple ring, along with a heavier earing he had designed as a present for his new friend. Helen had sorted out the body jewellery for the yoga session and was testing the shielding on the monitoring systems while Doris was fiddling with the fitting on a diving mask, usually used for mounting a small video camera, so that it would hold the miniature squid that had been delivered by drone in the early hours of the morning. I had been relieved that our mooring was outside the drone exclusion zone that covered Ile du Levant. Indeed, residents often sailed out to our bay in order to pick up such deliveries, so this wouldn't seem anomalous in any way.

I still had not decided whether our survey of Tan's yacht would be best achieved by scuba or if a long snorkel swim would suffice, overlaying the updated satellite images with bathymetry maps and modelled currents, when a detail caught my eye. "Buggeration!" I cursed aloud, causing three heads to turn in my direction, with matching looks of surprise.

I zoomed in on the image of the yacht and groaned. "What's the problem, boss?" Helen asked the question that seemed to be on the tip of three tongues.

"Fucking Tan's boat, it's raising anchor at this very moment. Shit!"

"Well, at least we're not losing anything critical. The squid would only have confirmed a quantum memory on board and given us its location, nothing really mission-critical." Doris sighed and detached the device from her mask. "And, on the bright side," she smiled at Helen, "I can go along with Rüdi to the orgy, while you guys search databases or whatever."

Seems like a justifiable cop out, but really not what we're here for. I sighed, a little theatrically. "Well, if we're here anyway, no point in twiddling our thumbs when we could double the chances of picking up some useful intel. Make it four for the yoga love-in."

"Boss, I'm impressed: we'll make a hedonist of you yet. We got enough charged up rings?"

Helen nodded. "If we make it one each, we're fine."

"Goody, goody. Let's get lubed up and then we're off to the buggery fest!" Rüdi leered at me, bursting into laughter at my grimace.

I glanced towards Helen, who seemed to be sharing my discomfort. *Maybe this is a bit above and beyond the call of duty, but there's no way I can back out now.*

***

Even though it was only our second visit to the villa, we were greeted like old friends by the Lanfranchis and Rüdi's new best buddy, David. I was bemused by the fuss made as the men exchanged nipple rings and then David's gushy response to Rüdi's present, seeing a camp side to my colleague that I had never suspected, despite my

180

knowledge of his sexual orientation. Doris was also hamming it up and I wondered if this was going to end up in a gang-bang before the yoga session had even started.

Now forewarned about the procedure, I found it easier to go with the flow, paired again with Brigid for all of the introductory exercises and the meditation. Then Lucy started selecting her groups for the main event. The bronzed Amazon recognised me immediately. "Ah, the neophyte. You looked a bit nervous yesterday and, to tell you the truth, I didn't expect to see you back again."

I forced a shy smile. "Yes, it's a bit hard teaching an old dog new tricks, but my young partner here swears she'll make a new man of me," I glanced at Helen, who grinned back, "so I'm doing my best. No pain, no gain as she puts it."

"Good lad!" she squeezed my testicles hard enough to make me wince. "Anyway, let's continue your education. I think Ingrid and her girls will look after you."

Ingrid: the mysterious Deutscher woman. So maybe I'll get something useful out of this. And her girls, so maybe I've lucked-out here. I could feel some of the tension easing out of my body while I watched Helen being teamed with David, one of the lesbian gardeners and a young black guy who I didn't recognise.

"Ingrid and girls," I whispered in Helen's ear. "I guess I missed a bullet here."

"And walked in front of a ten-ton truck," she grinned at my look of confusion and nodded her head over my left shoulder.

181

I turned to see Ingrid approaching, a riding crop in one hand and a huge dildo in the other. My gasp turned into a groan as I saw that she was closely followed by the two unforgettable, massively-endowed transsexuals. "Shite!"

Helen's giggle added insult to impending injury. *I just hope they come with that bliss stuff ASAP; this isn't going to be something I want to remember.*

***

Déjà vu all over again. I slowly became aware that I was back in the café from yesterday, with an equally worried Helen staring into my eyes. "Jesus fucking Christ," I groaned. "What the hell happened?"

"Well, I was a bit too busy to follow it all, but the Kraut woman seems to have taken a shine to you."

"Actually, she's a cloggy," I interrupted, now wishing that I hadn't asked.

"Anyway, she and her girls, God but they're well-endowed both above and below the waist, managed to keep you going for the entire session. With a bit of help from Lucy, of course."

"And a lot of drugs."

"Definitely, they must have been pumping Bliss and Viagra into you by the bucket load. Despite the fact that I had my hands full, well, actually a lot of other parts full also, I couldn't help but be impressed." She patted my hands, which I only then noticed were distinctly trembling. "Anyway, get that coffee down your neck and also the fruit juice. I dropped a painkiller in it, so you'll feel much better thereafter."

I managed to take a sip of coffee without spilling any, which seemed to help reduce my spaced-out feeling. "What happened to the others?"

"David invited Rüdi back to the villa for lunch and Doris is off with Tricia and Tracy, the gardeners. They're meeting up with some others and we can join them if you feel up to it."

"I think I'll pass on that; I feel completely drained."

"Not bloody surprising," she grinned, "I'm sure the video will drive your cred miles high when the team see it."

"Fuck, you really know how to salt a man's wounds, don't you? Anyway, how did it go with you and the others?"

"I only had a chance to exchange a few words with Doris, who seemed to have had fun. She told me about Rüdi's lunch date and I'm certain that he's like a dog with two tails."

"But what about you?"

"Well, it was a bit on the extreme side, but nothing completely beyond my comfort zone." She hesitated before gushing out, "it's the video of it being viewed by all of our colleagues that I find disturbing. A bit of kinky sex is fine, I just don't post it on the internet." She stopped again and looked into my eyes. "That's surely normal, isn't it?"

"Completely normal. I'm probably even more uptight about this than you are. On the positive side, if my action was all that you made it out to be, there's probably little chance of much time being spent viewing what you've been up to."

"There's that, I suppose," she smiled wanly, "and all the wild goings-on from Rüdi and Doris's cams. Not that that pair would be bothered a bit about the vid being on general release."

I started to feel a bit cheered up before she added, "But I guess your bit will still be the most popular by far."

***

We had a slow lunch in the café before Helen helped me limp to the port where our rendezvous with the others was planned, suffering from my abuse despite the painkiller. Doris had already arrived at our meeting point, but we had to wait almost an hour in a nearby bar before Rüdi eventually showed up. While the girls had been speculating wildly on what he could be up to, I had begun to worry, very aware that the superficial decadence of McKie's estate was the front for a key node of an extreme terrorist network.

"Bloody hell," he greeted us, with a smile that immediately dispelled my morose concerns," that's a truly weird place Lucy is running! We need to check out what David's ring has on it," he pointed to his left nipple, "but this isn't a cult as we know it, Jim."

"Less of the Trecky shit, Rüdi," Helen cut in before I betrayed my ignorance. "How can it not be a totally loopy sex-driven cult with WMDs that would make Manson weep?"

"No idea about Manson or mass-destruction weapons, but the sex bit seems much more consenting adults, not the spooky cult thing I was

184

expecting."

"And you learned all this over a brunch buggery-session?" Doris broke in, to my surprise.

"Actually, most of the buggery, and that very well done, I'll have you know, was pre-brunch, as you well experienced yourselves." He grinned in my direction, causing chuckles from the ladies. "Anyway, in the villa, it was a proper lunch, at a huge dining table. There must have been about twenty of us. Formal, I suppose you'd call it, in that we were all wearing these smock things, which were somewhere between transparent and translucent. Anyway, the most amazing buffet of finger food and some stunning Provence Rosé wine, which I thought wasn't produced any more."

"Jesus Christ, Rüdi, cut to the chase," Helen took the words out of my mouth.

"The bottom line: they're a really well-balanced, even if scary-smart, bunch of cookies. Not the slightest hint of religion of any shape or form, no control by Lucy or the other yoga instructors or spooky master-slave relationships. Just a bunch of free-thinkers."

"You'd bet your life on it?" I enquired.

"Mmm, well I wouldn't go quite that far. Anyway, let's get some images downloaded and analysed and then we can check if we're maybe barking up the wrong tree here."

I'd almost be glad to find out that this is some kind of false alarm, but the links to bioweapons seem water-tight, even if I can't guess what the goal would be.

***

Back on board, we uploaded the material from our rings and left the Brugg team with the job of analysing the complete video record using heavy-duty image crunchers, while we skipped quickly through the material from inside the villa. The ring that Rüdi had swapped with David had hours of blurry video due to the robe that seemed to be the ubiquitous garb indoors, but a reasonably clear audio record of conversations in a polyglot mixture of English, French, German and Italian, with languages often drifting within a single sentence. One of the women occasionally dropped in a word or two in what I guessed to be Dutch while two of the men had a brief conversation in what Helen identified as Portuguese, but with a very strong accent.

After initial chatter about the yoga session, with repeated references to Rüdi, who seemed to be a hit with both his male and female partners, the conversation drifted to the anodyne topics that might be expected for a group of friends living together: weather, news, politics and the arts. From our fast-forward through midday, afternoon and evening, there was nothing that seemed to have any relevance to our mission. Mid-afternoon there was an hour of clear video while David had a swim, worked out with free weights and then sunbathed at the poolside. Although there was lots of naked flesh on show, this material served only to emphasise that the residents were all in good shape and did not rely entirely on energetic sex to burn off calories.

After dinner, Lucy organised two pairs to play bridge, while David joined a group to watch a

World Cup football match in the basement media room. About 10 pm, the residents congregated in the main lounge for coffee and nightcaps and then, gradually, pairs or larger groups wandered off to bed. Unlike the yoga session, Lucy played no special roll in selection of bedmates, which seemed to be completely ad hoc. David initially entered a bedroom alone and showered in the en-suite bathroom but, by the time he re-entered, Lucy and one of her young toy-boys were sprawled on top of the huge circular bed that dominated the room.

"That lad's called Jesus, and fucking well named," Doris noted. "He really can raise the dead and you'll be screaming his name when he gets to work on you. Well, at least Rüdi was," she giggled.

"Too much information," I tried to keep the team on topic. "Do we have any idea what role he plays here?"

"Well just look at him," Rüdi rolled his eyes, "really black and ripped. I'd call him more beautiful than handsome."

"Absolutely drop-dead gorgeous," Doris confirmed.

"But is he eye-candy only?" Helen asked. "Well, apart from a really good shag, of course."

"I only talked to him very briefly," Rüdi answered, "but he was chatting away over lunch and seemed to be able to hold his own during discussions about the latest bird flu pandemic and its likely links to global warming. I wouldn't be surprised if he had some training in medicine or the life sciences."

"Whatever, we need searches on all those

living in the villa, but that'll come out of the Brugg analysis." I jumped quickly through the subsequent ménage a trois, despite Doris's objections, and then focused on the post-coital pillow talk. Although the three bodies were covered only by a light sheet, David's conversation with his wife was indistinct and partially drowned out by Jesus's snoring. The gist, however, seemed to be that David was leaving soon and would be absent for about a fortnight, in the company of Ingrid Deutscher.

Early in the morning, just after sunrise, David slipped out of bed and walked into a neighbouring room where a laptop was docked into a system very similar to the ones we had already seen with Jones and Tan. I slowed replay to real time and we waited with bated breath until the login started and our view was suddenly blocked off.

"Bollocks!" Helen groaned. "He's been swanning about in the buff for hours and then, as soon as it's getting interesting, he puts on a sodding t-shirt."

Just at that moment the video cleared enough to show the disturbance caused by a black hand moving into view and starting ministrations that rapidly induced a response of the penis that was just visible at the bottom of the screen.

"Bugger off, Jesus," David was clearly annoyed despite his evident physical response. "This is work, well above your level, so you shouldn't even be in this room in the first place. Just trot back and give my darling wife a good rogering to start her day in the manner in which it'll probably continue."

I stopped the playback and looked at the confused faces around me. "This is strange, don't you think? Lucy McKie seems to be the top of the tree in this cult, but David is disparaging about her in front of one of the lower-level acolytes. Rüdi may well have a point here; it doesn't seem to be the way that a typical cult would work."

"You know, there's something about all of this that I've picked up as weird, and now it's dropping into place..." Doris looked a bit uncertain, but continued, "...toes!"

Exchanges of vacant glances showed that this had gone above everyone's heads. "Toes?" I asked.

Most unusually, Doris seemed a bit embarrassed. "I can't say it's my main thing, but I've always been into toes – during sex, I mean. Sucking toes, having my toes sucked, it's kind of intimate, sensual in a BDSM kind of a way. Well, anyway, there seems to be a bit of that in the videos we've seen and, especially the new bit of David and Lucy, seems to give us an indication about the pecking order here."

"Toes?" I echoed. "Isn't this a bit farfetched?"

"Not at all," Rüdi answered, "very Dom-Sub kind of thing. I actually... with David... well we haven't come to that bit yet. It'll be on the other file."

Now I was really bemused; the entire op seemed to have passed out of my control. "So, it's all toes. That's the answer?"

I was relieved that Helen seemed to be as confused as I was, but then she hit the comm link. "There's something here that I don't understand, but

I feel that it's important. Everything we discussed has now been dropped into the Brugg AI analysis, so let's see what it comes up with."

Pirmin immediately came online, gushing. "Wow, thanks for the porn, guys, this'll keep the team here amused for weeks. Rüdi's street cred has gone sky-high, but the boss's performance is the stuff of legends. Can you even walk after that?"

"To work, for a minute," I sighed gratefully as Helen broke in. "What about toes? Analyse all the video we have from Tan's place and Lucy's villa and tell us if there's a link of some sort."

"Running already," Rashmi contributed in a more professional tone. "We can confirm that the sexual domination side of things is a lot more subtle than it seems and doesn't fit the profile of a normal cult. If, indeed, there is any such thing. Nevertheless, umm, the assessment is just getting summarised now. Anyway, there is something strange with regard to toes. I haven't the slightest clue how Doris picked it up, but all of the upper-level members of this organisation seem to have toe rings."

"Toe rings?" I interrupted. "This is even weirder than toes per se!"

"We're running enhanced images now," Rashmi added. "Yes, Jones, Tan, David and Ingrid all have identical rings on their big toes. These seem to be based on an Ouroboros snake or dragon encircling a plate of some form. Interestingly, many of the other members of the extended family here seem to have similar rings on their thumbs or pinkies. But without the plate, whatever it is."

"And, I bet you that kissing these rings is part of the sex play," Doris grinned. "That's how you'll nail down the master-slave hierarchy.

I looked at the beautiful young woman in amazement. *Preconceived ideas completely blown out of the window. I'd thought of Rüdi as the wild man of the team, but it's little Doris who's got the decadent background to provide insight into the mad conspiracy that we're up against.*

CHAPTER TEN

I couldn't see any advantage of doing more at Levant, so we sailed off that evening to Nice, where we caught a direct flight to Basel. The next week was focused on stripping all significant information from the videos that we had captured and integrating them into a consistent project database. As I summarised at the next project team meeting, we had both good and bad news.

The first bit of good news was that an explanation of the strange toe-rings had emerged. Image integration and enhancement indicated that the Ouroboros design surrounded a plate of diamond-like carbon. Doris explained how this could hold huge quantities of holographically-stored data and, based on what we had seen of the computer systems used by Lucy, Tan and David, could form yet another redundant security check. "This clearly connects all of the key players," she concluded, "and shows how serious they are about protecting records of whatever they are up to. I'm sure we could crack this wide open if we could just break into one of these computers, although, at the present, I haven't the slightest clue about how we would go about it. Anyway, we've got a geek team working on it."

"Yes, well that's part of the bad news. Rashmi, you're up now," I nodded in her direction.

"Yes, well, the boffins have a good idea about what one part of the plan involves. It seems that our terrorists have constructed a phage-like organism ab

192

initio. It's stripped down to a basic minimum and bears no similarity to any known natural virus. Actually, it's difficult to say if you'd properly describe this as an organism or an organic nanomachine."

"Is this dangerous, something that we've no immunity to?" the commander interrupted.

"Well, this is the strange bit. There seems to be no health threat here at all. From what we can see so far, it's simply too alien to do any harm. It has a lot of sulphur replaced by selenium and so replicates only very slowly, very much nutrient limited."

"Selenium, that's odd," Doris mused aloud. "There was something about high levels in one of our routine analyses, although I'm buggered if I can remember what it was."

Pirmin initiated the search and seconds later a file was projected on the meeting room screen. "Well, as you can see, you were very close with reference to being buggered. These are genital and anal swabs taken after your tantric orgy."

"What the fuck?" Rüdi looked worried. "Does this mean that we're now contaminated with this phage thing?"

Rashmi threw some data on the screen. "There's some kind of risk analysis, but it's well above my head. Urs, can you make any sense of this?"

The forensic tech reorganised the data in a spreadsheet and then scratched his head. "Well, if it hadn't been for that selenium gel, I'd have said low levels of infection, even if all your sexual partners there were carriers. With the gel, I guess higher infection levels are more likely. We don't know what the minimum infection level is to have an impact and, in any case, this would probably be undetectable in vivo until we've developed some better tools."

"But could it be like AIDS, hiding in our bodies until something sets it off?" Rüdi's voice had a distinct tremor.

"I would say the chance is zero, or as close as scientists ever come to a black-white answer. I honestly don't see this as any kind of disease or bioweapon, especially as it appears that the main conspirators are infected and deliberately spreading it to a small number of family and friends. If I had to judge, I would say that this is some kind of antidote or prophylactic, protecting the chosen few from an expected plague that would spread widely through the general population."

"You know, this makes a crazy kind of sense," I frowned as the implications became clearer. "Colmar could fit as a secret development facility aimed at scaling up more academic work carried out in associated universities."

"Very exotic life-forms would fit the links we saw to extremophile and astrobiology groups," Urs added. "But, if this cult is intending to bring about a global apocalypse, then they need not only something exotic, but also a delivery system that would avoid triggering the defences we already have in place to identify and fight pandemics."

"We need to be careful to avoid exaggerating the risk here. It is, after all, mainly speculation without any hard evidence." The Commander waved to stop my objection before continuing. "Nevertheless, it would be prudent to look at worst case scenarios. What do you think, Pirmin, you're a bioweapons guy?"

"Maybe we need to think less on normal terrorist weapons, which are generally targeted in some sort of way, and more in terms of pandemics, as Urs noted. The worst case, super-horror scenario would involve something novel, released in parallel at many locations. A disease that is highly infectious and has a long, asymptomatic latency period. To maximise impacts, if that's the goal, something with a high mortality rate but a long period requiring intensive care and frightening, Ebola-like symptoms could completely crash the global economy, adding to the primary disruption caused by the disease itself."

This gloomy picture caused a couple of minutes of silent introspection. "That's certainly a horror scenario, but I think, or I hope, we're missing something. The key players are certainly control freaks, but I don't get the impression of a nut cult. There isn't the feel of Aum, Manson, Jonesville or Waco. No divine revelations or spaceships or anything like that. As Rüdi noted, they're maybe a bit brighter or more successful than average, but otherwise surprisingly normal people."

"That's a bit one-sided," Helen objected. "What about the suicides in Colmar, the death trap in Marseille? That's hardly what you'd expect of normal people."

"You're right, of course, but I feel that they have the profile of people fighting for a cause, not

195

psychopaths or lunatic mass-murderers."

"Well, we can't tell until we get deeper in the organisation," the Commander concluded. "If we opened up what we have to the French and / or Italians, we could probably arrange a hit on McKie's villa or Tan's yacht."

"I'm sure that's not the way to go," Helen again took the words out of my mouth. "We have almost no chance of breaking into the computer systems in either case," Doris confirmed this with a silent shake of her head, "so I guess we're left with capture and interrogation. These aren't ragheads in a cave, though. They're professors, bankers, lawyers, industrialists. I'd be very surprised if they didn't have some plan in place to counter any such action."

"How about softly-softly in and out, with use of smart drugs to extract info and blur all details of the action," Rüdi suggested.

"Depends on our drugs being better than theirs and also the feasibility of a silent action on either a fortified villa or a ship on the open seas. The big problem, though, is that if we fail, we've tipped our hand. There was a lot of luck getting as far as we have and, in particular, we still have no idea how big their organisation is. If we break only a local cell and there's a lot more globally that goes black, we may have no chance of finding another trace before it's too late."

"I think Helen's right. What do you think, sir?" I passed the buck to my boss.

He looked uncomfortable, while the team waited with bated breath. "Yes, well, the global extent of the organisation is the crux here. We need to trace the links we have further. Where's this David guy supposed to be going anyway?"

"We've got searches for him and Ingrid Deutscher at all borders, with image recognition running on key CCTV locations in airports, harbours and train stations. However, not a trace so far," Pirmin reported.

"Um, I wonder…" Rüdi closed his eyes in deep thought.

"Come on, out with it, lad" I encouraged him, hoping that he wouldn't be intimidated by the Commander's intense stare.

"Well, it was over brunch in the villa and I was chatting to Jesus. It wasn't caught on the audio record, but I think I heard Ingrid ask what the weather was like in Sal or Sol, something like that. I seem to remember this was in French, although I wasn't paying a lot of attention."

"And what was the answer?"

"It was in English: *hot, dry and, as usual, very windy* or something like that."

"Okay, I know where that is," Helen announced.

"You do? I haven't even started a search," Pirmin sounded sceptical.

"I'm fairly sure they're referring to Sal, one of the Cape Verde islands. It's a popular destination for kite surfers and I spent a week there once, near the town of Santa Maria."

The meeting dragged on for another half hour, but my attention was elsewhere. *I'm not quite sure why, but a tourist island in the Cape Verde*

197

archipelago seems to fit. Of course, even if it does, it may only be a single stepping stone towards a global network of terrorist cells. Anyway, getting more information on the network is critical. It'd be so much better, though, if we had any clue as to what their timeline is and when their plot passes the point of no return.

***

Thanks to Rüdi's tip, locating our targets in Sal proved remarkably easy. Although it wasn't evident how they got there from the south of France, David, Ingrid and her daughter, Ruth, appeared on CCTV from the international airport, a day after we had returned to Brugg. Arrival late in the evening on a private charter from Lisbon had allowed them to rapidly complete customs in the executive reception area, where their few items of luggage were transferred to a large, electric SUV and whisked out of the airport. We traced the vehicle to the Hilton in Santa Maria, where there was a record of a man and two women checking into the Presidential Suite but, unfortunately, no video to corroborate who it was.

Helen and I looked at each other. "This stinks!" she commented with a frown. "This crowd don't like their whereabouts being known and holing up in the Hilton doesn't fit with them at all. I suppose no video since they arrived?"

"Nope," Pirmin confirmed. "I could dig a bit further though."

"Don't bother, it's all misdirection: smoke and mirrors. What other vehicles do we have leaving the airport at about the same time?"

"Shit there are loads, even though there are

fewer tourists now than when I was there about ten years ago. The private flight landed just after scheduled flights from Stockholm, Berlin and Lisbon, plus a TUI charter from Manchester."

I scanned some general background. "Makes sense, I suppose. The storms that thrash Europe every autumn and winter rarely come this far south. There's been a bit of loss of land due to sea level rise, but they don't have the storm surges that do so much damage elsewhere. So, tourism still struggles on there."

"Anyway, where could they be now?" Helen pulled us back on track. "Almost all the traffic is heading south, to Santa Maria, where the big hotels are. Maybe they went somewhere different?"

"Let's see. One anomaly might be this black minibus," a video clip appeared. "It left just before the SUV, so I doubt that they would have time to transfer their luggage onto it, but maybe that's not so important. It headed north east to the Pedra de Lume harbour, then disappeared."

"What's in Pedra de Lume?" I asked, just before Pirmin projected a map on the screen.

"Not much," he responded. "There's a new marina and a small, upmarket tourist resort, together with associated services."

"I seem to remember that there was a salt mine somewhere nearby. You could bathe in the brine there," Helen added.

"That's been closed to tourists for almost a decade now, taken over by some chemical company that makes direct use of the salt." A satellite image showed solar panels covering the entire floor of the

199

caldera. "Quite clever, actually, they can easily generate enough power for any processing required…"

"…and all activities are completely shielded from prying eyes," I added. "Do we know what the layout of the buildings underneath is like?"

"We've got drawings of the original plans for licensing and a series of satellite images during construction, which really don't show anything much. The only relevant part for us is the management accommodation. That's this villa on the north side of the caldera wall. Given that the plant is completely automated, including the transporters that shuttle material to and from the nearby harbour, there isn't even anything that we could obtain from workers. The only external staff regularly on site either service the solar panels or are domestics at the villa."

"Okay, I've been digging into ownership of this plant. It's called *Salex*." Rashmi projected a complex 3D network of names, about 10% of which I could identify as being Swiss-based and involved in chemicals, pharmaceuticals or investment banking. "It may look like a rat's nest, but it's typical of the layers of shells for any specialist manufacturing facility. It may mean nothing at all, but Deutscher's business overlaps with at least 5 of these links and David is a board member of an investment house holding 25% of the company's shares."

"Could be a justification for the pair of them visiting to check up on things, I suppose," Helen seemed unconvinced.

"But this wouldn't justify the level of secrecy associated with their trip," I added to complete her thought.

"There's also the daughter, Ruth. What's she doing on this business trip?"

"Jesus!" Pirmin interrupted. "Look at this, from the Salex website." There were several gasps as the file was projected.

"That can't be right: Sarah Kempf, CEO? That photo's surely the kid, Ruth, isn't it?" I peered at the image.

"Looks like her, but you can't have a seventeen-year-old kid running a company," Rashmi added.

"Could it be an older sister, who's married? That'd explain the name," Helen frowned in thought. "Do we have images of Sarah and Ruth that are good enough for full biometric scans?"

"Or anything more on Sarah, a CV or something?" I added.

Images flashed on the screen while Rashmi, Pirmin and Doris scanned open databases and hacked into others as required. After a couple of minutes, a very long time for this highly talented trio, I had to ask. "Things not kosher then?"

"Buggeration!" Doris was clearly pissed-off by their lack of progress. "If we had just looked at either Ruth or Sarah, we'd have a nice, credible background history. Put together, though, and they overlap as if Sarah is simply Ruth displaced by eight years. This is screwed-up on so many levels. But, without the comparison, there's not a single obvious anomaly."

I scratched my head. "So, if Sarah exists, she's Ruth's sister and just very young looking, at least in this website image."

"Also credible," Helen pointed out, "if the kid is travelling with mum to meet up with big sis."

"And," Rüdi added, "a twenty-five-year-old CEO is still very unusual. She'd have to be a very high flier, but certainly more credible than a teenager."

"Okay, we need to dig deeper into this," I decided. "In parallel, we should look into options for taking a closer look at this salt mine."

"The upper levels are going to love this," contributed Rüdi sotto voce, "yet another field trip to a prime holiday destination. If we don't get a lead taking us to a hellhole like Manchester or Milan, this is going to start looking a bit suspicious."

CHAPTER ELEVEN

Three days later we were in Sal. The decision to make the trip was confirmed when Tan's yacht anchored in the bay just off the port of Pedra de Lume, giving us two possible goals. I had taken Rüdi out of the intrusion team because he was now well known to David and all McKie's dinner guests, replacing him with Rashmi, who could be used if we ever needed anyone to get into close proximity to our targets. We flew to the island directly on a Helvetia holiday charter from Zurich, with package accommodation in a resort that included hotel rooms, apartments and villas. The resort had been built in the '20s, just before the collapse of the tourist industry, but seemed to have survived better than the deserted properties surrounding it. It was located close to the main tourist town of Santa Maria, about a kilometre further out than the Hilton, where David's party were supposed to be staying.

As I had not been involved with logistics, the relatively busy flight and bustle of hotel reception was a surprise. I commented on this after we had been dropped off at our apartment and received a guilty look from Helen. "Well, it's an adults-only place that caters for a niche market," she prevaricated.

"What kind of niche?" I noticed Doris and Rashmi exchanging smiles, confirming my suspicion that I had missed out on something.

"Well, mature adult sort of niche."

Rashmi burst into giggles. "Come on, Helen,

call a spade a spade. It's a swinger resort."

"Jesus," I groaned, "Why the fuck did you select a place like this? The Commander will go apeshit."

"No, it's okay, there's method in our madness," Doris interrupted. "This came out of the planning group, learning from our experience in Levant."

"Experience dragging me into wild orgies and distributing videos throughout the department?"

"I have no idea how those video clips got passed about," Doris struggled to keep a straight face, "but the orgies were just a bonus. The clincher was the absence of CCTV on the island."

"Didn't stop you getting enough video of me," I ground to a halt. "Shit, that's actually not entirely daft. Nowadays, there's closed circuit surveillance just about everywhere."

"Yes, exactly," Helen jumped in. "That's how we do 95% of our tracing. The amount of material available is huge, but the AI search engines can manage it given enough number crunching power."

"So that's why we're here?"

"Exactly! Although the risk must be small, we need to minimise any chance of our opponents linking us to Swiss security or any of our previous actions."

Anomalies now fell into place for me. "That would be why you insisted on us wearing those bloody awful sun hats."

"Yup. We've got Zurich departures spoofed, but we couldn't be sure about covering everything at Sal arrivals. No security cameras at all here, however, to ensure privacy of the interactions

204

between guests," Helen smiled smugly.

"Of course, it also increases the chance of Rashmi being able to see the now-legendary performance of her super-stud boss," Doris added, ensuring that my building acceptance of the situation was completely destroyed.

***

Although we had been travelling as two couples, our luxurious apartment had three bedrooms. I had assumed that I would be allocated one, but the women clearly had other ideas. The smallest was selected as our communication centre and the relevant kit from our luggage set up there. While it was being sorted out, Helen smiled in my direction. "Well, boss, which bedroom do you want?"

"Whatever, I'll fit in with anything you decide," I responded while setting up the unit that created a virtual Faraday Cage to isolate the room. This cut all external electronic links, with the exception of the optical cable that Doris was plugging into a small laser on our terrace, creating a link to a Swedish military satellite that we had borrowed bandwidth on.

"Fine, you're in the bigger one with me then."

It took several seconds before this response sunk in. "I think that'd be a bit uncomfortable for us all. I can squeeze into this room and you ladies can sort yourself out in the others."

Helen vented a theatrical sigh. "For God's sake, boss, lighten up. There're two single beds in this room, both covered with comms crap. The other rooms have king-size beds and en-suites. You have already had your evil way with both Doris and me, so you could have your choice of bedmate. Then again, if you want a change, I'm sure Rashmi'd be up for it."

"Come on, Rashmi's got a husband and two kids. And, well," I was clearly struggling, "Doris has a couple of husbands, who clearly outperform me in every way imaginable."

"That means you're going to bunk with me then?" She smiled in a most annoying way.

"Oh, stuff it, better the devil I know, I suppose."

"Devil? Is that what you're looking for?" She licked her lips salaciously and fluttered her eyelashes. "I suppose that could be arranged, although it might be better as a foursome with the rest of the team. Look on the bright side, it'll get you in the mood for the swinger action."

"What swinger action? The entire point of being here is to avoid CCTV."

"Yes, of course, but we also need to ensure that we don't display any odd behaviour that could bring us to the attention of a smart search engine." I jumped at this comment from behind me, not having noticed Doris returning to the room. "These don't just search CCTV, you know, also anything odd reported on social media."

"Okay, we hit the bar after we've showered and our tweets will fit right in with the other residents here," Rashmi added. "Naturally, no videos are allowed in common areas, but our presence will be registered."

I rolled my eyes, but my silence was a

concession of defeat. *I'm on a hiding to nothing here, so may as well just go with the flow. At least it won't be as extreme as McKie's yoga and there won't be a video record.* Somehow, I had a feeling that maybe this was more wishful thinking than a rational risk assessment.

***

While the ladies were showering and getting themselves sorted out for the evening, I checked the link to Brugg, updated the project database and had a quick video chat with Rüdi, who was acting as main liaison contact for this op. As I expected, he was fully informed about the accommodation that we were booked into and had checked out the amenities.

"There are two restaurants in the complex and a couple of pool bars that offer a range of snacks. That's food with a view, I'd guess, as the pool area is swimsuit optional," he reported. "There're also a couple of bars that look interesting... and an extremely dodgy nightclub."

"I dread to imagine what you'd consider interesting and I pale at the very mention of something dodgy," I responded in a bemused manner, wondering how to balance fitting in with the profile of those who frequent these places while keeping a focus on our project.

Rüdi was evidently prepared for my question. "The main bar is called *Hook Up* and is a relatively standard pick-up joint, with floor entertainment and wide variety of tail-for-sale."

"A wide variety in what way?" I interrupted as my suspicions began to build up.

"Sexes, colours, orientations, whatever," I could sense that Rüdi clearly considered this self-evident. "Anyway, there are live sex shows later in the evening, with audience participation encouraged."

"Shit! Well, we'll stay away from that."

"A good choice, boss, as that's the boring option. The other drinking hole, *The Wet Bar*, is a bit kinkier and, as you could guess from the name and the large number of Germans favouring that place."

"Okay, maybe the first option might not be so bad after all."

"Well, I did warn you: it'll be totally boring! Probably packed full of Swedes, Dutch and Danes. You should really check out the club though: *The Dungeon*. The reviews from the BDSM crowd are amazing. I've read that the gadgets are state-of-the-art. It was described as a cross between the Shinjuku Robot Restaurant and De Sade's Château de Silling. I bet Doris would really go for it," he attempted to mimic her crossed eyes, but failed miserably.

"You're just trying to wind me up here, you bugger! Anyway, I think it's going to be dinner in the restaurant and then a nightcap by the pool."

"Bugger, I am indeed," he smiled. "But just remember that any of the guys there who aren't straight gay are probably bi and you don't have me to keep you out of trouble."

I signed off before Rüdi could worry me more. *The CCTV arguments were good, but I'm not sure that there aren't more hazards in this bloody resort than from David, Tan and their retinues.*

***

I spent a further ten minutes checking that there had been no developments relevant to our targets on the island, then shut the system down and wandered back into the main living area. Rashmi was sitting on a settee, checking an interactive database on sports options available at the resort. She was clad in a simple white smock that was so sheer that it was completely obvious that the well-endowed young woman was not wearing a bra. I started in surprise, not so much due to her obviously pierced nipples, but more due to the subtle makeup, which emphasised her delicate facial features.

I've been working with this woman for years and previously noted mainly that she was on the well-built side, never that she's quite cute. I suppose it's the combat gear that does it – or the lack of makeup. That or I'm going blind in my old age, I suppose.

My stare had clearly been noticed. "So, boss, what's up? You not going to get dressed? The place is smart-casual, but top end, so something elegant wouldn't go amiss. I think Helen is done in the shower," she looked over her shoulder into what I guessed was my bedroom and, indeed, my roommate could be seen through the open door striding about in the nude while rubbing her short hair with a towel. "So, get a move on. Doris would be ready by now if not for that jail-bait gear she's squeezing herself into." The door to the other bedroom was also open but, although I could hear muffled curses, I couldn't see what our team nympho was up to. *Something that I'll find disconfiting, that's for sure.*

When I entered the bedroom, I was greeted by a fantastic view of Helen's arse as she bent to fasten high-heeled sandals, causing the skin-tight micro-dress she was wearing to ride up almost to her waist. "Now that is indeed a lovely sight," I commented, "but don't you think that nickers might be appropriate?"

The muscular blonde turned to smile at me while slowly pulling her hem down so that it just covered her shaved parts. "Doris assures me that underwear would be out of place, unless that was all that I intended to wear. I could wear this instead," she dug a minute transparent tanga from the case lying open on the bed, "so what do you think?"

I rolled my eyes, to her evident amusement. "Okay, whatever you think," I conceded defeat, "but if you drop anything, let me pick it up for you,"

I hauled my own, considerably smaller, case onto the other side of the bed and keyed it open. Then I noticed the glass wall separating off the en-suite bathroom. "I suppose you're just going to watch while I have a pee and a shower, are you?"

"Well, if I wasn't already dressed, I'd have been happy to join you in there. However, voyeurism is more fun in groups. Girls, do you fancy having a look at the boss in his birthday suit?" she shouted.

"Bloody hell, you'll do no such thing!" I scrambled to close and lock the door. "Helen's turning her back here," I announced in the general direction of the sitting room.

"No, I'm not," she replied in her most annoying tone. "I'm just watching as he peels off his trousers to expose a minute posing pouch, almost bursting with the huge erection caused by the sight of my bare bum," she fantasised while I stomped into the bathroom and, with my back to her, quickly peeled off my clothes. "He's kneeling in front of me, licking my toes while stroking..." Thankfully the massage-jet shower at maximum power drowned out the rest of her waffle.

By the time I left the bathroom, Helen had departed, leaving the door wide open. I couldn't see anyone from my side of the bed, so I prepared to dress in the clothes that had been thoughtfully laid out for me. The small, white jockstrap and the loose linen trousers were mine, but the strange sheer bolero shirt looked like it must belong to one of the girls. "Helen, what's this weird blouse thing? I'm just going to wear the shirt that goes with these trousers."

"Oh no you're not, boss," Doris scurried into the room, closely followed by the others.

"Come on, I'm getting dressed here," I turned a little away from Rashmi's blatant stare at my groin, as if sizing up my wedding tackle.

"Yes, so put on that stuff there," the girls broke into giggles as my testicles dropped out in my rush to get into my underwear, "probably best with your balls on the inside."

"Okay, I'm dressing," the elastic-waist trousers slipped on rapidly. "But what's with the blouse?"

"It's a shirt and well in keeping with the smart-casual theme. Well, for swinger, debauched, older

211

men, that is. This goes with it," she handed me a heavy gold chain.

"Christ on a bike, I'll look like Barry fucking Manilow!"

"Barry who?" Doris's brow wrinkled.

"Last century, well before any of us were born," Helen explained.

"Actually, before my time also," I protested, "he was my mum's favourite."

"Anyway, you don't look like him at all," Helen added, "Barry had lots of hair."

On a hiding to nothing here, better just shut up before I dig myself even deeper into the shit.

***

I was sure that my three colleagues were fully clued up on the resort but, to my surprise, they agreed to my suggestion that we head directly to the fancier restaurant for an Aperitif while we checked out the dinner menu. It maybe helped that I presented this as a recommendation from Rüdi. I initially felt self-conscious in my 20th century pimp rig-out, but was forced to admit that it did not seem out of place in the busy corridors and reception area. *If anything, this is conservative compared to some costumes, particularly in the case of some of the sad old blokes with much younger eye candy. Actually, the team fit in well, as there seem to be a significant excess of women amongst the residents and most of them are also tarted up to the eyeballs.*

Helen's thoughts were clearly mirroring mine. "What a bunch," she whispered into my ear, "it looks like the guys are throwbacks from the era of disco while the women should be in Amsterdam

212

windows."

"That's the top end, there's a good few of the women look like they would be more at home on the street, under Berlin red lights, while their partners were running dodgy sex-shops," I responded with a laugh, linking arms with her while our companions drifted ahead, casually hand-in-hand.

"I take it that you're not numbering me amongst them," she gave my arm a painful pinch, "unless kerb-crawling in Germany is your hidden vice."

"No, not at all, you're definitely up-market Amsterdam material," I reassured her, receiving a pinch to my bum this time. "But I can't help noticing that there're a lot of hefty, older couples about; I'd have thought swingers would have been younger and fitter."

Helen groaned. "Christ, boss, don't you ever surf internet porn? The professional videos may be populated by super-model nymphets and well-ripped studs, but all the self-produced, cheapo stuff shows it as it is: just ordinary people trying to spice up a love-life or break the barriers of convention."

"Oh, *break the barriers of convention*, is it? And here's me thinking they're just sad pervs."

"Hell's bells, you're so narrow minded," Helen's voice dropped further as we approached the restaurant. "Don't you know that variety's the… Oh, shit, no!" she gasped.

I had noticed a man approaching quickly behind us, but still started at Helen's response to his tap on her shoulder.

"Helen, good God, I haven't seen you for ages. And I certainly didn't expect to meet up with you here," he gushed.

"Phil, shit, you scared the life out of me. What on earth are you doing here?"

While Phil did the usual Swiss triple cheek kiss ritual with Helen, I looked him over critically. *Maybe mid-forties, but grey, balding and overweight, so gives the impression of being older. The purple Paisley-pattern shirt and lilac Bermuda shorts don't do him any favours and his gold chain is even chunkier than mine.*

While still holding Helen's shoulders, Phil gave her a theatrical, exaggerated wink. "I guess we're just doing the same as you, having a break from boring Switzerland and letting our hair down." He grinned while Helen looked bemused. "Not, of course, that I've got a lot of hair these days, but Sue here has enough for both of us." He turned and pulled forward a woman who had been standing behind him.

His partner could be a similar age, but appeared younger due to the thick black hair that cascaded to her waist, her heavy makeup and the skin-tight, red latex cat-suit she was wearing. *Well, he certainly goes for voluptuous. Her tits and bum are so huge that her waist seems slim even though she's certainly got a bit of a belly. Going to be tricky keeping my eyes above neck level, as that kit covers her like a thin coat of paint.*

"Sue, we met before, didn't we?" Helen scowled in thought while she did the kissing routine. "Yes, you were with Phil at the surveillance

214

tools workshop in Davos. Maybe three years ago, was it?"

"Ah, Helen, yes," Sue's face lit up in recognition. "You were wearing a uniform then, that's why I didn't recognise you immediately. That dress is very sexy and suits you much better, although your uniform could fit in also, especially in the Dungeon." *Even to someone as naïve as me, that sounds like a pick-up line.*

My confusion was quickly resolved when Helen suddenly smiled. "Yes, that's it, I was wearing my bike patrol leathers! I didn't think to bring them, I'm afraid, although I've noticed black leather seems to be back in mode with Doms."

"You can't beat a classic," Sue looked directly into Helen's eyes for a moment, before breaking the stare to glance in my direction. "But you haven't introduced your friend."

"This is my boss, I mean..." Helen stopped, clearly flustered as she belatedly remembered we were on an undercover mission.

"Oh, boss, is it?" Phil crashed in, apparently oblivious to Helen's predicament. "Somehow, I'd always thought of you as the Dom type, never a Sub. Well, actually, I hadn't considered that you'd be part of this scene," he waved his arms to vaguely indicate our surroundings.

"I'm Alan, pleased to meet you." As we shook hands, I noticed that Phil's were soft and distinctly clammy, while Sue's were surprisingly calloused, which fit somehow with her powerful grip. "Well, Helen and I aren't your usual Dom – Sub pair. It's more Boss – Underling, I suppose."

"That's what he says," Helen grinned mischievously. "I'd call it more Master-Slave. Anyway, I've just arrived and am starving and the boss here has a couple of other underlings in tow that he has to feed before forcing them to satisfy his perverse carnal cravings." Helen indicated our colleagues, who had spotted that we were no longer following and were waiting at the entrance to the restaurant, arms casually around each other's waist.

"Oh, you seem well sorted out," Sue licked her lips in a blatantly salacious manner. "We're meeting some friends in the Hook-up Bar, but we'll end up in the Dungeon about midnight, so maybe we could meet there if you're in the mood?" *Phil doesn't seem delighted by this idea, but it's clear that he's not wearing the trousers in this relationship.*

"I can't promise anything tonight, as I think we'll be well shagged out in a couple of hours or so. But I'm sure we'll bump into you by the pool or somewhere in the next few days, as contact is the name of the game here."

"I look forward to us having a lot of contact," Sue placed her hand on Helen's shoulder and let it run slowly down to her hip. "Maybe your Boss would be interested in swapping a Sub for an Underling?" She raised her eyebrows while swiping Phil with her handbag. "This bad boy needs a bit of serious bossing."

"We'll get back to you on that, I've got three hungry women with unsatisfied appetites," I responded before dragging Helen off.

"So, you're going to satisfy the appetites of all three of us," Helen whispered as we approached the others. "That's a bold statement."

"Well, we can start with food and then, when we get back to planning, I'll see what I can do about any desire you might have for a bit more excitement in your life." *That's the tricky bit, I've got a team here ready to hit some very dangerous opponents and we still don't have any kind of plan.*

***

Apart from some rather outrageously dressed clientele, the restaurant was unremarkable: a typical, top-end establishment offering artistically prepared fare with a general Southern European feel. *Apart from the view of the beach and the low prices, especially of the local white wines, it could be in Switzerland.*

Over aperitifs, the discussion centred on Helen's friend and the potential of this surprise meeting to compromise our mission. It was a bit of bad luck, but the fact of ease of travel from Switzerland and Cape Verde's enviable reputation for safety meant that such an encounter was actually not so unlikely.

"At least the nature of this resort helps," Helen pointed out. "We shouldn't have any pictures of us getting posted online and there's no reason that Phil mentioning my name would ring any bells. As far as he or anyone else is concerned, I would just be a cop from some special unit of the Aargau Kantonalpolizei."

"But your real name doesn't match the one you're registered here under," Doris pointed out.

"Sure, but someone would need to be already suspicious of something going on here to be

217

carrying out such a detailed search. The anomaly we noted in the Hilton along the road was spotted only because we had a focused target. Otherwise, it wouldn't have rung any bells."

"You're probably right, but we need to remember that this bunch take paranoia to extremes. In any case, we don't want anything to raise our profiles in any postings by your kinky friends. How should we play this?"

"Well Phil is much more of an acquaintance than a friend. I've bumped into him at meetings and conferences, maybe three times in the last five years. His company provides security tools and he often runs demonstrations at these functions. Typical salesman, though, always remembers names. I remember that he's called Phil only because of a terrible joke he made, which I won't inflict on you. Anyway, I think that, if we keep our heads down, we probably won't see him again."

"I'm not sure that this Phil is the concern, it's maybe more his partner," Doris frowned. "I noticed the way she touched you and suspect that she'd be very keen to hook up, as the term seems to be here. On the other hand, that might be a way of ensuring that we fit in: meet up in the Dungeon for a bit of partner swopping. Or maybe more partner swatting, I suppose," she added with a grin.

Rashmi laughed. "Does that mean that chubby Sue gets the three of us beauties to play with, while the poor old boss gets flabby Phil? Doesn't seem like a very fair swap, does it?"

"I wonder what Sue would do to us, in that case?" Doris mused. "I would guess she's the huge, double-pronged, strap-on type, well into exhibitionism."

Fuck, Doris sounds like she's actually interested. "Well, I think this is a moot point, as we're going to stay well clear of this Dungeon place. We don't know how the mission will develop and what kind of blow-back there may be, so any activities here that could make us stand out need to be avoided. Basically, the four of us sharing a room should fit the profile here well enough."

"Yes, Phil and Sue should be avoided," Helen nodded. "And they wouldn't be my first choice in any case."

"Definitely not," Doris broke in, "Rashmi and I were looking at some of the talent and there are some very tasty, young, black guys here. Look at those two with the crumbly couple at the table in the corner there."

"Very tight," Helen observed, licking her lips. "Local hookers, I guess."

"Jesus," I rolled my eyes, "this is going to look great on our expenses claim."

"Don't worry, boss," hidden by the table, Helen's hand slid up my thigh, "I'm sure we can get it charged to room service."

I groaned and shook my head. *This is not at all the way to start a mission, but it'll certainly be dangerous, so letting off a bit of steam could help reduce tension.* "Okay, whatever, but what about more important things, like dinner? Will this place do?"

"Definitely," Rashmi responded while the others nodded their heads. "The seafood looks

219

excellent. There's a fixed menu for four that's great value. Would that be okay with you?"

"Sure," I agreed without even looking at the menu. "Will I order wine?"

"That'd be great," Doris looked into my eyes. "We start with oysters, just to get us in the mood, so maybe Champagne would be appropriate. That'd definitely fit with an old guy accompanied by three foxy ladies."

I waved over a waitress, while quickly scanning the wine list for a cheap Cava. *It's going to be hard to control the girls later this evening, so maybe some pre-emptive retaliation is called for: like getting them as drunk as possible on this incredibly cheap wine.*

***

By the end of an excellent meal, we were feeling mellow and agreed that a walk along the beach would be the ideal way of aiding digestion. It was only eight thirty, but already dark with a new moon peeking through scudding clouds, driven by the constant breeze. A well-lit boardwalk extended along the shore, with restaurants and bars becoming more regular as we strolled in the direction of town. It seemed that about a half of these establishments were boarded up – either indicating the low season or a more general reflection of the decline of tourism as an industry.

Outside the resort, I felt that our clothes might attract attention, but this did not seem to be the case. *I guess our complex is one of the few places here that's still relatively busy, so maybe not so surprising.*

The stroll to the outskirts of Santa Maria took about 30 minutes and, by the time we were almost back, it was clear that our accommodation was very much a night-time place; the various pools and the bars around them were busier than when we left. Given that the majority of the clientele were nude or, at least, semi naked, we decided to return to a more conventional bar that we had passed, close to the entrance to the grounds of our resort.

"Looks like most of the customers here are residents of our place, maybe here just for even cheaper drinks," I commented, looking around while Doris ordered a bottle of Cava for the ladies and a draft beer for me.

"Yes, so nothing strange about us drinking here. However, we'll need to be seen at some of the bars where the action is. It's why people come here, after all," Helen noted.

"Well, I'm one old guy with a bevy of young things in tow, so an early night wouldn't be unremarkable."

"Maybe so, for the first night, but SM swingers are going to be doing a bit of mixing, just as Helen's pals suggested," Rashmi gave me a wink. "I volunteer to work out a plan for us."

"Certainly," I broke in, "you can do that just after we have the intrusion plans outlined for this salt flat villa and Tan's yacht. I think we're unlikely to be overheard here," the high-backed booth we had selected was well separated from the busier area around the dance floor and a couple of platforms on which naked pole dancers performed. "We'll need the planning kit to sort out tactical details, but that can get nailed down when we get back to our room. The first question is logistical, though. Do we work together on both of our targets or do we split them, have a pair focused on each?"

Doris looked around the table thoughtfully, pausing while our drinks were served, then slowly provided her input, clearly working through it as she spoke. "Rashmi and I both have hacking skills and all three of you have field experience. Of course, the boss having most of that. If we were going to form two pairs, an obvious team would be myself and the Ancient One, his experience compensating for my lack of it. This would leave Helen as lead of the other and Rashmi giving her technical support"

I waited for an immediate response from the others, but nothing came. "Okay, let's go with that, but with the caveat that it's for the planning phase only. We'll exchange ideas at regular intervals and integrate the Brugg team into the process. After we've got detailed plans, we can reassess whether or not we split up for the incursions and, if so, how we'll pair up."

"Sounds fine to me," Doris smiled, "so do I get to share a bed with my partner?"

"That doesn't sound optimal to me, given that you regularly service two super-stud husbands. The boss would need a fortnight to recover from a night with you! Probably the two team leaders should share a bed, with the aim of fostering communication between us. And, in any case, I've already bagsied him." The women laughed at Helen's response, while I tried to ignore the way that my choice in this matter was not being considered at all.

***

Back in our suite, I fired up the communication system while the ladies slipped into more comfortable working clothes. After a secure link with Brugg was established, during the time needed to set up encryption protocols, I stripped off my shirt and gold chain and chucked them into a corner of the room. I then set up a list of key developments since we left Switzerland, based on the expert system priorities.

"So, topless is the dress code here, is it?" Doris startled me when she appeared, wearing a t-shirt and loose shorts.

"No, well, I've still got to get changed. I'll just…"

My protest was far too late, Doris peeled the t-shirt over her head to expose her small but very well-formed breasts. "Okay, ladies, it's a topless evening. But that doesn't count for you, Rashmi, you slut. I saw you've no nickers on under that nightie thing, so you can just keep it on."

"Come on girls, we've got video online with Brugg. There are already enough whispers about why I'm suddenly sharing a bedroom with my three female colleagues, without all of you swanning about half naked." I could sense a note of desperation in my voice as I stood to gesticulate in the direction of the holo interface.

My plea was evidently picked up on the open line. "No, boss, honestly, we have no problems with the ladies appearing half naked. Anything at all, if it makes your cover better."

223

Bloody hell, Mister Boring! Where the fuck did Pirmin finally get a sense of humour from?

"Actually, I think completely naked would be de rigueur for a place like that," Rüdi added. "But, of course, the boss would need to fit in with the others. And it would give the sex-fiend a chance to extend his video creds with a bit of live action."

"Can we not just…" At this point Doris grabbed the elasticated waist of my trousers and pulled them down to my knees.

"Boss, how could you," Pirmin groaned. "That posing pouch is truly offensive to the eye. I think I may have to gouge mine out as a counter-irritant."

"It's not the posing pouch," Rüdi added with a laugh, "it's the flabby body wearing it."

"And the body hair, it's like a grizzly bear in sexy underwear."

"A greying, baldy, grizzly."

"For Christ's sake, guys, can we finish up with this?" The three women had been blocking my attempts to pull up my trousers, so I sat down to block any camera views below waist level. "And, Doris, t-shirt on now!" I scanned the others; Helen's translucent t-shirt and shorts appeared modest in comparison to the flimsy baby-doll that our new team mate was sporting. I rolled my eyes. "Fuck, Rashmi, knickers!"

Gradually this dress code was implemented, although based on me continuing to sit down, and the hilarity died away. *It's pre-action tension, causes folk to horse about. Anyway, I'm glad it's only my team at the other end of the line at this time of night. I dread to think what the Commander, or*

224

even worse Supersaxo, would have made of all of this.

I started by updating the Brugg guys of our ideas for the two planning teams. Both were nodding in their video window but, typically, it was Pirmin who cut to the chase. "Seems a sensible way to do things, but how have you split the targets between you?"

"Good question, we hadn't quite got that far…" *Better not add this was due to diversion onto discussion of our sleeping arrangements.* "Well, Doris, this was your idea. What do you think?"

"Um, yes, that's certainly something to be nailed down. The yacht is a target that we have a lot of data on already and any approach would probably be scuba, so the boss would be the one for that. The villa in the caldera won't be easy because it's surrounded by desert. There's absolutely no cover, so maybe needs something very stealthy from the air. With all her surveillance training, Helen would fit in there. What do you think?" she finished, looking around uncertainly.

"I think that seems logical enough. Although scuba options are hardly going to be easy, getting anywhere near to the villa without being spotted could be a lot trickier and Helen certainly has more technical background than me for stealthy stuff," I conceded.

Helen smiled enigmatically. "I think I may actually have an idea about that. But, anyway, let's get the updates and we can then have a first brainstorming on options."

Rashmi simply nodded and then Rüdi initiated

the summary of developments over the last 24 hours. *Despite the resources that we're throwing at this problem, output from our smart search engines is underwhelming. If spotted at all, this would just look like some kind of weird sex cult. Strange, certainly, but nothing like as bizarre as a lot of other swinger or BDSM alt-sex groups. Or even some fundamentalist religions for that matter. If not for the fluke of Achmed's abortive attack, we'd never have picked it up as any kind of terrorist activity.*

I was drawn back to the details of the presentation when the latest multi-spectral satellite images of the salt works and Tan's yacht were displayed. Although no images of the yacht's owner had been recorded, his harem and several of the crew had been identified sunbathing or swimming since it anchored. The yacht had docked for a couple of hours at a service jetty at the northern end of the marina, presumably taking on stores, but details were obscured by a canvas awning. During this period, the minibus that we had previously spotted running from the airport arrived from the salt mine and, after ten minutes in covered marina parking, returned to base. There was no proof, but clearly an opportunity for transfer of people between the boat and the mine.

The point where the yacht was moored was about 300 metres offshore, in the lee of a breakwater that sheltered the marina from the large waves that attracted kite-surfers to the area. Bathymetric maps showed that a scuba approach would be possible. However, Doris pointed out that,

226

if we were focused on remote sensing only, a submarine drone would be a better option.

At this point Helen nodded. "Yes, that's what I've been thinking over all evening. It was that tosser, Phil, that set me off. His company specialises in surveillance drones, stealthed ones that are almost undetectable. For the salt mine, we could use a glider. These are diaphanous and all-organic, so just about invisible and with no EM signature."

"How does that work?" I could feel my brow wrinkling as I struggled with the concept. "If it's invisible, how do you communicate with it?"

"Ah, that's the tricky bit. The survey needs to be pre-programmed and, during the op, downloads are one way only. These are short laser bursts to a receiver that needs to be in the line of sight. Full data records are available only after drone recovery."

"Sounds good," Rüdi commented while he scanned through the specs of the drone. "But maybe tricky to set up on Sal, with the constant strong winds."

"Yes, that a weakness," Helen agreed, "but I think it's doable if we launch upwind and recover downwind. Anyway, I'll outline a mission profile and we can link it to the weather forecast for the next couple of days."

"And I'll have a look at mini-sub drones," Doris added. "This is certainly more my thing than scuba. We should get details sorted out tonight and have the drones Fedexed to us tomorrow."

"I can sort out the logistics involved," Rüdi confirmed, "including having them labelled as leather bondage suits, which would fit in well with your profiles."

I restricted myself to a theatrical groan. *Definitely getting a bit long in the tooth for all this advanced tech, but my team seem to have everything well under control. Having seen them at play in Levant, it's easy to forget just how dangerous our opponents are. We had very close shaves in Colmar and Marseille, so anything that keeps us out of harm's way has got to be good.*

CHAPTER TWELVE

I slipped off to bed just before midnight, unnoticed by the ladies who were now running simulations of the actions against our targets. These were set up to occur in parallel, with the justification that, if one was spotted, setting up the other thereafter would be significantly more difficult.

My old man's bladder woke me around three, when I realised that I was sleeping alone. *Not sure if that makes me happy or sad but, at least, it's one complication less to worry about.*

When my internal clock woke me again at seven, I was surprised to see that Helen was now snoring gently by the far edge of the large bed. I carefully rose, grabbed shorts and a t-shirt, and slipped into the lounge, quietly closing the bedroom door behind me.

"Morning boss!" Rashmi's cheerful greeting caused me to jump as she peered around the large armchair that she was curled up in. "The coffee from the machine on the counter there is drinkable, just, if you want to kick-start your day here in windy Sal."

"Not a bad idea," I searched out a mug and then set the capsule coffee-maker gurgling. "How did you sleep?"

"Sleep? Who has time for sleep? I don't often get the chance of a wild lesbo threesome, so had to make the best of it. So, after six hours in bed, I'm completely knackered."

I took my coffee over and plonked down onto a seat facing the smiling young woman, noting that she was wearing only her transparent nightdress of the evening before – and no nickers. "I guess it's just as well that we have a rest day today, waiting for the kit to arrive," I sighed.

Rashmi grinned. "Just pulling your chain, boss! Helen did actually crash with us when she heard how loudly you were snoring, but no lesbo action, I'm afraid. We were all too exhausted."

"So how did Helen end up back in my bed?"

"That's only been for about half an hour or so, same time I got up. Doris started snoring then and she's even louder than you. We've decided that heavy duty ear plugs are going to be essential kit for this mission," she finished with a giggle.

I sipped my coffee while silently considering options for the day ahead. Gradually I noticed that Rashmi had shifted in her seat and I now had an unhindered view of her shaven mons. "Well, I guess we've got some time before the others emerge," I raised my eyebrows, "so maybe time for some sweaty action?"

The young woman looked taken aback, but then smiled salaciously as she slowly opened her legs to give me a better view of what was on offer. "Well, I'd be up for it, if you are."

"Great!" I bounced to my feet. "I'll just slip into my room and grab my trainers and we can head off for a run along the beach."

First, she looked startled, then annoyed, then finally grinned. "You were just pulling my chain, you old bugger! Okay, a run isn't a bad idea. I've

230

got trainers somewhere."

"And, hopefully, knickers also," I suggested, just as she stood and pulled the flimsy nightdress over her head. *Lordy, she's on the heavy side but really well-endowed. This is going to put a strain on my old heart when coupled to running on soft sand.* "And a sports bra," I muttered after her retreating back.

I entered my bedroom as quietly as possible, pulled trainers and socks from the kitbag lying on a luggage rack at the side of the bed and then stubbed my toe as I was walking back to the door. "Fuck!" I cursed involuntarily and then froze as Helen turned towards me.

"What's up?" she muttered sleepily, rubbing her eyes while farting extremely inelegantly.

"Nothing, go back to sleep," I responded. "Just going to shag Rashmi's brains out and then I'll make breakfast."

"Fine," she signed, turning away from me and letting rip with another fart.

I was still laughing while lacing my trainers when Rashmi appeared. She was wearing very short shorts and a skin-tight running top, which showed off her impressive frontal system and the fact that she was still not wearing a bra.

"What's so funny?" she enquired suspiciously, probably thinking that she was the butt of some joke.

"Just the lovely Helen. God can that woman fart!"

"Oh, that," she grinned in relief. "I'd take farts any day over stentorian snoring."

"Stentorian, the very word for it! Not an adjective that you hear a lot these days."

"Classical allusions," she confirmed. "Sometimes sounds a bit pretentious, but got more of a ring to it than just saying that something's really fucking loud."

"Yes, good old Stentor. I wonder if he had also mega-farts and not just a really fucking loud voice."

We managed to keep waffling on classically-themed English terms for the full fifty minutes of our run, admitted with Rashmi doing most of the talking after the first twenty, by which time keeping up with her pace took all of my breath.

Very fit, very smart and a sense of humour that really fits with mine. Just about enough to keep my thoughts away from her bouncing breasts for most of the run.

***

We arrived back to find our compatriots still in bed, now together in what I thought of as Doris's room. I only glanced in, while Rashmi headed for the shower, shedding sweaty kit in all directions. Helen picked up my presence, however, and managed to catch my eye. "Boss, thank God! I've got the hangover from hell here. I need pills, coffee and orange juice, but not necessarily in that order."

Doris peeked out from behind the naked body that had evidently forced her to the very edge of the bed. "Actually, skip the orange juice for me. Unless, of course, you can find some fizz to make it drinkable."

"Yes, right, Morning Glories for both of us, soon as you like. I think room service breakfast is

232

the way to go." Helen then pulled a sheet over her head, which was then the only part of her body not exposed to full view.

"What the hell did you really get up to after I hit the sack?" I mused aloud.

Doris smiled as she slipped out of the bed and proceeded to carry out a series of stretching exercises, certainly aware of the impact that this would have on me. "We did consider a totally obscene ménage a trois, I seem to remember. But then we decided to drink the mini-bar, just to get us into the mood. Can't remember much thereafter, though."

"Not bloody surprising! I remember looking at the booze in there, absolutely nothing mini about it. Much more like an industrial fridge."

"Please don't bloody remind me," Helen groaned, showing that she wasn't as far out of it as she pretended to be. "Just get pain-killers and shut the sodding curtains."

I was just beginning to feel sorry for her when she let off another horrendous fart. "Okay, chem-warfare here. I'm going to seal this door and anyone left inside will just have to suffer the consequences."

Doris was immediately by my shoulder. "Yes, definitely, seal it for Christ's sake. There's Geneva conventions against the use of anything like this." Unfortunately, she spoiled the dialogue by bursting into laughter and throwing her arms around my neck, the sensation of her naked body pressed against me destroying my concentration into the bargain.

I could just hear Helen mumbling under her cover. "Sodding comedians! I didn't hear any comments about my smelly arse when…"

I quickly stepped out and shut the door. *Too much fucking information for this time in the morning. Shit, shower and shave and I'll be in shape to face the rest of the day. Of course, that's assuming I can take my mind off the flesh on show, which gives me the choice of a cold shower or a bit of serious onanism."* I smiled, remembering my chat with Rashmi as I headed for my room and the shower.

I took off my trainers in the bedroom, before walking into the bathroom and stripping off my sweat-soaked training kit in the shower. *May as well wash it and myself at the same time.* I was soaping my face while treading on my washing when a warm, obviously female body pressed against my back while a hand slipped down my front in the direction of my groin.

"What the fuck?" I frantically attempted to rinse my face, succeeding only in getting soap into my eyes.

"Well, boss, my room has been rendered uninhabitable, so I need to make use of your facilities. I'm choking for a pee."

"Help yourself: the bog's all yours. I promise not to look – and won't be able to anyway until I get this fucking soap washed out of my eyes."

"Oops, too late!" Her right leg lifted to clamp around mine and ensure that I was aware that she was now pissing down my thigh. "Well, does this get you into the mood?" Clearly a rhetorical question as my response to her handling of my dick was unmistakable.

She was still dribbling as I turned to assist her clambering onto my erection and thrust to a rapidly achieved orgasm. *Well, that's my priapism problem sorted out without need of a cold shower. I guess old Onan wouldn't have needed to sin the way he did if he had a nymphet like this on tap.*

"Jesus, that was fast," Doris shook her head in disappointment. "Well, I guess you're going to have to make up for all the rug-munching that I didn't get last night."

I dropped to my knees, glad of the soggy kit on the floor of the shower as I hurried to comply. *Still a faint trace of urine, but overwhelming musk of her well-lubricated vagina. Probably essential, given some of her stories of double penetration by her two well-hung husbands.* She began to moan, lifting my hands to squeeze a pair of rigid nipples before her fingers joined my tongue and her body began to quiver. The build-up lasted for about ten minutes, before she came with a drawn-out scream.

Her orgasm seemed to have taken more out of me than it did her. I was still slumped on the floor of the shower when Doris gaily started to rinse herself down. Just as I beginning to get myself sufficiently compos mentis to offer to wash her back, she shouted out. "Okay, I'm done with him. Anyone else want a shot? Not sure he'd be much good to you now, but you're welcome to try."

I looked up directly into her eyes. "Salt my wounds, why don't you?"

"Sure thing," she grinned mischievously before

hollering. "Pissing on him seems to get him up, so I'd recommend that for starters."

I groaned and hid my face in my hands. *Just when I seem to be finally getting the ladies under control, I open my bloody mouth and they're running riot again. I've really got to sort this out before the real action starts.*

***

My luck seemed to have changed, as nobody was in the lounge to hear either Doris's noisy orgasm or her subsequent calumny. After she left in search of clothes, I was able to complete my ablutions in peace, then dress and order breakfast before my colleagues appeared.

Rashmi and I were sipping isotonic drinks, notably untouched during the rape of the mini-bar, when our breakfast trolley was delivered. I signed for it while Rashmi flirted blatantly with the waiter, whose loose cotton uniform only emphasised his body-builder physique. "Yes, this is definitely the resort for a woman who wants to get her mojo back," she purred after he left. "Ripped or what?"

"What've I missed?" Doris emerged just as Mister Universe closed the door, so then had to suffer an exaggerated description of his many attributes, while I laid the table for breakfast.

"Actually, I suspect he was probably gay," I interrupted when Rashmi was waffling about how well-endowed he was."

The two women looked at me in surprise, Rashmi momentarily speechless. "Of course, he was," she recovered. "But, in this place, certainly gay with a bit of bi added in. Probably happy to fill

236

any orifice available."

"Just like my husbands," Doris added with a giggle. While the ladies expanded on the virtues of bisexual hunks, I grabbed a coffee and a couple of croissants, deciding that it was time to head for our comms room to check on our operational status.

Although my main focus was trying to drown out my comrades, the project file update quickly captured my attention. The team assessing the images that Doris had captured from Tan's computer had been expanded to include a number of pandemic specialists and a story was beginning to come together. The weaponised delivery system was for a virus that caused only mild flu symptoms in most cases, but drastically decreased fertility. For a woman, this decreased chances of impregnation to less than 10% of normal, but it made men effectively sterile. This suddenly made sense of the virus spread at the Levant orgies: it immunised the carrier from the sterility plague.

Shit! Even at my age, I could end up one of the few guys on the planet capable of impregnating women. The shock of this revelation lasted only for seconds before the consequences of this plot became evident. *It'll take a while, but this will finally solve the over-population crisis that's proven impossible for politicians to address. Sort out a lot of other environmental problems also, even if too late to avoid the first impacts of global warming.*

My head was spinning. The basic idea could well be considered a justified response to the ineptitude of a generation of decision-makers: their total inability to get to the root of so many problems due to political correctness and the power of rabid religious and loopy bleeding-heart lobby groups. *Rüdi classed this bunch as above average intellect with a cosmopolitan viewpoint, so maybe it makes the entire thing understandable.*

Now a problem crystallised in my mind. *Do I work to kill this conspiracy, which will certainly be judged at the level of crimes against humanity by any international court, or withdraw because I sympathise with their goals? Or, even worse, would I compromise the actions of my team, who're committed to support whatever decision is made by our overlords in Bern?*

I was roused from my reverie by a tap on my shoulder. "Just leave that stuff for now. It's breakfast time and we're having Buck's Fizz. Even if you won't drink it, we can discuss the source of its crazy name," Rashmi added with a smile.

Back in the lounge the entire team were assembled, all relatively demurely dressed in shorts and t-shirts, although with bras clearly not considered necessary. Helen was looking much better and had evidently medicated away her hangover. The women were talking over reconnaissance of our targets and had already rented a car for the job. The main point being discussed was whether we should all go on this trip or only Rashmi, as the rest of us had at least some chance of being recognised by any surveillance that they might have in place.

I was on my second mug of coffee when Helen spoke up. "Why so silent, chief? You haven't said a word since you joined us and look downright

238

miserable. Not post-coital tristesse, is it?" She smiled in a teasing manner, making it very likely that she already knew about my shower encounter with Doris.

"If only it were." Three faces looked at me expectantly and I suddenly decided to get this problem off my chest. I outlined the news from base and slowly worked through my feelings with respect to the goals of the conspiracy. Very unusually this proceeded without any interruption or comment, although eyes widened when I described the actions of the virus.

After I finished, the women looked at each other and Helen seemed to be chosen to respond by some kind of silent selection process. "If I've got this right, we're all immune to this sterility plague, as would any others that we have contact with before it is released."

"Well, it seems to be an STD so, by definition, a disease that's sexually transmitted. The transmission efficiency appears to be very high for vaginal, anal or even oral sex – especially of the selenium-rich gel has primed you for action."

"But, knowing this, a vaccine could be developed surely?"

"Developed, manufactured and distributed globally, certainly. But that'd take months or years, even if the required resources were made available immediately. The only credible counter to this threat is to prevent its release in the first place."

"And just how do we do that?"

"I'm not sure that it'll be up to us for much longer. With such a global threat level, it'll have to be passed on to Interpol or, possibly, the UN Security Council."

"Who will then totally bugger things up," Rashmi interjected. "You know, this makes a lot of the pieces of this puzzle fit together. It was never a small anti-terrorist team that these conspirators were worried about, it was something much bigger, like Interpol. They had defences in place to cover up individual activities in case of security leaks, but not set up with comprehensive anti-intrusion measures. To me, this implies that they have their own people in place in key organisations to ensure that they're forewarned of any action against them."

"Christ on a bike! That aspect hadn't occurred to me. I need to get in contact with the Commander and Supersaxo ASAP to ensure that we don't open up this case. Rashmi, work with Doris to put your arguments together in a formal case outline. Helen, thinking cap on and try to find some options that'd allow us to accelerate a direct move against this crowd on the assumption that the kid gloves are now off."

***

The video meeting with the Commander and Supersaxo did not go well. Further analysis had shown that the weaponised virus was probably already under production in two forms: one with the symptoms that I had already seen and another with the additional functionality of decreasing the efficiency of the victim's immune system with increasing age. As the Commander put it, "this is terrorism of the most extreme form and we can't justify not bringing in our international colleagues."

We're now on a fucking hiding to nothing. Our partners will start crashing about and, if things go well, will take all the credit. If all goes tits-up, as I'm sure it will, we're the sacrificial goats who will be loaded with all blame!

I worked through the case developed by Rashmi and Doris, but little sympathy was evident. I then decided to up the ante. "This is all very well, but you've got to realise that these aren't your usual nihilistic anarchists. They're a highly qualified team who appear to have saving the planet as their primary goal. Crushing them without due legal process could be hugely unpopular, if it ever got out."

"If it ever got out, Herr Gruppenführer, was that a threat?"

"Certainly not, Sir, more of an observation. I really think that we can neutralise this risk if left alone to do our job. Bringing in anyone else at this point would just screw things up beyond belief."

The Commander was extremely unhappy and I could hear the ice in his voice. "Very well, you've got twenty-four hours. Pull this off and you're a hero, but otherwise your career is truly shagged." The video conference abruptly ended on that sour note.

I was stunned. I had always considered my boss a friend and had never heard him use language like that. I then realised that Helen had caught the end of this conversation and was signalling *fuck him* in no uncertain terms.

Okay, myself and my team against the worst terrorist threat we've ever seen and no support from my boss. Fuck him indeed. If he's not part of the solution, then he's part of the problem.

"Right, Helen, the kid gloves are certainly off now. Despite my uncertainties, we're under pressure to either solve this problem or do major damage limitation. How are we going to do it?"

"Well, funny you should put it like that, but I think we do have an option. We'll be burning a lot of bridges and gambling completely on being right, but I think it's doable."

"Christ, that's a lot to offer. What do we have to do?"

"Abandon everything else and go full out for an attack on either Tan's yacht or the villa at the salt mine. We go for broke, so get access to their database or crash and burn. Would you be up for that?"

I had to think over things for a bit before I responded. "Yes, I certainly am. But this is only with 100% support from the entire team. It goes pear-shaped and we all suffer."

"Of course, let's set up a group meeting now." Helen was clearly fired up about it.

Yes, but bad enough for me to get into something as radical as this. Do I have the right to drag the rest in? It's dodgy enough as a concept and we haven't even tried to work it into an action plan yet.

***

We quickly set up a link to Brugg and brought in Pirmin and Rüdi before I reviewed our present status, with particular emphasis on our vulnerability due to the disappointing lack of support by the

Commandeer.

It was clear that this came as little surprise to the Brugg team. "The Commander's been twitchy ever since we got the updated risk assessment on the virus," Rüdi noted. "I think the poor old bugger's completely out of his depth here and just wants to pass the buck. Did Supersaxo say anything during your meeting?"

"Actually, not a word, now that I think about it. Looked rather grim, though."

"I suspect the BND are fully aware of the dangers of opening this operation further, but it's difficult for them to over-rule the Commander. I'd guess that they'd happily provide any support that we requested, which we should bear in mind."

"Definitely," confirmed the taciturn Pirmin.

"So, for the op itself, do we all agree to go with Helen's blitzkrieg plan?"

"If we've got only twenty-four hours, I don't see that we've got an alternative," Doris said thoughtfully. "We'll have the drones by this afternoon, but what other kit will we need and can it be rushed to us in time?"

"Well, our goal is to get full access to one of the key computers," Helen pointed out.

Doris grimaced as she summed up the situation. "Okay, we know where that is on Tan's yacht and I have a good idea of how to break through the external security system on the boat, but only a recognised user can access the computer. Even if it didn't self-destruct, I suspect it would take months to hack the biometric locks on the system. If we could persuade Tan or Jones or one of the other key players to log in for us, fine, but I'm not sure how it could work otherwise."

Helen looked thoughtful. "Maybe we're looking at this the wrong way, based too much on our past experience with terrorists. Let me check a hunch. Rüdi, do you have the forensics on Colmar and, in particular, the self-destruct system. How was it configured and was there a timer?"

A side screen flashed through analyses of the post-mortem of our action and then froze on the information that Helen had requested. Rüdi summarised the key points. "Focused blast to completely destroy the lab and release traces of the gas used in the initial attack. Heavy reinforcing would minimise damage to the rest of the building. Oh, yes, here it is: five-minute timer."

"That's it," Helen smiled triumphantly, "five minutes is certainly long enough for anyone in the lab to evacuate into the basement…"

"…from which we have since identified a tunnel that leads to the basement of the building opposite, a small guest house," Pirmin added.

"Yes, that fits. These aren't suicide bombers like mad Achmed's mother. They're playing a serious game and set death traps for anyone closing in on them, but they don't sacrifice their lives for the cause. That's a weakness we can use."

"You know, the delay in the explosion at the Marseille Uni also points in this direction," Pirmin added. "A failsafe was set up to wipe out the lab in case of any intrusion, but the explosion was delayed, even after the entire department had been blown to buggery."

I could see that Helen wasn't happy with this summary of our incursion, but the point was certainly valid. "You know, this might be the most critical insight that we've had yet. If we went in hard, I mean really fucking hard, would this crowd have the balls to face us down? Lots of immature raghead nutters would, of course, as they expect a paradise full of virgins waiting for them. But these are educated folk with real lives that they stand to lose. If we put guns to their heads or, even better, to the heads of their loved ones, would they really sacrifice everything for the cause?"

There was a moment of silence before Helen sighed. "You really want to go there, boss? We'd be crossing a lot of lines. It's almost descending to their level. Can we go that far?"

I grinned savagely as options began to flick through my mind. "Well, we are Swiss and we have a reputation for seriously fucking up anyone who comes up against us." The team were not looking impressed by this bit of jingoism. "But we're also smart, with top end technology, so maybe we can appear to be the bastards from hell without actually compromising our core values. Would that work?"

From the smiles, my argument seemed to be convincing. But I had to ensure that expectations weren't too great, as this could be even more a threat to my plan. "The problem is that we need to scare shit out of this bunch of dilettantes, so they need to know that we're not making idle threats."

"In plain text, there'll be collateral damage?" As ever, Helen was straight to the point.

"I hope not. At least nobody who isn't in some

way supporting this plot."

"You mean we'll be judge and executioner, maybe with a bit of torture and other war crimes along the way?"

"Well, yes," I conceded, "although keeping offences against the Geneva Convention to the absolute minimum."

"That's what I thought. Well, I'm certainly in for that!" The rest of the team were nodding or mumbling agreement and thus we were committed. *So now we're off the leash and going to do anything at all to attack our opponents, despite the fact that we can't really disagree with their goals. This is going to be tricky, especially when they realise just how hard I am prepared to go!*

CHAPTER THIRTEEN

After I explained my general concept for the attack on Tan's yacht, we started preparing the detailed plan and programming for the drones. The tricky question was whether to focus 100% on Tan's yacht or also to allow for an attack on the salt mine. The key constraint was manpower, or actually womanpower in this case. There just wasn't enough time to bring in reinforcements, even if the Commander would be prepared to authorise them. If we could take down all security systems and attacked at night, the mine looked like a soft target. From what we could extract from all surveillance, this would be Ingrid, her daughter and David in the villa, with maybe a maximum of four overnighting staff, presumably two of which would be security. Apart from the additional difficulties of intrusion of a boat, Tan's yacht had a crew of eight, some or all of which with security training, plus his usual coterie of wives / mistresses and, maybe, guests.

Setting the time was also an issue. We needed to delay as long as possible in order to be able to carry out all required preparation, but the longer we waited, the more chance that our presence could be spotted and the entire operation compromised. In order to avoid this detracting from more serious issues, I proposed midnight as a goal; so, this was pencilled into the outline time plan and never questioned thereafter.

By the time that we had nailed down the fundamental outline of actions, including those to be carried out back in Switzerland, it was already lunch time. I suggested getting room service again, but was unanimously over-ruled. A pool bar was proposed as an alternative. This had the advantage of fitting in a bit of swimming to loosen us up for the night ahead. The Brugg guys decided that they would mirror us in their local pool.

"I guess I should dig out my trunks then," I saw the inevitable way that things were going.

"Not those hideous budgie-smugglers, I hope," Doris groaned.

"What's wrong with Speedos? They're comfortable and…"

"Completely inappropriate for a deviant resort of this type," she rolled her eyes theatrically. "It's swimsuit-optional, meaning almost everyone will be in the buff. What we're wearing is fine. We'll just peel-off when we get to the bar. Or, of course, you could just strip off now and let it all hang out. It'll be just like Levant."

Despite this plan, the girls changed clothes before we left: Doris wearing a colourful wrap, Helen a pale blue yukata and Rashmi something very short, maybe a Happi coat, with a ferocious looking dragon motif. Clearly no underwear in any case.

To my relief, our garb seemed to fit in well with anyone we encountered while we wandered through the resort towards the nearest pool bar. *Indeed, if anything, probably a bit on the modest side.* At the bar, I was able to point out that Doris hadn't been 100% correct. The staff wore minute tangas and a spectacular threesome, two men and a woman who looked like professional athletes of some kind, wore more conventional swimwear. Conventional in cut, but completely transparent. In some strange way, this seemed more provocative than simply being naked.

The sporty trio also stood out in terms of appearance, aged around mid-twenties and breathtakingly good-looking. Most of the rest of the flesh on display was much more pedestrian, with a diverse spread of colours, shapes and sizes. Ages were notably bimodal, with a majority being late middle-age and a smaller group being much younger. While I was taking in the view, Helen guided us to an empty table by the poolside, where we could strip off and hang our clothes on a conveniently placed rack.

Helen ordered a large beer while the rest of us went for sparkling mineral water. "Hair of the dog," she grinned and swallowed a first mouthful with a sigh of pleasure.

God, but that looks good! I'm definitely swapping to beer to wash down the food.

While we perused menus, I scanned the groups sitting in our vicinity. I quickly became aware that there was a distinct difference to Heliopolis. On Ile de Levant everyone was naked, but it became unremarkable after a while. There was a different vibe here, though. Bodies were being flaunted and physical contact made at every opportunity. When the waitress came to take our orders, she touched each of us on the shoulder, allowing her heavy breasts to rub against the back of our necks. At other tables, touching was even more gratuitous, often blatant groping without any pretence of subtlety.

Not just physical contact. I was bemused by the amount of direct eye contact whenever looking around. There was little doubt that invitations were being made and, from the movement between tables, probably accepted in many cases.

My musing was interrupted when Helen kicked my leg. "Don't look now, but Phil and the Dom from hell are heading in this direction," she whispered.

"Christ on a bike, this is just what we don't need. Have they spotted us?"

"Doesn't look like it, but they're heading for a table further along the pool. Bound to notice us eventually."

"Could we make a quick run for it?"

"Then I'm sure that Phil's mistress will definitely spot us. Maybe we just need to accept the inevitable and have lunch with them."

"We've got too much to do and don't need any further complications that could risk blowing our cover."

Doris, who was leaning forward to follow our conversation, suddenly smiled. "Maybe I can sort something out. Pass me over that tablet with the menu on it."

I watched bemused while she manipulated the pad, flicking quickly from the normal swipe menu options to a virtual keyboard where she rapidly typed in commands. I caught Helen's eye and saw that she was equally baffled.

"What on earth are you doing," Helen finally

asked, but was ignored until Doris was finally finished and she threw the tablet casually onto the table.

"Let's just wait and see if this works," she smiled in a smug manner.

"What works? The Gruesome Twosome over there are looking at menus now, but will probably spot us as soon as they've chosen."

"Maybe, maybe not."

"Come on, don't be such a pain in the arse. What've you..." I sat back in amazement as a waitress approached the couple and, instead of taking their order, led them off towards the main hotel building. "Jesus, how the hell did you manage that?"

"Not just a pretty face, am I? Actually, pretty everywhere else, don't you think?" she gave a little shimmy that caused her small breasts to sway in front of my face.

Rashmi gave one of the objects of my distracted gaze a playful slap. "Stop being such a tease, you tart, what're you up to?"

"Well, I just made sure that our Rubenesque Dominatrix has been selected by lottery to coordinate action in the Dungeon this evening. She's now going to lunch with the hospitality director to go over details."

"That's lucky. I'd no idea there was such a lottery," I responded in surprise.

"Actually, there wasn't until I created it. It's a new initiative from upper management. If you like, I could make sure that I win it tomorrow night."

"Hopefully we'll be well on our way home

before then," I responded automatically, reflecting that it was lucky that we'd be far too busy this evening for a visit to the BDSM den and pitying anyone who got caught up in whatever the pervy Sue came up with.

***

The gentle post-prandial swim had relaxed everyone and, as I had often seen, the break had encouraged lateral thinking that was reflected in the rework of our attack plans after we returned to our room. A consensus rapidly emerged that our chances were greater if we coordinated the hits on our targets to make best use of our limited resources, with a focus on use of stealthed drones. This was certainly trickier for the more exposed salt mine, but Helen's diaphanous glider offered a good chance of undetected intrusion. The main modification required was to repurpose it for gas delivery rather than its normal reconnaissance functions. The residents' villa had a covered terrace which, based on AI analysis of shadows cast by those moving around after sundown, as caught on satellite images, seemed to be used for al-fresco dining most evenings. This vulnerability could allow us to incapacitate the residents and, assuming defences weren't fully automated, open the way for a direct frontal assault.

The yacht was trickier. Moored in isolation in the bay outside the harbour, an approach by anything bigger than our smallest swimming drone would be relatively easy to spot if active and passive sensors were fully deployed. Our solution was to set up the drone to cut all external communications, allowing us to risk a cheeky direct approach in the early evening. Satellite images allowed us to identify a rocky cove beyond the marina that would be accessible by four-wheel drive and allow us to release both the drones: the glider to head inland on the prevailing easterly winds and the swimmer, looking like a small eel, to head south towards the yacht.

Most debate developed around how we split the attack. I was all for simply swimming out to the boat and boarding her when nobody was looking, but Helen was convinced that she could make a better surprise approach by kite-surfing. After much toing and froing, I conceded that, if we could time our approaches right, together we had a better chance to board and overpower the crew before they were aware of being under attack. The risks associated with this option were certainly higher than stealthier approaches, but time pressure made it the best that we could come up with. With the outline plan agreed, we spent the next hour thrashing out fine details. Additional equipment was delivered along with a hired 4x4 pickup truck and, after they arrived mid-afternoon, we programmed the drones with the help of the Brugg team.

Just before 5 pm, we loaded our kit, along with some snacks, and set off in the direction of the airport. As we drove past the runway, I spotted a large, ugly, heavy-duty helicopter sitting beside the goods transport hangers, confirming that our option for emergency extraction was now available. Although manned by Swiss special forces, this was formally registered as a hire for salvage operations.

Shortly before reaching the town of Espargos, we turned onto the main road towards Pedra Lume and then diverted onto a dirt track heading for the quiet Baia da Parda, ignoring multiple signs directing us towards the tourist traps at Shark Bay. At the beach, we dropped off Helen with her kite-surfing kit. I was rather worried to note that the only other surfer in view was on the horizon, a great contrast to the much busier kite beaches just north of Santa Maria.

As I helped Helen zip up her shorty wetsuit and stuffed her discarded clothes into a backpack, I patted her on the shoulder. "Are you sure that you're up for this? It looks pretty remote around here."

"Worry not, Auld Yin," she smiled. "The busy beaches are where the big waves are, for jumps and stunts. This is a touring board," she indicated the windsurfer now floating in the shallows, "which will be ideal for just cruising up the coast. With this relatively large sail, it'll be fast as hell with the wind behind it. Just make sure that you're where you're supposed to be when I'm heading for Tan's yacht. If you get your head clipped by this, your brains will be jam."

"Well, with that cheery thought, I'll be off," I hefted the backpack and chucked it into the back of the truck. "But, please be very careful," I whispered as I turned away.

I initially wasn't sure if she heard me or not but, just as I clambered into the spacious cabin, I heard her shout, "You too, you old bugger."

**

By the time we reached our target cove,

shadows were lengthening to remind us of our relative proximity to the equator. When we first arrived, a couple of men were fishing from nearby rocks. However, they packed up and left as the sun set, leaving us alone on our rocky beach. Although out of direct sight, we could hear sounds from the bars in the marina and groups were visible, enjoying sundowners on a few of the dozen or so boats moored in the bay.

After the drones were dispatched, Rashmi checked their progress while Doris and I lugged a small jetski to the water's edge. "Don't you think I should come with you now," she enquired while I stripped down to swimming trunks and dug out fins and goggles from a kit bag.

"Nope, we've got to stick to the plan. After we secure the yacht, you can shoot out on the jetski and do your hacking stuff."

"But maybe I could help."

"Nope, that's not happening," I interrupted. "We've got a plan and we stick to it. If all goes well, we won't need any help. And if it goes tits-up, it'll be better with you here to hit our second target."

I smiled after she turned and struggled back up the stony beach to the car. Despite her offer, it was clear that she was relieved to be spared another marine adventure. I rinsed my goggles and then put them on, together with the associated wireless throat mike patch and ear piece, checking my audio link to Rashmi and that the small inbuilt video camera was also functioning.

"How's Helen doing?" I enquired. "There's

supposed to be heads-up functionality in these bloody goggles, but the resolution is crap."

I could hear the amusement in Rashmi's voice. "Well, all we could get a hold of was sports kit, so it's really just intended for navigation, not planning military operations. But don't worry, I'll talk you through it."

"So, where is she?"

"I made very good time and passed the port about ten minutes ago," Helen broke in. "I'm going to tack round shortly and head further out from land. Then I'll come in fast, as if I'm heading for the marina, and just cut over to the yacht at the last moment. Shouldn't give anyone on board any advance warning."

"Okay, I'll swim off now. You'll be approaching towards the bow of the boat and I'll pass the stern, where there's a platform with a small speedboat tethered to it. Presently one of the bodyguards is sitting on the rear sundeck, but he doesn't seem to be paying much attention to his surroundings."

"Roger that. I'll set your hit for 15 minutes for now, okay?" Rashmi initiated the stopwatch function that ghosted onto the left lens of my goggles, which would also now be mirrored in Helen's glasses.

I gasped as I pushed off into the cool water, but quickly warmed up as I settled into a racing crawl that became smoother after I passed through chop close to shore and into the gradual swell of the deeper water. I kept my face down and allowed Rashmi to plot my course, bringing me along a wide curve that would pass the yacht at exactly the right time.

As I swam, I visualised Helen's approach. She was riding an over-weight board combined with an over-sized kite, which would allow her to take off when her foot clips opened and drift over to land on the fore sun-deck. To me, it seemed very tricky, but I was assured that that it would be no different to a standard parachute landing. No matter how smoothly this was done, it was inevitable that the guard would notice, so I needed to be in place by then.

At T minus 30 seconds, I switched to breast stroke and headed for the boarding platform, cursing under my breath when I realised that the guard had spotted me although appearing more bemused than concerned about my approach. I stopped just short of my goal at minus 3 seconds, treading water as the guard walked towards the stern, probably to warn me off.

I surreptitiously removed the dart gun from its holster as the parachute seemed to appear from nowhere and instantly collapse as Helen landed with a soft thud. The guard spun in surprise, then slowly collapsed as the fast-working drug from the dart buried in his back rendered him unconscious.

Kicking hard, I shot out of the water onto the dive platform, snapped my fins free, and clambered onto the yacht, just as Helen appeared, running from the bow. Together, we burst through the open door leading to the main lounge and waved our guns at the shocked group who were sprawled around, clearly enjoying a pre-dinner aperitif.

"Nobody move a muscle or we'll shoot," I shouted while I strode to the connecting door leading further into the boat, slapped a wifi repeater link onto the door jam, threw the drone inside and slammed to door closed.

"Okay, I have the drone," Rashmi confirmed. "I'll get as far as I can before I release the gas: should knock out anyone below deck as long as they're not sitting somewhere airtight. Assuming that you've got everything under control there, the swimmer drone will drill through the hull into the engine room and inject gas there also."

"Who've we got here?" I subvocalized to Helen through our closed link.

"Tan, wife, mistress, yacht captain, Prof Jones and a young lad I'm not sure about. Maybe one of the guards."

"Who're we missing?"

"Five crew, the guards and maybe one of the women, the ex-wife, if she's still on board. Maybe also the baby. Could well be nursing it."

"Okay, Rashmi, you've got the drone linked inside their Faraday Cage, so you can use active search tools to check that we don't have anyone unaccounted for."

"Now, just what the bloody hell is this all about?" Clearly the initial shock had worn off and Tan was not happy about our intrusion.

"All of you, shut it!" Helen commanded. "Just slowly move over to this settee here and cram together onto it."

"No way! I have armed guards and they will kill you if you don't get off my boat immediately."

Tan stood in front of Helen, pointedly ignoring her gun and seeming to have forgotten about me.

"My colleague told you to shut the fuck up," I kicked the back of one of his knees, causing him to fall heavily to the floor and the young man to jump to his feet while the women gasped. "And also to move slowly to the settee." I shot the youth in the foot, causing him to collapse with a scream of pain.

"Just what the hell is all this about?" Jones enquired in an impressively calm manner. "Is this a robbery? We don't have much cash, but there is some quite valuable jewellery that you can take, if you'll just leave quietly without hurting anyone. Take the little speedboat, you can be clear in no time."

"No, Professor Jones, Mister Tan, this isn't a robbery. We're just going to access your computer for a little bit and then we'll be off. No reason for anyone else to be hurt if you cooperate and do exactly what we tell you."

Jones frowned, then glared at Tan to warn him not to interrupt, confirming my guess on the hierarchy here. "So, you're working for Hashimoto then, are you?"

"Actually, we're not, but that's a very interesting question and one we'll need to go into after we've looked at your computer."

Now the professor looked confused. "Not Hashimoto? Don't tell me you've had another schism. Is it that mad bugger Easton?" She rubbed her forehead as she struggled to make sense of the situation, unaware of the impact of her words on my team, who were blocking comms with comments while they struggled to make sense of these questions.

"No, you're not even close," I smiled in a feral manner to add to her discomfort. "But, first things first, we need one of you to log into the computer in the study. Maybe best if you do it, Professor."

"Why don't you just hack into it, if you know so much about us?"

"We know that log in requires biometric confirmation. I'm sure that any attempted hack would give us little, apart from maybe a serious radiation dose."

Now Jones looked worried. "Well, you clearly know that we've got good security. But, even with the biometric log-in, we can't help. I could try, if you want, but it's time-locked. There's no chance of access before midday tomorrow." She rearranged her sitting position into half lotus and breathed deeply as if to calm down.

"Okay, let's give it a try anyway. Helen, you look after this crowd while Jones and I head off to the study. Rashmi will be here in a minute or two. Prof, you'll realise that I have to be careful, so I'll just pat you down now."

Her scowl would have stripped paint. "As should be very obvious to even the blindest of thugs, I'm wearing a robe over nothing. See!" She pulled the front of the diaphanous garment open to show off her bare breasts without any sign of embarrassment.

"Very nice, for a woman of your age," I commented, receiving another death-stare, "but I'm going to check you out anyway." I approached and slipped my hands into the opened robe, sliding them around her back, down her spine, up her sides and then down under her breasts and along the tops of her thighs before finally curving round her buttocks and finally patting the cushion she was sitting on. "There, that wasn't so bad, was it?" I grinned.

"And your female colleague here couldn't have done that?" She glared at me yet again.

"Just as well not," Helen interrupted before I could come up with a suitable response. "My sub is an older woman, not unlike yourself. I'm not sure I could have been so restrained." Slowly she took a hold of both the nipples on display and twisted them savagely, forcing a whimper from her victim. "It isn't for nothing that the anti-terrorist groups have a policy of focusing on the women first." She twisted the nipples yet again and then let go, smiling happily.

The entire lounge had gone silent, hardly breathing during Helen's demonstration of her sadistic capabilities. I wasn't sure whether to be impressed by her acting capabilities or to be worried that it wasn't actually an act. *Anyway, time to get things moving.*

"Okay, Jones, less chat and more action. Lead the way to the study, and don't expect any of the crew to help you en route, they'll all be out cold by now."

As a token act of defiance, the professor shrugged out of her robe as she stood and walked ahead of me in the nude. Just as she reached forward to open the door, she hesitated. "You said that you gassed the crew. Surely we can't go in

261

here?"

"Not a problem, short half-life stuff. Just get a move on."

At his point I picked up a flicker of movement in my peripheral vision, followed by a high-pitched scream. I spun round to see Tan's wife squirming on the deck, holding her stomach, while Helen stood over her with her pistol aimed directly between Tan's eyes. "Calm down, for fuck's sake," I growled before this was choked off by an arm clamped round my neck, making me strangely aware that I was wearing only my Speedos and was being strangled by a rather well-endowed, naked woman.

"Drop the gun," she whispered into my ear while her forefinger located a nerve centre under my jaw. "I've studied Oriental martial arts for decades and, although I've no formal gradings, I can..." I never found out what her threat was going to be, as she choked for breath following the impact of Helen's roundhouse kick to her ribcage. From the loud cracking sound, at least one rib was broken and, from the way she was coughing blood, broken bones had damaged her lungs.

The growing roar of the jetski had gone almost un-noticed during this action, but the crash of it hitting the diving platform caused all heads to turn towards the noise. The arrival of Rashmi seconds later, in black combat fatigues and carrying a huge assault rifle, was enough to quell further resistance from our captives, so that they meekly submitted to ties binding their ankles and wrists. While this was happening, I injected Jones with a powerful anaesthetic cocktail that caused her to sag back with a sigh of relief and allowed me to pull her to her feet with only the slightest grimace of pain.

"Let's just try this again," I commanded in a tone that emphasised that my patience was gone. "I need you to help me access the computer but, if there is any more silly-buggers from you, I'll shoot you in the guts. I can drug you up after that so you can still function but, if you survive, it'll take major surgery for you to be able to have any kind of normal life. I'm packing biowar gangrene here and I will not be buggered about with!" We looked into each other's eyes and I knew that she recognised what I was capable of.

With slumped shoulders, coughing blood along the way, Jones led us through the grandiose master cabin and into Tan's study. "It's not going to do you any good," she mumbled, "it's on a timer, I told you that."

"What's that about?" Rashmi queried over our comms link.

"Not a problem, just wait and see," I responded while helping Jones lower herself into the chair in front of the computer, avoiding any contact with her damaged ribs yet allowing the biometric certification to proceed.

The computer screen had come alive after she sat down, but displayed only a classic blue circle of death. "I told you so," she groaned, "it can't be accessed until tomorrow."

"Ah, is that so?" I grinned, while displaying the toe ring that I had spotted her removing while she settled into the lotus position and which I had recovered during the pretence of patting her down. "Then I don't suppose you'll object to trying this," I crouched down and shoved the ring onto her toe, manfully avoiding the view of her crotch that I had from this position.

I looked up to see menus flicking down the screen while Rashmi leaned over the professor's shoulder, muttering as she coordinated the hack with Doris and the Brugg team.

"It'll work better like this," I manoeuvred my colleague until she was sitting in Jones' lap, "which will let the prof and I have a wee chat while you work. As you can see, young Rashmi is leaning forward to avoid putting pressure on your ribs. But if I was to do this," I touched her naked flank, eliciting a squeak of pain, "it could get quite unpleasant. So, for a start, who are Hashimoto and Easton and why would you think we were working for them?"

To my great surprise, her sigh sounded more like relief than concern. "I think I've got it now. I've actually met you before, haven't I? It was yoga, in Levant, I'm sure of it!"

"Yes," I nodded, "we've been on to you for some time now."

She shook her head wryly. "It was your crowd in Marseille. Colmar also I guess."

I nodded silently, encouraging her to go on.

Suddenly she glared at me. "So, what happened to Jean-Pierre in the lab? He just disappeared without trace. Was he working for you?"

"No, I'm sorry, he was killed in our action. It was a mistake, actually, we didn't know that he would be there and would have preferred to have taken him alive. But he was working in a terrorist lab."

"Shit, he was a nice lad." She scowled in thought. "But what makes you think that he worked in a terrorist lab?"

"Might have something to do with a bomb attack at a Swiss border post and a hidden lab producing a weaponised virus," I glared back at her. "My colleague here was shot by one of your *non-terrorist* scientists, and I was one of the ones picking up a radiation dose in your own apartment, so don't even try the unsuspecting boffin bit on me."

"Now it all makes sense," she sighed. "You're a Swiss hit squad. Assassins. And we're in your cross-hairs, due to that stupid cunt Bernhard."

"You know the routine; I don't confirm or deny anything. But, let's start with Bernhard. Usually, the stupid cunt getting blamed here is Achmed."

"I give you that, Achmed and his entire extended family were mad, raghead wannabe terrorists. But he was also Bernhard's lover." She spotted my frown and continued. "Bernhard is Ingrid's ex and CFO of her company. When it was clear that the development done in Strasbourg needed to be up-scaled and Ingrid wasn't prepared to do this in Heidelberg, Bernhard came up with the smart idea of locating the lab with Achmed in Colmar. Does this make sense to you?"

"We know about the links to Strasbourg Uni and Ingrid's company in Heidelberg, so this clarifies the link to Colmar. It was a really stupid move though. You'd never have come onto our radar if not for the attack on us."

"But you wiped out the entire facility in Colmar. Why keep after us?"

"What part of *weaponised virus* are you not picking up on?"

"But we never intended to target Switzerland. That'd be silly."

"Never mind who you weren't targeting," I interrupted, noting that Rashmi had managed to attach some kind of memory to the cabled processing unit and was harvesting all key files as backup before attempting to disconnect it. "Who were you targeting and how do the others you mentioned fit into things?"

"Okay, long story short. We're a team working together to solve the biggest threat to the planet."

"Global warming?"

"Don't be daft!" Her professorial background came over in her scornful tone, "Climate change is a consequence, not the cause. Over-population is at the bottom of every environmental and socio-political threat we face. It's the elephant in the room that no politician will address."

"So, your elite group decide, unilaterally, to embark on a global sterilisation campaign."

"Someone had to do it. But problems arose due to internal differences of opinion in terms of how to achieve this goal. We, the European group, went for the milder option."

"Sterilisation is the milder option?"

"Yes, far too mild and long term for Hashimoto and the Asians. Their version of the virus causes spontaneous abortion that results also in about 99% mortality of the mothers. This not only stops growth, but rapidly leads to population collapse."

"Shit, the death rate would be horrendous!" I gasped.

"You have no idea. It's not just the direct mortality, you have to take into account global demographics. Fastest population growth and hence numbers of vulnerable women is in the poorer countries of Africa, South America and Asia. Just think of the impact of such deaths on the remaining numbers of young men. Wars would break out everywhere, with all the associated illness and famine resulting from socioeconomic collapse. This is the apocalyptic scenario that we're fighting to prevent."

"To prevent?" I shouted into her face. "You're one of the evil cunts who kicked this off in the first place."

Finally, her belligerent resistance crumbled. "I can't pretend I wasn't a contributing factor, but we were really trying to fight an existential threat. Doing nothing will result eventually in the population drop that sterilisation would achieve, but only after the planet has been rendered almost uninhabitable. When I think about this, I can almost sympathise with Hashimoto. But his approach is too brutal and too uncertain in terms of the final state reached."

"And the final state is what?"

"He aims for a global population of about 1 billion within 50 years. But it could be less, much less."

"Jesus suffering Christ! You're not kidding about an apocalypse! So how can we stop this?"

"There is only one credible option: release our virus as soon as possible. It then protects against all variants, including the one Hashimoto is developing."

"Not an option! We now have the details on your virus and can prioritise a vaccine. From what you've said, a vaccine against your bug will also give protection against variants."

"Don't you remember how long it took to develop vaccines against the different pandemics in the early decades of this century and the effort required to then vaccinate on a global scale. Technology has developed, certainly, but this is a completely novel, synthetic organism not just another bog-standard Coronavirus mutant. There is no way that you could protect even a fraction of those at risk on the timescale available. Only our weaponised virus can do this job, as we've already done all the required development. That's why we thought you were working for Hashimoto or one of his cronies. All our secrecy and defences have been focused on preventing them neutralising our counter to their threat."

I looked at the woman, suddenly looking vulnerable as she started to cry, but with tears of frustration rather than pain.

"You see now, don't you," she sniffed as she wiped her nose with the back of her hand. "You've got to help us release our virus before it's too late. It's the only sure way to prevent a catastrophe that'll impact even isolationist Switzerland."

As if I wasn't conflicted enough about this op, now I'm really between a rock and a hard place. Although clearly what we'd classify as a threat to national security, this crowd come over more as intellectual do-gooders and don't match our usual terrorist groups in any way. Our number one target has to be Hashimoto, but how can we defeat his bunch of genocidal maniacs without cooperating with Jones and her compatriots? It'd be easy to pass this up the command chain, but this'd just slow things down. No way a top career civil servant or politician is going to make a quick decision on something as critical as this. Especially as it all comes down to Jones' testimony on Hashimoto's capabilities. If this was a contrived fiction, we'd actually be helping implement global-scale sterilisation, particularly impacting the third world. If that ever came out, the present threats against Switzerland would pall into inconsequence.

I looked down at Jones. *I believe her. I really do. But how on earth do I sort out this clusterfuck?*

***

"Okay, boss, we've got the backup," Rashmi's voice broke into my reverie. "I'm just going to disconnect the processor."

"No, don't do that!" Jones shouted just as the cable clicked loose. I heard the door into the study slam closed and bolts engage, causing a distinct feeling of déjà vu. "Bloody hell, you need to logout with the disarm code before you can disconnect."

"So, you're now hoist by your own fucking petard," I shouted into her face before Rashmi could say anything. "How do we get out of here before I

269

get fried by gammas, for the fucking second time? If I'm going to help you, it's only if I walk out of here."

"Shite! From in here there's no way of resetting the source or opening the door. It can be done only from outside the secondary Faraday Cage surrounding this cabin."

"Come on, now, there's got to be a way. If we lose all the data here, there's no way that I can defend us against Hashimoto."

"Christ! Can't your team get something from Tan?"

"What could he give anyone that's not in this cabin? Is there a backup on board?"

Jones appeared to have aged years, thinking for a moment before shaking her head. "Nothing on board, but there is a duplicate at the salt mine. Do you know about that?"

Before I could answer, the door clicked open and Helen walked in. "Are you guys finished yet?" she enquired, unaware of the look of shock on Jones' face.

"Yup," Rashmi answered, "just the boss doing a last bit of mind fucking."

I smiled at the shaking woman, aware of the smell that indicated that she'd lost bladder control when the door slammed. "Yes, I forgot to mention that we knew also about the gamma trap on board, from a further op that you don't know about: Tan's retreat in Sardinia. We used a submarine drone to disabled it before we boarded, but left the auto-seal system just in case it could have set off an alarm. We did, of course, add a simple override."

"You bastard!" another death stare. "I literally pissed myself."

"I think we all noticed that," I grinned, "but it actually helped your case. You volunteered information on your base on this island and so, if you help us raid it, it'll strengthen my arguments to provide support in releasing your virus."

"Are you sure about this boss?" Doris asked over our comm link. "There's a serious risk that she could tip our hand early, sabotaging the attack."

"Yes, I'm well aware of that," I sub-vocalised. "We mine her for information, but ensure that there's zero chance of her compromising the op. In the interim, we need to lock down this yacht. Everybody on board immobilised and the engine together with all communication kit destroyed. We take Jones and Tan with us, but leave the rest. They should be able to get free at some point but I guess they're not going to want a huge hue and cry, so it'll probably stay quiet."

"And if they can't get free?" Helen inquired.

"Then they starve to death, I suppose. But, on the scale of my other concerns, this will bother me not a jot."

"We should get moving," Rashmi reminded me. "If you take Jones and Tan in the speedboat, Helen and I can tidy up here and will be behind you on the jetski. We could then be ready to head for the mine within a half an hour or so."

"Perfect, let's make it so." I helped Jones up from the chair, noting her groan of pain. "Okay prof, let's get you off this boat and then I'll dose you up with a bit more anaesthetic."

"I could actually do with a shower, you understand," the prof looked at me hopefully.

"I'm sure you could, but you can make do with picking up your robe in the lounge. It won't make you any cleaner, but might make us a little less obvious when we get back to shore."

CHAPTER FOURTEEN

Just a little more than thirty minutes afterwards, we set off in our pickup truck, abandoning both the jetski and the speedboat in the cove. Tan was bundled into the open back, while Jones was squeezed in between Doris and Rashmi in the middle of the rear bench seat of the over-dimensioned cabin. The professor had removed her robe and Rashmi was binding her ribs while Doris wiped her down with a handful of tissues.

"I know you too," the professor stated suddenly, peering at Doris's face. "And also, I think, the other woman who's driving. You were both in Levant, with the guy in the front." She started to laugh, but this turned into a cough that had her spitting blood. "Who'd have thunk it? Three Swiss assassins and all into tantric yoga."

"I'm really sorry that it's come to this," Doris patted her shoulder kindly. "Under different conditions, I'm sure we'd have gotten on fine, could even have been friends."

"Speak for yourself," Rashmi glowered, "I don't get friendly with anyone whose pals have tried to kill me."

"Goes for me too," Helen added. "You were lucky indeed that we had keeping you alive as a priority, otherwise threatening the old boss here would have earned you a slug between the eyeballs."

"Let's just calm down a bit, ladies," I ordered. "It'd be nice to avoid any unnecessary violence, although that doesn't happen often in the real world. So, Professor, do you want to help us finish this op without increasing the body count."

"For a start, let's just drop the gratuitous honorifics. Call me Chris: everyone else does. And yes, I'll help if it decreases the risk of someone else getting hurt. So, what do you need from me?"

"For a start, confirmation of who's in the villa. We guess Ingrid, her daughter and Lucy McKie's husband, David."

"Yes, that'd be them all. Except, of course, for the live-in staff. As I remember it there was a chef, an odd-job man, a couple of girls and two guards. The rest of the estate staff go home in the evenings."

"That matches what we worked out," I lied. We had spotted only one guard, although we had guessed that there would be more. "And what about other security measures, are they controlled from the house?"

"Usually, but there's a failsafe in case the comms links are cut. There are a couple of huge radiation sources that sit by the series of gates on the approach road. You could hack controls or simply cut your way through, but at each point the dose would fuck-up both your team and any electronics you were carrying."

"Shit! We didn't pick this up, did we?" I didn't realise that I had spoken out loud until Helen nudged me in the ribs. "Well, ladies, and guys back in Brugg, did we? Chris, you're looking a bit shell-shocked. Did you realise that we've got a team linked up here with audio and video comms?"

274

"I should have done" she looked somewhat bemused.

"Okay, put all comms on the speaker in this car," I commanded. "If Chris is going to help us get through this, she needs to know what's going on."

"Are you sure about this?" Helen's voice blared out before the volume was turned down.

"Yup, just switch out our secure comms now. We've an independent wireless link to Brugg, so they stay in the loop. I want Jones, Chris that is, to be integrated into the team. Also, I want the other observers in Switzerland cut out."

"Done, boss, but are you sure about this? The Commander will be very seriously pissed off and the BND guys will go totally apeshit."

"Do you see me giving even a small fuck here? You've heard everything on the yacht and I guess that, by now, first analysis must be coming through on the material we ripped off Tan's computer. What do you make of it?"

"Well, as far as I'm concerned…"

I broke in quickly. "Helen, you can throw in your tuppence worth later, but first I want feedback from those who weren't active in the op: that's Doris, Pirmin and Rüdi."

To my amazement and, I am sure that of the rest of the team, it was Pirmin who responded immediately. "As far as I'm concerned, Jones and her team are terrorists, legitimate targets." I could hear both Chris and Doris groan. "However, this Hashimoto guy has got to be the prime target, assuming he's not some kind of Keyser Söze."

"Well, I got the inscrutable reference to an

275

ancient movie there, even if nobody else did." I rolled my eyes, but continued. "I think you've hit the nail on the head, though. The key is getting some hard evidence to collaborate Chris's statements on the Asian threat."

"The technical background should be in the database you've just lifted."

"There's Exabytes of stuff here," Rudi interrupted the professor.

"Look for *virus x-variants*, there should be an entire directory covering everything we know about Hashimoto's work."

"Okay, got it. But it's still a couple of Tera."

"Yes, but a lot of that'll be molecular dynamic simulations. Just pull out exec summaries and give them to your virologists, who should be up to speed on this if they have been already analysing our work."

"Fine but, while Rüdi's doing that, how do we nail down Hashimoto's role and put a timetable on all of this?" I glanced behind me to face Chris, "Is there anything in your database that we could use as hard evidence?"

"I'm not sure," she shook her head in frustration. "We don't keep records of contacts, with everything face-to-face wherever possible. It helped reduce risks of information on our work leaking."

"Well, it would have worked if not for Bernhard and Achmed," I grimaced, reminded again of what a fluke that had been. "I guess we need confirmation from the key actors. In addition to yourself and Tan, that would be David, Ingrid and

276

the girl. But, first of all, the booby-traps en route to the salt mine. Any ideas?"

"Um, well," Doris started, clearly still working out a strategy while a map ghosted into existence on our visors, "these traps assume that whoever is intruding is unaware of their existence. There are two gates on the approach road but, with this truck, we can drive around them and just cut our way through the fence. The third is the tricky one, as it blocks entry to the cutting, which is the only road through the crater wall. We could try off-roading, as it may be possible to get access from the north-east, but it's very rugged. It would probably be easier and quicker to stop short of the gate and just go the rest of the way on foot. It's a bit of a scramble, but only a few hundred metres and should be easily doable."

"Sounds good to me, any thoughts from Brugg?"

"Doesn't seem to be a problem," Pirmin commented while expanding the satellite image of a potential route from the last gate to the mansion. "I guess Helen could probably jog this track and even the aged boss should make it with the occasional push from behind."

Again, Mister Dour, now with what would almost pass for a sense of humour. Strange!

"Let's go with that option. When we reach the last gate, Helen and I make for the mansion as quickly as possible. Doris gets some more drones in the air and coordinates all links from the truck. Of course, she also provides rapid evacuation should that be needed. Rashmi follows with Jones and Tan. All being well, we can carry out any interrogation in the villa, with the aim of being able to put together a nice package for the Commander before we leave. I guess it must be getting noisy back in Switzerland, eh?"

"Lots of brass screaming their bloody heads off," Rüdi chuckled. "We've put it down to a comms failure, so they're chasing after that. No indication that they even suspect that we have an independent link to you, so we should be okay for a bit. All the same, sorting out something sooner rather than later would help a lot."

"Yes, that's the plan. Coming up to the first gate now." Helen drove over a shallow ditch and then up to a stretch of chain fence about ten metres distant from it.

"Traces of gammas, caesium 137 again," Rashmi reported after she bailed out, before running to the fence and hacking out a section with a blade that went through the mild steel like butter.

"Dose?" I inquired after she jumped back into the car and Helen drove through the gap and headed back towards the road.

"Nothing. I guess the gammas are collimated to give the maximum dose directly above the source. We were far enough away from the trap that we picked up only traces of sky-shine."

Only a minute later, this procedure was repeated at the second gate and, a couple of minutes after that we pulled into a layby twenty metres before a more serious-looking, armoured gate that blocked access to the cutting.

"Wow, this isn't caesium we've got here. There's a wider range of gammas and... bloody hell, neutrons. What the fuck's that?"

"A sub-critical fuel assembly," answered Chris with a wry grin. "Only just sub-critical, so drive over that and you'll get an instant criticality excursion."

"Jesus Christ," Rudi muttered, "a nuclear bomb. Fucking extreme or what?"

"No, not a bomb, you just get a flash of criticality. This gives a massive pulse of gammas and neutrons. It's almost certainly lethal, you're disabled within minutes and dead within hours."

"At some point we're going to have a chat about these radiation traps, Professor Jones, but let's move out, staying very far away from that gate."

***

Just before I set off with Helen, we hauled Tan from the back of the truck, cut the ties binding his feet and injected the antidote to the drug we had used to keep him quiet. As soon as he came to, he started screaming protests until I jammed the barrel of my pistol between his eyes. "Chris, talk to this guy and get him calmed down. He will either come with us quietly, without any resistance, or we'll shoot him in the gut and then drag him to the villa. He should have a look into Rashmi's eyes, she's already been shot by one of your colleagues and will not hesitate to fuck him up if he tries to bugger about with us."

From the look of terror in his eyes, it was clear that he had received the message.

It was already getting quite dark as I set off behind Helen after she had cut a gap in the fence at a point about 50 metres from the gate. By the light of our head torches, we scrambled up what looked like a faint goat track, following the route that Pirmin had selected for us.

I was panting by the time we reached the crater rim, although Helen was breathing as easily as if this had been a gentle stroll in the park. We switched off the torches and went onto a heads-up virtual display of the inner crater and the path leading towards the brightly-lit villa created by synthesis of scans from Doris's drones. "Any sign of activity in the house?" I asked as I zoomed in on the stone garden surrounding it.

"Not a peep," Doris responded immediately. "I'm pretty sure that the gas has done its job, maybe also indicated by the traps being activated, if this is a default in case of residents being incapacitated."

"However, the traps could have been triggered by someone who's still conscious down there and spotted our attack," ever-cautious Helen added.

"Okay, we assume the latter as a worst case. Doris, get a drone into the building and start a search. We're heading down and will cut through the fence at the back of the building in about five minutes. Any threats there that we can pick up?"

"So far the only concern is a gamma source at the gate to the driveway into the estate. Seems a bit superfluous after the criticality trap, but it seems they have sources to burn."

Must remember to quiz Chris on that. "Right, do we have a drone with GPR?"

"Let's see, ground penetrating radar, doesn't seem to be an option. But I could configure a pair to run synthetic aperture multi-spectral scanning, which would be much the same."

"Okay, run them over our path, in front of us. Just in case of any more nasty surprises."

"Good, grief, boss, you're getting to be a scaredy cat in your old age," Helen whispered in my ear.

"You complaining?"

"No, just observing. The drones are in place now, so just follow me down."

"Maybe I should go first."

"No way, you'd just trip over something and hurt yourself. Follow carefully."

Helen jogged off without waiting for a response, so I simply dropped in behind her, doing my best to keep up with her pace on the uneven scree that formed out path. *Treacherous stuff, but unlikely to be suitable for mines or similar traps.*

By the time I panted up to the fence, Helen had already cut a gap and was cautiously moving towards a back door, which seemed to lead into a conservatory. Both the garden and the house itself were brilliantly lit, so I switched to normal vision.

"Door's open," Helen reported, pushing it open, "and nobody in view inside. How does it look, Doris?"

"I have our three targets slumped over the dining table on the front terrace. Also, one of the girls. The cook and the other girl are in the kitchen. There are locked doors to two of the bedrooms and the basement. Wait a minute, the odd-job man and one of the guards are in bed in the small bedroom at the back of the house, seem to be asleep. The other locked bedroom, clearly the master suite, appears empty. Well, I guess that's just one of the guards unaccounted for."

"Have a drone gas the couple in bed in case they're just shagged out rather than unconscious. We'll check the basement. Rashmi, you can make your way in and head for the terrace. Immobilise our targets and then prep them for interrogation." I waved Helen to my side. "Okay, I lead now. Doris, do we have anything on the basement?"

"Not a sausage, I'm afraid. No plans registered and completely shielded."

"Right, we do this the hard way. I'm at the basement door now," I rapped my knuckles against it, "very heavy duty. About to set a shaped charge. The door itself may be tough, but I'm not so sure about the wall around it. Looks like a fairly standard reinforced concrete. So just back off a bit now, I'll try to ensure the force is focused inwards and the door is blown out."

The explosion shook the entire house. "Erring on the side of caution there, boss?" Helen grinned. "We shouldn't need to worry about anybody downstairs hearing our approach, that blast must have burst eardrums."

I peered around the corner and saw that the door had been blasted loose and lay wedged in the approach corridor. "Not ideal, but could have been worse. I can squeeze past…"

"…so, Rashmi and I could walk past shoulder to shoulder…"

"…so, we need less frivolity here!" My head torch cut through the cloud of slowly settling dust, showing another door at the bottom of a flight of

282

steps. "Fuck, another door here and it looks tight. Also armoured. Helen, you got more explosive to take this out?"

While Helen set the shaped charges based on a scan to locate deadlocks, I stuck a sensitive microphone array onto the door. "Can we pick up anything inside?"

Pirmin responded after a few seconds. "The analysis indicates rather rapid breathing to the left of the door as you are looking at it. Yes, now got heart beats. Just over one-thirty, so this is a very nervous guy."

"Okay, get a drone in there with a flash-bang as soon as the door goes down."

"No gas?" Doris asked, to double check.

"Nope, I want this guy as confused as possible when I go in there. Okay, got to move as we're counting down here: three, two..."

Although she had been a bit more parsimonious with the plastique, in the confined space at the bottom of the stairs the explosion was deafening, despite our ear protectors. The door collapsed into the basement, just before a drone flashed past and another bang was heard within.

I spun low through the opening and dropped to the floor, my gun pointed at the shape in full battle kit who was trying to direct an assault rifle in my direction. His armour covered only as far as his groin, so I shot out both knees before sliding towards his slumped form and wrenching the weapon from his convulsing hands."

"Okay, we've got one down in what looks like a security control room. Actually, more like a

283

bunker," I corrected as I noticed corridors stacked with supplies leading further under the villa.

"Bunker is right," Doris confirmed, "you could live out a nuclear apocalypse down here."

"Just lucky that their blast doors aren't up to Swiss Luftschutzkeller standards," I smiled at Helen as she cautiously slipped in to join me. "Prep the action hero here for a bit of brutal interrogation. Rashmi, you here yet?"

"Waiting at the back fence for an all clear."

"All clear from my side. Doris, what do the drones say?"

"Everyone now accounted for and immobilised, so clear for entry."

"Excellent. Rashmi, set up on the terrace as initially planned. We'll be up in a moment, but feel free to start without me. We want anything that'll either support or contradict our present assessment."

Helen had already bound the guard's wrists behind his back and his legs at knee level while he was under shock from his knee-capping. She then injected him with a potion that would keep him conscious, before slitting off his armour and then clothes with a huge combat knife.

The slim man was clearly middle-eastern and very handsome in an almost androgynous way. Pieced nipples and circumcised, I noted absently, while his cries of pain increased in volume as he looked down at his shattered legs.

I grabbed him by the hair and throat and roughly dragged him onto a large leather swivel chair while Helen steadied it for me. "Okay, we can give you an anaesthetic to take away the pain of

284

that," I punched him in the thigh, rewarded by a screech of agony, "but first you need to tell us how to disarm the traps along the access road."

His screamed gibberish seemed to include a lot of cursing in Portuguese, so I silenced this by hammering the butt of my gun into the tape binding his legs together, causing him to black out for a moment despite his drugged state. I took a plastic bottle of water from my belt and poured it into his mouth, causing him to choke back into consciousness.

"Pay attention now," I slapped his face twice with the fist holding my gun, opening up a cut on his cheek. "This board in front of you controls all the CCTV and other monitors, but also has a panic switch somewhere that puts all defences on automatic. Logically, it'd be this unlabelled red switch, on the right-hand side. There would also be a way to disarm it, like the green switch below it. Is that how it works?"

The young man glared at me and then, as I lifted my gun in his direction, broke down. "Yes, yes, that's how it works. Green button and all is off."

"Helen, do you trust this little bastard?" She shook her head, looking sad to admit it. "Yes, well let's see. I have now hit green. Doris, how does it look out there?"

"Let's see. Dose rate from gate is unchanged. There's been no disarming of that trap."

My gun slammed into the guard's face. "So, you're a lying bastard. If we hadn't checked, we could have been killed. Helen, can I borrow your

285

knife?"

I watched his fear overcome pain as I first brandished the blade before his eyes and then grabbed hold of his testicles. "Well, this won't be so bad because, as far as balls go, you've got a spare." I plunged the knife through one of his testicles and he was again unconscious before I sealed the gushing wound with an emergency sealant.

I needed both another jab and a mouthful of water to bring him round again. "Okay, let's try this again. You're going to tell me how this thing works or no more Mister Niceguy." I grabbed hold of his wedding tackle and ran the razor-sharp tip of the blade across his stomach. "Not a little teaser, but the entire shooting match. I am going to remove your dick and scrotum before I stick this to the hilt up your arse. And don't think you'll get anything sown back on. I'll blow-torch your entire groin before I go."

I thought my threat alone was going to make him faint, but he managed to stammer an answer. "Both the red and green arm the defences, either of them will work. When armed, the only way to disarm is to switch both red and green together, wait ten seconds, and then switch both again together. It's true, really true, don't hurt me anymore." He broke down into sobs interspersed with grunts of pain.

I did as instructed and checked in with Doris. Shielding was back in place and radiation at the gate, which had opened automatically, was down to background.

"Right, you're clear now, so you can drive up

to the villa and get ready for extraction. Keep monitoring the link to Brugg to ensure it isn't compromised and we'll join you as soon as we can."

All we need to do now is find incontrovertible evidence that everything Chris has told us is kosher. How hard can that be?

***

The terrace was surrounded by a mosquito screen, which still allowed a view onto the array of solar panels covering the floor of the crater, gleaming faintly in the moonlight that appeared occasionally between fleeting clouds. Lighting over the long dining table was subdued, but quite sufficient to make out the glares of hatred on the faces of Ingrid and David, who were now awake but firmly secured to the heavy dining chairs set at one end of the table. Tan was tied up beside them and Jones sat nearby, although unsecured. At the other end of the table, the daughter and the serving girl were slumped forward on the table, but positioned to reduce the chance of them choking.

"I think we should have Ingrid's daughter to complete the set here," I nodded towards Rashmi. "We need to sort out exactly what this cabal is up to and it might be that young Ruth here will be a bit more open than the others."

"Just leave the girl out of this," Deutscher objected. "We can give you whatever you need."

"I hope you've grasped the situation that you're in. Your entire group is classed as terrorists due to the attack on Switzerland and normal operating procedure would be summary execution of all of you."

"But the attack wasn't..." David started to object before Rashmi walloped him on the ear with the butt of her rifle, causing him to slump forward with a grunt of pain.

"We don't care about excuses. I want you to stay quiet until explicitly asked to speak. Do not piss about with us or we will hurt you. We're not going to kill you, not yet, but we can inflict pain that'll make you wish for death."

Looks of shock were mirrored on the faces of all our captives, including Ruth who was now awake and tied beside the others. I gave them my best psychopathic loony grin while I waved Helen's bloody knife in their direction. They made a strange picture: Chris wearing only a bedraggled robe and a pair of combat boots; David in a dinner jacket; Ingrid wearing a long black gown appropriate to a formal dinner; and Ruth in a flimsy, semi-transparent chemise that would have been more appropriate to either a red-light district or a dodgy nightclub. *Or, perhaps, given that she appears to be wearing nothing under it, just the rigout for our kinky hotel.*

"Okay, this is how we're going to play this. David here is going to go with Rashmi and open up your main computer. Don't bugger about! We know all your tricks and have already accessed the one on Tan's yacht." I passed the knife to Rashmi, who cut the ties between his ankles and the chair legs. "The blood on this knife is from when I cut off the testicles of the guard in the basement," I exaggerated a little for effect, "but my colleague

288

here isn't as soft hearted as me."

"No kid gloves, got it boss," Rashmi's evil grin put mine to shame.

"Now Ruth, you're up."

Ingrid looked at me with tears in her eyes, but was clearly smart enough not to try to interrupt.

"I don't know anything, really," the spectacular redhead whimpered. "Just ask my mom, she'll tell you." She wiped her nose with the back of one of her bound hands and looked up at me like a beaten puppy.

"Oh, well, if you know nothing, I guess we can just shoot you now. That should make your mum a bit more loquacious." I drew my pistol and flicked off the safety, pointing it between her well-shaped breasts.

"No, please!" "Don't do it," begged Ingrid and Chris simultaneously.

"I'll talk, I'll talk," the girl screamed just before the sound of my shot resulted in a shocked silence.

At the last moment I had lowered the gun and fired between her legs, grazing her left thigh and causing a flow of blood that was quickly mixed with urine.

"I told you about this," I glared at the quivering young woman. "Do not fuck about with me. You're the fucking CEO of operations here and the little girl act just doesn't cut it. You have ten minutes to summarise everything that goes on in Sal and how that fits into your overall weaponised virus production plans."

Her resistance crumbled completely and she

talked non-stop for fifteen minutes, painting a picture that generally meshed with everything we knew or had recently learned from Jones. One notable addition was the role of her twin, Helena, who was in charge of virus distribution. As typical with this organisation, she operated independently and Ruth was unaware how far trial runs had gone. However, she was fairly sure that first batches of the virus had already been released.

I glared at Chris. "Why didn't you tell me this?"

"I knew Ingrid was organising release, but I don't know details," she looked sheepish. "It's all need-to-know, you see. I didn't, so was out of the loop here."

"Bugger! This won't make getting a balanced hearing from upper echelons any easier. How far on is Hashimoto with release of his virus?"

Ruth squirmed uncomfortably. "That's something I don't know, honestly. Helena might know, but best to ask my mother."

Ingrid glared at her daughter, but quickly recovered her composure. "Can I speak now?"

"Sure, Frau Doktor Deutscher. I guess you can give us more on the releases of both your own and any other virus strains."

"The distribution is trivial, as it's weaponised for efficient air dispersion. Release in a busy check-in area for international flights is easy and direct symptoms develop over a couple of weeks and resemble only a very mild cold. Just occasional coughing or sneezing, so there's little chance of it being picked up. Unlike Hashimoto's plague, loss of fertility is something that'll show up only over months or years and, even if it is traced back to a virus, by then it'll be too late to do anything about it."

"Well, what about your counter-virus? You're already spreading that about, as I know well. Couldn't we use that on a global scale?"

"That's my area," Jones cut in. "I guess you spotted this when you were infected in Levant, so you know that it's sexually transmitted. Although the active sites are similar, the sterilisation function is engineered into a highly infectious, completely synthetic nanovirus. The counter is incorporated into a herpes analogue phage vector, which is harder to transmit other than by sexual intercourse."

"But don't you also need selenium to ensure infection?" I interrupted.

"Ah, you had the lubricant gel analysed," she continued. "No, that's just to decrease the time between being infected and being able to pass it on. The vector itself is highly infectious and was based on one designed to increase sexual desire and decrease inhibitions."

"The date-rape virus that was reported about a decade ago!" Helen interrupted. "I thought that was an urban myth."

"That's the one: it's anything but a myth. Made a lot of money for a couple of very bright but unscrupulous post-docs, before they were traced back by a mafia don whose daughter was a victim. Tortured to death in a most horrible way."

"So how did you get a hold of it?"

"Interpol pulled me in to an attempt to reverse

engineer the virus. This work was dropped when the source was closed down, but I decided that its attributes made it also well-fitted to our purposes. Driving higher levels of sexual activity makes it a perfect STD."

Maybe this also explains to some extent the uninhibited sexual activity of this crowd. It's not all a weird cult thing, but a consequence of the virus that they've all been exposed to.

"And why can't you just engineer the protective functionality into another phage or virus?"

"I could, in time, but it's not a trivial job. Especially so as I'd need to ensure that the engineered version is both stable and safe. Not much good protecting fertility if it's lethal in 50% of cases. It was very much easier starting from a synthetic herpes. From where we are today, other options are non-starters."

I turned back to Deutscher. "And what about Hashimoto? Has his group also started tests?"

"Not as far as we know. They've had a lot of internal dissent. Hashimoto would like to release his variant, but is being blocked by that Nazi Easton," she almost spat his name. "He has almost finished testing a variant that is racially targeted, with a lower death rate, only about 90%, for Caucasians and Orientals. But it's effectively 100% lethal for racial groups from Africa and India. These variants compete against each other, and ours of course, so whoever gets wide distribution first will dictate how the global depopulation pandemic will develop."

"And your STD protects against all these

variants?" Helen asked.

"It should do. It was jointly developed with Hashimoto before we went our different ways."

An uncomfortable silence developed in the room until Rashmi appeared, dragging David by the shoulder. "What's up guys?" she asked cheerily. "I've hoovered everything off the computer here and then melted down both the core and memory. I guess we can blow this joint now. Should I call up heli-extraction from here?"

I paused for a moment, trying to see a way through the cat's cradle of potential responses to the threats posed by Hashimoto and Easton. "No, let's not rock the boat by drawing more attention to ourselves. The helicopter is at the airport, so get them to prep for a flight back to Switzerland. Officially, it'll be flying back empty. We'll penetrate the security wire and board without anyone noticing. Got that, Doris?"

"Setting it up now, boss. Rüdi will set the incursion route. Just get your arses on board and we're off."

"We've got yet another three passengers, so it may be a bit tight."

"Plenty of room in the back, as long as they don't mind a bit of discomfort."

"They don't have an option. Let's get this show on the road."

***

After we crammed into the pickup, I left organisation of further details to my team while I silently pondered our situation, my reverie broken only for a few seconds by the general tension as we drove over the criticality trap, evidently still safely deactivated.

As soon as we get to the chopper, full links are back and we can't play on a supposed comms failure. I've got about fifteen minutes to come up with a credible justification for the Commander, who isn't happy with me in the first place, to support Jones and her crew as the lesser of two evils. Three, actually, if we count that mad fucker Easton. If there is no way that I can do this, I either have to go over his head, which could get very messy, or go open with this all. Spread it through the internet, which I could probably do before I'm arrested and court-martialled. We've brought back the death penalty for treason, so not a good option for me, and maybe even the rest of my team if they can be linked to my actions.

The more I thought about it, going open wasn't a credible option. Either I would be quickly discredited, so it would all be for nothing, or the fact that first steps to limit fertility had already been taken would lead to global panic and violence against anyone who could be even remotely connected to the plot. No matter how sensible Jones' option was, a unilateral decision to prevent couples having children would lead to armed revolt. As the entire aim was to block Hashimoto, public awareness could well make this even more problematic.

It has to be the Commander, but maybe together with Supersaxo, so they'll need to come to some kind of Swiss consensus on how to respond.

We were nearing a gate that served as an

294

emergency entrance to the airport. The Brugg team had hacked airfield security, so the gate automatically opened as we approached and closed after us. The helicopter was sitting with rotors slowly turning about 200 metres distant, on the pad outside a maintenance hangar for light aircraft. Helen skidded to a stop and we piled out of the cab, aware of a couple of armed soldiers who were watching us from the open hangar door.

Helen seemed to read my mind. "It's okay, boss, we're clear for extracting a group of terrorists to Bern and the locals have agreed to stand by for this."

"Nice of them. Are we sure that none of those squaddies are videoing us?"

"They shouldn't be but, in any case, we're projecting electronic and optical dazzle that should mess with any kit they might be using. In addition, as you'll see, we've got hoods for our prisoners."

"I wasn't so worried about them, more about our faces appearing on *Zehn vor Zehn*. Anyway, keep visors down, everyone. Doris, can you set me up a secure link to Schmidt and Supersaxo as soon as we're settled in the chopper. I need to have the both of them and, if possible, somebody high up in the security commission. At the same time, you can open our normal encrypted broadband and download everything we've got to Brugg."

"Everything, are you sure?"

"Yes, starting with all we've got from the two computers. Even with our high-speed link, that'll take quite a while. While that's happening, you can grab all our drone and bodycam material, just taking out the few direct links to Brugg. There'll be such a vast amount of material that I doubt it would ever be noticed."

"Not unless someone was specifically looking for it," Doris warned me.

"Well, we just need to ensure that never happens. Depending on how my chat in the next few minutes goes, either everyone's going to be up to their eyeballs with the chase for Hashimoto or we just need to head for the hills when his virus ignites a truly biblical apocalypse."

I absentmindedly clambered aboard the massive helicopter and sat at the front of the rows of seats along its flank. *Will this really work? I'm sure that the Commander hasn't the balls to go for the hard decision on his own, but with NDB support, it could work. The national security commission is a bit of a gamble. They certainly think at a higher level and are the basis of Swiss security policy, but are renowned for being very conservative. Could I have shot myself in the foot here by aiming too high?*

***

I set up an electronic security screen and initiated the communication link as soon as we were airborne. I was wearing a full-face VR helmet, so the meeting participants ghosted into view as they joined. First an irate-looking Schmidt appeared, who was glaring towards me. "I have no idea what you are up to here, but…" He shut up abruptly as Supersaxo appeared.

"As you requested, Herr Gruppenführer, we're joined by a security commission representative,"

Supersaxo didn't look any happier, "Bundesrätin Zwicky." As he made this introduction, a rather prim looking woman joined the meeting. Probably late middle-aged from her position, but her rather oriental features, maybe indicating a Thai parent or grandparent, made her actual age impossible for me to guess.

Shit, a Bundesrat! I'd no idea it'd go this high. Some details of this op must have already passed up the chain of command, which explains why the Commander is shitting bricks, dreading what I'm going to say.

To my surprise it was Zwicky who got the ball rolling. "We're under time pressure here, Herr Berner, so I want you to give me the short, sharp, executive summary. Please focus first on demonstrable facts, we can come to your interpretations later."

I took a deep breath, starting slowly while I ordered my thoughts. I quickly covered Colmar and, from her nods, the Bundesrätin was already well aware of this background. I began to relax while I skimmed over the Marseille University intrusion, but her theatrical cough brought me to a stop.

"Is this right? You destroyed a university research lab to cover traces of your illegal intrusion?"

Let's see if honesty is really the best policy "Yes, I did, although the place was actually a death trap and would have probably had a major explosion sometime even without my help."

"What about collateral casualties?"

"We expected the lab to be empty when we

broke in. We surprised one student who was, unfortunately, shot dead in the confusion. He did, however, work in the lab producing weaponised viruses."

"Alright, what happened after that?"

I covered our raid on Jones' flat in only the vaguest terms, happy she didn't ask about collateral damage there, and quickly summarised our intrusion to Tan's island and the evidence gained on the nature of the threat. I gave Isle du Levant a similar treatment, but was stopped again by a cough after covering the protective STD virus.

"During this passive operation to spy on our enemies in a more subtle manner, your entire team was infected with a virus that you state is only sexually transmitted," she frowned.

"Yes, exactly. It was a very unexpected outcome from this mission." I waited for an explosion and could see Schmidt holding his breath.

"That's what I thought you were saying, alright go on."

I couldn't hide a sigh of relief, which seemed to elicit the smallest of smiles from Zwicky. I then covered Sal in more detail as, apart from my Brugg team, this would be new to everyone in Switzerland. I was very careful not to draw any conclusions, but simply reported the information that we had gained, in particular from Jones and the Deutscher women. "So those are the key points," I concluded, "although we have a vast amount of material from the two computers, which will be getting analysed by experts as we speak. Getting hard conclusions from that stuff, if possible at all, will certainly take some time."

"Thank you, Herr Berner, that gives me a much better idea of what's going on here. And, I think, it explains why you wanted someone from the commission to be present. Commander Schmidt and Herr Supersaxo seem to have done a good job supporting your team, but the issues raised are far above their pay grade. Actually, I worry that they're also well above mine, to tell you the truth. So now the tricky bit. Let me know your personal take on this. What do you think we should do?"

Shit, what a question. I was hoping that she'd have the answers that I need.

***

"Well, I'm not sure how to handle this," I started, hesitantly. "To be honest, I worked most of the time assuming that this was a simple terrorist bio-threat, best handled by neutralisation of all those involved and destruction of all of their facilities. I'm now a bit lost." I hesitated before going further, but again decided that honesty was probably the best course. "Even before I heard about Hashimoto, when we found out that the goal was to combat over-population, I couldn't help being sympathetic. Even if it's politically incorrect, we have to acknowledge that too many people expecting a western standard of living is driving not only global warming, but also the secondary attacks that we face constantly in Switzerland. If we could cut the global population by 50%, most of our problems would disappear. But..." I ground to a halt.

"But what?" Zwicky looked annoyed. "You've

299

been at the front of all this stuff, so you've got to have a grounded opinion of some sort. Let us have it, without ifs, buts or maybes."

"As you noted, it's very far above my pay grade," I responded belligerently. "Look, I would cut population in an instant if it was my job to decide, but it isn't. Even though she's clearly a brainy professor, it's not Jones' job either. Or that of any of her clique. You can look at what they're intending to do from one viewpoint and it's saving the planet; from another it's genocide that makes past atrocities look like peanuts by comparison. But it isn't actually killing anyone, it's stopping millions, or billions, from being born. Is that the same? That's an angels on a pinhead question, best left to philosophers or God-botherers."

"But, if it could be considered genocide, our job has to be to stop it, surely?" she goaded me.

"Maybe, I don't know. But Hashimoto changes the entire ball game."

"How so?"

"What he's aiming for, and even more so that bastard Easton, is 100% genocide and on a scale that dwarfs anything that could result from Jones' virus. This will be murder of hundreds of millions of women, together with their unborn children. It will also spark conflicts that will kill many millions more. True, overpopulation will no longer be a problem. But, if we did nothing about it, Switzerland would probably be destroyed along with all other developed countries that require a stable population to maintain their essential infrastructure."

"You said *if we did nothing about it*. What do you propose that we do to stave off your apocalyptic worst case?"

Zwicky seemed to be leading me by the nose to get to some particular conclusion, but I just had no clue what this was. "If it was up to me, regardless of any other action we take, I'd do my best to spread the protective STD throughout the Swiss population. This would be helped a lot by our relaxed culture when it comes to alternative lifestyles. Encourage everyone we know is infected to pass it on to the most sexually active members of our population and encourage its spread. Especially to those most important for supporting key services, such as medics, police, teachers, artisans. I don't know, your civil protection service must have lists."

Her smile was now clear. "So, you're suggesting we start planning for your team to shag the Bundesrat?"

Schmidt groaned and Supersaxo clearly muttered "Jesus fucking Christ on a bicycle," under his breath.

I hesitated for a moment. *Oh, well, in for a sheep as for a lamb.* "Not quite the way that I'd put it, but assuring protection of key politicians is clearly a top priority and the STD would do the job. The critical point, however, is to assure that we keep whatever we're doing as quiet as possible. We still don't have all of Jones' team locked up and have no control as yet on Hashimoto and Co. Pushing either of them into earlier releases of their viruses would compromise our defence, so has to be avoided at all costs."

Zwicky's grin shocked me, and probably even more so Schmidt and Supersaxo. "So, I need to push through something like an initiative to open state-sponsored brothels and encourage their widespread use, with my Bundesrat colleagues setting an example. That's a challenge that'll probably make your job easy by comparison. I'm going now and will leave you gentlemen with the job of chasing down all of the Jones mob, confirming the reality of the Hashimoto threat and, if it's real, eliminating it. And also keeping everything you're up to under wraps. You have effectively unlimited access to all our security resources and I can set up international links."

"Please don't do that," Supersaxo beat me to the objection, "Interpol leaks like a sieve and UN or NATO organisations are even worse. I can set up links to the Big Canton, if we need them for the Heidelberg link. They're at least halfway secure and they'll trust us enough to provide support without knowing all of the details."

"Somehow, I knew you were going to say that," her smile broadened. "Get your asses in gear and get me results." With this command her image vanished leaving the three of us staring at each other in amazement.

Finally, Alex issued a long sigh. "I thought we were going to get well reamed there. Of course, when I say we, I mean you, Berner. The shit always slips downhill. But, somehow or other, you've pulled the coals out of the fire."

"I'm not sure I'd put it quite as optimistically as that," I rubbed my face under the headset as the reality of the last thirty minutes began to sink in. "It could get bad if Helena's test virus distributions aren't stopped ASAP, but catastrophic if Hashimoto or Easton can even start their operations. We're running blindfold on a tightrope over a tank full of piranhas!"

"Oh, come on," Alex gave an encouraging smile, "it's not as bad as that."

"No, it's worst: the tightrope is greased, its ends are on fire and the piranhas have AIDS. Do you get the picture yet?"

Well, that seems to have dampened the little bit of cheer resulting from missing out on a bollocking from a Bundesrätin. On the positive side, Zwicky definitely had a mischievous glint in her eye when she provoked me into recommending passing on our STD to the Bundesrat. Could that really be what I'm reading into it, she's not a bad looking woman after all?

***

I emerged from my meeting into a barrage of questions on secure comms. "Okay, guys, wait a minute until I get my head together," I groaned.

"But, good or bad? Are we going to get reamed for this?" Rüdi sounded really worried.

"No, we're not getting reamed."

"But the commander was very seriously pissed off, that can't be good," he insisted.

"I'm not quite sure what he feels at present. We had Bundesrätin Zwicky in on the call. Actually, she was leading the entire thing."

All went silent for a moment. Then Doris muttered, "Präsidentin of the security commission?"

"The very one. I think the bottom line is that she's as shit-scared about this as we are, although she hides it better. The key messages are that we're still running things and we have to handle the threats from all the virus variants pronto."

"Just how are we supposed to do that?" Helen sounded baffled.

"Buggered if I know. The good news is that we have free access to any resources we may need. The bad is that this has got to stay completely quiet, no leaks at all."

"You realise that those points are contradictory," Pirmin pointed out. "The more we expand the team working on this, the greater the risk that it'll leak somehow."

"Tell me about it! Even Supersaxo knows that we can't bring in international support, although he reckons that the Germans would help without knowing all details. But I think even that should only be a last resort."

"Well, what's your cunning plan now, boss," Doris asked.

I rubbed my face and groaned aloud. "Back to base and then interrogate our prisoners, with a focus on finding this Helena and anyone else involved in production or distribution of the Jones virus. Additionally, we need to know everything possible about Hashimoto and the virus variants. Maybe some of that will come from stripping the computer databases we have."

"We can't do all of that ourselves," Pirmin pointed out.

"Yes, that's why you've got the job of

expanding the team, first bringing in folk who already know a bit about it, like the forensics techs. The rest of the team should all pass suggestions to Pirmin, anyone at all you know in the Polizei, special forces or NDB who is both smart and tight-lipped."

"Does that mean no women?" Rüdi asked provocatively, unleashing a wave of abuse from his female colleagues.

"Okay, calm down, we all know Rüdi is more of an old sweetie wife than any woman." I cursed under my breath at this diversion, but maybe such banter lowered the general stress level. "However, we can make things a bit easier by breaking our team down into groups with different access to details of what's going on. We can dream up a new project, biowar task force or something like that, to provide dedicated generic support on demand, rather than us having to go through normal channels. Within that, we can have a smaller team working on counter-terrorist actions outside the Swiss border. They can know a bit more about individual targets, but won't see the full picture. Expansion of the Zodiac core group only to the extent absolutely essential."

"Um, I suppose that could work," Pirmin responded cautiously. "It'll still be hard for us to do the most sensitive work, like the interrogations."

"True, these can only be done by those completely up to speed. Helen, why don't you work out a plan for that?"

"Okay, but what about the assessment of the databases that we have now?"

"Doris, that's something for you. Pass off as much as you can to the forensics team and the additional staff that Pirmin will round up. We could call it an exercise for the outsiders: given a database containing a potential threat, what can we extract with our best AI tools?"

"I can do that, but won't have much time for interrogations."

"You and Pirmin can skip these."

"Wait a minute, boss," Helen frowned. "These interrogations will be a lot of work. We currently have Jones, Tan, Ingrid, David and Ruth, but I'm left with only you, me, Rüdi and Rashmi."

"You can count me out also, I've got planning to do. But you're forgetting Schmidt and Supersaxo. They've both got the knowledge and experience to do the job."

"Maybe, but aren't you forgetting that you work for them, not vice versa?"

"And they both sit far under Bundesrätin Zwicky. I have to produce results soonest, so they need to pull their weight. I'm sure you can phrase that a bit better, but I suspect they might both be happy to be playing an active role rather than feeling that I've sidelined them."

Helen sighed, but nodded her head. "Anything else for now?"

"Nothing from my side, but take time to think things over and we'll have a formal planning session back in Brugg. Myself, I'm going to have a little snooze. It's going to get very busy soon."

How the hell am I going to sleep, having just been given a completely impossible job which, if I

306

fuck it up, could have consequences that I daren't even think about?

CHAPTER FIFTEEN

I woke with a start as the chopper landed, feeling strangely refreshed despite a crick in my neck from my cramped sleeping position. *Maybe there really is a way to cut this Gordian Knot, if I can just flesh out details a bit.*

I had apparently slept through a refuelling stop in Gibraltar and we touched down in the small airfield of Birrfeld at first light, to be met by a convoy of black limousines. Schmidt and Supersaxo stood together beside them. The Commander waved to me. "You travel with us; we're meeting again with Zwicky."

"Helen, get everybody to Brugg and prep for the interrogations. I guess I should have asked Pirmin to annex some extra space for us."

"Done already," he broke in. "We have the entire basement and will have more when we can get the rest of normal police operations based here transferred to either Baden or Aarau. We're not making ourselves popular with the rank and file, I can tell you."

"Excellent. I'll be out of touch for a bit, so sort yourselves out as needed."

As I clambered into the car, sitting in the back on a jump-seat opposite the others, I wondered how that was going to play out. *Dare I even mention some of my half-baked ideas now or should I wait until I've thought them though a bit more. Well, I guess I just play it by ear.*

***

Although neither of my fellow passengers looked happy, they seemed a bit less worried than they had before our last meeting. "So, Berner," the Commander started as soon as the door closed, "it seems that you've been moving fast to build up your force."

"Not actually me, that's all my team's work," I pointed out. "I've delegated all logistical responsibility, so that I can focus on planning."

"And drafted us in to help," he didn't seem to like this idea at all, although Supersaxo seemed amused at his reaction.

"I'm just trying to make best use of available resources in order to face up to an almost impossible challenge. I need more support, but can't risk any information leaks. This means polyvalent use of everyone available. Your experience here would be invaluable, but if that's not possible…"

"I'm not refusing," he blustered, "but this isn't the only job I've got."

"If there is anything more important than this, I'm sure the Bundesrätin would understand."

I thought he was about to explode, but Supersaxo intervened. "Come on, Hans, you know he's right. Either we help out here, or we take over the planning. What do you think?"

"Planning is my main function," he blustered.

"But field operations, against targets scattered across the globe, with devastating impacts if you get it wrong? I sure as fuck would rather be in support than take on that responsibility."

This is probably the NDB way of defusing the situation, but I'm not sure if I wouldn't be happier if

Schmidt had taken the leadership job.

On arrival in the underground garage of the Brugg office, a uniformed gofer was standing by the lift to guide us to a sumptuous conference room on the top floor. I had heard of this place, but never seen it in real life. *Normally reserved only for the great and the good.*

We were still settling into seats facing the holo display cube when Zwicky appeared in it, looking somewhat flustered. "Ah, good, Berner, you're back safe and sound. Hopefully with some good ideas about how we're going to sort all of this out."

"Actually, I slept most of the way back," I confessed. "It was an exhausting trip."

"I imagine so. You were sharing a bedroom with three of your female colleagues, I believe."

"Shit! Sorry! I mean we were sharing a suite, which was necessary for our cover. There were 3 bedrooms."

"Never mind, just trying to lighten things up a bit," she smiled. I couldn't help smiling also when I noticed that my compatriots were looking distinctly pale as the Bundesrätin made the depth of her knowledge clear. "Anyway, you're doing better than me, I've been living on caffeine, and a few stronger stimulants, since we last talked. I think the job might be slightly less impossible but, first, I want to know what you've come up with. Lots of really novel ideas come to us when we sleep: Kekulé, Mendeleev and all that shit.

Jeez, she's really goading me here. I wonder what she wants to hear. "Well, I did some up with a couple of ideas before I dozed off. These are just

310

some thoughts of my own," I emphasised, looking from side to side, "and haven't yet been discussed with my colleagues. No time to do so, actually. I landed only about fifteen minutes ago."

"I know all of that, so you can skip the caveats and arse-covering. What do you propose to do?"

"As I said before, we need to spread the protective virus as quickly as possible and get hold of the rest of Jones' team, going in as hard as we need to. Hashimoto is trickier. Our focus has to be on stopping him or slowing him down as much as possible. Frankly, I would target him and everyone else in his organisation for assassination, erring on the side of caution and prepared to accept collateral deaths to increase the chances of success." I exhaled and stared at Zwicky's face, afraid to look at either of my colleagues, sure that this was not the message that they wanted to hear.

Now her smile had real warmth. "I'm glad that you came out with that so bluntly, Herr Berner. My crisis management team took a couple of hours to reach the same conclusion. Now I have some good news. This Hashimoto is well known to our embassy in Tokyo and is actually quite prominent in our Chamber of Commerce and Industry there. From identifying him, it was easy to trace Easton, an American who is currently in Tokyo also. We've invited them both to a seminar on defence against bioterrorism, hosted by the embassy. We think they'll both turn up."

"Wow, that's good. I assume my team have all this info."

"Logged onto the project notice board about an

hour ago."

"I just need to see how this will all fit into my other plans."

"You can do that on the plane."

"What? What plane?"

"The one to Tokyo, leaving Kloten at three this afternoon. That gives you plenty of time to get everything sorted out before you go."

"I'm off to Japan, to do what?"

"For a start, the bio-terrorist colloquium. But I'm sure you'll find other stuff to keep you busy."

"There's just one problem with that, I've never been to Japan. Know nothing about it."

"Not a problem, the embassy head of security, Andrea Tamborini, will meet you and act as your local guide." She looked to the side, beyond the holo pickup. "Sorry, I've got to go now. We'll have a chat again when you reach the Tokyo embassy."

After she disappeared, we sat together in complete silence. *Well, I wasn't expecting that. Tokyo! I wonder how long it takes to fly there. I should try to make sure I get business class tickets, as I've been told that all resources are available to me. Somehow this just usually means more work, not perks.*

***

The day flew past, with a focus on obtaining as much as possible from the bounty stripped from the computers displacing any consideration of how I was going to handle the Tokyo trip. It was after one before Helen drove me to my flat. I chucked my kitbag from Sal onto the floor and then quickly crammed some fresh clothes into a backpack. I didn't even have a chance to empty my mail box.

On the way to the airport, Helen reminded me to upload my ticket and travel documents. I had the Swiss travel app and also an e-passport, but was surprised about all of the other documents that appeared on my Handy. "Christ, am I really vaccinated against all this shit?"

"Of course, you get it all automatically during your annual medical. But you don't need certificates for travel in Europe, that's all done through our bilateral agreements with the EU and the other Minor States. Intercontinental is a bit trickier, especially for Japan. They've suffered from several East Asian pandemics, in addition to the global ones that we're familiar with. Anyway, you not only have all this stuff, but also a Diplomatic tag that'll fast-track you though passport control and customs at both ends of the flight."

I was flicking though the file of travel documents when I came to my flight ticket. "Bugger me rigid, this is first class! How the hell did you manage to get this past Schmidt? I was dreading cattle class for this trip."

"Nothing to do with me, boss, though I'm jealous as hell. This came from Bern, along with the handshake for the Embassy security chief. Do you know how stupidly expensive Swiss first class is? A Bundesrat will fly it, but all the accompanying lackeys will be in the back, not even Business in most cases."

"I guess Zwicky must be salivating over my body and dreaming about me giving her the protective virus," I turned to grin at my colleague.

"You do know that she's a happily married woman, do you?"

"I didn't actually, but I can't help being devastating attractive to older women."

"Well, you just have to hope that you aren't," she laughed. "Her husband is a schwingen champion: built like a brick shithouse."

Oh, well, win some, lose some. At least I've got a mega-luxurious flight to look forward to.

***

Unfortunately, I had no time to savour the delights of the first-class lounge. After a super-fast check-in due to my diplomatic tag, I was taken through a dedicated passport and hand baggage control area and then driven to the departure gate. Maybe an indication of how ludicrously expensive first class was, I was alone in the cabin located at the front of the Swiss Airbus. In fact, there were only twelve seats spread over four rows of this wide-bodied plane and I had a hostess to myself, who seemed dedicated to loading me up with Champagne and nibbles even before the seat-belt sign came on to prepare for take-off.

As soon as we reached cruising altitude, her attention was relentless. After more Champagne and savoury snacks, I was faced with a menu for a five-course dinner and an extensive wine list to pair with it. This was dragged out over a couple of hours, before I finally reached coffee, chocolates and a fine Cognac digestif. The hostess, Brigit, chatted happily throughout, in a promiscuous mixture of English, German and broad Züritüütsch dialect. Although feeling guilty about ignoring work, I realised that this was my first proper meal since the evening I arrived in Sal, which seemed like a very long time ago.

Although it was still early evening according to my body clock, Brigit made up a bed for me on one of the spare seats and encouraged me to change into a *sleeping suit*, so that I could get my head down for a few hours before arriving in Japan, early morning local time. I washed down the offered melatonin pill with my second Cognac and crashed out, probably helped by my copious alcohol intake.

CHAPTER SIXTEEN

Next thing I knew, Brigit was gently shaking my shoulder, informing me that I had time for a quick breakfast before landing. Despite the fact that I had slept for only five hours, I felt fully refreshed and tucked into bacon and eggs, washed down with coffee and Bucks Fizz.

I may be walking into the lion's den completely unprepared, but at least on a full stomach.

I was allowed to disembark before my fellow passengers and was met by a petite Japanese hostess who guided me through VIP arrivals, made even faster by my lack of checked-in luggage. Barely ten minutes after leaving the plane, I was shaking hands with Andrea Tamborini in the executive arrival lounge and ten minutes later was seated with her in a black limousine heading for downtown Tokyo.

I should've checked in advance, but assumed that Andrea, as head of security, would be a man. Maybe also a consequence of my childhood, as my mum was a huge Andrea Bocelli fan. But this Andrea was all woman. She was tall, slim, with paged brown hair and wearing a very short black skirt and high heels that showed off her fantastic legs and tight bum. The open black blazer she wore over a white t-shirt did little to hide her flat stomach and large breasts. *Incredible physique and fit as a fiddle, by the looks of it.* Her face was rather plain, almost boyish, but lit up when she grinned: more cute than conventionally beautiful.

"So, Herr Berner," she started as we left the

kerbside, "how much background do you need on the operation here?"

"Jan, call me Jan please. I think it's best if you just give me an overview, assuming that I don't know anything." *Or, in truth, I was too busy pigging out in first class to read my briefing material.* "I assume that you have full clearance on Zodiac, so you don't need any background from me."

"Yes, Jan, I've got full NDB clearance to state security level, just a little bit above yours," she smiled impishly. "Supersaxo brought me up to speed after Bundesrätin Zwicky made this number one priority for the Ambassador. I don't need to say that this is highly unusual, but understandable given the threat. As instructed, nobody else in the Embassy has been informed and know nothing more than your visit is to give a colloquium, typical stuff that we do together with SCCIJ. The Chamber of Commerce," she expanded in response to my look of confusion.

"But this all seemed to go very fast, setting up this colloquium in particular."

"We're super-efficient here, all the best of Swiss and Japanese efficiency rolled into one." She giggled in a most attractive manner while I rolled my eyes in response to this hyperbole. "Anyway, to tell the truth, it was quite easy, as Hashimoto was already well known to us."

"He was? Oops, sorry for interrupting you."

"Not a problem." She closed her eyes and recited as if reading from a document. "Hiroyuki Hashimoto, 59 years old, very smart and extremely

317

rich. First degree in Biochemistry from Tokyo University; PhD in molecular biology from Oxford; almost took up a Professorship at Stanford, but went into industry instead. Two years with a genetic engineering start-up in Kyoto that was bought by Roche, which gave him the millions to set up his own company, developing protocols for RNA vaccine production. Expanded with daughter companies covering a range of microbial vectors for environmental cleanup. This is now the financial core of the company, with about a thousand employees and additional bases in Pretoria, New Orleans and Quito. The RNA side had a bilateral collaboration agreement with a company in Heidelberg."

"Deutscher's, I suppose."

"The very one. Anyway, since that fell apart about 2 years ago, he's been courting a couple of small companies in Basel, which is where we come on the scene. We did our usual screening and hit a problem with the RNA daughter: specifically its CEO, Leo Eastern."

"Ah, I wondered where he was going to appear."

Leo Eastern, age 45, is a high-flier. Degrees in Chemistry and Business Management, both from Uni Witwatersrand in Jo'burg. Recruited to Hashimoto's Pretoria operation and was running it within 2 years. Like all the senior executives in Hashimoto's companies, implication of sexual links to the others, especially Hiroyuki himself. Hashimoto is openly bisexual and Eastern is kinky gay."

"I'm not quite sure how you define *kinky gay*," I rolled my eyes, "and also don't think that I need to know. But this overall situation seems very close to what we've seen in Europe."

Andrea grinned, apparently savouring my discomfort. "Yes, we've spotted that. It's an incredibly effective way of ensuring the organisation stays tight. Everyone at the top is physically involved with each other and thus philosophical or commercial bonds are strengthened by emotional ones. There's nothing illegal going on here, but the reported sexual activities push the boundaries of acceptance, even in more permissive societies, so these encourage solidarity."

"Well, he may be kinky, but surely nothing that would rattle cages at the embassy."

"No, we couldn't care less who shags who and how, but Easton was picked up as potential right-wing extremist from our social media data mining. Quite open Neo-Nazi at Uni, but much more subtle since then. All operations that he heads up tend to predominantly recruit staff with far-right backgrounds and he provides donations to political groups with a similar leaning. This seems to have caused internal strains, as the main environmental cleanup activities tend to be supported by parties to the left of central."

"So how did this pan out, linking up with Swiss tech?"

"There wasn't enough hard evidence for us to put a block on it, we just flagged it for keeping an eye on. It's gone a bit cold over the last year. A couple of Memoranda of Understanding were signed, but we haven't seen much concrete happening."

"And Hashimoto's relationship with Easton? I got the impression that they had some fairly fundamental disagreements in terms of virus development."

"Yes, we've been looking into that for you. It seems that, despite policy disagreements, their personal relationship is still very close. Easton has been involved with Hashimoto's son for years and always stays with him whenever he's in Tokyo, which is usually for about a month every quarter. Although the son, Tatsu, is on the Hashimoto conglomerate board, he seems to be a bit of a dilettante. A rabid Imperialist and Mishima fanboy, his politics certain fit in well with Easton's."

"Mishima, I know that name."

"Very famous Japanese author and right-wing nutter. Maybe you recall his dramatic suicide in 1970?"

"Actually, I think it was a Stranglers song that my dad used to play all the time. Anyway, I know the guy you mean. So Tatsu is really into all this *young death is good* crap."

"Well, he certainly seems to idealise Mishima and has followed his steps in body-building and swordsmanship, also doing a bit of modelling. Can't write for shit, though," she laughed.

"Do you mind me asking you, have you all this stuff in your head or some kind of smart link that downloads it to you?"

"Just a good memory. Not quite photographic, but one of my many talents," she grinned

320

provocatively.

"You certainly seem to have a talent for pulling all this stuff together. What else is there that I should know? Like, where are we off to now?"

"We'll have a briefing update with your team later this afternoon, early morning Swiss time. We'll do that in the embassy. In the interim, we've rented a furnished flat for you, so I'll take you there first. We weren't sure how long you'll be here, so this accommodation option seemed more flexible, and secure, than a hotel. This was actually killing two birds with one stone. The flat is in the block where Hashimoto lives. He has a vast penthouse that comprises the upper two floors. You're 10 floors below this, in one of the Mori flats, which we thought could be a convenient base if you were attempting any kind of electronic surveillance. This won't be easy, though, as Hashimoto's residence is effectively decoupled from the rest of the block. Has his own parking garage, private lift and independent services. A little world of its own in central Tokyo."

I had been paying little attention to the scenery as the heavy traffic made its way along a freeway that seemed to run through continuously built-up areas. Although the flow was continuous, the three lanes of traffic seemed to hold to a relatively low speed, which I estimated to be about 80. Low blocks of flats extended to the horizon, with occasional clumps of skyscrapers. To the right, I could see a high tower with a characteristic shape come into view.

Andrea noticed my interest. "That's the

321

skytree, tallest building in Tokyo. The exoskeleton is a good example of Japanese earthquake engineering. If we have another big quake, being at the top there is the best place to be."

"I'll take your word for it," I couldn't help sounding sceptical. "Given the choice, though, I'd rather be on the ground."

"That's a sensible option only if you're in a park. In the last big quake, in forty-eight, most of the casualties were at ground level, either among the high-rises or on the freeways."

As this was pointed out, I noticed we were running parallel to a convoy of trucks with warning symbols that I knew meant that they were carrying liquid natural gas. *I wish Andrea had mentioned that only after we were safely off this bloody motorway.*

The security chief chatted on happily, clearly unbothered by such concerns. "You should be able to experience our earthquake engineering in a couple of days as we're expecting a direct hit from a super-typhoon. If you weren't aware that it was an engineering strategy, you could get worried at the way that the big buildings sway when hit by strong gusts of wind."

"That's something that I'd be happy to pass on. I guess everything must be getting locked down if such a strong storm is expected."

"No, not at all. During the season we get hit by about a dozen typhoons. Okay, not all as big as this, but nothing to panic about. People will get off the streets, but you can get just about anywhere in this city underground, so it'll just be life as normal."

"God, I can't imagine anything in this city

being normal. It's so bloody huge!"

"Yes, greater Tokyo has a population of about 40 million, about four times that of Switzerland."

"Christ, how can you manage security in a place like this?"

"It doesn't have the threats that we have," she looked into my eyes, as if to check that I understood the home truths she was about to impart. "The problem in Switzerland is that we're a safe haven. This during a time when the impacts of climate change are getting more critical and many countries are becoming effectively unliveable. We've closed our borders to all but the mega-rich, those who are responsible for all this shit and who made money out of creating it. It's not surprising that there are many who think this is extremely unfair. They can be easily mobilised to try to set things right, usually with their own political agenda." The cheery, smiley Andrea had vanished and this was someone much more serious.

"Although Japan is certainly better off than many other countries, it's only technology that's keeping heads above water, literally in lots of places. So far this century, they've had a giant earthquake and a submarine volcano, both causing huge tsunamis, and Fuji is rumbling. Temperatures in Tokyo average over 40 for months on end, overlapping with typhoons that bring humidity up to 100%. This is one of the unliveable places: it's just that the Japanese don't accept that. In any case, there are very few external threats and people here focus on the struggle to get through each day."

"What are you doing here, then, if it's so

hellish?" I inquired provocatively, hoping to break her out of this grim mood."

I succeeded. "Aikido," she replied with a glowing smile. "I was already 1st dan in Switzerland, but am now 5th, which is much higher than I ever dreamed. Also 3rd dan aikijitsu and 2nd dan iaido."

"Aikido, I seem to remember that's called *the peaceful martial art*. I'm not sure about iaido."

"Not so peaceful, your first move kills your opponent and the rest is about cleaning blood off your sword. Except, of course, for the *sword of the second*, which involves decapitating your partner after seppuku."

"So that's us back to Mishima," I added, just to show that I hadn't been completely baffled by all the martial arts stuff.

"Indeed, but what about yourself? Any interests in martial arts?"

"I did karate as a kid, but nothing since then. Of course, we all get unarmed combat training, but we try to be armed at all times, so not something that I've focused on."

"Ah, karate, that's good. I also have to brief you for meeting Hashimoto. He's 4th dan Shotokan, so you may have a conversation intro there. His wife, Shoko, is 6th dan. She was originally an accountant for a Yakuza gang before she met Hiroyuki and became his CFO."

"Well, I'm certainly not going to get into fisticuffs with this bunch. They're evidently a lot tougher than the European side of this conspiracy. I think you need to get me sorted out with a gun, a big one."

"That's something I can't manage for you," she laughed. "We're not big on firearms in Japan. I could, however, sort you out with a sword."

"Maybe a broadsword, a huge one?"

"Now you're getting silly," she giggled. "Anyway, we're almost at your apartment. You need to decide if you need to catch a few winks or, what I would recommend, work to adjust to the local time by having lunch. Ideally eat outside and let the sun help reset your body clock."

We had driven off the expressway at a complex junction and I could see that we were approaching a simple monolithic block of a skyscraper, which contrasted with many of the more fanciful shapes of buildings I had seen on the way in. "This is called the *Prudential Building*, even though it's a reconstruction of the original. We'll be dropped off at the side, where we pass reception and the guest lounge. You don't need to register or anything, as I have the key to the apartment. It's on the 37th floor and on the west side, so you'll have a view of Mount Fuji if it's clear. And also the approaching typhoon, when it comes."

Fuji view sounds good, but I'm not sure if I want to watch super-typhoons so high up. A Swiss-style, basement bomb shelter would be a much better idea.

***

The apartment was spacious and ultra-modern. Floor-to-ceiling windows in the sitting room looked over Tokyo, extending as far as the eye could see, with a range of hazy hills apparent in the distance.

"Fuji would be about there, Andrea pointed towards the hills, but it's not clear enough at present. Maybe you'll see it this evening."

"Very nice. But this looks like a very large flat for just me." I could see two large bedrooms in addition to the kitchen-dining area and a lounge that could comfortably seat six.

"It's actually not just for you," she sounded a little apologetic. "You're in that bedroom," she pointed, "and I'm in this one." When I looked closely, I could see signs that a woman had already installed herself, in particular with an array of cosmetics on a sink visible through the open door of the en-suite bathroom. "I'm supposed to look after you for your entire visit and I've heard you don't have problems sharing a flat with female colleagues."

Shit – who's been talking to her? "Yes, I see you've been talking to one of my underlings in Brugg, maybe Rüdi," I hazarded a guess representing the worst case, "You might pick up the wrong impression, though. They tend to couple exaggeration with a bizarre sense of humour, so take anything from them with a large pinch of salt."

"Actually, it was Doris I chatted to. My brother has a modelling agency and knows her husbands well. Probably shagged them both, and probably Doris also, if I know him. Anyway, I've met her at his parties a couple of times and so your visit gave us a chance to have a long talk."

Okay, maybe Rüdi wasn't the worst case. "Yes, Doris was on the Cape Verde team and, for our cover, it had to look like we were a group."

"Yes, you and the three women in a kinky swinger place," she grinned. "Sounds like a lot of fun."

"Don't worry, there was no fun, it was all work. I don't really think it's necessary for you to babysit me like this but, if we do share the flat, you don't need to worry that I'll pester you." As I stated this, I couldn't help looking her over. Her body was even more spectacular than that of the gorgeous Doris.

"Oh, I'm not worried," she laughed merrily. "Even if I wasn't a top-level martial artist, my partner will be overnighting with us, so you have a chaperone." I guess my disappointment must have been obvious, as her laugh turned into giggles. She kicked off her shoes and threw her jacket onto the back of a chair, dropping onto the sofa and patting the space next to her. "Take the weight off your feet and have a look at this," she removed a small device from her handbag that folded out to some kind of tablet.

I sat as she flicked through menus and then a holo appeared of a naked, heavily muscled Japanese woman in a classic body-builder pose. Her hairless body glistened with oil, emphasising even more her incredible muscle definition. "Oops, I guess I should have found one where she's wearing clothes, but I think this makes the point. She may look a bit muscle-bound, but that's deceptive. Yoko's a professional MMA fighter."

"Well, I certainly wouldn't like to come home to her with a broken pay packet," I saw Andrea looking at me quizzically. "An expression of my dad's," I explained while I looked at the image more closely. After I could eventually drag my eyes away from her body, I saw that Yoko had a classically beautiful, delicate face which contrasted markedly with her almost masculine physique.

"She's an incredibly sweet girl, except when she's in the ring, of course. Trained in a number of very different martial arts, Taekwondo, Krav Maga, Savate, Capoeira…, which gives her a big advantage over other fighters."

"And built like a tank," I accidently muttered out loud.

"She's certainly extremely strong and teaches body-building. But also yoga and tai-chi, so she's unusually flexible with it."

"Wow, I don't think I could handle that much woman."

"I'm sure you couldn't, especially as she's straight lesbian. More or less, anyway."

More or less. I think maybe a cold shower is called for before my imagination starts running away with itself. "Okay, I should dump my bag and have a quick shower. Then I'll take you up on al-fresco lunch."

"Excellent, I'll just slip into something more casual and then we can head out; in 15 minutes, say."

I watched in admiration as she bounced up from the settee, grabbed up shoes and blazer and strode off into her bedroom, noticing that she made no attempt to close the door behind her. *Cold shower, quick, before I do something daft that earns me a serious kicking from the bulky, but strangely attractive, Yoko.*

***

When I returned to the lounge, feeling fresher and dressed in casual jeans, t-shirt and trainers, I was faced by Andrea bent from the waist to buckle sandals, presenting a fantastic bum squeezed into small, very tight, white shorts. I resisted the temptation to swat the toothsome target presented to me and, instead, coughed theatrically to announce my presence. As she straightened and turned, a saw that the shorts were matched with a tight, white halter-top that clearly showed that her oversized breasts were unencumbered by a bra. *Must be quite a sight when they're together: Yoko is almost titless and Andrea has these huge boobs.*

"Um, I don't want to complain, it's not a problem," I started uncertainly, "but we're supposed to avoid drawing attention to ourselves."

I was beginning to recognise her giggle as a typical response to anything that discomfited me. "You mean this," she spread her arms wide, which thrust her breasts forward and required an act of will for me to move my gaze back up to her face.

"Yes, well they're very nice, your t-shirt, top thing, I mean. Spectacularly nice in fact, but a bit distracting, maybe."

"Well thank you for the complement. I take it that you enjoy the sight of a well-endowed woman. How large do you think my breasts are?"

I stared at her tits in confusion. "I have no idea how you classify sizes, but they're certainly very large. And also well shaped, if I may say so. Maybe XX or XXX, something like that?"

329

"Okay, close your eyes now." She waited until I did so. "Right, what colour are the earrings I'm wearing?"

"Are you wearing earrings? I suppose so. Maybe gold?"

"And my eyes?"

"Oh, they're... Blue I think."

"Open your eyes now." I gazed into her brown eyes and noticed that she was wearing large silver earrings. "I think I've made my point. It's not just you, or even just men, but almost everyone who sees us together will remember my boobs, but probably notice little else about me. It is unlikely they will even notice you."

"Doesn't do a lot for my ego, but I'm sure you're right. I'll just be hiding in plain sight. Okay, let's head off for lunch."

"Right, and there's the added advantage that you can ogle my tits for a couple of hours without risking a serious talking to from my better half."

I meekly followed the giggling girl as she headed for the door. *Ogling the tits will be highly enjoyable, but she's supposed to be continuing my briefing. How the hell am I supposed to concentrate with a view like that in front of me?*

***

We lunched on chicken wraps and beer, sitting outside an English-themed pub in a backstreet close to our apartment block. Andrea certainly was a magnet for attention, especially older Japanese men and, strangely, the young girls who wandered around in groups and wore quaint school uniforms. The girls almost managed to distract me from my colleague for a moment or two, whenever wind caught short skirts and revealed flashes of white pants. *Definitely not conducive to getting work done.*

Andrea chatted away throughout, fleshing out the background on Hashimoto, his family and company senior executives. The last two overlapped in a rather incestuous manner, with nepotism clearly rife in the organisation. The parallels to the European organisation were uncanny, with indications of sexual links between all the key players, their partners and their older progeny. After forty minutes of this monologue, I had finished a pint of beer and ordered a second while Andrea was still on her first half pint. By then, I had started to notice links that were not so immediately obvious,

As Andrea took a break to finish her sandwich, I looked into her eyes. "Despite all distractions, I'm getting a feeling that the organisation here isn't quite as simple as it first looks." She sipped her beer and raised her eyebrows, so I continued. "On the surface, it's Hashimoto who's the big boss and, apart from some differences with Easton, commands all the shots. However, all the links to the rest of his management, whether organisational or sexual, seem to run through, or be facilitated by, his wife, Shoko. Especially with Easton, I'd have expected conflict with Hashimoto to have broken out by now. But Shoko seems to hold it all together."

"That's good!" she looked impressed, or maybe surprised. "Our expert system assessment also came up with this. When we fed it with all raw data on the entire organisation, the best fit model had Shoko at the top, with Hashimoto having more of a figurehead role. That's in addition to his technical lead, of course."

"Could this son, Tatsu, be directly linked in here?"

Now her expression was definitely surprise. "Smart cookie! I wondered about this materfamilias role and looked at what could be mined from dodgy underground gossip. This is highly speculative, but there were suggestions of sadomasochistic links between Shoko and both her son and Easton. Wouldn't be surprising if it didn't involve a threesome."

"All of this without her husband being involved?"

"Looks that way. He seems to have been sexually involved with everyone on our list of suspects in some way or another, but no traces of BDSM or anything else kinky in that way, so far at least. Apart from a taste for group sex and incest, he's just a vanilla bisexual."

Unfortunately, Andrea caught me just as I was swallowing a mouthful of beer, so my laugh turned into choking. "Are you okay?" she slapped me hard on the back. "What's up?"

I wiped tears out of my eyes. "It was just your term, *vanilla bisexual*, which highlighted to me how ludicrous all of this is. We've got a genocidal psychopath here and it's fine details of sexual proclivities that we're using to assess how to proceed."

"It's fine for straight hetero types, but

proclivities are…"

"Hold on," I interrupted, "I may be your idea of a boring vanilla hetero guy, and I'm certainly not criticising anyone's lifestyle. Well, with the exception of mass-murdering maniacs, of course."

"According to Doris, you're not so straight vanilla hetero," she laughed, the moment of tension broken. "Society in the more advanced countries may have moved forward, but, in Catholic parts of the Tessin, they're not into the 21st century yet. My mother is still waiting for me to find a husband so that I can start producing grandchildren for her," she rolled her eyes in a comical manner. Anyway, sorry for going off on one."

"Not at all," I smiled reassuringly. "I'm sure Doris has let you know about my own insecurities."

"She hasn't at all, but I must ask her. You just don't look like the insecure type."

We sat silently for a couple of minutes, smiling at each other, before she helped herself to a mouthful of my beer. "Mine's done, she explained."

Somehow, we've passed from being colleagues to partners. This could really work, as long as I don't fall foul of her girlfriend.

***

We popped back to the flat after lunch, so that Andrea could change into something less provocative and more suitable for walking to the embassy: loose denim shorts, a baggy shirt and trainers. "By Tokyo standards, it's relatively cool today and the walk will also help reduce jetlag. It'll be about three-quarters of an hour."

"I've already taken melatonin," I pointed out,

"so should be okay."

"Fine, but the exercise will also be good for you, after spending eight or nine hours in a plane."

"Should I also get changed? This is maybe a bit too casual for an embassy."

"Not a problem. We're pretty casual anyway and the Japanese are still in Super-Coolbiz mode until the end of the typhoon season."

"Lead on. I'm sure it's going to be an interesting walk."

Despite setting a brutal walking pace, Andrea talked non-stop, providing a potted history of the evolution of our surroundings over the last century, explaining the odd mixture of architectural styles and the clear lack of any kind of consistent themes as we passed through the entertainment areas of Akasaka and Roppongi and into the smarter housing and embassies in Azabu.

By the time we arrived at the compact Swiss embassy, looking like a smaller brother of the Norwegian embassy opposite, I was drenched with sweat. "Sorry, Jan," she grinned. "I guess maybe we should have taken a taxi. Anyway, it'll be cool in the basement, where the secure comm room is. I'll just drop you off there and quickly bring the Ambassador up to speed. Would that be okay?"

"Fine, but is there any chance you could find me a towel? This t-shirt is drenched."

She used her tablet to open a side door and again to access a lift that descended into the basement. After shooing a technician out, she checked the link to Brugg and then scurried away while I scanned through updates on notice boards, prior to my scheduled meeting with the Zodiac team. Moments later she was back with a towel and a t-shirt, still sealed in its wrapping. "Swiss logo, we use them as prizes in competitions," she explained before disappearing off again, closing the door carefully behind her.

The interrogations had brought little additional to what Jones had already volunteered, although the technical input would probably help making sense of the huge volume of material taken off the computers. The Deutschers had been questioned under the strongest truth drugs that would not cause irreparable harm, confirming that neither had any idea where the elusive Helena was. Ingrid was still unsure about when and how the Asian group would distribute their virus, but was convinced it would be soon in order to pre-empt the European variant. Their major constraint was that widespread distribution had to be as closely synchronised as possible. Its highly visible abortion impacts would be spotted much more quickly than infertility, so they had to ensure that uninfected areas did not quickly identify the pandemic and close their borders.

As I was pondering this, Pirmin opened the tele-conference. The full core team seemed to be present on the Brugg side, now numbering sixteen when Schmidt and Supersaxo were counted in. "So, boss, you hit the jackpot yet again, rooming with the lovely Andrea." I could see Doris giggling on one side of the conference table while the Commander was glaring at her.

"It's a bit reminiscent of what we've found in

Europe," I noted quickly to get us back on topic. "The organisation has the same cult-like integrated hierarchy, with sexual domination seeming to play a key role in keeping everything tight. The problem is that there's an extreme right-wing link here, which makes at least part of the organisation less predictable on the basis of our experience to date alone." The Brugg team had access to Andrea's knowledge base, so this was not news, but my focus on it was clearly causing concern.

Helen summarised the key issues from the Brugg side. "It's reasonable to rate Easton as the greatest risk but, compared to Hashimoto, this is just like debating the difference of being wiped out by a big asteroid or a really bloody huge asteroid. You're screwed either way. The consensus here is that Hashimoto is a more credible threat, being at the top of the organisation. He's the one we need to focus on. We can get Easton afterwards."

Doesn't sound at all like Helen, more flowery language than usual. I think they're all shitting bricks on this and Helen's the chosen messenger to bring me to heel.

"I don't care about the consensus. I think Tamborini's assessment of the hierarchy is correct and it's the wife, Shoko, at the top. However, I don't think it really makes much difference, the threat is immanent and the goal has to be to take out everyone at the top of Hashimoto's organisation. Removing a few of them might reduce their chances of rapid deployment of the virus, but we can only be confident about removing the threat if we eliminate every one of them."

"That's going to be about fifteen people, with a couple more if we include sons and daughters who are clearly being trained up to enter key roles."

"Don't worry about trainees at present, we want those already at the helm in this conspiracy. If we do things properly, we could also take out a lot of those at the next management level."

"But with much greater risk of collateral damage," Helen pointed out.

"I can live with that. So, before we go further, have the tools been delivered to the embassy in the diplomatic pouch?"

Rüdi grinned. "The Tokyo Ambassador wasn't very happy about transferring something that he wasn't cleared to know about. His main worry was firearms and he seemed a lot happier when I promised that we had nothing of the sort in the package. He'd shit himself if he knew more."

"Good, well done folk. So, how's the planning going? Is this you again, Helen?"

"Not this time. As the focus is on megadeath, we reckoned Rashmi was best for the job."

I frowned and hoped that the new members of our team didn't get freaked-out by our flippant treatment of state-sponsored assassination. It certainly looked like Schmidt was ready to explode. "Actually, our focus is on preventing megadeath and it's only because of such a terrifying threat that we're even considering these measures. This isn't taking out loopy suicide bombers or those who encourage and support them, this is a focused attack on well-respected personalities, weasel words for the rich and powerful. Even worse, they're located in the capital city of one of our key allies and we'll assassinate them on the basis of evidence that we haven't made public or subject to any legal scrutiny. Collateral damage may occur, but should be reduced to the extent possible, as long as it doesn't compromise our goals."

To my amazement, Schmidt's frown disappeared. "Well said, Berner, I couldn't have put it better myself. So how do we proceed?"

"Rashmi, what do you think?"

"Well, I'm a bit disappointed about toning down the megadeath," she grinned, "but assassination of all the bad guys looks like a doable proposition. You've got the skin-contact toxin and you just need an occasion to spread it about, like the Apero after your colloquium. I assume a shake of hands, but maybe more intimate for our target ladies," again a wicked grin, which made me glare at her. "It's slow acting, so the impact won't be obvious but, after about 10 hours or so, anyone contacted will die from something very, very difficult to distinguish from a heart attack."

"Won't that be a bit suspicious, all these folk pegging out around the same time?" Supersaxo asked.

"Doesn't make any difference," I answered for Rashmi, having picked up on the clever part of her plan. "We'll be in the clear. Hashimoto's crowd will be forced to play this down, as they don't want to be in the limelight at the present stage of their operations. In any case, it could be a coincidence or maybe something like exotic food poisoning. If the toxin really is undetectable, what else can it be?"

338

"But what about collateral deaths?" I expected exactly this question from Helen, as it was one concern that I had. "This could be a well-attended colloquium and there'll be a lot of Swiss ex-pats and other top business types there. Not a good idea if they also drop like flies after the colloquium. Even without evidence of how it was done, they couldn't miss the link to the colloquium."

"Ah, this is the really clever bit," she hesitated, smiling smugly. "Anybody spotted a way to make Helen happy?"

"God, Rashmi, you can be a pain in the ass at times," I gave in.

"An extremely clever pain in the ass, however, as you will soon learn," she hesitated again, being even more annoying. "You see this is a biowarfare colloquium that the boss is going to give a wonderful presentation at. I know it's wonderful, 'cause I've written it for him. Anyway, he'll talk about transmission vectors and how to plan countermeasures. He'll mention the usual weaponised distribution vectors via water, air and contact. At the end, he'll mention that, after the recent norovirus and coronavirus pandemics, there's focus on the first two, with contact often forgotten. To illustrate this point, the room in which the colloquium is held will be sprayed in advance with harmless dye nanoparticles. As they leave the room to go to the Apero, all participants will have their hands swabbed and the number of particles present reported to them. As the talk will have emphasised that only one virus clump is sufficient for infection and an infected person could then shed tens of millions of such clumps every day, the point should be made very well."

There was silence as everyone tried to work out the point of this exercise. Finally, it was Doris who piped up. "The fluid for swabbing contains a barrier or counter to the toxin. Or, at least, the stuff used for non-targets does. For the victims, it's just alcohol or something inert."

"Very smart," Supersaxo conceded, "but isn't it a bit contrived, overly complex. Why not administer the toxin directly in the swab fluid?"

"Admittedly simpler, but not very smart," she responded, cheekily. "For a start, if Hashimoto is as paranoid as I expected him to be, he could reasonably refuse to be exposed to an unknown fluid. This kills your option, but doesn't affect mine. Also, for your case, Embassy or SCCIJ staff need to handle a very dangerous toxin and, if all goes well, will actually kill some people. Not a good way to go. I require these guys to handle only completely safe materials and have no direct role at all in the assassination, which is carried out by, and attributable only to, my boss. His job is killing people, after all."

"Masterful, Rashmi, indeed you're much smarter than me for this stuff. Anyone see any problems?" I looked over a sea of blank faces and noted that Supersaxo was wryly shaking his head. "Right, work that over with whoever you need, Rashmi. And send me my brilliant presentation. I should have a look to see what's on it before I appear on stage. I guess I also need to pick up the toxin and familiarise myself with how to handle it."

"Sure thing, boss, but we need to go through part two also." I clearly looked confused. "Well, this is aimed to take out Hashimoto and any of his compatriots who attend your symposium but, as you emphasised at the start, we need to take out everybody at the top. I've also got an option planned for that."

It should have been me bringing this up. I was so impressed at the colloquium plan that I got distracted. I can't let this happen again. "I assume it's as subtle and clever as the other one."

"Clever, yes, but not so subtle. After Hashimoto dies, a wake will be held as soon as possible. It's called tsuya and is a very formal occasion. All family, friends and colleagues will attend. It'll be easy to find out where it's held but, for security reasons, the penthouse is by far the most likely. We then blow it to buggery. Everyone there dies, which should be everyone with any significant role in his organisation."

"You're planning to blow up the entire penthouse at the top of a skyscraper in central Tokyo!" The Commander looked close to apoplexy.

"No, not at all, do you think I'm some kind of psychopath?" She favoured him with her best psychopathic loony face. "Sure, the Yanks would go for a drone strike that'd be a total 9-11 on that building, but the tailored slow-blast explosive that I've sent over produces a directed high-frequency pressure wave that'll destroy organic tissue, but do little damage to the structure of the building. Okay, there'll be collateral, as anyone in range will be jam: man, woman or child. But this is the good bit,

341

even the downstairs neighbours are unlikely to suffer more than a burst eardrum or two."

"You really think this would work?" The initial idea seemed like complete overkill, but it certainly fit the job profile. "Unlike a few suspicious heart attacks, this'll be very obvious as mass murder. It may be difficult to worm out the exact details, but this could never be sold as any form of accident."

"True, boss, this explosive is state of the art stuff, developed as a collaboration between us and the Israelis. It's very secret and wouldn't be found by any normal data-mining operation. However, we could fit up the Yakuza."

"The Yakuza?" This seemed to be too much for Schmidt. "What the hell have they got to do with anything here?"

"It's in background on Hashimoto's wife. True, there's no indication of any current link," Rashmi gave a conspiratorial wink, "but all we need is a credible narrative. After the explosion, an anonymous tip leads to a Yakuza house where samples of the explosive are found. Case solved, even if everything is circumstantial. Tokyo police don't manage their incredibly high success rate for solving major crimes due to dotting is and crossing ts. All that's needed is some highly incriminating evidence."

"Could work, I suppose," I closed my eyes to focus on the implications of this outrageous plan. "What about our colleagues in Israel, won't they be a bit unhappy about us revealing this new secret weapon?"

"Well, it's got to be used sometime and the

advantage here is that there are no clear links to either Israel or Switzerland. We can also make sure all that's found is a sample of the explosive, which would match the chemical signature that will certainly be found after the explosion. There won't be any trace of the firing mechanism, which is the real black magic here. Without that, all you have is extremely flammable silly-putty."

"As you noted, anything but subtle, but seems to do the job. A rather brilliant bit of work, Rashmi."

"Well, I just presented the overview, the entire team here has been providing input."

"Well, congratulations to everyone. Work this up into a time plan and I'll sort out required support at the embassy. By the way, does Andrea know about this?"

"Frau Tamborini hasn't been in the loop, so far," Doris raised an eyebrow at my slip of the tongue, "ensured deniability and all that. What do you think?"

"No, definitely keep it this way. I'll pass on anything required on a need-to-know basis. Okay, that's top priority out of the way, what next?"

Over the next quarter of an hour, we discussed expanding the search for Helena and prioritising distribution of the protective virus within Switzerland. For the latter, the key question was how widespread this could be made without it becoming obvious to our partners. We had to inform them as soon as possible, but agreed that this could be done only after the Asian risk had been eliminated. Once the cat was out of the bag, all hell would break loose. Thus, a range of scenarios needed to be developed along with storylines that would play down the extent to which we had gone our own way on this.

"This has to be you, Commander, working together with Herr Supersaxo and Frau Zwicky," I felt relieved to pass the buck.

"Thanks a bunch, Berner," Schmidt looked miserable. "I suppose I'll also be the one to tell the Bundesrätin that you're planning to wipe out a funeral party in central Tokyo?"

"I guess so, but you need to emphasise that it's our plan. We all agree that there's no obvious alternative." Now the Commander looked positively ill. "Right guys and gals, make it so while I head for dinner with the security chief."

The line closed to a chorus of theatrical groans.

So, the problem here seems slightly less intractable, but I can't believe an operation as complex as this is going to go smoothly.

CHAPTER SEVENTEEN

My misgivings came quickly true when Andrea joined me, having spotted that the closed meeting was finished. I saw immediately that she was disturbed by something. "I think we may have outsmarted ourselves," she started ominously.

"That doesn't sound good."

"As background for this trip, a social media history for you was created. The aim was to provide justification for your visit here without compromising your position. My assistant was a bit creative and added a link for the programme for your trip, which has you sightseeing today while details of your colloquium are nailed down. Unfortunately, this makes it clear that you're staying in Akasaka, which was spotted by one of Hashimoto's operatives. He has thus invited you to a reception in his penthouse. The mail just came to the address the Chamber created for you."

"That's not necessarily too bad, when is it?"

"This evening at seven."

"Shit, that's short notice. Nevertheless, we can't really turn down this chance for a bit of reconnaissance, can we?"

"I thought not," she smiled suddenly. "That's why we've already accepted on your behalf. You're invited with companion, so at least I'll be able to hold your hand."

"Would your girlfriend be happy with such hand holding," I smiled back.

"Oh, I'm sure she wouldn't mind, especially as

she'll also be coming with us. We'll both be holding your hands."

"I'm not sure that's a good idea," I frowned. "We shouldn't bring any outsiders into an operation like this."

"It's only a reconnaissance, as you noted. And you can be sure that we'll provide a fair amount of distraction, which could prove useful."

I thought through this for a bit, but couldn't see any obvious risk. Again, this was hiding in full view, being such a focus of attention that nobody would consider that it was part of anything surreptitious. "I can't see a problem. Does this mean that you'll be wearing your white kit from lunchtime, to maximise this distraction?" I asked hopefully.

"No, nothing as subtle as that. Yoko and I don't get a lot of chances to go to fancy dos like this, so we'll dig out our special glad-rags. I'm telling you, your eyes will pop out of your head," the giggle indicated that her concerns had vanished.

Jesus, doesn't sound like I'll be able to focus much on pumping Hashimoto and Co tonight, I'll be expending all my efforts to stop dribbling.

***

We travelled back to the flat in an autonomous taxi, which seemed to take a gratuitously complex route through a maze of back alleys. As always, Andrea chatted throughout, but I switched this out while I tapped the briefcase containing the contents of the diplomatic pouch and pondered options to turn this surprise development to our advantage. My presentation was scheduled to happen in two days, which was not as soon as I had hoped. *All that was needed was for Hashimoto, a very busy man, to decide not to attend and then the entire operation goes tits-up. I wonder if I can talk Andrea out of attending or, at least, not having the Japanese she-hulk accompany us. This could be tricky...*

I was still working through this problem when we were dropped off and I followed my roommate to our apartment. I had just about worked how to approach this when Andrea opened the door without using her key card and shouted out, "Honey, I'm home!" As we entered the living room, she added, "Oh, and I'm with Jan, so some clothes might be a good idea."

I almost tripped over a rug when I came face to face with Yoko, who jumped up from the settee, strangely clad only in a pair of pink, *Hello Kitty* slippers. Totally unfazed, Yoko offered me her hand. "Very pleased to meet you, Jan-san."

I shook hands, forcing myself to keep my gaze on her face. "Very nice to meet you, Yoko. You're just as, um, spectacular as Andrea said you would be."

Yoko's delicate face lit up with a glowing smile. "You are too kind." She slid her hands down the front of her body. "See, I have no titties, not like my girlfriend. She has huge ones," she mimed holding a couple of large melons in front of her chest while Andrea groaned. "Also, very big nipples. See, I have only very tiny ones," she rubbed them to make her point, and I could feel myself starting to blush. "It's very lovely when we make the fucking, but not so good for the wrestling.

Even with the oil, very big things to get a hold of. She can never…"

"Enough, Yoko, stop dicking about with him," Andrea burst into giggles.

"Sorry, mate," Yoko's pidgin English vanished and was replaced with an accent that sounded Australian. "Just pissing about, but you should have seen your face!" She laughed and playfully slapped my shoulder.

I managed to hide a gasp of pain. *Christ, that woman's strong – feels like my shoulder's dislocated.*

"Okay, love, we've got a schedule here. Jan's taking us to a fancy reception in the penthouse here, so we've got to get done up. Really done up, it'll be mega-posh."

Yoko very inelegantly sniffed her armpit. "I had a shower at the gym, but am still a bit whiffy. Probably need another shower."

"The bath in this place is big enough for two," Andrea grinned.

"Not three?" Yoko raised her eyebrows.

"Get in there, you slut," there was a loud crack as a very tight bottom was slapped. "We can leave the doors open, so he can listen to us shagging in the bath. I'm sure that'd be good enough to help him relieve some obvious pressure," she looked down at my groin and giggled again. "Lots of relief, that'll be, as you need to be presentable this evening. Remember, a properly dressed woman is more sexually arousing than one completely naked."

I'm sure she actually means improperly dressed, but I'll find out soon. In any case, Andrea's recommendation is not so daft. I watched the women head for the bathroom, Andrea shedding clothes as she went, noting that the doors were indeed left open and the sound of foreplay carried well into the lounge. *So, all my plans of cutting the ladies out of the reception have been completely pre-empted. It really seems that, in Tokyo, no plan ever does survive first contact with the enemy. Or even with the allies.*

***

After a long, onanistic shower, I shaved and dressed in cream linen trousers, with a matching shirt and slip-on loafers, aware that, due to the minimal contents of my hand luggage, the original plan had been to buy smart clothes for the presentation after I arrived in Tokyo.

I did not need to worry about what I was wearing; there was absolutely no chance of anyone noticing. Yoko appeared first, wearing a full-length ball gown in a shiny sapphire silk that clung to her body like a coat of paint. This made it obvious that not only had she skipped a bra, but also panties. Just to up the ante, the armless dress was split up both sides to waist level which, together with her ridiculously high heels, showed off her muscular legs to perfection. Although relatively modest from the front, it was cut down to the crack of her bum at the back. She smiled at my *rabbit in headlights* reaction and spun in place to make sure that I could fully appreciate the goods presented. "Maybe you might want to head back into the shower, mate."

I couldn't help grunting from the pain of her nudge to my ribs, but even that did not reduce the impact of her wardrobe. "I'm not sure I'd make it to the shower," I groaned. "You might be the most spectacular woman I've ever seen."

"Oh, so I'm just scruffy, am I? Not a touch on my lovely partner?" I tore my eyes from Yoko, to glance at Andrea, who was leaning against the bedroom door jamb: then I was glued to her. The contrast to Yoko was dramatic, she was wearing a very short, white skirt, a semi-transparent boob-tube that was filled to bursting point and more restrained high heels. Indeed, she had huge nipples, which were erect and threatened to puncture her diaphanous top. She spun round, mirroring Yoko's previous performance, causing the skirt to flare out and reveal the minute, transparent tanga she wore below it.

"Okay, I give in, you're the most beautiful pair of women I have ever seen."

"So, you've seen individuals who look better," Yoko started, but ruined her attack by bursting into laughter, probably due to my shell-shocked state.

I held up my hands to try to kill the humour. "Now, this is going to sound a bit strange, but the amount of flesh on display gives me a little problem."

"You think your erection will drive your blood pressure so low that you pass out?" Yoko giggled, setting Andrea off.

"Ah, a bit trickier than that. This reception was a bit of a surprise, but I think it will really help the project that I'm working on. The thing is that I'll need you to put some barrier cream on your hands and..."

350

Andrea quietened down immediately and gave me a hard stare. "Our hands and?"

"Ah, yes, any bare flesh that might be touched by anyone during the reception. But maybe hands would do it, I finished feebly."

Yoko raised her eyebrows and spread her arms wide. "You think nobody is going to attempt to catch a grope at this? I could wear a fucking suit of armour and someone would be trying to catch a feel. It may be true that, for some strange reason, men often get frightened off," she glared at Andrea, who had snorted inelegantly, "but I'm like a chocolate-covered schoolgirl for the discerning mature woman. Is that a surprise?"

The last question was clearly rhetorical, but I rose to the bait. "My experience with chocolate schoolgirls is a little limited," another snort from Andrea, "but I can see your point. Luckily, I have a lot of barrier cream, so we just need to cover any of your vulnerable areas."

"Who this we, white man?" she giggled. "I'm buggered if this is my problem. If you need this stuff on me, then get going," she turned and went into a bodybuilding pose that showed off the sculpted muscles of her back.

"Andrea, maybe you'd be a bit more comfortable with this?"

"You've got to be joking, why spoil her fun? She's a total pain in the arse, but funny as hell. You're the butt of the joke now, so get with it. After you're finished with her, you can do me. Then, after that, you can explain what this's all about.

Fuck, that's exactly where I don't want to go.

Well, at least I'll have something take my mind of it for a bit.

"Talking of butts, make sure you get right into my crack. As you can imagine, my lovely bum is a target for Sapphic matrons."

"No, don't worry about that," Andrea laughed. "Her arse is so well-used that it's like old leather, should be totally impervious without any treatment."

"I heard no complaints when you had your tongue deep into it just a little while ago," she retorted, before they burst into giggles once again. "Okay, we'll be a bit serious now, because, if we keep on like this, you're certainly going to burst your flies wide open."

I looked down at my prominent erection and groaned. *Despite the preparation in the shower, I'd never dreamed that I'd be faced with a challenge like this.*

Despite their promise, the girls continued to taunt me while I was cajoled into applying cream to more intimate bits of their anatomy. The only benefit of this was that Andrea forgot to chase me up on what exactly was behind this bizarre procedure.

After I finished, I quickly popped into my bathroom to wash my hands and prepare for the reception, running through scary thought of what could go wrong, with the aim of being more presentable when I returned. The girls were still making fine adjustments to each other's clothing when I returned, which almost undid all the good of my mental exercises.

352

Anyway, that's it now, nothing more I can do. Into the lion's den and completely up to me to ensure that no harm comes to these lovely ladies.

***

Although Hashimoto's penthouse was only eight floors above our apartment, we had to descend to ground level, leave the building and walk round to a separate private entrance. A guard at the reception desk nodded when Andrea announced us in fluent Japanese. *I doubt if he even noticed me and would probably have admitted the women without checking their credentials.* He could hardly take his eyes off Andrea's chest while he fumbled to open the private elevator for us.

The elevator had no obvious controls, whisking us rapidly to an entry lounge, where a hostess was waiting for us. "Welcome, Berner-san," she bowed and greeted me warmly in perfect mid-Atlantic English. "We are very glad that you were able to join us this evening. I heard you arrived only today, so I hope you aren't jet-lagged."

"Things feel a bit spacey every now and then, but basically I'm fine – and looking forward to meeting Hashimoto-san."

"Welcome also Tamborini-san and Takeuchi-san, the Chamber informed us you were accompanying Berner-san." She bowed again and, apart from a twinkle in her eye, seemed unperturbed by the costumes of my escorts, who had now attached themselves to my arms.

"Ah, may I now introduce you to Hashimoto-san," she waved a man forward who had just entered the lounge.

353

Hashimoto was short, but his immaculately tailored suit showed off his broad shoulders and slim waist, indicating that he was in very good shape. Indeed, if I had not known his true age, I would have guessed him to be in his early forties.

"Berner-san, very good to meet you," he bowed and offered me his business card. His English was perfect, with the slightest trace of a West Coast accent.

As I had been previously instructed, I took the card in both hands and carefully inspected it before shaking his hand. "Hashimoto-san, it's my honour. I'm afraid I don't have a business card, though. I should also introduce my minders from the Chamber – Andrea Tamborini and Yoko Takeuchi."

Somehow the two women were exchanging business cards with our host. *Where the hell do they conceal those? They don't have handbags and there's no way either of those rigouts have pockets.*

"You are lucky to have such very beautiful minders," he inspected them without a trace of embarrassment. "Come with me. I must get you a drink and introduce you to the others."

We followed him onto a room that must take up about half the area of this floor, with windows comprising three of the walls. Immediately we were approached by a waitress, who offered us flutes of Champagne. As I was introduced to the thirty or so guests, I was relieved to note that only Hashimoto was wearing a suit and that most men were as casually dressed as I was. The women were more glamorously attired, a couple almost rivalling my pair in terms of provocative outfits. I was interested

354

to note that, although I was introduced to wives, sons and daughters, almost all seemed to have some position in Hashimoto's business empire. *This is even better than the Colloquium, almost everyone on our hit list is here.*

I was being introduced to a young woman, a daughter and HR manager who was wearing a negligée of a filmy material that made it impossible to be sure, but strongly suggested, that she was naked below it, when I suddenly became viscerally aware of what I was actually doing here. It was likely that all the guests here, plus some of the staff, would be dead within a day or two. I was assassinating them as surely as if I shot them between the eyes. This must have registered on my face, as the girl asked if I was feeling unwell. I passed it off as jetlag, which seemed to satisfy her.

The next hour passed in a blur. Much of the time involved a discussion of bio-attack countermeasures with Hashimoto and his Head of Science, a rather severe-looking, middle-aged woman. She was wearing what seemed to be a rather modest black Cheongsam with a pattern of gold dragons, until I noticed it was split even higher than Yoko's dress. I tried not to get distracted by her shapely legs and evident lack of underwear while overviewing the different possible goals of terrorist attacks and how these relate to associated bio-weapons. I was quizzed in detail about how quickly attacks could be identified and defences mobilised, which was linked to blatant marketing of their capabilities to provide support, which could be improved if they were to partner with a Swiss company. *Ah, this is what the invitation is all about. Makes sense: these guys are smart cookies and will try to get the jump on their competition in any emerging market area.*

I acknowledged that there certainly could be synergy here, but emphasised that I had no responsibility for contracting support work. Nevertheless, I promised to check with the embassy and have them pass on appropriate links. Hashimoto seemed very pleased with this result, and happily accepted my excuse of leaving early due to increasing jetlag, helping me to round up my escorts, who were now part of a group of five women who were laughing as they chatted in Japanese, with a lot of body contact that came very close to gratuitous groping. *Well can't say I wasn't warned about this, but probably as well we're leaving now as I don't want them getting too friendly with my victims.*

***

The women were in good spirits on the way back to the flat, clearly having enjoyed themselves. Shoes were kicked off as soon as they entered our lounge and they then dropped together onto the settee, showing off very distracting areas of smooth flesh.

"That was great," Yoko slumped back with a contented sigh, "the booze was really top notch. I didn't get a chance to sample much of the nibbles though."

"What?" her partner elbowed her in the ribs. "You were grumphing away like a pig. No wonder you're so fat."

Yoko responded to this calumny by nipping a very prominent nipple, causing a squeak of pain. Andrea grabbed her chuckling aggressor and forced her arms back, before the attack turned into a deep kiss and wrestling morphed into sensuous caressing.

"Ladies, could you please restrict that to the privacy of your bedroom. Anyway, Yoko's reminded me that I ate nothing at all and I now feel distinctly peckish. Is there somewhere nearby where we could grab a quick bite?"

The mention of food had a wondrous effect, the girls breaking apart immediately. "Dinner, that's definitely a great idea. We just need to get into something more casual."

"And have a shower. It'd be a good idea to wash off that barrier cream."

Andrea looked at me quizzically. "Actually, that just reminds me, I was going to ask about that."

"Whatever," Yoko jumped to her feet. "We can chat about this while we're eating. So, Jan, are you going to help us rinse this stuff off. There's loads of space in the shower." She was about to say more, but squealed when Andrea slapped her bottom.

"Get in there, you bi slut. Anyway, there wouldn't be room unless he could get rid of that silly-looking erection. Right, we'll be ten, fifteen minutes max. You can sort out your priapism problem in the interim."

I quickly went into the bathroom and scrubbed my hands before setting up a secure link from my tablet to Brugg and downloading the video from the camera that masqueraded as a button on my shirt. Due to the time difference, it was just after lunch in

Switzerland and I was able to assemble most of the core team, Helen, Pirmin, Rashmi and Doris, for a quick debriefing.

There was a dazed silence after the news that I'd pre-empted Rashmi's carefully developed plan, but they all acknowledged that the opportunity had been too good to miss.

"Bloody unbelievable," Doris commented as she scanned the synthesis of the party video, "you've accounted for just about everyone on our hitlist. Maybe Rashmi's megadeath option won't be needed."

"Who's missing?"

"Actually, it's three of the big ones. Shoko, the wife; Tatsu, the son; and Easton, the Nazi."

"Shit, that's not good," my previous elation disappeared. "Those are all key players and, if Andrea is right, maybe this Shoko is the most important. Do we have any idea why they weren't at the party this evening?"

"Not a clue," Doris responded. "But your mike is very sensitive so we can mine the audio record for clues while we're doing the auto-translate from Japanese to English. It'll take a little while, but I'll get back to you after the scan has run."

"Fine, I need to go for dinner now, but I'll contact you again thereafter."

"Have fun with the girls," Doris laughed.

"You sound jealous."

"Oh, I am. I've seen video of Andrea's partner and she's luscious. Wouldn't mind waking up between the two of them."

Now that's a thought that's doing my priapism

problem no good at all.

***

We ate in an Asian fusion restaurant located in the ground level of the apartment building. We were all in shorts and t-shirts, with the girls still notable, but not so spectacular in this pedestrian attire. Even before we ordered, I pushed to control the conversation in order to pre-empt Andrea's questions.

"So, Yoko, what's with all the different martial arts that you seem to be into? I've been trained to fight, but mainly with firearms and weapons like tasers, gas sprays and electro-batons. Do your arts really help you against them?"

"Of course, the focus of these arts is on unarmed combat or defence against conventional cutting or blunt force weapons. Not a lot of help against a high-powered gun at a distance handled by a professional, but often very useful if your assailant is close up and naïve enough to think that having a gun puts them in control. Even better if you're a little girl up against a big man; over-confidence is the worst thing you can bring to a fight."

"Well, you're not very tall, but I certainly wouldn't give much for my chances against you."

"Just as well, as you have none," she grinned to take the bite out of her words. "But look at my skinny lover, would she frighten you?"

"Well, yes. But mainly because I know you'd kick seven shades of shit out of me if I touched her."

"Not a stupid answer that," Andrea commented. "Should I order for us, while Yoko sorts out your misconceptions? Would white wine be okay?"

I nodded while the girls exchanged knowing glances. "Yes, definitely better not to mess with me. But you underestimate the large-breasted one at your peril. I did the first time I fought her. That's something I won't do again."

"What, mixed martial arts? I can't see Andrea in an octagon somehow or other."

"Of course not, silly," I manager to roll from one of Yoko's rib-cracking nudges. "I'm talking about wrestling."

Andrea had been chatting to the waitress when she suddenly appeared to pick up on what was being said. "No, Yoko, I don't think you need to go into that. I mean you really don't want to tell Jan how I completely thrashed you, do you?"

"This sounds fascinating and I certainly want to know how on earth anyone was able to thrash you, especially wrestling."

"Because I'm built like a concrete outhouse?" she raised an eyebrow.

Treading on dangerous ground here. "Well, I wouldn't quite put it like that."

"That was exactly how he put it, or a more Brit English equivalent thereof," Andrea threw gasoline on the fire I was trying to put out.

"Yes, I know I'm heavily built, but I'm happy with my body as it is," she posed and flexed her dramatic biceps. "And my lover is also happy with it…"

"Very happy, if not very, very happy," Andrea squeezed the muscles to show that they were rock hard, before starting to kiss them.

"Oh, I definitely believe you both, and think your body is truly fantastic, but I think you understand my scepticism about you losing a wrestling match to Andrea. Did you let her win?"

"Who, Yoko?" Andrea giggled. "Choosing to lose? She'd fight to the death to win a game of tiddlywinks against a 5-year-old. Okay, you may as well tell him now. It was oil wrestling."

"Oil wrestling? I've heard of mud wrestling, but that's a new one on me. No, wait a minute, I remember having seen something about olive oil wresting. But doesn't that involve swarthy Turkish farmers?"

They were both giggling now. "You couldn't be more wrong," Yoko wrapped her arm round her partner while she poured wine. "Just swap that picture in your mind for one with naked girls wrestling."

"More specifically, the two of us," Andrea raised her glass and we had a silent toast while my brain over-heated with this image.

"What, this is like pole dancing, in a club full of dodgy guys?"

"Well, you do get those also, but this case is strictly ladies only and it's not play, it's a real competition. A lot of the MMA women are really into it."

"The lesbians and bi ones, anyway," Andrea interrupted. "Also, quite a few high grades from martial arts that include any form of grappling. It's an incredible test of your technique."

"And extremely erotic, of course."

"Especially if you're a masochist who likes getting well thrashed," Andrea blocked a slap and defused potential escalation with a deep kiss.

"So, Andrea thrashed you at this oil wrestling. It still seems unlikely."

"This was my point about over-confidence. Unless she beat me to death with her huge knockers or poked me in the eye with the deadly acorns that she has for nipples," she wriggled to escape as Andrea started to tickle her, "she looked like she hadn't a chance. But that Aiki stuff works particularly well against stronger opponents and so she had a lucky win."

"Yes lucky, because she was caught out. But I still beat her 9 times out of 10."

"No way, more like 40%, when you get lucky again."

"At least 80%, if not more."

"No way more than 60%."

"I'm not so interested in the exact success rate," I broke in, "but I have enough problems working out how women covered in oil can wrestle, much less how Andrea can beat you."

"Yes, it requires a lot of skill."

"Except for the case of the fan-girls who just come along to be groped by their idols," Andrea added.

"But how does it work? I can't imagine how you can get a grip on anything. Except maybe hair, I suppose."

"All the hair grabbing is for bimbos in boys' bars." Yoko shook her head, as if in despair at their foolishness. "The rules quite clear in our wrestling

362

clubs: no punches, kicks or other blows; no grabs of face or hair; a kind of classical wrestling or grappling."

"In the nude, which does give a couple of other options."

"And added erotic aspects."

"Um, I think I'm beginning to get the idea. So, Andrea is better at this?"

"She's amazingly sneaky with her arm and leg locks."

"And my tits are so gorgeous, that my opponents are shell-shocked."

"Well, they often waste too much time going for grips on the deadly acorns."

"And the next they know they're in a headlock with a fist up their bum!" the girls finished together, bursting into yet another fit of giggles.

I sat back to enjoy the cabaret: the women spinning increasingly unlikely yarns that, nevertheless, seemed to be based on a Tokyo subculture that was weird beyond my wildest imaginings.

The meal involved many small dishes of spicy food, accompanied with different types of rice, bread and crackers, but I ate without noticing it, completely entranced. They squabbled constantly, but this almost seemed like a form of foreplay, as it inevitably ended in a kiss or a hug.

My tension had disappeared by the time I paid and we headed back to the apartment. Unfortunately, when the girls disappeared off to the bathroom, yet again leaving doors open, I realised that it was time to link up with Brugg. Now I had to face up to the reality of what this operation involved: searching out and assassinating the last of my victims.

***

My unilateral decision to upend our entire plan for the Tokyo operation had caused chaos in the Zenith team, especially those having to field questions from Bundesrätin Zwicky. This was not only Schmidt and Supersaxo, but also Helen and Rashmi. As soon as I logged in, Helen warned me that the Commander wanted to set up a special link with Zwicky ASAP, but I might want to delay that. She then passed me to Doris.

"Good news boss, the audio mining came up with a link to our missing targets. Their absence was evidently noted, with several people explaining that they were together for a special dinner at a Fugu restaurant. That's…"

"Yup, I know, the fish that kills you if it's not handled properly. But I guess that they'll have left if by now, if they were there during the reception."

"Yes, but there was one interesting, whispered conversation, which seemed like salacious gossip. This suggested that, afterwards, they were heading off to a club. It seems to be very dodgy, even by the standards of some of the places we've visited."

Shit, thank God the Commander isn't on the line yet. "Christ on a bike, how fucked up is it?"

"You'll love it," I groaned when Rüdi joined in. "Very specific: gay, old men and young boys, but with a hard BDSM edge. It's been rumoured to include everything up to and including snuff, but it's very exclusive and very tight, run by the

364

Yakuza. Most of the rumours are probably pure fantasy, but it's certainly at the extreme edge of what's already a very bizarre sub-culture."

"Fuck, Rüdi, they should have sent you here instead of me!"

"No way, Jose! I'm gay and into a lot of queer shit, but you wouldn't get me within a mile of these lunatics."

Now that has me really shit scared. "Right, if we assume that they're now in this place, can you get me into it?"

"Funny you should ask, boss," Doris sounded very smug. "Not only can I confirm that the terrible threesome are in said club, but I can get you in as a guest of Shoko Hashimoto."

"Good, make it so. What's the name of this place?"

"Kamen no kokuhaku, seems to translate as Confessions of a Mask. Weird or what? Anyway, details downloaded to your tablet."

"I can't really pass up on this chance, can I?" *Is this a rhetorical question or am I really hoping that someone will come up with an excuse for me to get out of this?*

"I guess not, boss," Pirmin answered. "I suppose we need to stall the Commander and hope to get away with it when you come up with some really good news afterwards."

"But you better take Andrea with you," Helen added. "You're not armed and these are tough customers."

I can't get the giggling girl in the sexy clothes out of my head, but Helen's right. This woman's head of security, and can out-wrestle Yoko, so I've got to bring her in. The mission is far too important for me to fuck it up trying to be macho.

"Okay, Doris, set that up. I guess I'd better gird up my loins and then beg for some help." ...*even if I still have doubts whether I want it or not.*

***

When I returned to the lounge Yoko was again clad only in slippers and Andrea was wearing a very short robe that I identified as a Happi coat. She spun to show me the rather suggestive manga schoolgirl image on the back. "What do you think? I've got another one like this if you want to slip into something more relaxing."

"Nope, wouldn't work," Yoko quickly added. "It'd be too loose at the chest and would never close over his belly. However, I've got another pair of slippers and you could dress like me. It's very relaxing."

My eyes automatically ran over the naked flesh on display. "Not for me, it's not," I raised my eyes to heaven, setting off the giggles again. "Anyway, I was checking in with Brugg, so I need to have a chat with Andrea. Work stuff."

"It's okay, Jan, Yoko is security cleared. Full check when we moved in together."

"Even then, this isn't like any normal operation. I think I need to talk to you alone."

"But whatever went on upstairs was part of the op and Yoko came along. Actually, I think you need to let us know a bit more about what actually happened there."

"I really can't and, to be honest, I think it's best

366

that you don't know. Presently I'm working with the Zodiac core. Not even the Bundesrätin has been briefed as yet, so there's a chance I'll get well reamed after this happens."

"I get the distinct impression you want me to help you with something."

"Very perceptive! I'd prefer not to involve you, but you know the stakes here."

"Without going into details, does this involve something dangerous?"

"I'd be lying if I said it didn't."

"And I could help reduce risks, increase the chance of success?"

"I think so, maybe. But my team are sure that it could help a lot."

"Including Doris?"

"She's the one setting up details now."

"Well, I think I'll agree to anything you propose. So, now, would our chances be improved if my girlfriend here tagged along?"

"Okay, she could break my back with her pinkie. But, as she admitted, there's a difference between modern combat and martial arts. We can't even think about including her."

Andrea patted her lover's head. "I suppose this little shrinking violet would just get in the way. All those black belts don't really count for much. But I did forget to mention to you that she's also reserve Ozzy special forces. Two tours in the Middle East. She's probably seen more real combat than you have, despite your advanced years." The women smiled smugly at each other then turned to face me. "So, is she in or out?"

"Bugger, I don't know. Okay, she's in, but only because the consequences of failure are so catastrophic. I don't have time to go into details now, but I promise you that I'll give you the entire story when we get back." *If we get back.* "But we need to get moving fast. What do you know about a place called," I checked my handy, "Kamen no kokuhaku?"

For the first time, all trace of amusement vanished from the faces of the women. "You have got to be joking!" Yoko gasped.

"Well, you're certainly not vanilla anything, if that's where you want to hang out. That place is the stuff of urban myths. It's supposed to be the most extreme SM in Tokyo, which is quite something. Also, lots of wild, gay sex, involving very young boys."

"And run by the Yakuza," Yoko added.

"Well, you could say that about half of the strip bars, gambling dens, soaplands and perv-clubs in Kabuki-cho. But that's missing the point. Kamen no kokuhaku is ultra-exclusive: members and their guests only. It's so exclusive that nobody knows how you can actually get membership. I guess that, if you have to ask, you're already disqualified."

"I've heard that it's hereditary, passed down by the top members of the Yakuza organisations. It seems to be the equivalent to a church for these gangs, one place where a truce holds and is immune to their normal squabbles."

"Anyway, the bottom line is you can't get in, unless you're thinking of taking the place by force. For that you'll need more than us, at the very least a couple of police swat squads. Even if you could organise this on short notice, which is probably impossible, there's no way that the Yakuza won't get a warning. They've got informants at all levels of the police."

"Well, actually that's the easy bit. Doris already has us registered as guests of Shoko Hashimoto, who is a member. Actually, if I remember details from the associated file correctly, the son, Tatsu, is also a member in his own right."

"Of course," Andrea swatted her bow. "Shoko's got high level Yakuza links and a strangely close relationship to her son, the Mishima fan-boy." She clearly noted my look of confusion. "Kamen no kokuhaku, in English *Confessions of a Mask*, is the title of a Mishima novel. It has a homosexual theme and often linked to previous works glorifying shudo, that's man-boy love, and suicide. It's just the place you'd expect to find Tatsu and maybe his mother also, if she's as kinky as some of the rumours suggest."

"Well, if we can get into the club, what would we come up against?"

"Well, there'll be lots of Yakuza guards: in a place like that almost certainly armed with swords. Even though I can't imagine that anyone seriously thinks that place would be raided, it's just normal practice for the big gang bosses. It's said they don't go for a shit without a bodyguard present. If anyone discovers our intrusion, it'll be Mortal Kombat in a very big way. So, do you think you can get your hands on a couple of assault rifles?"

"Don't you think that'd make us a bit

obvious?" My rhetorical question drew wry grins. "Anyway, if all went well with our invitation and the Yakuza don't mess in, what'll the problems be?"

"Well, that depends on where your targets are and what you're intending to do with them," Yoko frowned. "I take it you don't want to just have a quick chat."

"Well, I know where they are. It seems to be a private room in the basement. It's called," I checked again, "Sado kōshaku fujin. Does that mean anything to you?"

The women exchanged worried looks before Andrea spoke up. "The title of a Mishima play. It translates as Madame de Sade, which might not be a good omen if this is Shoko's usual hang-out."

"But, if can get into this private dungeon, then we're maybe facing our three targets and maybe a guard or two. Surely that's doable?"

"I'd say at least one guard, but also whoever else is participating in their SM fantasy. I can't see it just being the three of them working their kinks out together."

"Good point, I guess we just have to hope that they include a lot of bondage with their SM. But it would be doable?"

"Not completely impossible?" Yoko looked at her partner.

"Only slightly impossible, maybe even highly improbable?"

"Of course, this assumes that your chubby colleague can actually fight…"

"I'm sure he can…"

"Without a gun…"

"Well, maybe…"

"Up against an expert swordsman?"

They looked at me and the silence drew out. "Well, I'm game if you are," I stated, hoping I sounded more confident than I really was.

"I think we're already committed," Andrea concluded. "Just try not to get us killed."

"And you've got a good incentive," Yoko grinned with a feral light in her eye. "If we can't protect you, you're very likely to receive a sound buggering before they torture you to death."

Fuck, that's an incentive that I don't even want to think about.

CHAPTER EIGHTEEN

The ladies brightened up as they took over the task of dressing us up in a manner appropriate to this club. The first challenge was making me look the part, as the ladies reckoned there would be very few gaijin in such a place. Nevertheless, Easton's presence indicated that any of Shoko's guests would not be excluded. They started with a pair of latex shorts, apparently used by Andrea for some kind of grappling training. Luckily, these were extremely flexible, but stressed to bursting point when I finally squeezed into them, after being stripped and coated with oil by Yoko. To provide extra re-assurance, I added my own belt to reinforce the waist. Even then, my belly hung over the top in a rather ridiculous manner. This was hidden to some extent by the Happi coat donate by Yoko, which fit my shoulders surprisingly well, but barely tied over my gut. *Must really do something about this. At least it's served to cheer up the girls, who evidently enjoy making me look ridiculous.*

The women disappeared while I was trying to fit on a pair of zori sandals that were several sizes too small, quickly returning fully dressed. To my surprise, they were wearing matching desert-camouflage combat suits, complete with tan boots that laced up to mid-calf.

I scratched my head. "How's this going to work? I look like a rent-boy, a bottom of the range one, and you two would fit in as part of swat team."

"Ah," Andrea smiled, "this is just for the taxi."

Simultaneously the women zipped the fronts of their suits to below the navel, demonstrating that they were both bra-less and strongly suggesting that no other underwear was present. "Same tactic as before, we capture attention and nobody spots how ridiculous you look."

"Yes, especially if one of those watermelons falls out," Yoko laughed.

"No, it'll be okay," she gave a little shimmy and immediately her huge left breast popped out. "Well, I just need to zip up a wee bit."

I was greatly cheered by their giggles, but they did little to cure my fundamental misgivings about this entire action. "Right, both of you zip up and we can hit the road." I surreptitiously clipped the pouch from the diplomatic bag over my belt, hoping that it didn't show. *Hopefully I won't need this stuff, but better safe than sorry.*

***

The autonomic taxi drove quickly along main roads, through Yotsuya to Shinjuku according to the bilingual map displayed. Then it wound through a labyrinth of narrow lanes crowded with pedestrians, a number of whom were clearly very drunk. Our destination turned out to be a bare steel door set in an ugly cube of a building, four stories high and clad in material that resembled orange marble. There was no name or any other indication of what it could be or how it could be entered. Nevertheless, when we approached the door, it opened silently, no doubt in response to a signal from my comm unit, which resembled a bulky watch. We seemed to be attracting attention from passers-by, but I was not sure if this was due to us entering this club or the fact that the girls, linking arms on either side of me, had their suits zipped down. Based on a quick glance, it looked like Yoko's zip was even lower than before, clearly showing her smooth mons. *Well, if I was a guard, I sure-as-shit wouldn't be looking at me.*

The outer door closed to isolate us in a small entry lobby, with walls, roof and ceiling mirrors and a small screen displaying a message in Japanese. "We're being scanned and that's a list of proscribed articles; firearms, tasers and the like."

Shit, I hope there's nothing to pick up in my kit. No sooner had I started to worry than the inner door opened, allowing access into a short corridor leading to a large bar area. The walls of both the corridor and the bar were covered with framed pictures, posters and newspaper cuttings. Although text was mainly in Japanese, it was clear that this was a shrine to the author who provided the name to this club.

Lighting was very subdued, but our entry seemed to have caused less interest than I had expected. Between the bar and tables distributed around the periphery of the room, a central area lit by spotlights provided the floorshow. A naked young man, hardly more than a boy, was roped to a frame resembling a St Andrew's cross and being whipped by another lad, clad only in a loincloth. Nearby, a middle-aged man, similarly naked and strapped face-down to something like a vaulting-horse, was being buggered by a much older man who was wearing a bizarre harness of leather straps,

374

buckles and pointed studs. A naked boy stood to the side, dropping hot wax from a candle onto their victim's back. From the scars on his back, the boy played a bit of the M in addition to the S side of this perversion. As we neared, I could see that both of the tortured men wore ball gags, which explained the grunts and whines rather the screams and curses that would be expected to result from such treatment.

The audience were difficult to make out, both due to the contrast in lighting and my desire to avoid rubbernecking. Nevertheless, I noted mainly couples or groups of men who were either in Japanese attire: Kimonos or Happi coats for the older ones, loincloths for the boys; or were clad in leather and latex. In both cases the main difference with age appeared to involve the density of tattoos on display. Prime audience locations seemed to be booths at the back, the couple I could make out both contained old guys with retinues of naked catamites. Or possibly, in one case, a pair of twin boys and matching androgynous twin girls.

"Stop ogling," Andrea nudged me and whispered, "you've got to make it look as if you're at home here."

"What, you're okay here?" I whispered back.

"Hardly, I'm pissing myself. Anyway, keep straight ahead. The sign there shows the way to the private rooms downstairs. Upstairs is open and, strangely enough, the Japanese translates as *multi-user dungeons*," she snorted.

"Okay, Doris couldn't get anything on internal layout. Where is the Madame de Sade room?" We had passed through the main lounge and into a lobby with a lift and stairs running up and down.

"The sign indicates that, at the bottom of the stairs you go left for *Middle Ages* and *Kyoko's House* and right for *De Sade* and *Patriotism*. The four rooms down here are all named after rather extreme Mishima works."

"Wonderful, probably all full of right-wing fuckwits." At the bottom of the stairs, I peeked through a heavy curtain closing off the corridor to the left, to see that it was again decorated with Mishima memorabilia, but otherwise empty. To the right, however, guards stood in front of the two doors into the private rooms. In both cases, the heavily-built men wore kimonos and were carrying sheathed swords. As soon as we pushed through the curtain, the men grasped the hilts of their swords and the nearer one issued what was clearly a challenge in Japanese.

Yoko responded, clearly trying to explain why we were there while Andrea slipped closer to me and whispered a translation. "This guy isn't impressed by an electronic invitation. Nobody interrupts the Hashimotos when they're in that room. Any invited guests enter with them. That's it, he's telling us to bugger-off in no uncertain terms." This was emphasised by him starting to draw his sword.

Yoko turned away as if to leave, then whirled into an incredible flying back-kick. The heel of her boot hit the side of his head with an ominous crack and he crashed against a wall, knocking down a photo of a young Mishima, before he slumped to the floor while Yoko landed in a low crouching posture. I noticed that the other guard had drawn his sword and was moving towards his colleague's assailant just before I was roughly pushed to the side and Andrea moved to intercept him.

I started to move behind her when Yoko grabbed my arm. "Don't get in the way, she knows what she's doing." The guard was clearly perplexed by the approach of the unarmed woman, and even more so when she gave a little shake that exposed both of her breasts. He backed off a couple of steps, then suddenly attacked, his blade slicing towards Andrea's neck. For a moment it looked like it would be impossible for the woman to avoid being decapitated but, in a sinuous move, she stepped inside the blow and then her attacker was flying over her back to smash face down into the floor with his sword arm caught in a vicious lock that was clearly extremely painful. His scream was muffled by Andrea's knee, which was pressed against his cheek, and died away when Yoko jumped forward and her boot crushed the man's larynx.

I felt totally drained, but the women were not even breathing heavily. "Do you think anyone heard anything," Andrea asked while she replaced her boobs and zipped up her suit.

"I doubt it, that went relatively quietly. Also, there's the heavy curtain and this seems to be the kind of place that a muffled scream wouldn't raise an eyebrow in any case." I quickly checked the guards. The first seemed to have a broken neck, but was still alive, while the second was unconscious but clearly struggling to breath. I extracted knock-out patches from my pouch and slapped one on each of them. *Probably superfluous, as these guys are no threat in the near future. But better safe than sorry.*

I checked my comm unit, but there was no external signal at all. Nevertheless, when we approached the door to the Madame de Sade room, I could hear it unlock and it then slid silently aside. *Thank you, Doris!*

Yoko led us through the door, sliding her feet forward in a way that made no discernible noise. I followed with Andrea at my shoulder and saw that our entry had not been noticed by those within, their attention clearly elsewhere. At the far end of the room, two young men were shackled to the wall. One of them was facing forward and whimpering as his thighs and belly were lashed by a cane wielded by a wiry Japanese man with a rising sun tattoo covering his back. The other victim was facing the wall, grunting as he was being buggered by a muscular gaijin sporting a huge, tattooed swastika. *No gags here, these bastards want to hear the suffering of their victims,*

To the side, two girls were tied together on a heavy wooden table, with the face of each forced into the groin of the other. An older woman with intricate tattoos that covered her entire body, with the exception of face, hands and feet, was watching the men with rapt attention while she absent-mindedly tortured the girls with a device like a soldering iron, ignoring their muffled screams. The entire setting was so weird that the fact that nobody present was wearing a stitch of clothing hardly seemed worth noting.

"Fucking hell!" Yoko cursed aloud, causing the tableau facing us to freeze before our targets turned slowly to face us in a manner that was almost comical.

Tatsu and Easton were obviously enraged, but Shoko seemed unperturbed. "I don't know how you gaijin got in here," she spoke clearly enunciated English, without a trace of an accent, "but you might have a chance of surviving the evening if you leave immediately and run very fast." She smiled in a way that radiated pure psychopathic evil. "You may have heard that these are snuff rooms, which generally isn't the case. However, we would be happy to make an exception in your case." She casually lifted a heavy knife from a side table and tossed it to her son. "If they're not out of here in two seconds, start cutting. But try not to kill them immediately, or at least not the women. I quite fancy playing with them."

I absently noted that the door had closed behind us as we moved apart to face the grinning youth. "Good, you're not running. I hoped that would happen," Shoko smiled with pleasure. "I'm sure Tatsu can manage this alone, but maybe you could help, Easton-san, so that he doesn't accidently kill them too soon."

The South African selected a metal baseball bat from a rack on a side wall and smiled while he flexed his muscles to show off his bodybuilder physique. He did, however, look a bit silly due to his blood-covered erection.

"Nazi for me, knife boy for you and, Jan, keep out of the way," Yoko whispered before the women

379

slid forward, to the evident amusement of the two men.

I was about to object, but then noticed a brief frown on the face of the Hashimoto matriarch. *She's not a dumb as the men and has spotted that these women are not the walkovers that she first took them for. As I remember it, she's a lot higher grade than her son, karate with a weapons speciality.* Then I noticed for the first time, that she was not quite naked and had silky scabbards high on both thighs. *Sai, that's it. Christ, I wish I had a gun.* I slid slowly along the wall behind me, noting that she was focused on the obvious combatants. *A really fucking big gun.*

With my back to the wall, I had an unimpeded view of Tatsu's first feint with the knife and Andrea's condescending smile as she casually slapped it aside. Yoko and Easton were facing each other, but seemed in no hurry to start fighting.

"What is it with weedy Japanese boys and big knifes or swords?" Andrea goaded him, probably using English to ensure that Easton could understand what she was saying. "I can see that you've got a tiny dick, but surely there are other ways of compensating? It must be humiliating with your boyfriend here; he'd hardly feel anything when you slip that up his bum. Do you fist him or use a…"

Shoko looked to be on the point of saying something when Tatsu cracked and, with a scream of rage jumped forward and stabbed at his tormentor's stomach. He flew through the air and, although attempting to breakfall, crashed heavily into a rack of whips and dildos. Andrea faced him with an even wider smile. "That all you got, boy-fucker? Just watch what you're doing with that blade as you may accidently cut off your micro-penis. Not that it'd really make much difference though."

Shoko angrily shouted something in Japanese at her son, but he was beyond listening. He charged forward, slashing with the knife and was thrown across the room to smash into the table holding the girls, missing his mother only due to her rapid move to the side. Easton clearly couldn't help watching this turnabout and grunted when Yoko's fist sank into his solar plexus. Despite his evident pain, he attempted to swipe at the woman with his bat, but that was easily blocked before Yoko brought her knee into his groin and then proceeded to clinically beat him into a pulp with a flurry of punches and kicks.

Andrea had remained in place as she watched Tatsu fight his way to his feet, seeming dazed and having lost the knife in his fall. A very faint hissing sound drew my attention to his mother, who had drawn the sai and was waving her son back. She reinforced this with a stream of Japanese that, even without translation, was clearly dismissive.

I started to worry as Shoko slowly faced up to Andrea, but then relaxed when I saw that Yoko was now brandishing a whip that seemed to be based on a cat o' nine tails. I now focused on Tatsu, who was slowly bending towards his knife, glaring at Andrea with a look of pure hatred. *No way is this bastard backing off just because his mum told him to!*

381

Luckily, everyone in the room seemed to have completely forgotten me and Tatsu was completely oblivious as I edged behind him. His fingers had just reached the hilt when I jumped onto his back, one arm round his neck and my other hand jamming the soldering iron into his left eye.

His blood-curling scream was all the distraction my companions needed. Yoko's whip cracked across Shoko's face while Andrea turned to avoid a blade that seemed to have been thrown as pure reflex.

I forced concentration back to my own fight as Tatsu dropped forward onto the floor, cracking the elbow of the arm I had round his neck and causing me to drop the soldering iron. Despite his evident pain, he managed to smash the back of his head into my face, breaking my nose and drenching us both in a spurt of blood. Although my eyes were watering, I could see that the squirming man had almost reach the knife and, in desperation, reached around and stuck two fingers into his cauterised eye socket and wrenched. As he his back arched in agony, I rolled off him, grabbed the knife, rolled back and jabbed it as hard as I could into his ear. I was amazed that he was still squirming when I struggled to my feet, but a heavy stomp to the back of his neck stopped that.

I was now aware that the women were beside me, looking concerned. "Shit, is all that blood yours?" Andrea required, then she noticed my nose.

She turned to her partner. "Just looks like a broken beak. You want to sort that out?"

"Okay, but you hold him, I don't want blood all over me."

382

I was grabbed from behind while Yoko reached forward to straighten my nose, which was as painful as having it broken in the first place. "Right, now to stop the bleeding." Her fist shot forward, her knuckles impacting on either side of my nose. "That'll bruise the capillaries, so you should be fine now. Just need to get the worst of the blood off you and then we can shoot the crow."

Behind a screen in the corner of the room, there was a very small shower and a wardrobe that held the clothes of those present. I stripped off my blood-stained Happi coat and dropped it on the floor, leaning into the shower to wash blood off my face and upper torso. I then selected a yukata that must have belonged to Easton, at the last moment remembering to transfer the videorecorder pin from my discarded clothing. Finally, with a sign of relief, I yanked off my zoris and replaced them with a much larger pair from one of the men.

"Can we go now?" Combat adrenaline seemed to be wearing off and Andrea was shaking slightly.

"Just a minute, you two drag the guards in here out of the way while I collect the samples we need." The women obeyed without questions, but both were evidently curious about what I was up to. Tatsu and Easton were both dead, the latter looking like he had been run over by a truck – several times. Shoko was unconscious but still breathing, although from the angle of her head it looked like her neck was probably broken. It took only moments for me to find veins and punch the little extraction vials into them in order to obtain the few millilitres of blood that we needed for analysis. This was a low priority goal, checking that Hashimoto's crew were using exactly the same protective virus as the Europeans and hence confirming that their STD would work for all virus variants. Nevertheless, the chance presented here was too good to miss.

Minutes later we were strolling back through the bar towards the exit. Little had changed except that the anal rapist clad in straps had been replaced by a naked youth in Yakuza tattoos who was being egged on by an older gang member wearing a loincloth and a hachimaki headband. I realised then that the girls' suits were again unzipped to the crotch, but nobody at all seemed to be paying us any attention.

We left the building and caught a taxi within seconds, piling in and slumping together onto the cramped bench seat in the back. *Jesus, after all of that, our exit was a bit of an anti-climax. Not that I'm complaining though.*

My slip into self-congratulation was spoiled by Yoko, who whispered into my ear. "That was a demolition charge that you slapped onto the wall as we left the torture chamber, wasn't it?"

"Not exactly… Well, kind of…"

"Explosive, yes or no?"

"Yes, but…"

"What's the kill radius? How much collateral do you expect?"

"Tricky to estimate, as it was dimensioned for a much bigger room. I'm pretty sure that impacts won't go beyond basement level, ground floor at the worst."

"But nothing outside the building?"

384

"With the heavy-duty sound insulation they have in there, I would say no chance, All you'd feel is a little ground tremble, which wouldn't even be noticed here in Tokyo."

"Thank God," she sighed. "That place was full of complete loonies and their removal from the gene pool can only be a good thing. Now, I suppose you need to tell us exactly what's going on."

"I need to report back home as soon as we get to the flat, but immediately after that, I promise."

"Oh, well, if you try to renege, I guess we can always torture the details out of you. The de Sade dungeon there gave me some ideas."

Wonderful. What's going to be trickier, telling the Commander and Zwicky what I've been up to or letting the girls know what I did at Hashimoto's reception?

CHAPTER NINETEEN

At the apartment, I immediately scuttled of to my room while then ladies went into a huddle, talking quietly with arms around each other, staring into each other's eyes. After carefully closing the door, I established a secure link to Brugg and downloaded my video record, while Pirmin assembled the core team and set up a later meeting with Zwicky and the top brass. Although it was approaching midnight in Japan, it was only late afternoon in Switzerland.

"Well, to my utter amazement, we've done it. I've only been in the country about," I quickly checked, "14 hours and we've completely decapitated the organisation here. Whether it was Hashimoto or his wife who was actually pulling the strings, they're both gone along with just about all of the upper echelons of this plot."

"Well, we've no evidence that most of them were actively involved." Helen frowned.

"But no evidence that they weren't. Even circumstantial evidence is good enough for me in this particular case. There have been, or will be, collateral deaths. But this was inevitable and the numbers are less than we had any right to expect."

"I've just quickly scanned your video file," Doris smiled. "How do you manage to get into such truly screwed-up situations? Anyway, do you want me to redact this before it goes up the chain of command?"

"No way. Everyone, up to and including

Zwicky, needs to know exactly what was needed to achieve the goals that we were set."

"I knew you were going to say that. Fine, the file is now open to all in Zodiac at our clearance or above. The bit with you wriggling about with that naked Japanese guy is a bit graphic, though," she laughed.

"Whatever... I couldn't care less. I've also got blood samples from all three of these nutters, so I need to get them back to you ASAP."

"I can't see how anything can get traced back to you," Pirmin pointed out. "The bomb in the club basement will be handled internally by the Yakuza; there's no way that they're going to be running to the police. Nevertheless, potential links between you and the spate of unexplained deaths at the top levels of Hashimoto's company could emerge, so it's a good reason to get out of Tokyo soonest."

"I've implemented that already," Doris added smugly. "You have a seat on the Swiss flight back from Narita tomorrow at eleven. It's the equivalent to the flight you arrived on today, maybe now yesterday your time?"

Jesus, could we really have started off with an almost impossible project and have it nailed down in a single day? And all of this due to events we hadn't planned for. Can we really have dodged a bullet like this?

"Fine, let's go for that. What else is critical? How about Helena, the Deutscher daughter?"

"Good and bad news there," Rüdi spoke up. "The good is that she's been shot and killed by German security after we gently suggested that she was linked to terrorist activities. The bad is that she'd already released the virus at the Frankfurt international departures terminal. This is where our isolation strategy fell down: we hadn't given our contacts in the Big Canton enough information to allow them to realise just how serious the risk was. So, the airport wasn't closed down."

"Buggeration! And flights were going to?"

"It's bloody Frankfurt, easier to list where flights weren't going to. I think Iceland, Greenland and the Antarctic are okay, but I wouldn't go on the barriers for anywhere else, especially as intercontinental flights focus particularly on regional hubs."

It really sounds like Rüdi's losing it, but maybe that's quite understandable under the circumstances. "Right, so there has definitely been at least one release and, possibly, a few before that. The critical point is that the vector there is closed down and we can assure nothing more from that source. As I'm fairly sure Asia is also down, from now on it's pandemic control and that's not our problem."

"I hope that's the case," Pirmin sighed. "Anyway, we're going to open to the management levels now."

We were joined not only by the Bundesrätin and my superiors from the security services, but also a half dozen others I didn't recognise.

As ever, Zwicky came straight to the point. "As I understand it, you have already assassinated all the targets on your hit list, is that correct?"

"Well, some aren't actually dead yet, but will

be within a couple of days. This includes Hashimoto and his wife, the prime targets. We also have eight out of ten of his senior executives which, given the tight linkages between them, are almost certainly key members of this conspiracy. The missing ones are currently in South America, on honeymoon together. I don't think they're on the critical path, but it might be worth eliminating them at some point. Further, we've also got an undetermined number of managers and other employees impacted by our actions at Hashimoto's reception." *Shit, sounds not so bad when presented like that.*

"So, the Asian threat is gone?" Zwicky frowned at me and, out of the corner of my eye, I could see the Commander hoping for a positive answer.

"I wish this case was simple enough to give you a clear yes-no answer, but it isn't. I guess it's probable that, after removing everyone from the top, Hashimoto's organisation will either fold or will take so long to recover that we can neutralise it at our leisure. However, we can't guarantee that there isn't another senior player we haven't spotted or an autonomic protocol that will lead to release of the horror or super-horror viruses. I really doubt it though. It's nothing better than a gut feeling here, but it doesn't seem the way that these cult-like conspiracies work. The person at the top simply does not delegate responsibility."

"Okay, Berner, say that you're right. What do we do now?"

I shrugged hopelessly. "Above my pay level I'm afraid, Frau Bundesrätin. We have either reduced or eliminated the genocidal options, but the population control virus is loose already. We currently have one airborne virus that spreads rapidly and a defensive STD that is inherently slowly spreading. I have already proposed a strategy to limit Swiss vulnerability, so it's up to the Bundesrat to decide if and how to implement it. For crisis management at an international or global scale, I don't have a clue."

She frowned again, clearly not getting the answer she wanted. "Let's put it this way, if you were me, with my surprisingly modest pay, what would you do?"

I mirrored her frown. "Well, number one, I'd bury all traces of the Asian conspiracy. Keep an eye on developments, of course, but keep it from our partners. If this becomes common knowledge, a single miscarriage would be sufficient to cause a panic."

"And we wouldn't need to try to spin your killing spree in Tokyo."

"That's a further benefit, but not the main consideration. Open knowledge of the potential infertility pandemic will cause enough chaos without adding further fuel to the flames."

"You don't think we should bury this one also?" Her grim smile indicated this was a rhetorical question.

"It would be great if we could, but the cat's already out of the bag there. Even if initial distribution has been greatly limited compared to that planned, we couldn't possibly mount any response without international support. We'll need to build a credible story about how we discovered it, but if we tie it into ongoing counter-terrorist actions, we can be a bit vague in key areas. Probably best to initiate it as a highly confidential memo to top Interpol brass. It'll then be common knowledge within days."

"And what about the protective STD?"

"That's a tricky one. I assume we've initiated some moves to spread protection in Switzerland, so we need to get knowledge of it into the open, but preferably without any sign of a link to us. Doris, what do you think? Any cunning plans," I passed the buck with a sigh of relief.

"Well, we need some way that details of this virus can be found, but wouldn't have any link to us?" she thought out loud. "So, what if we post an information note on a deep black website used by right-wing extremists? The source is effectively untraceable when going that route, but I can add a few wrinkles to make it 100%. We can word it so that it looks like it comes from Helena, so it'll be picked up quickly after intelligence agencies know about the pandemic. She's dead, so no way the post can be contradicted."

"But this is a black website. How can we be sure that anyone relevant will ever find it?" I wondered.

"Easy, 'cause I happen to know that it's actually run by the CIA," she responded, with a typical smug grin.

There was silence for a while as all participants thought through the plan. "Well, that's as good as anything my team has come up with," Zwicky looked as if some weight had been lifted from her shoulders. "I now need to bring this team online, to go through implementation options with the senior Zodiac members. You're excused this, Herr Berner, as I know you've had a long day. Just get back to Switzerland as quickly as possible and we'll have a full debrief." With that the link closed abruptly.

Shit, I don't know whether that went well or not but, in any case, it's done for now. All I need to do is let the girls know what I've dragged them into, which may be a lot trickier. But Zwicky's right, it has been a hell of a long day!

***

As a bit of procrastination, I then had a shower, very carefully removing caked blood from my nose before applying an anaesthetic spray. I felt much better when, wearing only my stolen yukata, I headed back to the lounge. The women were sprawled together on the sofa, Yoko again wearing only slippers and Andrea her lurid Happi coat.

Andrea started as I settled into an armchair angled to face them. "I've quickly run over all I know and Yoko told me about this demolition charge you placed. What else has been kept from me?"

"You know all of this is an action in response to a credible threat of a bioweapon attack that would global impacts." I paused to work out how much detail to pass on.

"Is this the work of the mad cunts in that dungeon?" Yoko asked. "Mister Hashimoto and most of the others seemed quite nice. Obscenely rich, but otherwise okay."

Nothing for it but complete disclosure. It's only fair, as I would have left that club in a bodybag if not for them.

"What Hashimoto-san and his coterie were planning was anything but nice. Anyway, settle down and I'll give you an overview, with none of the sensitive stuff held back. As will become clear, this has to be kept totally secret. Even the Ambassador isn't fully informed. Let me work my way through it first, then I'll clarify any details that aren't clear."

I talked for 20 minutes straight, true to my word in not attempting to soften any of the terrifying details of the threats posed. When I finished the women sat silently for several minutes while the details sunk in.

Andrea was distinctly pale and her permanent cheerfulness had vanished. "So, we murdered everyone at tonight's reception?" Her voice had a distinct tremor.

"No, I assassinated them. You knew nothing about what was going on."

"But I knew you were up to something."

"Come on, love," Yoko gave her a crushing hug, "you've heard the man. These were evil, genocidal loonies. It was easy with the psychos in the Mishima club, they really looked the part. The avuncular appearance of Mister Hashimoto doesn't reduce his culpability."

"You reckon that it's okay for us to be judge, jury and executioner?"

"No, not us, me! It's my job, remember." I broke in. "When you see a terrorist with a hand

393

grenade you don't read him his rights or ask if he wants a lawyer, you shoot the fucker between the eyes. It's a much trickier call here, but the stakes are so large that there's really no option. I confess that I had a bit of a crisis of conscience upstairs, especially when I met some of the younger employees. But, as far as we know, they're aware of what's going on and, regardless of how active their role is, they have to accept the consequences."

Again, there was a long silence before Yoko gave her partner a kiss on the brow, which seemed to draw some of the tension out of the room. "I think it'll take a while for all of this to sink in, but what's the present situation with the counter-virus? You said the European one had already been released, with air transport hubs being key targets. That would include Tokyo, wouldn't it?"

"I imagine so. But, even though it's very infectious, it'll take time to spread significantly. We're already working to protect key Swiss infrastructure, which will certainly include the Embassy. Presently we're using the STD form directly, so if Andrea gets it, she'll pass it on to you."

"But that'll take a while. However, you're already infected with this and can pass it on?"

"Yes, I was infected a while ago and so am a carrier, with a high likelihood of passing it on."

"To anyone you have sex with!" she smiled. "This means we can jump to the front of the queue if we shag you now. And this'll also protect us in the off chance that the lethal Asian variant is released."

"The blood samples I have will confirm it, but I'm almost certain you'll be protected against all variants. So, if you weren't lesbians, or I was a gal, shagging would be an option."

"Well, actually, I'm bi. Or, at least I used to be before I met this lovely lady," she added in response to a dig in the ribs. "This means that, if you shagged me," another hard elbow to the ribs caused her to grunt, "not for enjoyment, of course, just as a medical prophylactic, that'd work."

"Well, I could try very hard to get no enjoyment from the process, although that might be a serious challenge."

"And I could pass it on?"

"Any exchange of sexual fluids, vaginally, orally or anally, so I believe. You should be infective within a few days, a week tops."

"Okay, but Andrea would be immediately protected if she…"

"No way!" Andrea glared at her lover. "You know I'm not into sex with men and I'm having nothing to do with seminal fluids. It's bad enough you shagging him. Even if this is a sensible option, I'm happy to wait until you're infectious."

"Ah, this comes to my related question," Yoko placed a hand over her lover's mouth to prevent further interruptions. "If we had sex, what are the chances of me being infected from a single encounter?"

"It seems to be over 90%, maybe 95% or thereabouts," I answered, unsure what point Yoko was making here.

"This means that our optimum strategy, if we

wanted to be certain of protection, would be for you to have sex with both of us. Ideally, we'd both be infected but, even if not, the infected one would then pass it on to the other."

"Yes, you can't argue with statistics. I think you'll have a lot of arguments with your girlfriend however."

Yoko removed her hand quickly, anticipating her partner's attempt to bite it. "I concede that it's sensible. I'm even, with great reluctance, prepared to let you shag him. But I'm having nothing to do with spunk. The very thought of that in my vagina, yuck!"

"Well, maybe oral?"

"Double-yuck, even worse," she mimed sticking fingers down her throat.

Well, anal then? That wouldn't be too bad. You've had worse things up your bum."

Maybe too much information there, but Andrea actually seems to be considering this option!

"Oh, fuckity-fuck, okay. Only because it improves protection for both of us. It's only going to happen while we're going at it, as I'll need something to distract me from the horror of it all. But only this one time. I'm not going to experiment with bi, regardless of anything you say."

"You've got a deal," Yoko pulled her into a passionate kiss. When they eventually broke off, she grinned. "Right, big boy, get your bare arse onto that bed. You're going to experience something that men can only dream of."

Christ on a bike, I didn't see that coming. I wonder if I'll get through this without cracked ribs, not to mention a full-blown heart attack.

***

My encounter with the women was surreal as they, especially Andrea, treated it as if it was necessary but unpleasant foreplay to the Sapphic action, which was what they were really building up to. *Something like putting on a condom would be for a man.*

Yoko was the self-appointed choreographer for the event. After Andrea and I stripped off, and she removed her slippers to show solidarity, Andrea was carefully positioned near the end of the king-size bed, with legs widely spread and the backs of her knees at the edge and her feet on the floor. "So, we're going to do scaredy cat first."

"Why, why not you first?"

"Simple my love," Yoko kissed her engorged clitoris, "by the time Jan gets close to you, he'll be on a hair-trigger." She now kissed the end of my erect dick, making me very aware that she was dead right. "Now I get on top of you," she lowered herself onto her lover, grinding her crotch into the woman's face, "which will provide you with a bit of distraction," with one hand she ran her fingers over the fleshy labia and used the other to prise the tight buttocks apart to allow her pinkie to penetrate the now openly-exposed anus. "Mmm, that's good," this last presumably in response to whatever Andrea was up to.

"Jesus, can we get on with this! Otherwise, I'm going to come in your face in a matter of seconds."

"Don't you dare," Yoko commanded, seriously. "Just think of what would have happened

397

to you in that basement if we hadn't been there to look after you. I'd imagine double anal with your testicles in a vice while Shoko does her branding bit on your willy. Or something like that.

That did the trick. With that picture in my mind, my erection is starting to wilt.

"Now you can lubricate that in my twat and… Oh, shit, cancel that, I've fingers and a tongue deep in there. In my mouth, then, but you'd better not come!"

"Easier said than done," I mumbled as I was repeatedly licked, sucked and spat upon, interspersed with licking and spitting on the target anus and the fingers being used to penetrate it.

I had just about reached breaking point when my balls were savagely crushed, forcing me to yelp in pain. "Not yet, I told you, she's loosening up nicely." Now three fingers were being inserted, eliciting groans of pleasure. Just hold on."

A combination of pain and flashbacks to the Kabuki-cho club managed to keep me on the edge until Yoko's mouth disappeared and my dick was directed into Andrea's tight arsehole. I came immediately, but a steely finger jammed against my own anus prevented me from withdrawing. The security chief was bucking like a bronco while the cunnilingus got more frantic, eventually climaxing with a scream, which allowed me to slip out and slump backwards onto the floor. *Completely spent, in more ways than one.*

After a few minutes I had recovered sufficiently to lever myself onto the edge of the bed. The women were wrapped in each other's arms, taking turns for slow, sensuous face and neck licks and nuzzles. Yoko rolled free, onto her back. "So, you two, that wasn't so totally awful was it."

"Not the worst ten minutes in my entire life," Andrea giggled. "But you're not ever getting me to do that again."

"Well, at least not until the next pandemic," Yoko grinned at me. Anyway, that was fine for foreplay, but now it's time for the main event. Now, get onto your feet, you buxom bitch you," she leaned forward to playfully bite a huge, erect nipple, rewarded by an exaggerated squeak. "Jan, you're on your back here."

"I can't think of anything I'd rather do, but I'm totally shagged out. If I lie down there, I'll be asleep in ten seconds. Even if you have Viagra by the kilo, there's no way I'm getting hard again in the near future." *I don't suppose this pair would have any of those tablets they used in Levant – not anything that they'd ever need.*

The women ignored my remonstrations, whispering to each other while arranging my body to meet Yoko's requirements. *Well, the previous mood of gloom seems to have gone completely, if all the giggling is anything to go by, so that's something positive anyway.*

I closed my eyes and was starting to dose when Yoko straddled my face and started to rub a wet, sticky vulva over my mouth and nose. Despite this distraction, I couldn't help noting the hard, sculpted muscles of her stomach and thighs. She then leant forward and started licking my sticky penis and belly, while stroking my balls and fingering my bum. *Christ, for a lesbian she's certainly knows what she's doing on the fellatio front.*

Despite my worries, I could feel my member beginning to slowly rise from the dead. Then Andrea appeared above me and, after favouring me with a salacious smile, started to lick her lover's bum. *Jesus, this would raise Lazarus. Yoko might get her dose of seminal fluid after all.*

After my erection met Yoko's standards, she twisted around to slide it into her vagina and then interlaced her legs with those of her partner in a way that seemed possible only for yoga experts, giving me a strange flashback to Isle du Levant. Andrea was now on her back on top of me, her body arched and weight supported by some grip she had on her partner. She then started to writhe, presumably to make clitoris contact although, from the resulting grunts, Yoko's fingers were also in play. Very slowly Andrea's movements intensified and I could feel Yoko gripping my dick with her internal muscles, which were evidently as powerful as those on the rest of her body.

Just as the rapid breathing of both women indicated an approaching orgasm, Yoko shouted at me. "Jan, grab her nipples and squeeze hard, really hard. The bitch is just about tearing my tits off."

I did as commanded and was rewarded by a scream, which even surpassed that from her previous orgasm, drowning out whatever Yoko was shouting. My abuse of her nipples also finished me off and I came, feeling myself being milked by the shudders passing through Yoko's vagina. I don't know how long the lesbian climax lasted and what happened thereafter, I was sound asleep.

CHAPTER TWENTY

I was awakened by now-familiar giggles, slowly realising that I was lying very close to the edge of their bed while the girls were wrapped together at the other side, with either tickling or whispers, or maybe both, causing the hilarity.

"Well, Yoko, you were right. That was indeed a night to remember." I twisted myself to get a better view of my bedmates. "What do you think, ladies, should we try that again. It would improve the statistics quite…" I was silenced when Andrea swatted me in the face with a pillow, causing a shock of pain from my still-sensitive nose.

"Well, I'd give it a go, if I didn't think it'd be pointless," Yoko looked at me scathingly. "At best, you've only got one shag left in you, and it's holding you together."

"Can't say you're wrong," I admitted. "Now, what have we on for…? Oh shit, I forgot completely, I'm flying out this morning. I better get packed PDQ."

Andrea looked up from nibbling her lover's shoulder. "Relax, you've got tons of time." I now noticed that, despite the bright morning sun shining through the windows, it was only a little after seven thirty. "Have a shower and get packed. We can have breakfast in Starbucks downstairs and the limo is already booked to pick us up at eight forty-five. You've got diplomatic fast-track so might have time for a glass of Champagne in the lounge before you

402

board for ten hours of pandering before you land in sunny Switzerland."

***

I remembered this when, fourteen hours later, I deplaned at Kloten. Andrea was right except for the pandering. I shared the first-class cabin with one of the other Bundesrätinnen, who was returning from some conference. This meant that I was generally ignored and the service was terrible. *What a contrast to the trip out! Thank God I'm not paying for this with my own money.*

I was met in the arrivals lounge by Helen, who asked for the blood samples and, after I had dug them out of my bag, passed them to the young man accompanying her, who left at a run. At a more leisurely pace, she led me to a police car, illegally parked at the front of the terminal, and drove off quickly, blue lights flashing. "So, you've to rush me back to Brugg for the debriefing," I sighed. "Any chance we could postpone it until tomorrow, I'm totally knackered."

"I'm sure you are. Your pal, Miss Tamborini, was chatting to Doris earlier this morning."

"Christ, no! Just what I didn't need."

"Anyway, don't worry, Commander, we're heading directly down to the Tessin, where you're taking charge of our new unit. In our sparkling new offices."

"The Tessin, why on earth there? Oh, and what's this commander shit?"

"We've been working over everything uploaded from Tokyo for the last 24 hours and the consensus is that it all went perfectly."

"More by luck than judgement."

"That's certainly true. But the key was that we, you actually, made the best of your lucky breaks. I think that, if anyone had been running a book for this op, a success like that would be a 100:1 rank outsider. Zwicky also thinks your assessment of the threat was spot-on. Hence you're now a Commander."

"Are you sure? That's three steps up. You must mean assistant deputy or, at best, deputy commander."

"I know for sure. What else could explain your driver being a deputy commander?"

"Jesus…" I was shocked to silence by these completely unexpected developments.

"All the other core members of the team have also been promoted. Some will move down to join us in Locarno at some point, but Pirmin is now head of the Brugg office and will keep those who have logistical problems moving to the deep south."

"But Ticino, Locarno: why on earth there? You could hardly get further away from Brugg and still be in Switzerland. It's one of the few areas where tourism is still important and they've very little else."

"You've got it in one. I knew you were brighter than you look, which is just as well with the two black eyes you have now."

"Have I really? Looked a little bruised this morning, but," I activated the selfie camera on my comm. "Shit, I look like a fucking panda. No wonder everyone was avoiding me on that flight. Oh well, could be worse. I'm definitely in better shape than the other guy."

"Anyway, it'll be about 90 minutes to Locarno with the blues on and, otherwise, you've got the day off."

"Great," I settled back in my seat. "Just take your time and fill me in on everything that's happened since I left. Bugger me, that was only 48 hours ago and half of that was spent travelling."

I almost dozed off while the new deputy commander filled me in on developments related to the European variant and the initial moves to spread the protective STD without risking information leaking about the threat it protected against. Unwitting infection during sex had many clear advantages here, although other options could be considered after the existence of the slowly emerging pandemic was openly acknowledged. *Could be that Yoko's choice will prove very prescient in retrospect.*

The rest was in depth analysis of my actions and their potential consequences. I had been a little worried that Doris would be pissed off at me circumventing her meticulous plans, but she had, typically, just modified them to fit with the new reality. In particular, planting evidence to support a yakuza role in the Mishima club blast had been quickly implemented. For these boundary conditions, any link to us would probably be lost in the gang war that would inevitably result.

Hashimoto was already dead, a bit earlier than expected, but to the great relief of all involved. His company had declared worldwide closure for 7 days of mourning, which was interpreted as a cover for

405

the chaos that must have resulted from having so many top executives dead or dying. In any case, this would make it easier to spot any unusual activity, if there was any last-ditch attempt to manufacture and distribute their variant. This had inspired Doris to come up with another cunning plan, spreading rumours of imminent financial collapse of Hashimoto's entire business empire. With nobody at the helm to actively fight these, this could be a self-fulfilling prophecy.

Gradually I became aware of everything that had been happening in the background. I had, naturally, been focusing on staying alive while hitting some specific targets, but the team had been able to see a wider picture and pulled it all together wonderfully.

"Christ, you guys have done a brilliant job! No wonder Zwicky is so happy and everyone is getting promoted. I had no idea how well this was all fitting together."

"Of course not," she turned to smile at me, "below your pay grade. But we underlings also have our uses."

"I think I can just retire now and let you run the entire show. Locarno must be a good place for a pensioner to settle down."

"Not in the near future, boss," her smile widened. "The fact that we discovered this threat was a fluke – and taking down the main actors involved a lot of luck. But there's an entire infrastructure that we haven't nailed down – the supporters of the European and Asian groups, who must be high in Government or security organisations. We don't have proof as yet, but we have suspicions about the President of Interpol and several members of her Executive Committee. We're going to need someone like you on the front line, who is open to lateral thinking, and prepared to do the things we really need to do, regardless of how politically incorrect these might seem."

"Sounds like a poisoned chalice to me," I frowned. "On the other hand, if given freedom from political interference, a small Swiss team might be ideal for this job. I guess if we sold it the right way, we could probably attract some of the best of the counter-terrorist group."

"I'm sure that's the case," she confirmed.

I started to feel pleased with myself before she added, "Of course, there's also all the videos of you getting into the most bizarre sexual situations. The entire team love these. I really hope Andrea set up the video option in her bedroom."

Video option? This cannot be happening to me! I'm retiring, fuck the pension, I'm not going through all of this yet again!

***

I was still sulking when we pulled into the underground garage of an apartment block in central Locarno. This was on the lakeside and very close to the ferry terminal. Helen led me to a very plush penthouse flat on the seventh floor. "We've rented the entire floor to put up staff moving down here. It's all holiday accommodation and now very cheap. This place is very well situated, as our new office is just a couple of blocks away."

"So, you're moving down here also?"

"Certainly, like you in this temporary rented accommodation until we get proper digs sorted out."

"Nearby?" I asked suspiciously.

"Couldn't be closer, we're sharing a bedroom."

"Why? This place is huge. Couldn't you take one of the other rooms?"

"Just fighting off the opposition. Oh, sorry, the distractions from the rest of your team."

"What, Doris? I certainly hope that, whenever I find I find out whatever the hell we're doing here, I can tempt her to join us. But I can assure you, the thought of the competition that I have for her affections will ensure that she's not a distraction," I faced a meaningful stare. "Or, at least not a serious one."

"No, not Doris," she glared at me, "the rug-munchers you assaulted in Akasaka!"

I was momentarily dumbfounded before I caught her drift. "What, Andrea and Yoko, they've got nothing to do with anything going on here."

"Seems that they have. This is all since you had your evil way with them and probably from pillow talk that's best left unmentioned. It appears they've decided that, with the shit that's likely to go down internationally even in the best case, they'd be better off here in the land of cows. Seems that Yoko has an assured citizenship and, weird as it may seem, they've requested to work with you. Probably only 50%, as they plan to open a dojo of some sort."

"Come on now, that's just taking surreal too far. No way!"

"Remember the Japanese link. There we have

no clue how the local organisation was run – it can't only be Yakuza, there needs to have been support also from upper levels of the Japanese politics and probably the police. Andrea would be ideal to lead up that side of things."

"Mmm, well, I can't deny that she's got both the security and local Japanese knowledge that we need. But I got the feeling that she'd be uncomfortable working with me."

"Ah, boss, so much to learn," she smiled and moved closer to me, starting to remove my clothes. "They arrive in a couple of weeks and will be billeted next door. I've heard that, after thinking about these pandemics, they're considering having a child and you're top of the list of potential sperm donors."

Well, I certainly didn't see that one coming!

THE END